The Last Defender of Albion
Tristan Black Wolf

I0634719

ISBN 978-1-883688-08-0 (trade paperback)
ISBN 978-1-883688-09-7 (eBook)
Cover art by Edgard Aedo

Dedication

This one is for

Edgard Aedo

for more than a quarter century of friendship,
mutual support, and laughter.
Thanks for sharing the journey

The Ritual of Question and Response

As some members of each species rose to sapience, they retained their link to the instinctual need for the comfort and warmth of touch. With sapience also came a conundrum. Non-sapient animals ordinarily do not mate out of season; for them, cuddling and touch do not have a sexual component. Sapient beings can enjoy sexuality at any time, but they wanted a way to separate the need for physical comfort from overtures to sexuality.

The solution became the Question and Response. By formalizing the request for physical yet non-sexual intimacy, sapients created the framework for a social compact between those who wish to experience it.

The Question, which might vary in form, is, "May I share my fur with you?" The Response, given only if the furson wishes to join in this compact, is, "It is warmth to us both."

The Question and Response carries with it the responsibility of listening, paying attention, sharing the moment of emotional and mental intimacy along with the physical intimacy. If both parties wish it, the progression to sexuality may occur, but it is never expected, never demanded. The purpose of the ritual is for both parties to be safe within their shared physicality, for mutual comfort and aid.

1: Crime Scene

A lot of things may be said to swarm. Bees do it, as the old song goes. So do football fans at the stadium gates. Groupies at a rock concert. Relatives at a will reading. The swarm that I see most is cops around the house where somebody turns up a body. Especially when the house is located in a fancy neighborhood.

The whole damned thing could have been an April Fool's day joke, except that this year had decided that April 1st should also be a Monday, har de har har. As it turned out, there was still some cosmic or karmic mischief lingering the next day. See, I only got the call that Tuesday morning because I was the next detective in the barrel. Some joke, huh? Wait — the punch line takes some build-up to get to.

As far as first looks go, the case wasn't anything spectacular, like a burglary-cum-homicide, a vendetta killing, or even something juicy enough for the next creepy ghoul-monster-serial-killer movie (a franchise which, rather like its subjects, simply refuses to die). This was a suicide. Or, as the captain put it, "Just a suicide." As a rule, homicide detectives are not dispatched to such scenes; we do, after all, deal with homicide, not suicide. But in the same way that rank hath its privileges, money speaketh loudly, whatever the crime. I had been sent off on this fool's errand because Thomas Christian Thaddeus Glover, feline male, age 47, of average weight and build, had significantly above average means. That kind of clout means that the ranking part of the rank-and-file had to look into it. The pressure could have come from friends or enemies in high places, financial or political leverage, whatever; I'd seen it all often enough not to give a hot flying anything at this point. Make an appearance, that's all that was required of me.

No one had bothered to suggest why the cat would want to pull his own plug. Maybe some big problems at the office, maybe money trouble that nobody knew about. From what I'd heard about him from the captain, as well as from various public information sources, he didn't seem the type to be blackmailed — too damned straight for that. Then again, none of the other categories seemed to fit either, at least not at first glance. I'm not sure if I was being paid to think or maybe paid not to think. "Any death under unusual circumstances must be investigated" — thus it is written in the Sacred Rule Book. Simple truth was that no one cared if you offed yourself (with the possible exception of life insurance companies and anyone you owe money to), but somefur has to go through the motions, and I got tagged for the job. Even if I did my job right, I didn't expect it would take very long.

Nasty little traitors, expectations.

I levered myself out of my car, noticed that the sky was clearing. Some of the other cops were clearing, too. I hoped both were good signs.

"Detective Luton?"

The patrol padded over to me, a new pup on the job, much too cheerful, his uniform much too creased. Ears forward, tail reasonably respectful, eyes bright, golden fur clean and brushed to regs, still hot for this new game he had found to play. I'd have felt unkempt and shabby, if I'd given a damn. I noted the name tag, wondered if it would still be on the rosters in six months. "What've you got, Parsons?"

"You're gonna love this one, sir. One body, two weapons."

I felt an ear twitch. "What?"

A thin forefinger, bearing a carefully clipped claw, wrapped circles around his temple. "Looney Tunes," he said with confidence. "A nut case suicide. They haven't taken the body yet; still there in the library. See for yourself — unless you've just had breakfast."

* * * * *

There are days when it just doesn't pay to be canine. It was still strange to me that the young Labrador in the new uniform wasn't overwhelmed by the smells of a fresh body. Granted, the usual issues regarding the extrusion of various bodily wastes hadn't happened yet, but the blood and brains were enough to set most of us to using practically anything in a tin to help deaden the sensitivity of our noses. I may be only 52, but I'd already had too much of it ten years ago, when still a newbie at the detective game. One thing about collies like me: We tend to be tenacious. Oh, and practical.

That whole pension thing. About a year left to the magic two-oh on my shield, not that I'm counting.

The scene was plenty grisly enough that I didn't need a coroner to tell me the cause of death. The gun was still clenched in the victim's left forepaw, and it was clear that the entry point was the left temple, exiting through the right side of the head — what was left of it.

"Like I said, Detective: Whacko."

I also didn't need the running commentary, but Parsons seemed to be operating on a different script. Pardon the stereotyping, but Labs can be yappy if they're not given a firm paw at an early age. I chalked it up as another indicator of his occupational virginity. He'd adapt or go; that would be up to him. Meanwhile, back in the adult world, I was doing everything by the numbers — checking the scene, looking for clues to confirm the obvious, making mental notes of things to mention to the M.E., and to run a check on Glover himself — but I felt that I was already late to this party. "Has Forensics been here?"

"Been and gone."

"Everything? Photos, sketches, prints, fur, fiber, ingress, egress?"

"And a partridge in a pear tree. The M.E. is running behind schedule — caught in traffic. We're waiting for him to okay us to take the body and the weapon. Weapons," he corrected himself with an almost gleeful swish of his tail.

I knelt by the desk chair, a plush but efficient design like everything else in the meticulously kept study. (Note to Self: Check for a housekeeper. No self-respecting heterosexual male is this neat.) Glover himself was already dressed-for-success, ready for the office or perhaps, in this case, for his funeral. I still couldn't say for sure if he was the tiger he appeared to be by other fur color and markings; too much of his head had been blown away. My guess was a magnum shell, something that mushroomed out and probably lodged (if any of it stayed intact) in the opposite wall somewhere. Even so, one ear appeared to have the correct colorations for him to be *panthera tigris*. It would only be important for identification purposes, and his new widow would probably give us that if pawprints and DNA didn't do the job. (Mentally, I corrected myself: A member of the Bar would have pawprints and, depending on his law firm, DNA records as well. No respectable shysters [pardon the oxymoron] would let members of their firm not have identity markers in some private repository somewhere. The more perceived power you get, the greater the paranoia.)

I looked carefully at the second weapon. Glover's right forepaw had clutched spasmodically about the shining gold hilt of a brilliantly polished short sword. I could still smell the metal cleaner on it; not a smudge, fingerprint, or blemish on the entire length. Symbols or runes of some kind had been etched down the center of the blade, and they had oxidized sufficiently to stand out in beautiful relief.

"Nothin' like a little certifiable flip-out to renew your faith in natural selection, eh, Detective?"

"You like natural selection, do you, Parsons?"

"No likin' or dislikin', Detective. Just is."

"That's what they say, isn't it? It is what it is."

"Yah, and that's how it is."

"No flies on you, Parsons."

I let him try to figure out what that meant while I kept looking things over. The desk pad contained a series of scribbles, notations, question marks, doodles — no doubt all the components of a forensic psychoanalyst's wet dream. It also contained, in a carefully marked-off section, several scrawls that appeared to be the same as the sword runes. No, check that — not the same, but similar. An ornate pen holder lay up and to the right of the desk pad; the only pen in view lay on the right side of the pad itself, virtually pointing toward the scrawled runes.

"Some mess, huh?" continued Parsons jovially.

I could see no suicide note. Not everyone leaves one, of course, but it was another fact to put into my mental list. I stood and scanned the room. Nothing disturbed; shelves of hardcover books, many appearing to be collectables, slip-cased, gilt lettering on the spines, perfectly filed away and kept free of dust (yeah, there's definitely a housekeeper; subconsciously, I added the unnamed maid to the list of people to question). Two paintings, tastefully framed, hung precisely in carefully measured niches; to my untrained eye, they looked like originals, although I couldn't place the artist any nearer than 19th century.

The Lab forced a brief chuckle. "I tell ya, they'll never get it out of that carpet."

The floor was covered from wall to wall in a thick white pile, easy on the hindpaws, beautiful but cold. On one wall, a mini-bar stood well-stocked and orderly, each element of its finely polished oaken rack precisely placed. All of the glasses were set and clean, the bottles reasonably full. Even the pipe rack was immaculate, perhaps to the point of being merely decorative. There was no scent of tobacco anywhere, and even housekeepers can't take away that smell well enough to keep it from a nose like mine.

"Are you in charge?" The heavy-set pug who had just entered the room regarded me with respectfully professional uncertainty through Coke-bottle-bottom glasses perched above his pinched muzzle.

"Not necessarily," I responded. I extended a forepaw as the traditional litany exited my lips unadorned. "Detective Max Luton, Homicide."

"I'm the M.E.," he snuffled, taking my paw briskly, smiling. "Daimler, Bertram Daimler — like the car. A little out of date, and I don't idle so good, but I'm still running." He released me and set down his black bag — a prop guaranteed to identify him in almost any situation. Just to keep it official, he motioned to the ID tag clipped to his coat; it was proper issue, and no one else would want to be here anyway. He reached into the bag, removing and then snapping on a pair of equally proper issue gloves while I assured him that everyone else had come and gone.

Parsons padded toward the desk, and I intercepted him. He whined at me, "They want to bring in the gurney to bag this guy."

"Another few minutes, Parsons."

"You want me to stick around?"

"Take five and go mark a tree. Our guest of honor," I said to the doctor, indicating the body and moving back to let the old dog work.

He considered briefly. "Standard disclaimers." I nodded. "Victim appears to be the tiger known as Thomas Glover, according to photos and other information on file. We'll get verification of that along the way. The obvious C.O.D. may not be it, depending. Some clever bugger might have poisoned him, then staged the suicide scene, hoping we're not thorough."

"How likely is that?"

"Too ridiculous to be credited, but bets are made to be hedged." Daimler continued peering through his thick lenses, the occasional grunt or murmur probably meant to reassure me that he really was taking all this seriously. "You've noticed the obvious?"

"Yes."

"Good. Nice to have a homicide detective I don't have to train." He considered further, brought out a probe from his bag and managed to maneuver himself to the victim's left and crouch next to the body. "Anyone hear the shot?"

"Wife called it in early this morning; she says 'something' woke her."

"I'm getting a little old for this," he growled softly, maneuvering himself to find a way to insert the probe into the space between two shirt buttons and then into the body. I had to give him bonus points for not simply pushing through the cloth itself. "What's her definition of early?"

"Nine-one-one call is recorded as being at 6:24."

After a sufficient time, he removed the probe and nodded. "Close as makes no odds. I'll try to be more exact, if it proves to be important."

"Probably won't," I admitted, offering him a paw to help him unfold himself from his squatting position. "Anything else for preliminary?"

He shook his head. "At the risk of dating myself, what you see is what you get. They can take the body, and..." Another headshake. "There's no nice way of saying this: I'll make sure they scrape up whatever they can, see that it's properly analyzed."

"Thanks, Doc."

The old pug removed the gloves and reassembled his bag. "I'll get a proper report to you as soon as I can. Since it appears to be suicide, you'll ask about...?"

"The usual suspects." I padded to the doorway and performed the faintly unpleasant task of calling for Parsons. The Lab appeared all too quickly, along with a pair of suitably-attired attendants with a gurney in tow. "Make sure you bag'n'tag, and I want a make on the gun and the sword."

"How can there be a make on a sword?" the patrol asked sarcastically.

"I want to know what it's made of, who made it, where it came from. It may tell us why he had to keep hold of it, even at the last."

"Because, maybe, he's a fruitcake?"

"Is Mrs. Glover available?"

He jerked a chin toward the front of the house, where I knew the living room to be. "In there."

"I'm going in to talk with her."

"I'll take you in."

I leaned into the pup's face, feeling my ears rise and go backward. "Parsons... who's your boss?"

He blinked. "McPherson. Sergeant McPherson, out of the two-six."

"Wrong answer. You got called into a case I'm working on. You're on my detail, and I'm the one you have to make happy so that you can keep moving up your ladder. So unless you want me to call McPherson at the two-six and get your tail stuck on parking meters for the next six months, I strongly suggest that you get to work on getting that gun checked out and to get more information about that sword. Fail to do so, and I'll see that you discover a new form of parking meter duty that involves being seated, suddenly, completely, and without lube. Do you need me to write that down for you in words of single syllables?"

Give him credit: The pup didn't piss himself. "No, sir."

"Get on it."

He looked like he wasn't sure if he should salute or genuflect. I didn't give him time to do either. I had a grieving widow to talk to.

* * * * *

As it turned out, I was only partially right: I would be talking to a widow. Helena Glover was a tigress of self-imposed regal bearing, too thin for my taste, and too thin for a tigress, I would have thought. She looked almost too thin to have born three kits, although their faces showed in photographs on the wall, all in pride of place, all with the sort of smiles that parents inflict upon their children when evidence of their perfection requires proof in still life. All three were away at boarding school, no doubt being put through their paces.

I sat on the sofa, mindful of my tail and hindpaws. This was one of those living rooms where not a whole lot of living was expected. The tigress herself sat stiffly but calmly in the smaller of a matched pair of wingbacks, his'n'hers thrones of careful design. I gave her a moment or two to ready herself for the onslaught of questions that she was expecting. I'd been nursing one of those "bad feelings" that cops are supposed to get about certain cases, so despite the idea that I was probably there mostly for procedural window dressing, I had a pretty good idea of the information that I was going to get. As a famous barrister once said, "Never ask a question unless you're sure of the answer."

"Mrs. Glover," I said softly, bringing out my notebook as a prop for the show, "I know that you've been questioned already, and I apologize for putting you through it all again..."

"Get on with it, Detective."

Her voice pitched low, raspy, almost masculine, as if deepened by a good number of years of scotch and cigarettes, neither of which was in evidence in this part of the house. At that point, I reckoned that the high collar about her neck was not merely a fashion statement. I decided against pressing the issue. "Yes, ma'am. You found Mr. Glover?"

"I heard the shot."

"About what time?"

"Not too long after I got up."

"That would be...?"

"A little after six. Before the alarm. I felt that I was awakened by something, but I didn't know what it was. A sound, maybe. Anyway, I felt that I wouldn't get back to sleep, so I was getting myself ready to begin my day when I heard the shot. I came downstairs to see—"

"That was bold of you, Mrs. Glover."

She actually looked at me for the first time. Anyone needing to get the truth out of someone else will tell you that body language usually speaks louder than spoken words. Her tail held resolutely still, although one ear flicked in irritation. Ears, as a rule, are much more difficult to control, as are pupils which may dilate or shift when the subject is irritated, surprised, or disingenuous. In this case, I figured "irritated."

"I have a license for my own weapon, Detective, and I practice at a shooting range at least twice a year. I may not be able to predate openly, but I can defend myself quite well."

I nodded a demurral. "Please continue."

She gathered herself. "I came downstairs — yes, with my pistol — heard nothing, saw no one. The alarm system was undisturbed, the main outer doors locked. I went to my husband's study and found..." She trailed off, seeming for the first time shaken in her resolve.

"Did your husband have any visitors last night?"

"No." She reached for a coffee cup that was likely on its fifth recharge. I was only mildly surprised that she wasn't taking something stronger, but perhaps she realized how easily I'd smell it on her.

"How would you describe your husband's mood recently?"

"Fine." Her response came swiftly. "He was fine."

"And when he came home last night?"

"Fine."

"Nothing worrying him?"

"Thomas was always worried about something."

I nodded, letting the little fibs grow larger in their own good time. I moved the pen around to make it appear that I was writing down the holy writ of unimpeachable testimony. "Do you know what he was working on recently?"

"He rarely spoke of his work."

"I'm sure his office can tell me, particularly if it has any relevance."

"I doubt that it does." She caught herself just a little too late, shifted slightly in her throne, trying to recover. "He specialized in real estate law. I believe that his latest case involved squatters on some country land. Some... commune." She spat out the word as if it were distasteful to her refined senses. "The client wanted them evicted, and Thomas spearheaded the case. He was to present it to the court today. I had set my alarm early; I wanted to make sure that he would be there on time, because he was—"

Again, the tigress caught herself, although this time it was the tip of her tail that gave the game away. She had begun speaking the truth, and her body was reacting to it automatically. There was little doubt in my mind that the words she was about to speak were *because he was upset*. I let the point go.

"You found him in his study. Was the door open, closed...?"

"Closed and locked."

My expression asked the question.

"There's a set of keys for every room in the house, Detective. They're inside a cabinet door, in the utility room. When I got no answer from Thomas, and when I realized that I could smell cordite from inside the room, I fetched the key and opened the door."

I nodded, pretending to make a note on my pad.

"Aren't you going to ask if I unlocked the door, killed my husband, then relocked the door behind me?"

"Did you?"

"No!"

"I didn't think so."

"One of your fellow officers seemed to think it possible."

I shook my head. "The average beat cop who dreams of being a detective one day also dreams up ridiculous scenarios, trying them on like bad clothing. If you were going to go to such lengths, you wouldn't have ruined your alibi by leaving the house alarm undisturbed and the doors and windows carefully locked. I'm sorry if they offended you."

"I'm not easily offended."

That was particularly easy to believe. I shifted my hindpaws slightly, trying to prevent my back from tightening up, as it had a tendency to do these days. "Considering what you found there, Mrs. Glover, it may be ridiculous to ask if you noticed anything missing, out of place, unusual...?"

She finished what was in her coffee cup and set it back down. "Not that I noticed. I did worry about an intruder, of course; that was why I noticed that the French doors to the patio were closed. I couldn't tell if they were locked, at that distance, and I didn't go to look. I was shocked, of course. When I couldn't find any sign of an intruder in the house, I ran to the kitchen to call nine-one-one. I didn't notice anything unusual."

"You recognized the sword?"

Once more, the veneer almost broke. I kept my eyes soft, waited for her. "I don't know."

"It wasn't familiar to you?"

"It wasn't something that was kept on display."

"It belonged to your husband?"

"So far as I know."

"What do you know about it?"

"Nothing."

Between the terse answers and the hardened expression in her eyes, my keen detective skills told me that I wasn't likely to get more information out of her on this topic. Changing directions seemed best. I brought out Formulaic Homicide Investigation Question #47. "Can you think of anyone who might have a reason to kill your husband?"

"He was rich, and a lawyer, but he didn't go around making enemies. He was generous to the best charities, an active member of the Bar Association, even spoke at a few conferences. He wasn't the type to stir up trouble. Even so, anyone who has Something is the enemy of someone who has Nothing." She frowned at the coffee cup, reached to the front of the arm of her chair and pressed a button that otherwise looked like part of the stuffing. I fancied that I heard the buzzer that must have sounded somewhere in the offing, but it could have been my imagination.

"I asked that we not be disturbed, Mrs. Glover; I won't be much longer. Just don't blame your staff."

The look on her face became harder. "Well?"

"Am I to understand that your husband had no enemies?"

"He did not."

"No one who might—"

"Detective Luton, the answer is no. There have been no life-endangering cases, no crime bosses, no threats, no black lists, no one at all who would want to kill him."

"Very well, then. What about suicide?"

Her face changed significantly at that point. Her voice came out as a soft choke. "What?"

"If we rule out murder, then it must be suicide."

"No." Her headshake made it final.

I paused, calculating the right effect, setting my ears just so, shifting my hindpaws a little. "Mrs. Glover, if no one else could have killed him, then—"

"It couldn't have been suicide. He had his whole life..."

The silence rebutted her without any assistance on my part.

"Impossible," she reiterated softly.

Closing my notebook, I stood slowly. "Mrs. Glover, with that insistence on your part, I must ask you not to leave town for a while. I can't make any charges, because there's no evidence. You've made yourself into the only suspect in a murder case; I have little choice in the matter. I can see myself out."

She made no move, and I thought for a moment that I might have gone too far. Taking a tip from the famous television detective, I turned back to consider her more closely. "Mrs. Glover, your husband was right-paw dominant, wasn't he?"

A blink, a nervous *thap* of her tailtip, something registering or not. "Yes. Right-pawed, yes."

I nodded wisely. "Thank you."

"Detective?"

"Yes, ma'am?"

A long pause. "Why?"

"I can only try to find out, Mrs. Glover."

Her eyes glazed slightly. I turned to leave, her voice haunting me. "Couldn't... couldn't be..."

2: What the Maid Saw

I made my own way out of the formal living room, past another uniform in the hallway. I nodded at the large Shep, a fellow older than Parsons, one who also had a far greater sense of decorum (if that's the phrase I was looking for). He nodded in return. "Anything you need, sir?"

"Directions to the kitchen."

He gestured toward my left. "Quickest way is through the dining room."

"Makes sense," I smiled, sneaking a glimpse at the name tag, then hesitating.

The dog chuckled. "Pah-DEE-ya. Everyone does that."

"I wondered if it was more like the sounds in ar-mah-DILL-oh. Thanks for helping me out, Officer Padilla."

"Anytime, sir."

I moved off, daring to feel that the day might not be as hopeless as first I feared it might be. Cops like Padilla were always good to find; they had a sense of empathy toward others. He helped me avoid a moment of embarrassment by telling me how to pronounce his name. As burned-out as I get these days, I still hope for more like the Shep — in general, in the force, and in those I could work with. Luck of the draw stuck me with Parsons, so I'd live with it.

Navigating my way through an ornate dining room (the type no one in his right mind would use on a daily basis), I padded back into the warmth of a kitchen worthy of the old money that the Glovers pretended to. Generally speaking, "Winchester Heights" was a fancy name for a bunch of McMansions, carefully constructed for ostentation, designed to be mammoth buildings set like architectural sumo wrestlers squatting on perfectly-kept grounds. Having staff for gardening, landscaping, exterior and interior building maintenance, and household servants was a given; if you couldn't afford them, you couldn't live here. I made a wager that there were rooms in this house that were elegantly appointed, designer decorated, carefully kept, and never once used by anyone for any purpose. It was possible that the Glovers didn't even know that they were there.

That was the difference between old and new money. I confess a weakness for a variety of British television programs, and my sense of manor houses made with old money was that they were useful as well as ornate. Even those rooms that look like they should be attic spaces, with dormer windows and a half-dozen sets of stairs to get to, were used by yowens growing up. A whole section of the place would be given over to the house staff, with their own dining areas, modest but well-kept living quarters, and the atmosphere of private gossip and intrigue that became known as "what happens below stairs." Although that sort of thing didn't happen often on this side of the pond, I hoped that some member or members of the staff had picked up on something, even if they didn't know it.

At a kitchen table tucked into its own nook (mentally, I placed a further wager that Mrs. Glover had never stooped to using it), a female white mouse of perhaps twenty-some years sat almost as stiffly as did the white collar of her traditionally-designed gray housekeeper's uniform. Her furless tail was still, her eyes clear; I figured that the tension was partly due to her not understanding why she was there, and partly shock over hearing of her employer's death. Sitting with her, an older female panther in a similar gray uniform held the mouse's forepaw in gentle commiseration. The feline had been there longer, both in terms of service and in terms of who had arrived first that day; the cook would no doubt have been in to prepare breakfast for her employers, and it was she who had kept the coffee pot going.

No matter how quiet I thought my approach, the feline's ears pegged me before I was halfway across. She looked up first, followed by the mouse. I introduced myself, took out the shield to make it official. The panther took up the duties. "I'm Bessie Long, the cook; this is our housekeeper, Allison Doyle. An officer told us to wait for you, 'though the missus...'"

I nodded. "She buzzed while I was there. I think she wants more coffee. I also told her that I had asked you to stay here until I saw you, so you aren't to be blamed. Let me know if she says anything to the contrary."

The panther rose with the fluid grace of her kind, a smile on her muzzle. "I'll make a cup ready to take through. Saves time."

"Let me ask the officer in the hall to take it through. It's sort of a detective thing." My smile was intended to take the sting out of it; instead, I noticed that it made the mouse at the table more nervous. I turned back toward the feline, who busied herself at the counter near the stove. "Does she often take this much coffee?"

"I think it's to give herself something to hold on to that feels normal." The comment was made with a distant compassion. She felt a responsibility toward her mistress, and she was herself compassionate, but not out of a closeness with this employer. The preparation of the brew was quick, made out of ingrained habit, almost without thinking.

"Is so much caffeine healthy for a bereaved tigress?"

"It's been decaf after the first two cups; she hasn't noticed."

That got an appreciative nod from me, and I padded back to the door I had come in by. "Officer Padilla?" I called. "A favor from you."

The big dog made his way through, nodding genially to the maid and the cook, who passed the cup and saucer to him. "Thanks for waiting on her ladyship," the panther winked at him.

"Is that what I should call her?"

"For the sake of your tail, please don't!" The cook laughed gently. "Just 'Mrs. Glover' is plenty."

With an understanding smile, the Shep moved off to deliver the fresh, decaffeinated brew to the mistress of the household, without (I felt sure) supplying the honorific along with it. I wouldn't have trusted Parsons with the job, if only because the pup would have spilled half of it before he'd gotten back to the living room.

The cook resumed her place next to the young maid, once more taking the younger female's forepaw into her own. The mouse still had a quiver about her, one that most cops would think came from guilt. They wouldn't be entirely wrong, but I also wagered they'd misinterpret it. I supposed it would have been a good time to bring out some charm, but I'd left it in my other overcoat.

"Did you have questions for us, Detective Luton?"

"Just a few, thank you. I've already been told that neither of you was here prior to Mrs. Glover telephoning nine-one-one; is that correct?"

"Yes." At a gentle squeeze from the panther's forepaw, the mouse nodded.

"I'm looking for information about the household in general, if that's all right." I indicated a bench across from them, and the cook waved me to it. As I sat, I took note of the view. The breakfast nook wasn't in some dark enclosure; two sides of it were made of what appeared to be double-paned glass, looking out onto a meticulously-kept garden of seasonal succulents, or whatever they were called. I'm bright about a lot of things, but gardens, landscaping, even mowing a lawn was not among them. What I did know was that the view was beautiful. Spring may not have sprung, officially, but a lot of these flowers didn't care.

"Ms. Long, may I ask when you arrived this morning?"

"When the kits are away at school, I'm told to get here to have breakfast ready by seven-thirty on weekdays," she said, either from a practiced rehearsal or from having it ingrained for a number of years. "That's for Mr. Glover; he gets to his office about nine, generally, and he usually keeps it simple. The missus, she could want just about anything, but her schedule is... flexible."

I let the comment pass with a nod. "You arrived today at...?"

"Not quite seven." Her yellow eyes were half-lidded. "I was stopped at the gates by an officer. He didn't want to let me in, until the missus insisted. Word was passed by someone or other, I'm guessing."

"So you were physically in the house at...?"

"Gettin' on for seven-forty-five, I'd say. I had waited out front, to see if the missus wanted me sent home, and when she finally found out I was outside, she sent the word down. I was let in through the back door, like always. Started coffee. Don't think she knows how to work the coffee pot."

I allowed a small smile to agree with her. I took a breath, putting things into a mental timetable; it was creeping slowly toward ten-thirty now. "Are you here through the day, to cook other meals?"

"Weekdays, if the missus goes out, I can have the middle of the day to myself." The panther leaned back a little, her tail making a lazy sort of twitch behind her. "If she's here, I can do the grocery shopping after she's done with breakfast. I get a list, most often, although I can stock up on things we use up regular. I get dinner ready for seven at night, and I can go home after I clean up."

"Long days."

"Pay's okay. I have afternoons out, or take a nap in one of the guest rooms."

"Lot of years?"

"Seven. Since they moved in here. I worked other big houses; this one's 'bout the same."

I nodded, actually making notes for a change. "How was Mr. Glover to work for?" The panther looked cagy for a moment. "I'm not likely to talk to Mrs. Glover again, and I need to know all I can from you. This is between us."

She nodded, although she still had some guard up. "He was always very reasonable." The implication in her tone of voice was that "the missus" was not always so. "Simple tastes. Easy to cook for. Had some favorite recipes that he asked to be sprinkled in among more usual foods. Bad day at the office, he'd call to ask if it would be trouble to make a certain dish, and he was always very grateful for it. Didn't use his buzzer if he could pad his way here. I'd tell him it was no trouble for me, and he'd say that he needed a chance to get away from his work for a few minutes while I fixed up some tea or cocoa for him. He'd sit at this table and talk to me."

"Just talk?"

The yellow eyes turned on me, fully open and hostile. "Mr. Glover wasn't like that."

I held up a placating forepaw. "You know I had to ask."

She paused, backed down from her boil. "Yeah, suppose you did. No, he wasn't like that at all. He was just bein' pleasant. He treated me like a cook, not a slave. He didn't demand; he asked. Said that's why he didn't like the buzzer. Sounded to him like a scream, not just a signal."

"You served dinner last night?"

"As always."

"Anything special?"

"He didn't ask for a special meal, if that's what you mean." The panther took stock of herself and the moment, getting my drift. Her face showed pain at the thought of it. "I have a trick with meatloaf that he liked, and it was a joke sometimes, 'Meatloaf Monday,' like we had it all the time. Just happened to fall..."

Her voice trailed off, and I waited a moment before asking gently, "How did he seem?"

"Quiet. Not so unusual; him and the missus didn't talk much during meals, not for a long while. He was still polite, still turned a smile to me to thank me. It was... well, lookin' back, it was..." She took a long breath. "Nothin' I'd expect from that. Nothin' made me think there was that much wrong."

"It's not something you can actually see, they tell us. Not something you could know."

After a moment, the cook nodded a little. "Such a shame anyhow. He was a good furson. Treated me good."

I nodded, then turned to the white mouse. "Ms. Doyle, what was he like to you?"

"Same."

She continued to avoid my eyes. I put the pen and notepad back into my pocket and brought out my softest voice. "Ms. Doyle, are you all right?"

"A'course I am."

I flicked a glance to the panther, who nodded and leaned a little closer to the mouse. "Allison, how about I make a cup of tea for us? I know you don't much like coffee. How about you, Lieutenant? Which would you like?"

"Tea would be very nice, thank you. If Mrs. Glover decides she wants more than coffee, she can wait for it."

The panther allowed herself the tiniest of smirks. She squeezed the mouse's forepaw again and rose to tend to matters. I shifted, trying to make myself look as casual as possible. "Ms. Doyle, how long have you been working for the Glovers?"

"Three years."

"That's time enough to develop some loyalties. I promise I'm not here to dig up dirt or anything. Must seem like it; cops always have ulterior motives, don't they?"

An involuntary darting of the eyes told me that I'd struck home. Behind me, I heard the panther getting water from the filtered tap to make the tea. Her movements were efficient, and I had solid reason to think that her ears were trained on my every word.

"Ms. Doyle... may I call you Allison?"

She nodded curtly.

"Allison, would you tell me what it was?" She didn't answer, although her tail shook once through before she could stop it. "You appear rather young. I'm thinking it was a time ago, probably juvenile, so the records are sealed. I promise you, I'm not here to expose anything. Please answer one thing. Look at me at tell me that you've had no trouble since."

She turned her terrified, defiant eyes on me, but still she wouldn't or couldn't speak.

"You're in a position of trust in this household, and you're worried about losing your job. You won't, not if I have anything to say about it. Allison, I won't hold this over your head. I need you to trust me, trust that you can talk to me in confidence, and I'm guessing you haven't been able to trust that before. Not with a cop."

The older female returned to the table and reached out for the younger's forepaw again. "Allie... I won't let him hurt you. I think maybe we can trust him. If he throws anything to the missus, I'll call him a liar to his face."

I smiled a little. "And I'd deserve it, too."

The young mouse let fly with a kind of laugh that sounded more like a frightened snort, but she managed to loosen up a bit. "Took a car," she managed.

"Like a joy ride?"

She shook her head. "Had to get away from him. He... he would..."

"I think I understand. How old were you?"

"Sixteen."

"I hope juvie was better to you than he was."

A tiny smile emerged. "Not by much."

I chuckled softly, then looked to the panther. "That's why you defended Mr. Glover so firmly."

She nodded. "He wasn't like that, not to us, not to anyone I ever saw. The records on Allie were sealed, but she wanted to come clean with him when she answered for the job. It was considered GTA, so the files said nothin' about the beatings that damned rat gave her. Mr. Glover, he got the whole story from her, gently. Never did anything, just took her forepaw as she got to crying, offered her the job on the spot. Called me in, told me the whole story, told me I was to help watch after her, in case she got any flak from anyone — ground crew, guests, the kits, his missus, anyone. He wasn't no saint, but he was fair."

"Then help me find out what happened to him."

The tea kettle began to whistle as the panther nodded. She gave a squeeze to the mouse's forepaw again and rose to finish preparing the tea. After a long moment, the young housekeeper managed a small sigh and nodded as well. "Okay. I'll try."

"Thank you, Allison. I'll try not to be such a damn cop."

Despite herself, the mouse giggled (nervously but rather cutely, I thought), and I smiled with what I hoped would be viewed as non-predatory encouragement. I've been told, by a few females in my day, that my eyes had a certain quality that they described as "seductively needful." Apparently, what I had thought of as being a sympathetic look had some tinge of lustful predation to it. I made an effort to keep my ears at a friendly angle and my tail still. I would have had no designs on any female so young, but particularly not one who'd suffered abuse, and at such an early age, and doubly so not one who was connected to a case.

"Let's start with the easy stuff. What time did you get here today?"

"About eight-thirty. Bus was a little early today."

"That's strange by itself!" I smiled, hoping to keep the ice breaking. The smile she gave me made me think it was working. "Which is your stop, to get here?"

"Tolbert Street, about three blocks. Guess I'm still sort of on winter schedules." She must have registered my confused look. "If the streets and sidewalks are icy, I walk slower. Don't want to slip."

"Neither would I. Good thinking. So, about two hours ago?" She nodded. "You were stopped at the gate too?"

"Yes, sir. I was told—"

"Allison, would you like to call me Max?"

A pause. "If you wanted."

Too far. "It's just that 'sir' makes me feel old." I smiled again. "Not a problem. What were you told at the gate?"

"They didn't say much, just called up to the house to make sure I was supposed to be here. Bessie told me what happened."

I wanted to tell her that it took some guts to face down a bunch of cops, given her experience, but that might also be too far. Sometimes, I can actually figure out that it's better for me to keep my tongue behind my teeth. "So you usually get here about eight-thirty?"

"Ish," she said. "Usually, Bessie's the only one who notices."

"I ain't your time clock," the panther smiled. She set down a tray bearing three mugs of hot water, offered me a china bowl with several types of teas in individual bags. "Sorry for the 'instant' treatment, but I didn't know how much time you wanted to spend here. I'll fix real tea for you sometime." She sat, smiling at the mouse, then turned back to me. "Allison's most flexible between us, probably. The missus doesn't want to be disturbed by the cleaning up, so it's the upstairs done anytime after nine, downstairs after lunch."

"Does that include Mr. Glover's library?"

The mouse nodded. "His study, yes sir... urm, yes."

I kept the smile soft as I selected a packet of Constant Comment. Just opening it released the scent of spices into the air. I can be a slave to my nose. So sue me. I took out the bag, put it into the cup, let it soak and sink into the mug to do its work. "Did Mr. Glover ever work from home, Allison?"

"Sometimes."

"Recently?"

She paused, taking a packet almost at random, as if wanting something to do with her paws. As the panther selected Earl Gray, silently encouraging her again, the mouse found her tongue. "A few days this past week, and he was here yesterday."

"He didn't go to the office yesterday?"

"I think maybe he did in the morning, but he came back, or maybe he didn't go after all. Anyway, he was there in the afternoon when I came in to clean. I think I..." The moment stretched. "I think I interrupted him."

"What makes you think that, Allison?"

"I didn't expect him to be there, see, and I just walked in."

"The door was unlocked?"

"Yes." She squirmed, her round ears splaying a little. "I usually knock, just to be sure, but yesterday, I was distracted."

"Music?" the panther asked, and the younger female nodded. The cook looked back at me with a smile. "When Mr. Glover and the missus are out of the house, I let her listen to her music box, whatever it's called these days."

"My phone," the mouse blushed. "I stream music on it, and I'd gotten new songs this week, so I was listening to them."

"Must be good tunes," I agreed. "Was Mr. Glover upset?"

"Oh, no, he wasn't like that..." She paused, looked embarrassed. "Well, he wasn't... I mean, not usually, and not yesterday either. But it was..."

I nodded encouragement. "Just tell me what happened, Allison."

One last hesitation, a flick of an ear, and the mouse plunged in. "It just felt different. I mean, I'd goofed up before, and he was pretty good about it, but he was always... usually, he smiled, being nice, as if he didn't want to hurt anybody's feelings. This time, it was like he was sad. I apologized all over myself, and he said don't worry about it. He looked like he was going to ask me something, and then he stopped. He just looked at all the papers on his desk."

"Could you see what they were? I mean, if they're just lying there, in plain view..."

"Not to read, no, but... well, you know how lawyers seem to have papers tucked into a piece of blue paper, so that it's all stapled at the top?"

"Yes. I think they're called 'legal covers,' and a lot of firms use blue or beige. It's meant to look professional, I think." I finished dunking my teabag, the liquid in the cup seeming about the right color. "It does stand out, though; you can tell at a glance that it's supposed to be a legal brief of some kind or other. Were there a lot of them on his desk?"

"That's the thing, see. Other times, I could see maybe three, four, a half-dozen of them, scattered around. There was only one, and it was over to one side. He was looking at something else, papers in that old-time plastic-backed binding, what's it called?"

I thought back to self-bound sheafs of paper from clubs and some official offices back before emails, PDFs, all the electronic abolition of dead trees. "Comb binding?"

"That's it." She nodded vigorously, her eyes bright, her ears forward. "When I walked in, he closed it up."

"Like he was trying to hide it?"

"Well, not really, I mean, he didn't do it fast, like he was ashamed of it or something. He kept a finger in the place where he'd stopped reading, or I guess so. And he wasn't sharp with me or anything, so it's not like he was reading porn or something, like some males would do. I asked him if he wanted me to come back later, and he said tomorrow." She paused, frowning, blinking a little.

"Allison?"

"Sorry," she flinched a little. "Just... I don't know if..." She shook her head, trying not to smile. "I know, I know — anything could be important. Like on the TV shows."

I nodded, smiling gently at her. "Yeah. It's corny, but it's true. What were you going to say?"

"Well, he said it twice. 'Tomorrow.' The first time, it was like he was just giving me information, as though he'd said the whole sentence, like, 'Come back tomorrow.' And then he looked away from me, and he smiled a little, and he said it softer. 'Tomorrow.' Like he was thinking about..."

The mouse shuddered once through, violently enough to bump the table and jostle the mugs a little. Bessie reached across, taking Allison's forepaws in her own, shushing and holding tightly. "You couldn't have known, Allison. Don't you take that on, hun; it's nothin' you done."

"No, it isn't," I agreed.

"I know, I know," she said, her muzzle quivering. "It's just... remembering like that. It feels like maybe I *should* have known, like..." She stopped again, squeezing the panther's forepaws, regaining herself slowly. I remembered my thoughts about her having courage, and I adjusted them up a notch. I waited until she had gathered herself enough to nod, release her grip on Bessie, and moved to sweeten up her tea with honey. After she'd had a fortifying sip, she nodded once more and looked at me with a more steady gaze.

"Shall we just enjoy tea for a bit?" I asked gently.

"Only if you're done with questions."

"Just one last one, if I may." Her smile was strong again. "Could you read the title on that comb-bound volume?"

"Not all of it," she admitted. "His forepaw was over a lot of it. I thought I saw the word 'Manifest,' like maybe it was some kind of inventory or something." The young mouse sat up just a little straighter. "Got my GED."

"And scored high, I'm sure." I raised my mug in salute, and the two females returned it gently. I let the flavors of orange and sweet spices dance on my tongue as my mind tried to imagine what a real estate lawyer trying to evict squatters would need an inventory of, much less how or why it would be linked to his murder.

3: The Firm Law

I'd like to have lingered over the tea; it was warm, as was the kitchen, and the company was good. I learned that other required services to the McMansion were provided by independent contractors. No big snows for the past few weeks or more, so no one to clear the driveway and walks; gardeners and groundskeepers not expected until the next day. In this distressingly electronic age, no newspaper delivery, and the mail carrier didn't get closer than the cluster of boxes at the foot of the lane. No one beyond the cook and the maid would have any information about what went on in the house, what Glover was like. No doubt, I'd find that he treated tradespersons well, perhaps tipped appropriately or even a little extravagantly, but not too much. Not flashy, just genuinely generous. "Nice" would be the adjective used. A flabby, lame word that unintentionally slights the recipient.

With the rest of the merry band of blue-suits and snoops out of the way, it seemed inappropriate for me to linger. Usually, I'd have been Rhett Butler about it, but I took into account that both cook and housemaid might be in for even worse treatment if I kept them from tending to Her Highness' needs. I made my way to my car — the only one left on the lane, at this point — and climbed inside before getting out my cell phone. Every time I take it out of my pocket and brush a pawpad across the surface to wake it up, I'm reminded that it's not really a phone; it's a small, powerful computer that, almost as an afterthought, can connect by voice (and video, if desired) to similar compact devices, laptops, computers, and even — as I imagine yowens everywhere shuddering at the thought — land lines. I had so few contacts that the "Recent Calls" section of the phone (oh, excuse me, the phone *app*) had all the numbers I needed to dial. I touched one and held the small rectangle with appropriate reverence while it allowed itself to be reduced to the function I used most.

"Crandall," grumped a harsh voice.

"Luton, checking in," I allowed.

"Remind me."

"Glover. Called in as a suicide."

The pause on the line was expected; it was the duration that would make the difference. Captain Ambrose Crandall, who avoided using his first name at almost all cost, suffered also from a few clichés that made his life difficult when dealing with those who wouldn't see past them. He was a bulldog, known for being tough and for not tolerating impertinence or incompetence well. Tenacious, hard-working, by-the-book, Crandall was as incorruptible as it was possible for someone in today's police force to be. As I mentioned before, money talks. Sometimes, it talks to people way above our pay grade, and we get our instructions filtered through the layers.

A short pause was the time it took the cap'n to remember specifics of the case I'd mentioned. A longer pause might mean that he was figuring out if he had room to go by the Book or the Boss. A significantly long pause would mean that he was trying to figure out which rules to bend and to find a good reason for doing it. Either that, or precisely how much tail he was going to chew off, and by what method.

Short pause. "Routine?"

"Glover was right-pawed, the gun was in his left, and the sword was in his right."

"Say again?"

I did.

This pause was covered by a deep inhalation. I braced for chewing, although I didn't think things had gotten quite that far. "Okay," he began, breathing out slowly. "What have you got?"

"Daimler will have the autopsy later, but he doubts he'll find anything other than the obvious. CSI will have the photos for us; the gun is being traced, and I've requested that the sword be analyzed for composition, any hint of who made it, all of that. Wife denies any hint of suicidal tendencies or any threats made by others. Only household staff is a cook and a housemaid; they didn't have much to add. I'll make a report on them today."

"Background?"

"Clean," I said, hoping Allison's juvie record wouldn't pop.

Brief pause — the thought-gathering type. I could almost hear his wheels turning. "You want something."

"The law firm. Just to make it complete."

"What are you sniffing, Luton?"

"Just trying to make it add up, boss. If it's a murder made to look like a suicide, not only was it bass-ackward, it was also too weird to put the sword in his paw. Even the wife isn't sure where the sword came from; as she put it, 'it's not on display.' It had to have been brought out from somewhere, which brings us back to suicide, seems to me. Even if it's really suicide, same questions apply. I want to see if there's any further motive for murder or suicide. Workplace is next."

"Avoid ruffling fur, feathers, or overstuffed egos. Keep it civil."

"You want me to look stupid?"

"Just innocent should work."

"Too late."

"For both of us." He hung up before either of us could take that further.

I set the superbeast on the dash, picked up the folder from the passenger seat, and thumbed through it. The background sheet on Glover included his work address. Finding it would be easy. I've been told that I could rig the All-Knowing Slab to respond to anything I cared to call it, but I haven't gotten around to making it answer to a proper name like HAL, Colossus, or Joshua. I'd rather go classical and holler out, "Omniscient Oracle of Delphi, I beg a boon." Instead, I called up the right app, spoke the address, and let some allegedly female voice give me directions. I'm told I could get other voices as well, and I might look into that, just so I could have someone I could call a friend.

Making myself stop dwelling on such happy matters, I started the car, put it in gear, and followed the electronic breadcrumbs to wherever I was supposed to go next.

* * * * *

The law firm of Langston, Kilgallen, and Mondekirke took up an entire floor of a downtown mid-rise, which was fine with them since they owned the building. They owned a lot of buildings, according to various sources (including their own PR department), and the firm was known for what used to be called "sharp practice" until the distinction was blurred by phrases like "a healthy bottom line" and "strong economy." I'm sure that "caveat emptor" should have been in there somewhere, but it's not politically correct.

A badge can get you past security well enough; it's not always so good with secretaries. I arrived on the 11th floor (not the top, which I thought odd, until I considered how much money they'd make from renting the top floor) and was met by a well-dressed Shiba Inu who welcomed me with that flavor of artificial bonhomie reserved for those who really don't want to have to deal with you. She escorted me through the lobby area, which was decorated in classic Conservative Ostentation style, past some rooms that appeared to be for general consults, and finally into another waiting area, where she passed me over to another secretary who had just padded out of a nearby office. I reintroduced myself, offered credentials (which the ringtail regarded with a wholly professional level of disdain), asked to speak to someone about Glover.

"Mr. Glover hasn't arrived this morning," she informed me. "Perhaps you'd like to make an appointment?"

"I'm here on official business, not personal. I'd like to speak to Mr. Glover's superior, perhaps one of the partners."

"Do you have some complaint against Mr. Glover?"

I stole a glimpse at the sign next to the door that she had come out of. "Ms. Watson, do you work with Mr. Glover?"

"I'm the firm's general manager."

"Then I must report to you that you'll have one less person to manage. Thomas Glover is dead."

Perhaps because she worked for a law firm, perhaps for more personal reasons, the ringtail didn't flinch at the news. "When?"

"This morning."

"Was he in an accident?"

"What happened to him was quite intentional. Perhaps I could speak to someone in charge now?"

She showed no sign of fluster, instead moving to a desk that was bare save for a phone. Sitting in the chair behind it, she made a call to someone else, saying only that "Detective Luton needs a few moments of Mr. Langston's time." After a moment, the word "Official" came out. Something more was said on the other end, and the kinkajou disconnected. "Ms. Stokes will be with you in one moment."

I did my best to keep my stoic as much as she, wondering why it was necessary for either of us. The office manager of a large law firm probably had a lot to do on any given day, yet Ms. Watson sat with her forepaws folded on the empty desk before her, her dark eyes looking at some point past my right hip. Torn between what used to be called "common decency" and professional duties, I hesitated asking any questions for just long enough to be addressed by a well-dressed female cougar bearing down on me from somewhere further down the corridors.

"Detective Luton? Jeanine Stokes, confidential assistant to Mr. Langston. May I ask what this is concerning?"

"I believe you just did."

"Then perhaps you'd care to answer me."

"Thomas Glover is dead."

A response at last, although I mentally banged my wrists together above my head: personal foul, unnecessary roughness. The cougar paused, long enough to tell me that there was a connection of some kind. What kind, or how deep, I couldn't say.

Her brows came together briefly. "Detective..." Swiftly, her demeanor became professional again. "This way, please."

She led me down a hallway, bringing me through her own large office before knocking on the door to the inner sanctum. The "come in" was chiseled, all business, but not necessarily unkind. The cougar opened the door and waved me through, following to introduce me to the big boss.

It was a corner office, of course, complete with huge windows to emphasize the point. On one wall, a solid mass of law books, notably a sizeable selection from *Corpus Juris Secundum,* all kept in pristine condition. They were a form of collectable, by this time; everything was computerized, from cases to the cross-referencing database, with no real need to go back to "dead tree" editions. Like everything else in the office, including a desk of a size that could be used as a runway for small planes, and chairs that had to have cost a packet at Ethan Allen, it was a carefully-designed set piece to reassure clients that every possible contingency for success had been covered. The more subtle variation of this truth is that the success would be guaranteed for the firm and only tangentially for the client. Again, the phrase "caveat emptor" again came to mind.

Rising slowly behind his desk, the great gray rhinoceros, clad in finely-tailored clothing likely to be worth a month or three of a working fur's salary, provided his best imitation smile while his black eyes maintained their calculating assessment of the situation. Gregory Victor Langston dealt in real estate at levels to rival the worst land barons of earlier centuries. His was a household name in the same way that other infamous names become well-known: He did things that made the rich puff out their chests and the rest of us wonder just how badly we'd be affected. He did not offer a forepaw to me; that, I suspected, went to those who closed deals with him.

"What is this about, Detective..." He flicked a glance to the secretary, who provided my name for him. Secretaries do that.

"I regret to inform you," I said, breaking out the diplomacy as per my orders, "that Thomas Glover is dead. I've been assigned to the case."

"What 'case?' What happened to him?"

"It appears to have been suicide, although there are some unusual aspects that I'm looking into."

The cougar made some small sound that I couldn't decipher. Langston's beady black eyes flicked disapprovingly in her direction, then back to me. "What is it that you want of me, Detective?"

I got my notepad out, as the lawyer's mental script would have demanded I do. "Just being thorough. What can you tell me about Glover's current work?"

Resuming his chair, the rhino followed the script that I expected. "You know that I can't discuss cases with you."

"Of course not, sir. I just need background, if possible."

"Why?"

"As I say, I'm being thorough. The body was found this morning and, given the circumstances, I can't be sure if it was actually a suicide or a murder made to look like suicide."

"What circumstances?"

"I'm sure you know that I can't discuss specifics of the case, sir."

Rhino hides aren't supposed to "bristle," but his attitude made it clear that I had scored the point. "A lawyer, by nature of his profession, has enemies, including the law itself."

"Then you suspect murder?"

His laugh was probably meant to be good-natured. "Not at all. I thought you might want a quote for your prehistoric notepad. Honestly, Detective... papyrus and quills?"

"I wouldn't think that you'd prefer I used electronic equipment. These days, they seem capable of recording so very much."

My technique wasn't going to win me points with my boss. My hope was that I hadn't riled the attorney enough for him to complain, merely to comply. I got lucky.

"No," the pachyderm said in low tones. "I doubt that Glover was murdered. He didn't have the right temperament, if you follow me."

"I'm not sure that I do."

"Detective, I'm not a criminal defense lawyer, although I certainly am aware of that area of the law and of the rudiments of your own profession. To be murdered, one must be deserving of it, in someone's eyes. Your concern is murder disguised as suicide, so you assume either the cover-up of a crime of passion or premeditation."

"I can say that circumstances preclude a cover-up."

He flipped over a forepaw. "Premeditated murder implies that the victim is something, has something, or has done something, heinous or important enough to merit being killed. Glover doesn't fit that profile."

"He didn't do anything?"

"Not sufficient to warrant this, no." From an ornate box at the side of his desk, Langston produced a narrow cigar that might even have been paw-rolled. He did not offer one to me, not that I'd have taken it. "He was a quiet, competent, hard-working... legal hack, for lack of a more gracious term. A good worker, precise, thorough, but not enthusiastic. I had the idea that he had become a lawyer for reasons other than the law. That's a mistake."

"How long had he worked for you?"

The rhino considered briefly as he fired up his high-class stogie with an electronic lighter that looked far too small for his large forepaw. "Twelve years, thereabouts." He proceeded to build a fog bank around himself, either unaware or uncaring of the rules about smoking indoors in this state. "Came from a smaller firm in Massachusetts, wanted a bigger field for his particular knack for real estate law."

"Before that?"

"Public defender, upstate New York somewhere. Rochester, maybe Syracuse, somewhere. Got there fresh from law school."

Langston's ability to pull that from memory so quickly spoke either to a remarkable memory or to Glover being more important to the firm than the rhino was letting on. I made more scribbles in my notepad, if only to make it look good. "A good real estate lawyer. So may I assume that the case he was working on had something to do with real estate?"

The pachyderm smiled very quickly. Lawyers do that when they're uncomfortable or preparing to snap shut the trap. "You aren't easily sidetracked, Detective."

"Actually, I am. I get my attention pulled away by darting squirrels and flying disks. I just have this peculiar quirk that lets me remember when a question hasn't been answered."

"My answer was that I can't discuss specifics of the case."

"Glover specialized in real estate, and I know that it had something to do with evicting squatters." To the concerned look on the rhino's features, I replied, "His wife."

"Figures," he grunted, making more fog.

I flipped a page in the notebook, wondering how long it would take to get the stink of that overpriced cheroot out of my fur, not to mention my nose. "Was the case serious enough to warrant getting Glover out of the way?"

"Wouldn't do any good. Glover prepared it all, and he'd present it in court to answer challenges, but I'm the attorney of record; the case itself would go on without him."

"Naturally."

Cold, obsidian eyes marked me where I stood. I remained immune to what he probably thought of as a Medusan stare. "That's all the time that I can spare you, Detective."

"A final question." I gave the statement credence by pocketing the notebook and pen. "Do you know anything about a sword in Glover's possession?"

The merest fraction of hesitation. "No." He turned to the cougar. "Jeanine, I need you to put someone in Glover's place immediately. I'm sure the Detective can find his own way out."

Turning to the feline, I saw a moment of hesitation in her as well, a flash of the real furson behind the professional exterior, before she silently indicated the door. I thanked her, moved through her office and into the hall, momentarily wishing that I'd thought to bring a ball of twine with me on the way in. Before I had a chance to feel too lost, I saw a face I recognized. The general manager's anxious black-and-white tail told a complex story that I only caught part of. Ringtails aren't common in my world.

"Do you need something, Detective Luton?"

I returned the courtesy. "Looking for the elevators, Ms. Watson," I said, working to put a smile on my muzzle.

"This way. Would you mind if we stopped by my office on the way? I need to pick up some papers."

"Of course," I demurred. It was an easy code to decipher; I wondered why she felt compelled to use it.

I recognized the small waiting area, once we'd found it again. I followed her into her office, discovering that, for a firm which dealt in real estate, the bosses had no concept of allocating space. Langston's office was unnecessarily huge, while the furson overseeing the essential needs of organizing the whole show was put into a space overcrowded by the materials required to make it all work. The waiting area felt larger.

She didn't close the door; she simply kept her voice low. "The case was supposed to be heard this morning. The judge's chambers should have called by now, with an angry notification of the absence. With no one there to represent the complainants, the respondents may get a judgment in their favor; at the least, they'll have a reprieve. Here." She passed over a paper that looked very official.

"This is...?"

"A copy of the docket information. The court will have the filing. It's public record."

I considered the information. "Why is Langston being so cagey? He would have to know that we'd find all this out eventually."

"He gives nothing for nothing." She glanced at the door, then back to me. "I think he sometimes gives nothing for something."

My nose twitched, and not from the smell of that stinking cigar. What stayed my further questions was twofold: That sort of fraud wasn't my case, and I didn't want to get the ringtail into trouble. I had the feeling that there'd be enough of it without my hiking a leg on the pile.

"Thank you, Ms. Watson," I said softly. "May I contact you if I need you further?"

She reached behind her, taking a business card from a small stack. "My direct line is on there. Please, let me know what you find." She paused before saying, "I don't think he'd have had anything to do with it."

I knew who she meant, nodding as if I understood what "it" might be. I gave her a card of my own, jutting my chin to the door. "Let's not draw attention."

Her eyes thanked me as she led me out of her office and back to the lobby. The Shiba Inu was nowhere to be seen, nor was anyone else. The elevator arrived in short order. She shook my forepaw, thanking me for visiting, asking that I let her know if there was anything else that I needed. I thanked her in return, promising to do so. I stepped into the car, carefully avoiding looking at the surveillance camera. I knew there was one here; I didn't know what others were in play, other than one in the office's lobby (obviously), and it wouldn't make any difference to know. Living in a police state, even the police aren't safe, if they aren't part of the right type of police.

I shook my head as the doors opened on the ground floor. I had too many bits of misinformation whirling in my mind, and I needed a lunch break, perhaps one that would last for a decade or so. Signing out at the security desk, I asked casually if there was a good place nearby to catch some lunch. The Dobie behind the faux-marble counter 'llowed as how the place around the corner had a good buffet spread; just take the stairs inside the doors to get to it. I thanked him, and he stopped me before I could leave.

"Tell me to back off if it's private, but what's this about?"

"What's what about?"

"That shield is for homicide. Who got killed?"

"A guy named Glover."

The Dobie looked stricken. "Aw crap, not Mr. Glover?"

"You knew him?"

"Worked for the big guns upstairs. Wouldn't have thought he was a lawyer, 'specially not for that bunch. He was a nice guy, ya know? Called me by name, said hello when he went by. What happened?"

"Still working on that."

"Ah. Yeah." He shifted on his hindpaws, looked apologetic. "Sorry."

"How was he yesterday?"

"Mr. Glover wasn't in yesterday. I thought he might be feeling bad or something." He had the good grace to look a little ashamed.

"Did he seem worried lately, off his game, any changes in behavior?"

The guard considered a moment, nodded slowly. "Now ya come to say it... He'd been kinda quiet last week. Started off okay, then got quiet about, say, Wednesday, I think."

"Quiet, as in worried, distracted...?"

"Distracted, or maybe..." The dog wasn't stupid, it seemed to me, just hunting for words. It felt like he was trying to be accurate for me. I gave him credit for that when he said, "Lost. That's more like it. Ya know the kind of look I mean?"

"I think I do," I nodded. "Started about Wednesday, you say?"

"Yeah." He also nodded, more definitively. "He hardly said anything to me on Thursday or Friday, not even when he left with that box."

"Box?"

"Yeah, a wooden box. Maybe this long," he held his forepaws about a meter apart, "slim, maybe 50-by-30cm."

"He took it from his office?"

"I guess so. I mean, he was leaving the building with it. I didn't think to stop him. Did he steal it or somethin'?"

"No, I don't think so. You had no reason to stop him. He wasn't acting furtive or anything?"

"No; regular, like always, just quiet."

The pup passed his vocabulary test. Someone I'd call smarter than his job description. "Any idea what could be in the box?"

Again, he considered carefully. "My uncle is a Marine." He smiled a little. "Not active in the service anymore, but he always tells me that 'ex-Marine' isn't a real word. Anyway, he's got a sword used for full-dress occasions, and he keeps it in a wooden box, about that size and shape. That's what it reminded me of. Was Mr. Glover ever in the service?"

"Not that I know. Besides, how often does your uncle kit out in full-dress?"

"Once every several years, unless there's funerals involved."

"And he wouldn't take it to work?"

The Dobie smiled. "Not the kind of equipment you need to drive a truck."

"Might be good for directing your way out of a traffic jam." We shared a laugh, and I passed a card to him. "If you think of anything else, let me know, okay?"

"You bet, Detective... Luton." He read the card and nodded, sticking out a forepaw to shake. "Nathaniel Cole." He grinned at me. "Gonna go there?"

"Not on a bet." I pressed his pads properly, wondering if this Nat was a singer too.

"Thanks." He sobered a little. "Let me know what you find out."

"No lynching."

"Always tempting, never followed through. I might be a rent-a-cop, but I hope I know enough to follow the law."

"With that attitude, you're not a rent-a-cop. I'd call you a security guard who might benefit from sitting for the exams. Just a suggestion."

"Really?"

Remembering Parsons, I nodded. "It's cliché to say we need better recruits. It's also true. Give it some thought."

"You think I'd make it?"

I smiled at him. "Quizás, quizás, quizás."

His laughter sounded good in my ears as I left the building.

4: Of Dumplings and Dumps

The Dobie security guard was right about the Flaming Grill Buffet. It was surprising that the place could afford the space for five full islands of food, much less the kitchens and the spacious dining area, located as it was in the heart of downtown. Perhaps it was because they took the below-street-level space underneath one of the huge car parks. It was a chicken-and-egg story, since some dozen city blocks of underground space had developed into a warren of corridors and mall areas where shops and restaurants vied for the traffic of offices far above them. They must have been doing well, as they had been there for some time and, judging by the modest crowd in the place, were reasonably popular. I have no idea how these things work; I just doubled down on the potstickers and let my Primary Care Physician panic about my weight on his own time.

"May I join you?"

I was surprised to see a certain ringtail, a plate balanced in one foreapaw, iced tea in the other, her dark eyes holding mine directly. Glancing quickly around the tables, I said, "Sit down."

As she slid into the high-backed booth, I noticed her body language — nervous, determined, perhaps angry (at whom or what?). My own habits had positioned me to be able to see the entrance, and the office manager of Langston, Kilgallen, and Mondekirke folded herself into the corner of the booth, well out of sight. I didn't imagine that such stealth was necessary, but I let her set the tone.

"Nat told me you might be here," she offered by way of explanation.

"Office staff have to check out at the guard's desk?"

"Card swipe. I took the chance of asking him if you'd talked to him."

"Checking his loyalties?"

"Checking mine." She drew a breath, let it out slowly as she bit the end off of a spring roll, then proceeded to use the soy sauce bottle properly, sealing one opening of the cap with a digital pad, then making a tapping motion to allow small amounts of sauce to begin filtering down through the layers of vegetables and wrapping. I decided that the female was a regular to this establishment.

"Whatever you want to tell me, Ms. Watson," I offered, letting her take her time.

"Chelsea."

I took the chance that it was her first name and not referring to the fancy west side of London. "Max."

She made her way through the spring roll in a time period somewhere between gourmet and glutton. I filled in the time with bacon-wrapped shrimp, adding cardiology to the list of Physicians To Panic list. I did my best to keep my ears and tail still; I had no idea what might spook her. I wasn't at all sure what to expect from her, but whatever it was that she would tell me, I wanted it.

"We weren't close," she said first, rearranging pork fried rice on her plate. "It's nothing sordid."

"I didn't presume, Chelsea."

The dark lips in her pointed muzzle curved up in a smirk. "You'd be the first."

"If you weren't close, what were you?"

She did her best not to sigh. "Do you like your job?" Looking up at me, she didn't wait for a response. "I like my job in the same way that one likes critical open heart surgery: It's necessary to sustain life. I take the paycheck, and I earn it in more ways than one. Law firms like LK&M are a major part of the reason that it takes twice as much money to survive as it probably should. They absorb real estate and inflate its paper value beyond any ordinary furson's ability to buy a home, then work with banks to double the costs again with interest. A lawyer doesn't ask what's right; he asks what's legal."

I thought waiting was best, and I gave myself over to my own spring roll, dipping it in some duck sauce.

"Thomas," she paused very slightly, tasting the name as much as saying it, "was good at his work without being a complete bastard about it. It's why I said that he couldn't have anything to do with it. Langston wouldn't involve Thomas in anything that wasn't simple black-letter law, nothing that had any wiggle room in it, nothing that could involve a conscience."

"You're saying he had a conscience?"

"What did Langston say?"

"It was learned counsel's opinion that Mr. Glover had chosen to become a lawyer for reasons other than the law."

The ringtail's appetite seemed to be a product of necessity rather than pleasure. She had chosen, by my eye, small portions of three dishes, with a single spring roll (now dispatched) and the pork-fried rice, which was soaking up sauces from the three dishes. She would spear a bite's worth and convey it to her maw with efficiency rather than gusto. Having finished one of those bites, she nodded slowly at my description.

"Accurate," she assessed. "Langston and his partners are word-twisters and evaders of the law. Thomas wanted something closer to fairness."

"Seems to me that would make him unpopular."

"Unusual, maybe. He was a public defender, long before he came here. I had the feeling that the old job seasoned him somehow. He seemed more likely to defend a poor sap caught up in some legal trouble rather than work in conveyancy."

"Pretend I don't know what that means."

"Preparing documents for transferring ownership of property." The words tumbled from her maw as if by rote, which is what a lot of legal work seemed to be concerned with. "It can be simple, straightforward, which is the type of work Thomas did. It can also be fraught with complicated clauses, loopholes, and traps that can negate or convolute the intention of the conveyance. Do you have any land holdings, Detec... Max?"

"They say I'll own my house in another twenty years or so."

"Did you ever want a house in the country?"

"About as much as I want a luxury cruise. Neither one is in my foreseeable future."

She managed a smile at the comment. "If you purchase land, be careful to find out if you're also buying the oil, mineral, and gas rights to the property. If not, it's at least possible that the owner of those rights could plant an oil derrick in your living room without needing your permission."

A bit of bacon-wrapped shrimp didn't quite make it to my maw which, under ordinary circumstances, would be nigh-on impossible. "You can't be serious."

"It's extremely unlikely, for any number of reasons, but it's theoretically possible, under a strict interpretation of the land conveyance contract. That's the kind of thing that LK&M specialize in."

"But not Glover."

The ringtail's tail shifted a little behind her as a shiver briefly overtook her. Shaking her head, she said, "I can't believe that he could keep his paws clean in every way, but I know that he tried. He couldn't be a crusader, at least not under the corporate banner. I have reason to think that he did some pro bono work, legal consulting, reading over a conveyance contract for instance." She looked down at her plate. "It wasn't secret, but it wasn't broadcast, either."

"You'd think it would be good PR, proving how the Big Bad Law Firm does good works."

"You assume that they want that sort of image. LM&K are more in a position to be feared, and they like the 'iron fist inside a Gucci glove' thing. It gives our high-dollar clients the impression that no one will be able to touch them, no matter what the other side might try."

"Is that true?"

"More often than I'd like." She stirred her food around a little more. "With Thomas gone, I have even greater incentive to leave."

I considered various implications of that statement. "These pro bono cases. Anything that might have to do with the law firm's business?"

"No. Conflict of interest, even if it's free advice. Thomas would not allow himself to be put into that situation."

"Would any of those pro bono clients be upset enough to kill him over it?"

Another headshake. "If anything, they were grateful to him for clarifying their contracts."

I let the silence stretch as I considered making another pilgrimage to the serving islands. "Chelsea, are you all right?"

She brought her dark eyes up to meet mine, seeming to wrestle with the answer to my question. "You probably know the saying about dancing with the devil. I wasn't coerced. To manage a law firm's office takes strong skills. I have those skills, and I'm good at what I do." She toyed briefly with the food on her plate. "Maybe it's time to find somewhere else to be good at it."

"I'm sorry for your losses."

The plural caught her ear. "There might yet be a gain."

Sometimes, I'm able to read signs. I excused myself for another round of food. The ringtail merely nodded. My first plate was made of appetizers, so I helped myself to a modest sampler of a few main course items, skipping the rice — too filling. I returned to the table to find myself alone once more. She had tucked a few bills under the lip of her plate. The money covered her meal and a modest tip. She was considerate of a cop's salary, which was another point in her favor. There was a time when I'd have made a point to pay for a female's meal. There was a time when I'd have had a female to buy a meal for. I took my time over the pepper steak and tried not to think about it.

* * * * *

I stayed downtown long enough to get a copy of the court documents for the case that Glover was supposed to have faced down that morning. The clerk asked if I knew anything about why neither the complainant nor his attorney had appeared. When I explained the reason for Glover's absence, the clerk became a little more cooperative. I took just the brief that the judge had to consider; there appeared to be a whole tree's worth of paper supporting the complaint, and I hoped that I wouldn't have to wade through it. It should be enough just to find out who "the other side" was.

Returning to the office was always an experience in contrasts. It had the comfort of being familiar, the closest thing I had to "home," these days; it had the annoyance of being perversely regimented. The phrase "law and order" was often a juxtaposition of clashing terms. In theory, these offices were where we upholders of the law can order ourselves and our paperwork; drowning in the latter, overcrowded by the former, it was amazing that we could get anything done.

I set the court paperwork on my desk, making sure that I could find it amid the rest of the paper clutter, and padded my way to the open door of the captain's office. I knocked on the frame, and the bulldog looked up at me with softly appraising eyes. His attitude was always one of beneficence until the situation proved that another approach was needed. "Glover?" he asked.

"Yes."

"Law firm?"

"Interesting, as far as it went. Lunch was even better."

I gave him an outline of the office visit, along with the highlights of the office manager's lunchtime input. He considered it for a few moments, looking for all the world as if he should have a fat stogie stuck in the corner of his maw, lit or unlit, something for him to chew on. Remembering Langston, I was just as glad he wasn't one to give in to the stereotype.

"You got the court filing?"

"On my desk."

"Worth following?"

"About the only lead we have, this early."

"Need backup? I imagine the two-six can spare Parsons."

"I can spare him, too."

"That bad?"

"Yappy."

Crandall leaned back in his chair, nodding sagely. "He'll learn, or he'll wash out."

"So hard to find good help, these days."

"Glad you're so eager to see the respondents in the real estate case. I've heard the phrase 'hostile possession' out there somewhere."

"Going into real estate, Cap'n?"

"Soon as I hit the lottery."

* * * * *

The property was further out in the country than I felt easy about driving to, so late in the day; I chose to put it off until the morning. I used the evening to go over the essence of the complaint, using the Internet to explain a few concepts to me. Squatters have some rights, depending on many circumstances; they could also take ownership of a property, although it wasn't exactly easy. Squatters in an abandoned building, or in an apartment that a landlord had told them to vacate, walked a fine line between squatting (a civil matter) and trespassing (a criminal matter). I'd like to have seen Glover's notes about his visit, but those would fall under Langston's "privilege" umbrella.

The drive was decent, for another semi-predictable April day of cloud and early-morning drizzle. At least the state road was reasonably well-kept. The All-Knowing Micro-Monolith had some trouble locating the chunk of land I'd asked it to take me to; the location didn't have a physical address, not even a rural route number for a mailbox. I didn't imagine squatters would want one, and the landowner (from what I could tell) had no immediate plans to develop it. No driveway had been made to get into the acreage itself. There was what was called a "fire road," although the term "mudslide" might have been more accurate that morning. I only hoped that my old sedan wouldn't get stuck. I figured I'd be all right, but I wouldn't have wanted to make book on it.

A logging road would have been a straight cut, I'd been told, since those big trucks hauling a load of 15m pine trees wouldn't want to make tight turns. The fire road was meant to get 8-10m trucks of equipment to battle possible forest fires in this heavily-wooded area. Not every tract out here had a fire road running through it, and they generally aimed for an easement between two properties, which made for the possibility of curves in the road to follow the property lines. Yeah, I'd gotten an education the night before.

There was something of a curve in this fire road, and just past said curve is where I found the encampment of squatters. A half-dozen tents, from small two-person tents to the larger, almost palatial-seeming family tents, for starters. Some measure of construction to one side had yielded a larger tent from which smells of cooking emanated. The overall décor was Army Surplus, and not nearly so well-kept as it ought to be, with the general sensation of a lazy fur's oath of "good enough" plastered on top of it. I saw the quick-and-dirty construction of a pair of potty sheds to one side, each likely to have a chemical toilet at best. It was hardly paradise.

The drizzle had let up by now, leaving only residual drops falling from breeze-jostled pine needles. A few specimens of the group were outside of their tents when I arrived: an overweight bull (which is saying something); a lanky, underfed fox with a very nervous look about him; and a ewe, clearly pregnant. All were clothed, if barely, in cast-off clothing that had seen better days long before they were cast off. The term "living rough" seemed an understatement.

I pulled up a short distance from a few other vehicles on what seemed a reasonably compact verge, while the trio marked my every move. The sound of my engine had roused a few others from their various occupations and brought them out, making a total of seven so far. I saw no weapons but, having a perverse wish to keep living despite various reasons not to, I moved slowly, making my way out of the car, closing the door softly, standing next to it, trying to look like a harmless, friendly collie, ears neutral, tail still, waiting for them to make a move.

"And whadda *you* want?" the bull grumped at me.

"Name's Max Luton. Yes, I'm a cop; no, I'm not armed, and I don't have any warrants or papers. Just here to talk."

"What about?"

"A homicide."

"We're not killers," the ewe spoke up even as a large ram — her mate, I assumed — came up to put his arms protectively around her.

"I have to talk to anyone connected with the deceased."

"Who died?" the bull wanted to know.

"Thomas Glover."

"Never heard of 'im."

"The lawyer?"

I turned to answer the fox, who still appeared nervous. "Yes."

Explaining himself to his cohorts, he said, "He came here last week. To remind us about the court date yesterday. He didn't show..." He blinked, making the connection.

The bull charged on. "And the judge ruled in our favor, 'cuz he didn't show. We get to stay here."

I didn't challenge him. "You can see why I need to ask you questions."

"That's not how we do things."

The voice came from what I took to be the cooking tent. A matronly coyote padded out of it, moving a little closer to me than the others, but still a good five meters away. She was dressed a touch better than the others, or at least the clothes looked to be better cared for. A large cook's apron, bearing a logo from a fast-food chain, covered her ample front. "I'm called Pearl, or Mama, but not to you."

"I haven't earned that right."

She nodded slowly. "Respectful, for a cop. Keep it that way, and we'll get along."

"Fair," I acknowledged. "I'm guessing you didn't all go to court yesterday."

"Nope. Just five of us. The rest stayed here."

I paused, looking at the coyote squarely. I could see that she knew the drill; who wouldn't, after all the cop shows on television?

"No, we can't prove it," she said. "Can't prove a negative either."

"True," I nodded. "Let's skip that for a minute. Tell me about Glover's visit here last week. How did he seem? What was he like?"

"Typical tiger," the bull grumbled, "and rich besides, and a lawyer, even worse. Come into our home to tell us we hadda get out."

"You'd already been served papers. Why did he come here?"

"He came to verify our claims," Pearl said, her forepaws to her hips. "Squatters have rights. We've made improvements to the property. We found this space, unoccupied, unposted; moved our tents here late last fall. Got through a cold winter, started readying for a garden." She jutted her chin to an area beyond the cooking tent; I was too far away to see what she was talking about. "We're not hiding here, and we have no issues with the law. We're squatters, not criminals."

"I'm not a judge. I just want to know about Glover. I only met his corpse."

"He was here to get us thrown off!" The big bull advanced two paces toward me. I held my ground. "We're workin' hard here, just to have a place to live!"

"He was here," the coyote admonished, "to do his job. We talked about this, Isaac. We knew from the start what we'd be up against."

"Then you were okay with his visit?" I asked.

"No," Pearl acknowledged before Isaac could start up again, "but he came here with a job to do. He was right reasonable respectful, didn't pry. Asked to look around. We showed him what we're doing to establish our claim as squatters."

"What did he say to that?"

"Wasn't his place. He was working for the land owners."

"Conflict of interest."

"He wanted to."

I turned toward the ewe, who looked at me gently. I asked, "He wanted to help you?"

She nodded. "I could see him holding back. Conflict of interest. He used those words twice."

"You spoke with him?"

Another nod.

"How did he seem? Besides conflicted."

"He was..." Her hesitation reminded me of the Dobie back in town — considering, trying to be accurate. "I don't know how to read faces, like some can. He just seemed... sad, maybe. Lost."

The hackles at the back of my neck enacted a cliché, and I was glad that my overcoat collar covered it, or the bull might have thought I was going to mount an attack. I regained myself enough to ask, "How long was he here?"

"Maybe twenty minutes," Pearl told me. "After that, he packed himself into his fancy four-wheeler and left."

"You said that was Wednesday, right? Week ago today?"

"Yes."

I nodded. "Thank you for your time."

"You clearing us?" the fox wanted to know.

Weighing my options, I decided to take the chance. Addressing myself to Pearl, I said, "I was at Glover's law firm yesterday morning. Gregory Langston, senior partner, told me that he's the attorney of record, and that Glover was more or less just his proxy in the courtroom. The papers you were served with would have that information. Once the judge hears the reason for Glover's absence, he will issue a continuance, I imagine. One way or another, the land case isn't over. In terms of Glover's death, you're cleared, as far as I'm concerned. You have no motive for killing him."

The bull issued a snort so strong that it could be taken as an assault in some states, and it was a threat clearly enough. "We're not violent!" he insisted.

"I think it's time for you to leave," Pearl said gently. "We're about to have an early lunch. Isaac, Wally, Beatrice... how 'bout you help set places?"

The ram and ewe moved toward the cooking tent, while the bull held his ground, staring at me with black eyes that I did my best not to flinch from. None of the other watchers flicked an ear or tail, not sure how this would turn out.

"Isaac." The coyote's voice was firm, but not raised.

Again taking a chance, I padded slowly backward, preparing to open my car door. This broke the standoff without making the bull look like he was capitulating. He moved toward the cooking tent, eventually taking his eyes from me.

"Drive safely, officer," Pearl told me.

Nodding, I got into the car and, with no sudden moves, aimed myself back down the fire road. The distance to the state highway seemed longer than it should have been, and I was inordinately grateful for the lack of traffic. Barely slowing down for the turn, I took off from the fire road and forced myself not to break the sound barrier to put that bull far behind me. The reaction was visceral, irrational, based on memories of thugs and ruffians long past. He was clearly capable of the violence that he violently protested against, but I didn't credit him with the idea of breaking into a house, being lucky enough to find and use the owner's gun, then staging a suicide, especially with the sword.

Come to that, none of the squatters seemed to fill that bill. From what I saw, they were too lazy for it. If they made camp just before winter, they'd had a minimum of four months to get their campgrounds together. Considering the numbers that I saw, they could have erected the tents in a day, the wooden structures in a week. Even factoring in the cold of a relatively mild winter, they just hadn't been doing that much for themselves.

My wits returned from their brief vacation, and I found myself wondering what Glover saw. The players, sets, and props were the same for him as for me, but what plays did we see? The lines were different, the outcome different, even the actions of the players were different. My play was about seeing no reasonable motive or means to commit the crime; what was his about, and what did he think and feel after his visit to this backwoods theater? I wanted to see his notes more than ever, and I had no idea if I could get them. Langston played too close to the chest; as a certain ringtail had told me, he gave nothing for nothing.

Perhaps I could arrange another lunch date.

5: Of Mice and Menace

I'm not one of those hardcore city dwellers who doesn't like the country. My relief in returning to the city was exclusively that of feeling that I had escaped a physical threat. Rationally, I knew that the response was entirely out of proportion to what had happened. I wouldn't care to try taking on the big bull, whether in the woods or a dark alley somewhere; I also had to admit that the confrontation wasn't likely. Some other factor was at work, and I couldn't say what it was. I don't scare easy, as a rule, but something about the encounter had put my fangs on edge.

Good food usually has a comforting effect on me, and on this particular day, I knew exactly what I wanted. It might be just the carnivore in me, or perhaps it was a subconsciously Freudian railing against my unknown fears, but a gravy-covered country fried steak, bordered by mashed potatoes and sweet corn, remains unbeaten in my list of comfort foods. At the table of my local hole-in-the-wall, where they knew me best for that order, I pushed aside my feelings about the angry male I'd encountered earlier today and thanked, with silent grace, the non-sapient being that had given up its life for my nourishment. As an afterthought, the bull at the encampment came back to mind, and I wondered whether he should be considered sapient enough to avoid the same fate. Abashed at the thought, I made myself concentrate on appreciating and enjoying my food rather than disrespecting it.

Back in my car, I made reasonably sure that I wouldn't belch during my check-in with the boss. I activated my Infinity Device (Pocket Edition) and dialed... pressed? Swiped? Digitized, using a single digit to touch the screen? Whatever. It rang for me.

"Crandall," came the familiarly crabby voice.

"Checking in, cap'n."

"Communing with the great outdoors?"

"Complete with commune."

"They kept you a long time."

"Lunch."

A short pause on the phone. "Tell me you didn't visit Jo and Phil's..."

"Okay, I won't."

The bulldog voiced a passing comment about the legitimacy of my whelping and a mild threat against the continued functioning of my most personal equipment.

"I'm guessing you're stuck with the local mess today."

"Accurate in more than one way. Tell me about your blissful morning."

I can't say my description demonstrated any measure of bliss, but it did get the general idea across. The boss managed a bark of a chuckle at me.

"I'd be cheering on the bull."

"Nice of you."

"Allow me to make it worse. We may have another lead after all. Someone named Willy Keaton." He gave me an address far enough away from the precinct to make it irritating, and he damn well knew it. "Threatened Glover for serving him with papers."

That put my ears forward. "Glover himself? Not a cop or a minion? Why would he do that?"

"A great question to ask Keaton. I knew you'd make a decent detective one day."

"Fried steak, corn fresh-cut from the cob—"

"Obscene phone call." He hung up on me before I could get more graphic about how smoothly the potatoes were mashed or how the butter and gravy made everything all slick and sticky at the same time. This was not new banter between us. It was, however, almost enough to make me want to go back for second helpings.

* * * * *

Keaton's neighborhood was picture perfect, save for a certain set of eyesores, all of them from his house and yard. The chain-link fence was the only one on the block, and it reached almost to the edge of the sidewalk. A mailbox stood on a post just inside the fence, and fence links were anchored into the outer surface of the box itself, which was the type that allowed only flat items of limited thickness into the slot at the upper portion of the box. House numbers were painted on the front of it, but none appeared on or near the front door. Security floodlights were evident above the front door and the doors to the garage. I almost expected a sign declaring *ABANDON HOPE ALL WHO ENTER HERE.*

Paradoxically, the gate in the fence bore no padlock. Perhaps Keaton had a non-sapient pet who enjoyed the freedom of running around the yard. Given the set-up, I'd not have been surprised if the pet was uniformed and patrolled the perimeter on a tight schedule. I let myself in, making sure that the gate latched properly behind me. Padding up to the front door (itself fitted with a metal barricade), I found the buzzer and let it ring for a civil length of time. The response didn't take long.

"Get out of here!" a voice shouted from behind the door. "You're trespassing!"

"Mr. William Keaton?"

"Who wants to know?"

"I'm Detective Max Luton—"

"Invasion of privacy! Harassment! Get out of here!"

"—Homicide," I finished, when he took a breath.

Considering the tirade that went before, the silence was remarkable. "What's it to do with me?"

"Routine questioning, Mr. Keaton. Shall we talk inside?"

"Who died?"

"Thomas Glover."

Anticipating Keaton's next move, I reached into my jacket pocket for my shield. I heard only one lock slide before the door inched its way open. Holding the ID in plain view, I waited for Keaton to swing the door enough for us to size each other up. The brown mouse was of shorter stature, his round ears pert and slightly flushed. Slim, his casual clothing surprisingly crisp, his hairless tail guarding his hindpaws, he looked at me with whiskers twitching as if sniffing for deception. "You're still trespassing."

"Official business. Your gate is unlocked, and there was no way to announce my presence without coming up to the door." I gestured behind me. "I made sure that the latch was in place after I entered."

He paused, as if sizing up what sort of retort was called for. "So what are you here for?"

"I'm investigating the death of Thomas Glover."

"Nothin' to do with me."

"He served papers on you."

"Illegally!" the mouse spat, his tail giving a quick lash.

"What happened?"

"Came up to the door, like you, bold as brass. Identified himself as one of the muckety-muck lawyers in that firm I'm suing. They'd been trying to serve papers on me, countersuit, and I refused to talk to any of them."

"They didn't go to your lawyer?"

He raised himself up as high as he could go, proclaiming, "I represent myself. I know my rights."

"What happened?"

"He said he was here to help me. He wanted to talk about the case without having to go through the courts."

"You fell for that?"

"I fell for nothing! He started telling me things about the three bases for my lawsuit against his firm. Told me that the points I was suing on had 'broad interpretations,' as he put it. Sounded to me like he was giving up the game, switching sides, so I opened the door to hear more. That was when he pushed the papers at me and served me for the countersuit. I'm protesting; he did it unfairly, illegally. I know my rights."

"I'm sure you do, Mr. Keaton. Why would he tell you all that? Conflict of interest, isn't it?"

"All outlined in the countersuit. Most of it, anyway. He said something about the use of *Kelo v. City of New London* being limited by state legislature. That wasn't in the brief."

"Did it help?"

He wrestled with a response for a moment, long enough for me to take him off the hook.

"How did Glover seem?"

"Seemed like a damn lawyer, that's how he seemed. Used a trick to give me papers I didn't want."

"And some advice, against his own interests." That was a guess, considering that I had no idea at all what that court case was about. "When did all this take place?"

"Two weeks ago." The rodent seemed more secure about himself on this point. "I drafted a letter to the bar association to complain about his trickery."

"Have you mailed it?"

He nodded vigorously. "Return receipt. I should get it soon. They usually reply promptly to the receipt."

"You've had dealings with them before?" This did not surprise me, and he made no response to it. "Do you get any satisfaction from them?"

"They protect their own, so no, I don't hear from them often."

"Does that make you mad?"

"It should infuriate any sensible citizen!" he declared.

"Mad enough to do something about it?"

The mouse gave me a withering stare, although I declined to be withered. "I already did something about it. I would not resort to murder. I know my rights."

"So you've said. Can you tell me your movements from, say, Monday evening to Tuesday morning?"

Keaton's ears shifted slightly as his posture became defensive. "I was... indisposed."

"Here at home?"

"No."

"Where were you?"

"I was... out."

"Where?"

No answer.

"Any witnesses where you were?"

Grinding his teeth a little, he finally admitted, "On Monday evening, I was in the company of two males in uniform who were attempting to violate my civil rights."

I leaned forward slightly. "Would you care to be more specific?"

"They claimed that I had run a stop sign, but it was at a corner so overgrown that I couldn't see it. Clearly entrapment. They kept me for nearly three hours."

"For a traffic stop? Why didn't they just give you a ticket and move on?"

"They couldn't cite me without a driving license." He once more attempted to raise himself to full height. "I don't require one. I'm allowed to make use of public roads, in all circumstances. It's black letter law. They can't prohibit my use of the roads. It's my right to go where I please."

"Three hours?" I asked.

"They were trying to arrest me, to imprison me for exercising my freedom to go where I please, to do with myself as I please. It's the same reason that I refuse to pay income taxes."

"Is that black letter law as well?"

"Taxation without representation. I am disallowed to vote, therefore I have no say in who represents me, therefore I am not represented."

"Who's stopping you from voting?"

"They say I require government identification to register." His tail lashed briefly before settling around his hindpaws again. "It's a conspiracy."

* * * * *

When I got back to the station house, Captain Crandall was out. For all I knew, he was taking afternoon tea, or maybe even a nap, but he wasn't in his office. I sat at my desk and tried sifting through old information and digging for new stuff. Police work is boring, plodding; benevolently, the term "grindingly thorough" is sometimes applied. I'm a collie, not a bloodhound, but the phrase "sniffing down a lead" still has its applications. The Internet has yet to create "scratch 'n sniff" technology, but give 'em a few years. My variation was dubbed "Google-fu" by some wag of a writer, so I'll stick with that. Granted, cops have access to a few things that Google (claim that they) don't. I broke out the proverbial fine-tooth comb until the boss got back.

I was lost in the maze of information deep enough that the bulldog had to clap me on my shoulder to get my attention. "Pull your head out and get into my office," he said with professionalism, tact, and sympathy. I backed out of the screens, toned down my cynicism filter, and joined him at his desk.

"How was Keaton?"

"Brings new fullness to the term 'pipsqueak.'"

"Not a suspect?"

"I think the statistical term is a 'non-zero chance,' but it's a shot way too long to believe." I told him about the would-be dust-up on the night before we found the body; the precinct records had the details, including covering the hours between 7:15 and 10:00pm. There was still time afterward for the mouse to have tried something, but I think that the encounter probably left him without the stomach to get up to any more mischief for the rest of the time involved. Short form: He just didn't fit.

"Tell me you've got something else."

"Some time sneaking into bank records."

"Sneaking?"

"The 'suspicious circs' got me a little access without the need for a warrant."

"So that's what got you pinged."

I let my crossed eyebrows speak for me.

"It's why I got back here this afternoon."

"What 'ping'?"

"R.H.I.P. You first."

Never argue with the boss when he's got something on ya. "Glover's bank records are pretty straightforward, with one anomaly. There are regular payments into something called HLR Limited, an LLC setup of some kind. They started maybe five years ago, monthly payments at first, then semi-monthly, going up as time goes on."

"Blackmail."

"Looks like it."

"How much?"

"Over $400K, over the five years."

"Nice work, if you can get it. Here's hoping the IRS doesn't get curious."

"Glover's records, we can peek at. A dive into the LLC would require a warrant."

"I'll see if I can find a judge for it."

I nodded. "Okay, cap'n. What's this 'ping' you spoke of?"

Crandall leaned a short distance back in his chair. "Fibbies."

"What did I do that got the FBI on my tail?"

"Not yours. Glover's, or at least his bank accounts and business transactions. You know how they feel about domestic terrorism."

Considering all of the crazy turns this case had taken, this one shouldn't have taken me by surprise as much as it did. Clearly, the bulldog was enjoying my confusion as I tried to wrap my brain around all that I'd seen and learned about Glover over the past few days and attaching it to the term "domestic terrorism."

"C'mon, Luton," Crandall managed to grin at me. "We both know what 'subversion' meant, back in those glory days just before we got whelped. Didn't your dam ever regale you with stories of 'hells no, we won't go' and other proof of 'anti-government behavior'? My, what a sheltered puphood you must have had."

"I'm just trying to imagine what sort of 'undesirable' Glover could have been. If cookie cutters came in millionaire size, he'd be one of those."

"Recently, sure. No one starts out that way, unless you're a trust-fund pup. Our background says Glover worked for it, so he had to start with something, somewhere. That's what you get to find out."

"Lucky me."

"Like a five-leaf clover."

"Five?"

"Inflation."

"Even the leprechauns," I sighed, getting to my hindpaws. "How long, do you think, to get the warrant?"

"You just show up tomorrow, as usual. If you're lucky, you can bring me a bagel and schmear."

"Why is that lucky for me?"

"You might be able to trade it for a warrant."

"What do I get if I bring a coffee, too?"

"A big, sloppy kiss."

"One bagel it is."

* * * * *

"Chelsea Watson."

"Can you talk?"

I held my Omniscient Device of Audio Connection carefully against my ear, almost hearing the unspoken consideration. "One moment, please," the ringtail said with efficient grace. I imagined that I could hear a door close. "Depends on what about," she answered my question softly.

"A little more background, if you know anything about it. Willy Keaton."

"He'd throw a fit, if he heard you call him that."

"I was more formal at his door."

"What did you go to see him for?"

"My cap'n heard that he'd threatened Thomas Glover for serving him papers."

Her voice smiled a little. "He'd threaten anyone for breathing too closely near him. If you check public records, you'd probably find that he's got a few dozen lawsuits on file at any given time. He's an unpleasant nuisance, but he didn't have anything do to with what happened to Thomas."

"I figured that much. I want to know why Glover was sent to serve papers. That sounds a little below his pay grade."

"I don't have details, but I can make a guess. Keaton represents himself, so the idea would be to get him to agree to something that would twist a ruling into LK&M's favor. Thomas was probably sent to investigate, to intimidate, to cut a deal if it would be in the firm's best interests."

"Things he wouldn't do."

"Not if he could help it."

"What changed?"

She hesitated. "I'm not sure that anything had changed. He was told what to do, and he went. He didn't have to like it."

"Do you feel that it might have made him start thinking about leaving the firm?"

"Calls for speculation." The small smile returned to her voice. "I truly don't know about that, Max."

"I'm still looking for some motive for suicide."

"Not murder?"

"The self-esteemed senior partner seems to think that Glover didn't have the right temperament to be murdered. He wasn't worthy of it."

Several seconds of silence passed before she spoke again. "Do you agree?"

"I'm just chasing down leads, Chelsea. They could all turn out to be useless. It looks more like suicide to me. I'm no shrink, but I do think in terms of motives. In general terms, there are no clear motives for suicide, the way that there are usually clear motives for murder. The greatest commonality in suicides... there's a tipping point, a trigger of some kind, something that makes someone actually do it. I'm starting to see things that might build up to him taking that last step."

"Serving papers?"

"Seeing how things and people were being affected by law, by law firms."

I had the sensation of a nodding head, for whatever reason. "That's relatable."

"Except Glover felt that he couldn't leave, so he..."

My pause was meant to indicate that I was waiting for agreement; instead, she said, "That doesn't feel right."

"How so?"

"Pressure, yes, but not the idea of not being able to leave. He could have jumped ship, found another firm, even hung out a shingle, if he wanted to. This... I know this isn't proof, but it just doesn't feel right."

"The facts seem to be telling me it's suicide."

"Not for this reason." This time, the feeling was one of a shaking head. "If he did kill himself, it wasn't because of the job."

"Chelsea, I—"

"Have to go." The line cut off suddenly.

Could have been legitimate; could have been denial. I couldn't tell for sure.

* * * * *

Wednesday night has been movie night ever since Barb left me. I had my choice of whatever I could find streaming or the collection of DVDs that I'd pick up at random times and places. Anything cheap that hadn't been popular enough to make it to streaming was probably in my collection.

One day, we won't own anything anymore, and some blitz will make it impossible for us to entertain ourselves without paying for it, over and over, even if we're not using it. Like everyone else, I've been going along with it, not really having known much of anything else.

Some bit of perversity in me chose the film *Country* from my collection, which I watched while having my dinner. After the extravagance of eating lunch at Jo and Phil's, I balanced my food budget by having a can of soup for dinner. I wasn't quite so pitiful as to eat it cold out of the can, but the most I could do to make it edible was to add some hot sauce. This melancholy (don't even *think* of trying on that pun) meal matched the equally sentimental film, and I took the time to be grateful that I don't drink. It was an "out" for a lot of cops, but "out" had other meanings for me, with the Glover case, and I wasn't ready to go there yet.

Country (1984, Jessica Lange, Sam Shepard, Dir. Richard Pearce) was about land, families, the farming bust, the Reagan-era move to destroy small farms then let the agri-business lobby gobble up more land for almost no cost, and the cost of progress on the average fur. There's no question that the Glover case was eating away at me, for reasons I still couldn't fathom. The ringtail office manager was right: If it was suicide — and everything pointed to it being suicide — it wasn't about the land deals, not even about the laws surrounding land, not even about the law firm. Murders come in several categories, generally some variation of professional, accidental, or personal. Self-murder is personal, and the motives can be obscure. Eventually, it might make some kind of sense, somehow, but not always. This case might turn out to be one of those We Just Don't Know situations.

I tried not to sigh, failed. There's a term that AA uses, "dry drunk," to describe someone who's stopped boozing but hasn't done the emotional healing to stop bad habits and behaviors associated with the starting or continuing the boozing. I was never a drunk, so I'm not a "dry drunk." Since AA can explain everything, the term was broadened to encompass any form of addiction that one might be recovering from. I don't have a history of addictions, so AA will tell me that I'm in denial of one form or another, and that's about where I drop them off at their local meeting to suggest that they address their addiction to finding addiction in everything. Maybe I'm just not ready to give up being a wise-ass.

The particular behavior that I refer to is that peculiar urge to telephone someone when my brain decides it's time to bail whole buckets of angst from my sinking boat. I had tried calling Barb a few times after she left, because it was supposed to be one of those civil separations and divorces, the kind that real adults have. Staying in touch with her wasn't the best idea, and she knew it before I did. I tried calling my pup, my son, a few times... okay, it's supposed to be *our* son, isn't it? He didn't spring from my loins fully formed, and neither was Barb merely some intermediary incubation device. But that use of *our* stems from being a couple, and she's not here, so he's *my* son now.

Yeah, this is what "dry drunk" sounds like, they tell me. Maybe I should become a drunk for a while, just to legitimize my use of the term.

I looked first to the phone, then to the four photos that I still keep on the wall, each in a not-too-cheap frame. There's one of me and Barb and Michael, when he was still a small pup. Young, not small. My sire's genes passed through me and into him — tall, lean yet solid, perfect coloration, with a sense of a mane around his neck. His eyes were Barb's, and maybe a greater balance of temperament than I could offer. In that picture, you almost couldn't tell the difference between them, where eyes are concerned. In that sense, Barb had never left. I suppose some photo wizard could let me perform Cancel Culture on her and excise Barb from the photo; I wasn't that much of an asshole, at least not yet.

The other three photos were of Michael — a high school graduation photo, posed next to his first car, a used beastie that he worked hard to get and maintain; a college graduation photo, degree in paw, and a lovely young husky at his side (with effort, I could remember her name — Leota; I'd liked her, Barb less so, but it hadn't mattered; the two had separated after about a year together); and the most recent, with Michael and his two business partners standing in front of Unicorn Keep, the tea shop that I was sure would be a folly. Three years now, and they were eyeing ways to expand.

I looked back at the phone again, trying to resist it. The device was seductive, in its way. It was a phone, a device made to resemble one of the old designs, back when Bakelite was considered stylish, or at least functional. Fashioned like the old candlestick phones of as much as a century ago, its only concession to modern times was the push-button keypad on the base instead of the old rotary dial. A land line, so it would work even if the power went out (yes, I had "power bricks" for the Rectangular Cuboid of Infinite Function, but if the cell towers are down, you're screwed). It required the use of both forepaws, unless the base could be left on the table. This forces you to concentrate on the fact that you are speaking to someone, communicating, paying attention, actively listening.

Have I mentioned that I hate Bluetooth devices?

Unlike the original models, the earpiece of this phone was comparatively light, making it less likely that my forepaw would get tired holding it. The base was heavier, so that it wasn't prone to falling over. The push-buttons allowed up to 100 phone numbers to be stored for speed-dialing. There was no possibility that I'd ever fill up that list. According to the instructions that came with it, I'm told that I'm allowed to say that I programmed the phone, but I'm hesitant to claim such technological wizardry. I lifted the earpiece and "dialed" (that wholly antiquated term) star-zero-one.

"Hello?"

"Hi, Michael."

"Dad! Good to hear from you." The voice agreed with the words.

"You busy?"

A few words, muffled to my ear, then back. "Trey can handle the front for a bit. Let me get back to the office..."

He was at the shop, as he so often was, but he had his own Delphic Oracle Device on him. I let myself be slightly less offended by the Bluetooth tech; he used it to be available. That might make it a good thing, at least in this one instance.

"There, that's better." The background noise had faded. "Howya goin'?"

"You first."

He chuckled. "The store's doing well, and so am I. Thank you for visiting Short Attention Span Theater."

It was an old joke between us, so I took no offense. "Two thumbs up," I offered, as the usual response. "Glad to hear it."

After my brief silence, he prodded me gently. "Your turn, dad. Did you forget your lines?"

I kept this pause shorter. "Having one of those cases."

"Can you talk about it?"

"Not in specifics."

"That's understood," he said, not unkindly. "How can I help?"

"Mostly by being there." I smiled a little. "See? I'm learning."

"I know it sounds mushy to you, Dad, but I think it helps."

"So do I, Michael. At least now we know what it means when I call you 'pup.'"

He snickered a little. "I'm glad we got that cleared up. I can be proud of that, rather than thinking it was your way of trying to hold me back."

"Talking helps." I paused, just a moment, to make myself commit to that phrase. "I don't know if the name Thomas Glover has hit the papers where you are."

"I don't remember it, in print or on the Net." I heard the grin in his voice as he teased me about the advancements in modern technology. I had been the one to remind him that the online Project Gutenberg was, in itself, an irony that could be seen as bitter or hilarious. He had chosen the latter.

"He's not exactly famous, but he was rich enough to have the Powers That Be demand that a homicide dick investigate what looks at first like a suicide."

"That's pretty specific, Dad."

"Still in bounds. I'd be overstepping if I started talking about what the investigation is finding."

I could almost feel him nodding. "That's what's got you worried."

"That's my pup."

"Okay," he said softly, the smile in his voice again. "Nothing about the case. Can you tell me how you're feeling?"

"A lot of individual words. Lonesome. Tired. Worn-down. Useless."

He paused for longer than I thought the comments merited. I must have hit on something with him.

"You need some time, Dad."

"What else is new?" I hoped that my smirk made it across the phone lines.

"I mean it. I'm worried."

At last, the penny dropped. "No, Michael, it's not that bad, I promise."

"You'd said that the case was bothering you..."

Nodding, I said, "I see the connection, pup. No, I'm not thinking of ending it. It's more like..." I weighed the consequences and risked a little more. "Telling tales out of school... There's little doubt that it was suicide, at least to my way of thinking. It's the 'why' that's bothering me."

"There's not always an answer, Dad."

"I agree. I just feel that there ought to be, for his one."

After a short pause, he asked, "Would you think it self-serving if I suggested that a cup of tea might help?"

That got a chuckle out of me. "Is that home-style medicine or a business model?"

"*¿Por qué no los dos?*" he replied, also chuckling. "I'll even give you the family discount."

"Now you're making an offer I can't refuse."

He didn't rise to the Brando imitation. "I'll sweeten the deal: I'll make it for you myself. The house has a spare room, you know. Take a few days off, change of scene, all of that brochure hype."

I wouldn't have concealed the smile in my voice even if I could. "Gotta get this one closed before I can do anything else."

"Weekend off?"

"Probably not, but I'm not avoiding this time."

Before I could apologize for telling the truth, my son spoke for both of us. "Thank you, Dad."

I breathed evenly for a moment. "I still do that."

"But now you know you're doing it."

"So I can try work through it."

"That's my sire."

I had to smile again. "I do listen, sometimes."

"Dad... is that why this case is bothering you?"

Not so very long ago, I'd have bitten his head off for being "presumptuous." He wasn't a shrink, but he'd gotten help even when I didn't, so he'd been helping me as best he could. He was pretty good at it, or maybe it was just that I didn't want to lose him like I'd lost Barb. "I'm not sure. What are you hearing?"

"You said there ought to be a 'why' for this case."

"I feel like I'm missing it." I nodded slowly. "Like I'm not listening."

"Brace yourself," he said, and I could hear the grin. "I'm gonna ask it."

"Go for it."

"How does that feel?"

He had discovered — or maybe we did — that keeping it light worked better for me. By not being too serious, he got me to take it seriously. "That fits. There's just something I'm not hearing, not seeing." I paused, hearing something in the background from his side of the conversation. "I'm betting you're needed."

"You win. Are you okay, Dad?"

"Enough to sleep. Tomorrow, I'm gonna go back and listen. New ears, new eyes."

"Good choice. I love you, Dad."

"Back atcha, son."

We ended the connection softly, and I sighed. It was time for bed, even though it was a little earlier than usual. I made myself run through the litany of phrases that my son had given me to "check in" with myself. Some part of me still thought it was crap; another felt the tether that my son had thrown to me, that I still held on to. Perhaps not every drunk used alcohol. Perhaps there's such a thing as a healthy addiction. Maybe I should try tea.

I looked again at the pictures on the wall, looked at Barb, tried once more to let go of the bad feelings, hold on to the good, all those things that are supposed to be "healing." I wasn't angry with her anymore, but I still had trouble remembering the good times. It was easier to blot it all out than to admit that I wasn't everything I thought I was, that I did as best I could, then and now, and that the only thing I could change was what I would do now. What road would I take now.

My last thought, before getting up to go to bed, was that Robert Frost was a jerk.

6: Perceived

Thursday morning saw me getting a bagel and schmear from a local shop, just in case the cap'n actually meant it. I chose cinnamon raisin, on the off-chance that he might have a sweet tooth. If he didn't want it, I'd eat it. Until he mentioned it, I hadn't thought of having a bagel for a long time. It's something Michael would have in his shop. Maybe that had helped push me into calling him. Whatever the case, the bagel was good insurance.

I did not, however, bring coffee.

Thinking it best to provide food quickly (bulldogs are *so* insistent on proper mealtimes), I paused at my desk only to take off my overcoat before approaching the canine's den, paper bag carefully kept in view. The cap'n afforded what he called a smile. It passed, if you knew what you were looking for. He then raised his own paper bag. "Snap."

"Hostage exchange. Cinnamon raisin."

"Everything. An extra tub of cream cheese, in case you feel slighted."

"Deal."

"Break room. Everything bagels are messy."

As we proceeded to Checkpoint Charlie, I managed a glance at my desk phone. I noticed the message light on the official line blinking. It was an old-fashioned sort of thing that I appreciated. I'd have to get to it later, although my curiosity was itching like a bad cliché. I suppose it's a sign of optimism that I still hoped for some sort of break, whatever it would look like.

Retrieving the aforementioned tub from the refrigerator, Crandall indicated a table. I set my bag down there before getting a couple of cups of alleged coffee from the pot. I had often wondered about the department springing for one of those "pod" machines, but the idea never got past the "gosh, wouldn't that be different" phase. I doctored the sludge as best I could, returning to the table with cups of caramel color without the accompanying flavor. The pods got another passing thought.

"Warrant's on my desk," he told me, swapping bags. "Bagel, then bank."

"Alphabetical order today."

"Don't make me stab you with the same knife we use for cream cheese."

"Seems unsanitary." I took up the knife in question and added a little more cream cheese for the sake of decadence and safety. I passed the utensil back to the cap'n, properly. He kindly refrained from using it on me.

"Daimler passed along his report. Probably in your email. Want the highlights?"

"Surprise me."

He took a healthy bite of bagel first, just to build up the suspense. I lit into my own. Pays to be sociable. "Confirmed that it's Glover, through DNA; also confirmed GSR on the left forepaw. Angle of entry suggests gun shifted as he tried to pull the trigger with a non-dominant paw. A little more angle, he might have lived."

"I wonder if that's good or bad."

"We're not responsible for delivering bad news, as long as it's true." He caught my glance. "Forensically true."

"Caveat noted." I chewed on the information along with another bite of bagel. It wasn't actually news; more like confirmation. "No surprises, then?"

"Bloodwork clean, COD obvious, no health issues. Pathology's conclusion is pretty much negative for everything."

"So nothing there as motive, but it's still suicide."

"You've been sure it was suicide all along."

"Yup."

"Even though Glover was right-pawed?"

"Yup."

"Why would he shoot himself with his left paw while holding onto that sword in his right paw?"

"Because the sword was more important."

The bulldog put on the face that made me imagine him chewing a cigar, moving it from one side of his mouth to the other through some long-practiced mandibular magic. I was just as glad that he stuck to using his mandibles to grind the bagel into submission. "One last thing about the tigress. Insurance?"

"I checked. The policy was old enough that the usual suicide clause wasn't an issue. She'll get her $250K soon enough, along with whatever else might be in Glover's will. I think her disbelief was genuine; she really can't believe he had any reason to kill himself."

"Which means that the Powers That Be are going to be upset, too." The cap'n wasn't given to sighing, but his entire demeanor made me think about his heaving a huge one. "They want it wrapped up quick, and they also want it wrapped up with their conclusions intact."

"Rock, meet Hard Place."

"And I'm stuck in the middle."

With you, my mind filled in, substituting clowns and jokers to their respective approximations. We sat quietly for a while, chewing, swallowing, all that mealtime stuff. I'd like to imagine that I was actually thinking things through, but I've been trying to stop lying to myself so much. After a while, I tidied up the remains of my repast. "Thank you for breakfast."

"Same."

We padded back to his office, where he gave me the holy writ. "Anyone expecting me at the bank?"

"Probably not. Start with the branch manager, see where that gets you."

"Glad you thought of that, cap'n; I mighta missed it."

"And that's why you're not sitting at my desk," he garrumphed, and I probably deserved it. "Try not to stir up too much; remember, we're still catching heat for this one."

"Even with Daimler's report?"

"Especially with Daimler's report. The privileged simply don't off themselves."

I bit off *More's the pity* before I put my tail in danger. "I'll check in."

Crandall looked like he was going to say something that he, too, decided not to say. Given the feelings that this case was stirring up, that was probably a mercy.

* * * * *

The General Manager of the New Guardian Bank was an older squirrel who probably had heard far too many cliché comments about his choice of career, so I resolutely refused to add to the pile. We both behaved courteously, just doing our jobs, no cause to believe a crime had been committed, just dotting and crossing. Accounts of the sort that I had asked to see were handled by one of two Special Services Managers, a term that probably also saw its share of abuse. I had no wish to appear grim, but it was difficult to maintain decorum when faced with so much straight-line fodder.

Special Services Manager Lavenia Keel took me into her office, which was larger and better appointed than Chelsea Watson's. It was possible that the bank respected her more than the law firm respected Chelsea; likewise, perhaps the bank wanted to flatter its customers, and Chelsea didn't have visitors all that often. I let cynicism place that bet.

The black panther epitomized the word "sleek," her demeanor telling me that she had both experience and the self-discipline to keep herself in fine fettle even as her half-century loomed not far in her future. A bank like the New Guardian was created to keep furs like myself at arms-length, but she disguised the institution's repugnance for the poorly dressed quite well. She seemed in no way inconvenienced by my visit, a tactic to put most coppers off guard. I stayed focused.

"Ms. Keel, can you tell me the purpose of HLR Limited?"

"Any LLC is formed to gain the benefits and protections of a corporation without the difficulties of maintaining one, or even dissolving it, should the need arise. Beyond that, I can't say."

"You can show me records of transactions?"

"That's all, yes. Let me pull up their records for you."

She tapped away at her computer keyboard for a time, while I let my eyes graze on the trimmings and trappings of her office. On the wall, a few certificates of educational accomplishment, although I couldn't read what in, from this distance. A few prints of calmingly banal location scenes, the sort sold by the yard at starving artist and estate sales. There appeared to be a small framed photo on her desk, turned away from the front of the room so that customers would not be frightened by anything personal. It occurred to me only then that I'd not looked through Glover's office at LK&M, since it had seemed irrelevant. I realized, sitting here, that it would still be irrelevant. "Professional" offices weren't meant to be personal, which is why his study at home was so important to him. It was neat, not sterile. I cursed myself an idiot for not pressing further about one particular clue.

"Here we are," the panther said, turning the screen toward me. I saw dates and figures, unsure what else to read into them.

"I see deposits and check numbers, and that looks like invoice or reference numbers... but not payees."

"The accountant for the LLC would have that information."

Nice sidestep, I thought. "It might save some time if I could see the check images."

"Of course." Her smile was absolutely professional; the sense that her predatory instincts were frustrated by my having caught her omission came entirely from my own instincts. I hate being prey.

She clattered on the keyboard again, shuffled through some screens, finally dealing up some images. I noticed that the checks were not hand-written. All, with rare exception, were made out to hospitals and clinics. All, with no exception, were signed by Helena L. Glover.

* * * * *

My phone call caught Bessie just after she'd made a grocery store run, and she was glad to help. I asked her to enlist Allison's assistance, getting the two of them to go into Glover's study. It was time that I got a look at the comb-bound book that the maid had seen on Monday.

"Won't that make the missus upset?"

"If you catch any flack, tell Her Majesty that I asked you to do it, and I'll be there in thirty minutes, with more questions for her."

I was as good as my word. My arrival time was nearer to twenty-three minutes, at the moment that I rang the bell. Allison answered the door, looking nervous.

"We haven't found anything yet," the young mouse told me. "We've been looking everywhere that we can see."

Setting a forepaw very gently on the young mouse's shoulder, I said, "Try places you can't see. Desk drawers, behind things, anyplace that looks like it could hold that comb-bound book that you saw."

"If I find it, should I leave it alone?"

"It's okay; I'm not worried about fingerprints. I just want to see what it was that he was looking at." I smiled at her. "Good thinking."

After a moment, she smiled back and led me into the formal living room, where Her Majesty was expecting me. As before, the tigress was seated in her throne, her own pride of place in the room. I was not invited to sit down. She was none too pleased with my being there, and she let me know it with every word and movement.

"Have you found my spouse's murderer yet, Detective?"

"Mrs. Glover." I kept my voice soft. "The forensics is conclusive. Your husband killed himself."

"No." She shook her head firmly, twisting her neck against the high collar of her shirt. "That's not possible."

"Mrs. Glover..."

"He was right-pawed! Someone shot him and put the gun into his left paw. He did *not* kill himself, he did *not*..."

I waited until she had composed herself again. "Mrs. Glover, what was your maiden name?"

Her body froze momentarily, a startling action for an apex predator species. It took several seconds for her features to fall into a posture that made me think of surrender. "Ridley."

"Helena L. Glover, nee Ridley. CEO of HLR Limited. You sign all of the checks, so you must know what they're for."

"Don't be an ass, Detective."

"Would you explain the secrecy, Mrs. Glover?"

The jerk of her head suggested that she had almost let herself spit. She regained herself once more, righted her face, and replied, "Discretion. Thomas set it up; something to do with healthcare advantages, as well as to keep the payees out of our community accounts. Information leaks from too many sources."

"Why was it an issue?"

"Do you really want the lesson, Detective? Would you learn it?" Her glare could have been considered third-degree menacing in its own right. Her rough, rasping voice continued. "The meaning and value of privacy changes as you ascend the social ladder. The saying that 'knowledge is power' is even more important when image supersedes truth. Gossip is a deadly game, when fortunes are involved."

"The payments into the LLC looked like blackmail, from the outside. Is that what you were afraid of?"

"Only secondarily. The richer you are, the more the vultures hover, and the more that people guard being seen with you, being involved with you, in business or in other financial matters, like charities and fundraising events. Again, Detective, appearance supersedes reality, always."

"And you were afraid that people would begin to shun you if they knew you had cancer."

She glared at me, daring me to say anything further. I held my tongue to see if she would admit it for herself. After several long moments, she spoke.

"Thyroid."

"I would have thought that was operable, treatable."

"If caught properly, yes." Her eyes grew cold, more with resignation than with anger. "The goiter was diagnosed incorrectly; the treatment sped up the cancer. It was a pernicious little fiend. By the time it was properly assessed and treated, the cancer had metastasized into the lymphatic system. Surgery would have been useless. Radiation therapy, bone marrow stimulation... the last chance is chemotherapy, at which point there would be no keeping it quiet."

"I would have thought your condition would generate more sympathy than shunning."

"My death would rally monies for research; my suffering and survival would be considered self-serving and burdensome." Her lips twisted in a mocking smile. "I don't plan to die for them, but I will live as best I can for as long as I can before giving them the satisfaction."

Pausing, respectfully, I asked, "Do the kits know?"

"Shelton does. He's the oldest." She spoke dispassionately. "Head of the family, now."

"May I ask..."

"Sixty percent survival rate, ordinarily; chances are that I may have another six months that'll be worth living, then the last tango of chemotherapy, which may or may not end well. You may take that in whatever way you wish."

An appropriate response took a little time to form in my mind. Of course Glover knew all of this; he had to have set up the LLC himself, and he funded it entirely. He was planning for the long haul, to be here with her through whatever might happen. It was why the tigress had been so certain that it couldn't have been suicide. He would have fought for her, till the end. And yet...

I took a long moment before saying, "Thank you for telling me, Mrs. Glover."

She demurred silently.

Excusing myself with a nod of my head, I padded back into the hall and paused there, getting my breath back. There was more than enough drama in this story to fuel a television limited series, and all I wanted was an explanation that, ignoring the irony, I could live with. With all that surrounded this act of finality, it felt more necessary than ever for me to know the "why" of it.

The door to Glover's study was open, and I took a moment to glance in before disturbing Bessie and Allison at their work. The large desk had been discreetly covered by a thick white tarpaulin, as had a certain section of the carpet just beyond the desk. I felt sure that the females had been told why the tarps were in place, yet they continued to search diligently. I knocked very gently on the open door; they jumped a little at the sound, whipped around to see me. "Sorry," I offered softly.

The mouse climbed down from a small step-stool that she was using to look behind books on a high shelf, and the panther padded around the large desk to address me directly.

"Pretty sure I know what you're lookin' for, Detective, but it's hiding pretty good."

"I thought maybe it had fallen behind some books," Allison added, "so I got out the step to look back there."

"More good thinking, Allison. You've both done a lot, and thank you." I managed a smile. "That's actually a lot of what a police detective does. Believe it or not, it helps."

"Should we keep looking?"

"Maybe we could take a break from it to look for something else. I'd forgotten something that I'd heard a few days ago. Mr. Glover took home a box from his office, a wooden box about so big." I pantomimed the shape in the same way that the Dobie security guard had. "Have either of you—"

"Yeah, yeah," Bessie said, remembering. "It's over here…"

The feline led us back to the desk. In another life, the freestanding cabinet behind Glover's desk might have been a credenza, with its sliding panel and shelves built into the sides. On top, some framed photographs of his kits, a trophy for some sports battle at a charity event, and the telltale lack of miscellany that had made me suspicious of the neatness. The panther slid aside one of the panels below and withdrew the box in question. Deep brown, probably walnut, well-polished to the point of being almost slippery, it was precisely the size and shape to have held the sword. Bessie passed it over to me, and I set it down on the desk with a vague sense of reverence.

"What did he keep in there?" the cook asked quietly.

"It's a storage box for a ceremonial sword," I replied.

"Is it still in there?"

"No, he had it in his paw when he…" I cut myself off. This was the room where it happened; no benefit to painting a picture they'd been spared from seeing.

"Are you gonna bring the sword back, or…?"

It was impossible for me not to have opened the case, but it was from sheer curiosity rather than from any brainstorm that had allowed me to make some impressively brilliant deduction. The lid swung open noiselessly, and the thing inside the box stretched itself as if waking from a nap. The comb-bound sheaf of papers had been folded along its long dimension and had lain curled inside the interior until released from a position that it had found uncomfortable at best. In large and only slightly decorative font, the title read THE TRIBAL MANIFESTO. Below it, in a respectable faux script was the word *Timewind*.

* * * * *

I traded a receipt for both the box and the manuscript, then drove back to the cop shop. Something in my gut told me to leave them both in the trunk of my car. It bent the rules into shapes it wasn't meant to form; according to my last inventory of shits, I had none left to give. I told myself instead that I had some reading to do tonight and would wait for a chance to reunite the sword and its proper container. It was sheer technicality that allowed me to say that the items were not part of the crime scene, just as it was technicality to label suicide a crime. Self-murder, when successful, leaves no criminal to prosecute; in this country, it's no longer on the books. It's worth noting that *attempted* suicide is still a crime, a fact that actually encourages those who are considering it to do the job right.

Girding my stomach as best I could, I chose a cheap meal at the precinct mess. It fell within the definition of "food," and the meal itself could be awarded "fair attempt." It wasn't bad; it just wasn't good. It tasted like, somewhere in the process, someone had given up. Uninspired and uninspiring, on par with the can of soup I had last night, but enough to get me through the rest of the day. I made up my mind to look for sandwich-makings at the grocery, wondering what the modern, adult equivalent of a "lunch box" was.

By the time I got to my desk, I felt less than enthusiastic about cleaning up the paperwork. A good time to check the phone messages I'd ignored earlier. I pressed keypads for passcodes and retrieved only one somewhat terse message from a very officious, official-sounding officer of the FBI, requesting that I return his call, etc., etc. I wrote down the information, followed instructions, and found myself connected.

"Agent Parks."

I resisted saying *and Rec,* in case he didn't have a funny bone. "Detective Max Luton, returning your call."

A short pause, some clicking of keys. "Why are you investigating Thomas Glover?"

"Fine, thanks; how are you?"

This pause had sharp edges. "Do you like playing games, Detective?"

"Depends on the game, Agent. This isn't one. I don't care for being disrespected."

"And I don't care for people stepping onto my turf without being invited."

"What's your turf?"

"I'm watching listed groups for suspicious activities."

"Glover was part of such a group?"

"Yes, and he could be dangerous."

"Not anymore; he's dead."

That seemed to have struck home. The voice, when it returned, was strangely concerned. "Who killed him?"

"He did. It was suicide." After a moment of quiet, I asked, "You didn't know?"

"I was only told that someone was looking into his finances, particularly in connection with a shell company called HLR Limited. We've had it under watch for some time now."

"You don't know what it's for?"

"It doesn't seem to be for anything at all. There are no business transactions that we could trace, no real trail to follow. There was no cause for a warrant so, contrary to popular belief, there was only so far we could go. I assume that his death allowed you some sort of look into his records."

I outlined for him how I persuaded the bank officer to let me see check images, then the conversation that I'd had with the tigress that morning. "We had thought it had been blackmail, as a motive for Glover's suicide."

"We thought it was to hide money for subversive activities."

"Agent Parks," I said softly, offering the diplomatic bone of using his name and title, "what sort of subversion are we talking about here?"

He sighed softly, and I had the feeling that he was mentally questioning his choice of career. It was something that I could relate to. "He was once part of a group called Timewind. It appears on our records under the category of potentially seditious and/or socialist organizations which may or may not pose a threat to our way of life." Parks paused to let me know that he had finished quoting the party line. "His participation appears to have been minimal for a number of years, but there is a watch on his financials all the same."

"How long has he been associated with this group?"

"The notes say, over 25 years." Behind his voice, I heard keyboard clicks. "First listed when he applied to law school. Standard background check. The school apparently didn't care about his affiliation, but it got him flagged as part of our Timewind file. The public defender's office in Syracuse probably got more details, but they took him on anyway."

"He did well enough there to go into private practice."

"Real estate, yeah." A short, faintly surprised pause; something must have appeared on his screen. "How the hell did LK&M take him in?"

"You didn't know about that?"

"Not me, personally. I got tapped when you pinged Glover's accounts."

"Next fur in the barrel, huh?"

A snort told me that he still some sense of humor left. "I can neither confirm nor deny the existence of the barrel." A short pause before he added, "Would you send me your report, Detective Luton? It seems that our information supply line is not as efficient as we like to think it is."

"Be careful that your bosses don't hear that."

"We have a reputation to uphold; if we don't know everything, we can't keep the country safe."

"Electronic or traditional?"

"Electronic is the new traditional," he quipped, then gave me his contact info at the Bureau. "Thank you for your cooperation, Detective."

"We're all on the same side."

"Make sure your own bosses don't hear you."

We rang off. My evening's reading just got more interesting.

7: Translation

I almost called out sick on Friday, but I didn't know the medical definition for the kind of sickness I had. Is there such a thing as a hangover caused by dreams, whether from sleep or when awake? Either way, I couldn't make a reasonable case for staying away from work because I felt sick at heart. That's not something recognized by an HMO, and there aren't any other institutions that had legitimate cures. Some made claims, taking the form of fads that last for a few years or a few thousand. They didn't hold answers either.

The causes for my malaise were many. The main one was my trying to read *The Tribal Manifesto,* which was no walk in the park. I don't know why idealism, in any form, has to be so badly written. Part of the problem was that there clearly was not one author and there certainly was no editor. The only attribution for the material was to "Timewind," which was the name of an organization or group. The styles were all over the place, disjointed, disconnected beyond the central idea of utopia based upon love, cooperation, and everybody being together and thus more than the sum of its parts. The most notable thing appeared in the first few pages:

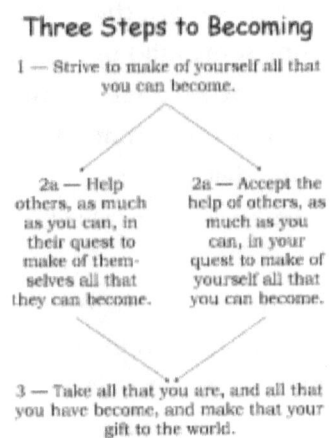

Three Steps to Becoming

1 — Strive to make of yourself all that you can become.

2a — Help others, as much as you can, in their quest to make of themselves all that they can become.

2a — Accept the help of others, as much as you can, in your quest to make of yourself all that you can become.

3 — Take all that you are, and all that you have become, and make that your gift to the world.

It would do little good to point out the numbering mistake.

In terms of the "free love" generation, the book was assembled about 30 years past those happy hippie days of the country's history. Except for the time difference, it would have fit right in. There were a few hints that some of it may have come from that time and stitched into the rest of the booklet. I tried to read as much as I could, but I ended up skimming most of the 97 pages. No index, no table of contents, and no real sense of organization. It actually hurt to imagine that this was what Glover had been looking at on the day before he killed himself. The cynic in me had to observe that the booklet wasn't *that* bad.

The skies matched my mood: gray, low, and about ready to piss down on everything just because it could. I wasn't in any mood to eat, but my stomach rumbled. I decided to teach it a lesson by going through a drive-thru place and getting what they claimed was a "breakfast sandwich." I didn't buy a cup of their "coffee"; why pay for their swill when I had free swill of my own at the cop shop? I could always top it off with an alleged "sweet roll" from the vending machine.

Pulling into an available parking space, I shut off the engine and sat in the quiet for a few minutes. I couldn't understand what was digging at me so much, what was yanking my chain. I didn't have the urge to get a drink or six, since I just didn't like the stuff; I did wonder if this was the type of feeling that pushed someone toward the bottle. Like AA's "dry drunk," I was angry, hurting, wanting some kind of release from this strange pain. There was a desire to have something take it away, like a magic pill that would cure everything, the literal meaning of "panacea" (I got it from a crossword puzzle), something that would require no greater effort than to take the drug. Easy solutions, no work involved, no needing to understand the "why" of anything.

That, it finally occurred to me, was the reason I wanted to understand Glover's suicide. It would either solve my own problem, or it would give me permission to follow his path.

The idea sat in the car next to me, a quiet companion floating silent suggestions in the guise of answers. It was strangely calming.

* * * * *

I can't describe my mood when I sat at my desk with my cup of bean juice, because I wasn't sure that I had one. I wasn't hosting the Idea, as far as I could tell. I simply had no particular mood or emotional response to anything. I think they call it "detachment" in the shrink circles. My sense was more that my inventory of shits was actually less than zero. I suppose that would mean, in order for me to give a shit, I'd have to be given some shit, and that didn't seem like much of a good idea either. This whole shitty system needed an overhaul.

Contemplating the mixed blessings of a refill from the communal pot (there's an image to be twisted) had caused me to delay at my desk long enough for Crandall to find me and call me into his office. He sat, I stood, just because that's what we usually do. "Updates?" the bulldog asked me.

"You know most of it," I replied. "Only new wrinkle is this association with some latter-day hippie-dippie group called Timewind. I don't think there's much connection there."

"That's what the Fibbies gave you."

"Yup. Glover had been 'associated' for over 25 years, but he hasn't been actively involved in some while."

"Nothing?"

The "manifesto" seemed irrelevant to anything, and I didn't want to mention it, maybe for personal reasons. "Not that anyone is aware of."

Crandall pulled that face again, the one that made me think of Langston and his cigar. The two seemed almost commingled in my brain, which I counted as yet another curse against me. "The upstairs wants this cleared by this afternoon; your job today looks like paperwork."

"Any hints on how they want this essay written? The content won't be to their liking."

"Write it up straight, just like you found it. I can sign off on objective facts, but not on maybe's and could-be's."

"Motive?"

"Not our jurisdiction," the bulldog shook his head. "Motive is only important if it helps to track down a murderer for prosecution. Suicide ain't a crime, if it works. If the brass wants to distort it, I've got a news channel for 'em."

I didn't have the chance to make even a non-committal comment before a soft knock on the door frame caught our attention. We both turned, and I had just enough time to wonder about synchronicity before the Shep indicated the box he was carrying. Shaped like a banker's box, its most noticeable item was something wrapped in cloth, perhaps to protect it, perhaps to protect whoever was carrying it. It was, after all, about a meter long and difficult to carry without its proper box.

"Forensics sent me over, Captain Crandall," he said. "This is from the Glover crime scene."

"Thank you for bringing it, Officer...?"

"Padilla," I filled in, pronouncing it properly. I moved aside to give him room to maneuver. "How did they tap you for courier work? I thought Parsons was assigned from the two-six."

"He called in sick today."

Small blessings, I thought. "Cap'n," I said over my shoulder, "I'm gonna take over your other desk for a minute."

"There's a surprise."

The Shep set the box down where I showed him, and I wasted no time bringing the sword out of its wrappings. I handled it carefully; the office wasn't blessed with the space to fling it around.

"I was wondering what that was," Padilla said. It was then I remembered that he might not have seen inside the study that he had been guarding.

"It's the only witness to a killing," I said. "Did Forensics come up with anything?"

"Let me check my notes." The Shep reached inside the box to remove a few sheets of paper, which I found happily old-school. It would seem that not everyone kept his life inside the Tricorder Communicator Mark Negative Two Hundred. "Careful shavings from the blade showed a unique blend of metals, not something commercially available in bulk, so to speak. Someone had to make this combination as an individual batch. Ultrasound showed that the blade itself is secured into the hilt by a... 'modern form of traditional method,' which doesn't tell me a lot."

"Me, either," Crandall volunteered.

"Tells me that the smith is a craftsman." I turned the blade over in my forepaws, admiring it carefully, now that it was safe to touch. "I have no idea how a sword is made, beyond movies showing someone banging the hell out of some extremely hot metal. I don't know what a 'traditional method' might be, but the telltale is the word 'traditional.' Absolutely not factory made; this blade was made by a single, talented fur who had a purpose for making it."

"Pretty fancy for a butter knife," the bulldog observed.

"Looks like it would hold a pretty sharp edge."

"May I have a look?" The Shep extended a forepaw, and I passed it carefully over to him. He looked it over intently as I went through the few other items in the box. The various plastic pouches and sleeves protected their mysterious treasures, and a file folder at the bottom appeared to have more case notes. All contents were free to be returned, now that forensics was done with them. I had no idea if anyone in the Glover family would want them.

"This doesn't change the report," Crandall grumped. "It's still suicide."

"Yes, it is. I still want to know why."

"Not our jurisdiction," the bulldog repeated his earlier statement. "We do the 'how' thing."

"Albion."

My head turned swiftly to Padilla. "What?"

He blinked a little. "It's the name of the sword. Or at least..." The Shep indicated a set of six runes at the base of the blade, where it joined the hilt. "Here. I was surprised by it."

"The runes?"

"More the name." Looking a little embarrassed, he glanced at the boss, then back to me. "Albion is another name for Great Britain, specifically England. Some conflated the word with Excalibur, King Arthur's sword. According to one version of the Robin Hood legend, Albion was the only one remaining of the Seven Swords of Wayland, imbued with the power of light and darkness. It was the sword of justice that the Hooded Man carried, both for its symbolism and for close combat."

"You can read these runes?"

"I'm a little rusty, but I can read that much, at least."

"What is it?"

"A guilty pleasure, mostly." He grinned at us before continuing. "The runes are from Tolkien's *The Hobbit,* originally. Some of the medievalist groups would use them to make things seem more authentic, or at least arcane."

"Great," Crandall observed. "More whackadoodles to the party."

I ignored him. "Padilla, do you think you can read the other markings along the blade?"

He hesitated. "Let me check something."

When he reached for his pocket, to find his Digital Direct Dial-up Doohickey, I waved to stop him. "Let's get something with a bigger screen."

I sat him in front of the computer at my desk, figuring he'd be able to look up the information he wanted faster than I could. It took him almost no time at all to find the web page he needed.

"Tolkien's runes were an alphabet, one rune per letter. He could have gone for something more like the Cyrillic alphabet, which uses one symbol-letter per sound." The Shep nodded at the screen. "This is more familiar, direct substitution... Do you have some paper?"

My sour mood from earlier lifted as I supplied a legal pad. He provided his own pen from his shirt pocket. There may yet be hope for sapientkind.

Even with the cap'n and me looking over his shoulders, he still made quick work of the job. It took him perhaps 40 seconds to translate one side of the blade, half that for the other side, as the lettering became familiar to him again. "Some of it is guessing what letters make sense to come next," he said, "like playing Wordle."

"I hate that thing."

"Why, Cap'n?" I asked him.

"Guessing five-letter words more often brings out my four-letter words."

"Here we are," Padilla offered.

I read the words on the pad. "Justice by word and need, honor by loving deed."

Crandall grunted. "This was in the paws of a lawyer?"

"Ex-lawyer." I hadn't meant to emphasize the descriptor so much, but the Shep cringed a little. I tried to make my eyes apologize to him. "Any thoughts?"

"It sounds like an oath of fealty. Combined with the idea that the blade is named, I get the feeling that it's... well, it's meant to be a warrior's weapon. Symbolically, I hope." Padilla paused before asking, "This was at the crime scene?"

"Clutched in the victim's right forepaw. He had shot himself in the head with his left."

"Was he left-pawed?"

"No, right-pawed."

"Not staged?"

"No; coroner says it was definitely suicide."

The Shep considered for a moment. "This sword was important to him."

I let my *I told you so* to the cap'n be just a quick glance. "Let's pretend that he thought of himself as some sort of warrior, a fighter for justice. He did start off in the public defender's office."

"Luton," the bulldog snorted softly, "how does this help?"

"You're looking for motive," Padilla said, his eyes narrowing slightly. "Did he leave a note?"

Realization smacked me in the head. "Yes."

I padded quickly to Crandall's office, trying my best not to rip through the contents of the box like a young pup at his Christmas presents. The documents associated with the case lay flat at the bottom. The desktop pad had been photographed and documented six ways from Sunday, the full-size images electronically cut into segments that could be printed by laser. I found the sheet with the section of blotter that I was looking for. Back at my desk, I handed it to our resident translator.

"From the notepad on his desk," I explained to the Shep.

He nodded quickly and set to work on his legal pad. "Yes," he murmured quietly. "A note. Almost a confession."

I did my best not to rush him. I knew enough that, if I watched him too closely, I'd try to anticipate the words, maybe end up rushing him after all. I tried to keep an eye on the walls around me. Y'know, if you don't watch them, they close in on you. I heard the sound of the pen being tossed onto the pad.

"No justice by words, no honor in my deeds," the officer read aloud. "I have betrayed us. Albion, forgive me."

"Short," Crandall observed. "Who's 'us'?"

"Does it say?" I asked Padilla.

"I don't think so. There's only one more word. Well... name, I guess."

"What does it say?"

"Airdancer."

* * * * *

The brooding skies had finally decided to let out their frustrations in a long, cold rain that felt like tears of exhaustion. No question, a shrink would label that as "transference," and my available shit balance was still zero or less. I did my best not to take on the emotion too closely, maybe because it was "emotion" (dangerous stuff, that), maybe because I needed to concentrate on the long, winding state road that wasn't all that different from the one I'd been on only a few days ago. This one headed in a different direction, taking me deep into the forests of the northeastern part of the state. It was a road that passed through few towns, and I'd taken advantage of each one, for taking on fuel for the car and for me, and for leaving off excess water of my own. With all these trees, I could probably find one to hike a leg on; I felt some strange need to be mildly civilized, at least while some mild version of civilization was available.

Capt. Ambrose Crandall had tried valiantly to keep me from pursuing this. He put out every reason he could think of, from wanting to get the case closed because of those in higher pay grades than ours, to wondering if I were really in enough of my right mind to be pursuing this clueless clue. I pulled out all the stops, including taking him to Jo and Phil's for lunch, cajoling him with "a more complete report" that he wouldn't have to take responsibility for if he didn't want to, and threatening to use his first name around the office. He wanted me to take Padilla with me, but I put my hindpaw down on that one. The Shep is a helluva good officer, and I'd welcome him on any other case out there. This one, I told him, was personal.

That was a risk, one I won't dignify with the term "calculated." I told him of the wooden box for the sword, of *The Tribal Manifesto,* and my certainty that I needed to make this journey alone, if only to see if my hunch was correct. I must have said something right, because I was on my way that afternoon, determined to find my answers, and maybe those of Glover as well.

Padilla's information about the sword included a very short list of furs who were known to use the composition of metals contained in the blade. I only needed to see one name and location to confirm my suspicions. Artisans of a certain type tend to band together, just as any group of like-minded people would do. This one group of artisans would no doubt appear on many other lists, as they were members of Timewind.

The unexpected roar of an eighteen-wheeler from around a somewhat cramped curve broke my reverie, making me realize that I was getting close to a turnoff I'd need to take. I would probably get some instruction soon enough from the voice of divine guidance emanating from the all-knowing Oracle of A. G. Bell's Nightmare, but I still had printed directions. Some things shouldn't be left entirely to chance or technology, especially on the infamous dark and rainy night. The semiannual curse of Daylight Savings Time had visited us already, but the heavy clouds and rain took away the daylight with far greater efficiency. I was actually glad to be driving the old clunker; a few more bangs and bumps wouldn't show.

I already knew from Agent Parks that Timewind was in the FBI files. They were likely to be in the files of the CIA, ATF, DEA, TSA, NCTC, CCTV, LMNOP, and the rest of the alphabet soup of watchdogs, not to mention state and local wannbes. There were no criminal charges against them, from any source, nor any civil cases on file. Even the IRS seemed satisfied that whatever legal structure they had chosen was, in fact, paying its fair share. (That, in itself, no doubt made them suspicious; willingly paying taxes may be considered by some to be an un-American activity.) They were not some renegade biker gang, nor were they politically active, at least not collectively. What seemed to put everyone's fur up was that Timewind referred to itself as a "tribe," while not making any claim to First Peoples or species identity. Clearly, this made them "other," therefore probably communists, socialists, anarchists, ultra-liberal, anti-establishment, foreign arms dealers, druggies, pushers, sex-slave-traffickers, yowen-molesters, satanists, demon-summoners, witches, shape-shifters, cryptid-abettors, any-or-all of the above. They were called by the thousand names of fear, paying the price for being different.

I can't be sure just when it dawned on me that I had known of Timewind, in a tangential manner. Part of their means of livelihood was what used to be called a cottage industry in loose-fitting cloth garments that appealed to members of various medieval groups. Other artisans created jewelry that might fit the period, along with various plates, bowls, cups, and utensils designed to mimic the times. I discovered this when my pup Michael became interested in, and briefly involved with, the largest of the groups, called (simply enough) The Medieval Society, or MedSoc for short. Some of the clothes still fit him to this day; even though he's not active in MedSoc anymore, the garments themselves are simple, comfortable, long-lasting. Back in that day, Barb had thought him "dashing," and I'd had a stick too far up my tailhole to admit it was true.

MedSoc itself was labeled a "cult" by the Establishment, and it didn't help matters when one of their area groups (referred to as a "kingdom," with all the attendant rigmarole) got the worst possible press for allegations of sexual molestation of minors. The old axiom about one bad apple was bad enough; the evidence, trial, and resulting convictions made it nothing but worse. Since that time, a great many groups, including the sponsors of renaissance festivals, put themselves at arms — or perhaps pole arms — distance from MedSoc itself.

I shook my head at such memories. That "kingdom" was several states away, and everyone in Michael's "shire" and "kingdom" were horrified. The incident was in no way typical, but it put a bitter taste in everyone's maw. A lot of their gatherings and events were cancelled because of that pall. It was as unfair as everything else in the world, and my pup got a taste of it the hard way. Nothing "happened," but simply having a tangential association with "one of them" could be enough for some furs. Commies in the 50s; hippies in the 60s; homosexuals in the 70s; immigrants, the homeless, indigent, or poor in every decade... there's always someone out there to blame for things not being "like they were," or simply not to your liking. Michael felt sure he'd lost a graduate teaching post because of it, but in some ways, that was a blessing: Because of that rejection, he found his way into creating Unicorn Keep. Sometimes, we need a good kick to put us on our right path.

That, I had surmised, was what Glover had failed to heed. In the seat beside me, the Idea murmured something I didn't quite catch. It felt like agreement, or maybe encouragement.

I turned my mind back to Timewind. The group had come together nearly 30 years ago, as a self-described "experiment in communal living." My research, and what little I'd been able to tolerate reading in their *Manifesto,* told me that they were both serious and jesting. According to the Fibbies, the original group pooled their talents and resources, finding a plot of land that had "fallen into escheat." I needed more law-degree stuff to really get that, but the upshot was that they had acquired nearly 35 hectares of land for as close to a song as made no odds. They had since survived by selling artisan-produced goods and working their land. I had no information about the status of the land, the inhabitants, or the buildings or lack thereof on the land. That thought made me cast my mind back to that grubby group of squatters, except that Timewind apparently owned their land and, so far as I knew, were still in business. There was a website, at least, and a link to a free electronic download of *The Tribal Manifesto.* I declined the offer.

There was little information about the membership of Timewind, beyond the original nine and a few later arrivals who might have let their affiliation be known publicly. It was very likely that some more were tarred with the same brush (as the saying has it), whether they were part of the group or not. Some may have left the group, for a short or long time, for work, education, a break, whathaveyou. Artists and farmers need their space, sometimes. Sometimes, they go out to take on new challenges. Sometimes, people just drift away. That might have been what happened to Thomas Christian Thaddeus Glover.

The tiger who had been known as Airdancer.

8: Precipitate

"In 500 meters," chirped the allegedly female voice, "your destination will be on the right."

I could only hope so. It felt as if the clouds had blotted out the sun entirely, and the increased rain had done the rest. I wasn't sure that I'd be able to see my destination with a floodlight, much less my ancient vehicle's hi-beams. I was alone on the state road, the last town being some ten klicks behind me, and I was battling my way down the rain-obscured road at maybe 55kph, one eye on the odometer, hoping to count five hectometers. At this point, I wasn't sure my math skills were up to it.

My mood had been somewhere between sour and neutral, that strange mixture that seemed to suit the Idea sitting next to me. I try to accommodate my guests, even when they weren't welcome. I realized only tangentially that "unwelcome" wasn't entirely true.

"Your destination is on the right."

I hoped that my destination wasn't merely the sign. Well-maintained, designed to look like rough-hewn wood, the sign bore Timewind's name along with the notation that they were "Artisans in Clay, Metal, Wood, Fabric, and Life." If there were any lights, they would have to have been spots from below, and they weren't on. I activated my turn signal out of sheer habit; I doubted that there was another driver on the state road for several klicks around. I turned into a wide gravel road which, like the sign, was well-maintained if, at the moment, mud-strewn. I passed over some cattle guard grating, noticing as I turned in some split-rail fencing making a boundary parallel to the road. Once past this, the road rose gently toward a general darkness made mostly of lofty pines on either side.

As I slowed my pace to maybe 25-30kph, I hoped to find some indication of habitation reasonably soon. The road was good enough, but I could still feel the tires slip a little, once in a while. The curve through the trees seemed to follow either a ditch or a naturally-occurring small creek, off to my right. I had the vague impression of yellowish light somewhere up ahead, along with something softly blue behind me. I checked the rearview, seeing nothing through the rain covering the back window, flicked my view back forward. Once more, the impression of soft yellow lights, not too far ahead, although the rain continued to put blankets between me and just about everything else. The blue light was definitely somewhere behind me...

back seat?

My eyes shot back toward the windscreen again as I shouted and swerved to my right to avoid a huge shape that had appeared suddenly in front of me. The brakes worked, but the road didn't. I missed the looming shape, slid off the road a bit, ending up sideways in the ditch/creek, leaning into it at about a 30-degree angle. After a few moments to catch my breath, I used a fresh batch of air to blister a few appropriate epithets at the non-sapient cow that had seemed to come out of nowhere, then tried to take an inventory. The car was reasonably whole but definitely stuck. The headlights were still on, but even if I could get the engine to turn over, I had little hope of being able to get out of this ditch under my own power. I couldn't even see where my Magellan-Bell-Bezos Machine had escaped to. As far as I could tell, I was intact. Just stuck.

"Ayooah!"

I looked through the rain-obscured window to see a strong lantern light bouncing along the road toward me. I made out two shadowy figures coming toward me, a horse-drawn cart not far behind them. If this was a rescue party, they should give lessons in precognition to other first-responders.

"Haloo!" one cried, getting closer. "Are you all right?"

I figured it was time to get a little wet. Pocketing the keys and turning off the headlights, I tried opening the door. I had the sensation that the door was unlocked but unwilling to open until I promised to renew that gym membership. The two figures had reached the car and, mercifully, they kept their lantern beam at an angle rather than directly on my face.

"Are you hurt?" the feline face asked loudly.

"I think I'm okay. Door's at a bad angle. L'il help?"

The feline stepped aside as the larger of the two shadows — a bear of significant size and, as I was to find, muscle — moved into place. "On three," he called. "One, two..."

Push and pull led me into a swift soaking and the lightning-quick reflexes of the feline, grabbing my arm and steadying me. My hindpaws gained some purchase and, soon enough, I was out. I fought the ancient reflex to shake, especially since it wouldn't do a lot of good.

"We haven't another cloak," the bear called over the sound of rain, guiding me toward the cart. "Crawl up and get under the tarp; we'll take you back to Starhold."

"I need—"

"Don't worry about it," the cat told me. "That car is stuck until daylight. We can get it sorted in the morning. Quick, get under the tarp!"

The worst it could be was dry.

* * * * *

Dry and dark. By touch, I found several tools, what felt like wooden posts, and various other implements that might be used on a rural property like this one. I had to guess, since items outside of a basic urban tool kit were also outside my understanding. Sounds beyond my close enclosure were muffled by the loud drumming of rain against the tarp. I heard the two of them calling out to one another, calling to the non-sapient horse who had stood so obediently in the rain. I felt the cart jerk and come around to head back up the gravel drive, the horse seeming quite sure where to put his hooves. The cart did not hurry, telling me that the bear was encouraging rather than insisting. Plus one for treatment of non-sapients. A few minutes passed in an oddly lulling rocking motion, the relentless pummeling of the rain, before I heard and felt the cessation of the battering of the tarp. My rescue vehicle stopped. I heard a few other voices along with the bear's, three perhaps. No sense hiding.

Breathing slowly, I raised myself to my knees, shrugging off the tarp as carefully as I could, not to make a puddle in the space around me. I was inside a large barn, warm, well-made, well-lit, and well-kept. I could see wood beams and structure of good quality, worn more by use than by time. Five non-sapient horses stood quietly in stalls just beyond, the sixth stall waiting for the powerful bay that was receiving a rubdown with dry towels, tenderly attended by an eerily tall, lean white wolf who murmured low, reassuring sounds, exuding a feeling of loving gratitude. The feline, his cloak's hood pulled back to reveal the unmistakable ears and cheek fur of the lynx, led a very wet roan-colored cow by a loose rope into another part of the barn. I heard sheep bleating, the sounds of chickens' clucking caroming off the walls and, above me somewhere, something rustled in the loose hay of the loft.

"Saved from the ravages of the storm!" laughed a nearby voice. The female padded toward me, shucking off a large cloth cloak from around her head and shoulders, passing it up to me. "Here, this one's dry; put it around you before you catch a chill."

I took it from her, unable to break my blatant staring into the most riveting ice blue eyes I'd ever seen. The Husky looked back at me, unabashed, as if my response were a familiar one but not expected as her due. Her black-brown mask blended perfectly into the fur that framed the cream-colored fur of her ears and of the rest of her muzzle. Her smile was friendly, welcoming, without the slightest hint of guile or insincerity, and her lush tail offered a brief wag, as if to reinforce the image. In all, it was a look that held few emotional barriers of the kind that I had become so accustomed to in the city, and my own drenched tail attempted a wag in response. Perhaps in her mid-thirties, she wore loose-fitting cotton shirt and pants in a muted dusty rose color, a dark cabernet-colored cotton sash tied at her waist, and her long, dark headfur lay pulled behind her head, held with a simple, narrow cloth ribbon, also the shade of the sash.

"Thank you," I finally managed to mutter. The cloak rested easily on my shoulders, perhaps more warm in my mind than in fact.

"Ayooah, Oaknail!" called a voice from above me. "What have you found there?"

Turning toward the voice, I looked up into the loft to see a young red panda, twenty years (if that), grinning down at us from behind a large lump of hay. The lean firefox wore no shirt, and my immediate impression was that he wore nothing else either.

Beside the cart, the larger of my two rescuers looked up with a huge grin of his own. "By the Hermit's lantern," the brown bear huffed gently, "are you up there again, Oray?"

"It seemed quicker than returning to the house when the storm broke."

The Husky offered a bit of a smirk in the yowen's direction, calling up, "Did the storm catch you out too, Starshine?"

I heard a distinctly young-female giggle from the loft, very close to the young red panda; for his part, he seemed to blush a little, gave us all a greatly exaggerated shrug, then fell back into the hay, his laughter joining that of his companion and the delighted chuckles that rippled through the small crowd around me.

"No need to stay up there all night," the big bear chuckled from deep in his chest, offering a forepaw to assist my descent. "Welcome to Starhold. I am called Oaknail, and to your right is Darkstar."

My second savior, a warm smile on his face, pressed pads with me gently. "I'm glad that you weren't hurt. Ginger seems to have gotten confused when the rain grew harder, wandering off instead of staying with the rest. She's back in the stalls now, acting as if nothing had happened."

"I hope that I didn't spoil the milk."

The feline laughed amiably. "I doubt it, although I appreciate the concern."

"Rainmist," said Oaknail, gesturing to a buxom, light cinnamon-furred river otter who, like Oaknail, appeared to be much nearer my own age. I wondered if she might be one of the group's founders, as I'd assumed the bear to be.

"I think we need to get your innards warm along with your outards," she chuckled softly. "Shall you join us for dinner?"

"Of course he will!" the bear boomed with the sort of tone which assumes that all good hospitality should not only be accepted but reveled in. "Rainmist has made a beef stew that's been simmering for some hours. The smell alone has been driving me mad all day; once you've sampled it, you'll never want to leave. Heartsinger," he added with anther gesture.

The tall, lean white wolf who had been tending the non-sapient horse earlier padded up to me with a shy smile and an outstretched forepaw. I took it, looking into his warm golden eyes, feeling the unmistakable sensation that he desired, most of all, to bypass the usual chit-chat between strangers and discuss, gently, matters of interest and importance between friends. "Welcome," he said in a baritone of crushed velvet. "I hope you'll stay."

"And Lightwing."

I turned back to the beautiful Husky who had lent me her cloak. The smile on her muzzle remained warm, and she reached out a forepaw to me. I took it gingerly, as if afraid that she might shy if my grasp was too firm. "Welcome," she said softly.

"Well now," Oaknail burst forth in loud goodwill. "What shall we call you?"

"My name is—" The word *detective* refused to form in my maw. "Max. Max Luton."

"Welcome, Max," the bear said again.

"Come," Lightwing urged, squeezing my forepaw instead of releasing it. "You and I can fit under the tarp long enough to get us back to the house. Darkstar, do you have some clothing that might fit Max?"

"I'm sure I do."

I shook my head. "Really, no, I—"

"Don't worry about it." Darkstar appeared next to me without a whisper of sound or movement. "You'll need to get out of those clothes and towel off before you catch a chill you can't shake... pardon the pun."

"The stew will be ready by now, and I'll wager Moonsong has made biscuits to go with it. That should help chase away all ills." Raising her voice, the Husky called over her shoulder, "And if you two want to eat, you'd better come join us soon!"

Giggling from the rafters. I put my head down to hide the smirk on my muzzle.

* * * * *

Lightwing and I shared the tarp as we trotted through rain not quite as plentiful as before. I held it above us as she put an arm around my waist to stay close. I had a fleeting memory of sharing an umbrella this way with some female, long ago, college days, now forgotten as anything but sensation triggered through muscle memory. I tried not to think about how friendly it felt.

The area we headed toward appeared to be a particularly large portico at the edge of a particularly large structure. I couldn't gauge what I was seeing, although it (for lack of a better word) felt huge. As we halted our trot into the cover of the portico, the last of the six of us to arrive, Lightwing and I shook off the tarp behind us and sighed briefly, that universal expression of feeling good when coming in from out of the rain. We shared a chuckle, and I turned my head upward to realize that overhead heating fans were blowing warm air into the area.

"I've got this," Lightwing offered, taking her cloak from around me. She moved to one of several wide brass pipes set into the walls and hung it over, spreading it out. It was then that I realized that none of my hosts wore plastic or rubber rain gear; all had cloaks.

"Connected to our heating system," Heartsinger offered in explanation, gesturing to the pipes. "With the rains here, it seemed more practicality than luxury."

I found the brass warm to the touch. "The fans don't...?" I began.

"Less energy efficient. They're just on for about a minute, to help us dry out our fur a little before going inside."

Oaknail stood at the arched stone of the entry to the house. Swinging wide the large oaken door, he boomed warmly, "Welcome to Starhold."

He allowed me to enter first, and I padded into an entryway that opened almost immediately into a huge living room area. The space looked warm and welcoming, with quite a variety of furniture to choose from. As I considered briefly, Rainmist padded smoothly past me on quiet paws, calling out, "Halloo, Moonsong!"

"Ayooah!" came an answering call.

"Set us another place, would you? We have a storm-tossed visitor as our guest tonight."

"Wonderful!" came the enthusiastic reply. "About the guest, I mean. Is all well?"

"Will be; we'll get him dried out and presentable." The buxom river otter fetched a wink and a grin at me. I'm not sure, but I might have blushed.

"Come," said Darkstar, again appearing at my side without a murmur of sound. "Our rooms are upstairs. Let's find you a towel or two and some dry clothes."

The six of us trooped up wide wooden stairs, risers carpeted in a well-kept runner. The staircase curved slightly to our left, emptying onto a landing which then led into the last dozen steps to the second floor. Oaknail had already begun shucking out of his shirt and, from the corner of my eye, I noticed Lightwing placing a forepaw gently on Rainmist's arm before she completed an apparently reflexive motion to remove her own shirt. I didn't get the feeling that my hosts were Naturists so much not concerned about it; having a visitor, they showed respect to me, in case I might not be comfortable with such a casual attitude. Rather than focusing on the otter's flying buttresses, I instead tried to take in the nature of the house itself.

The feeling that the structure was huge returned, with reinforcements. I had the impression of perhaps a half dozen large rooms on each side of a hall wide enough for three to walk abreast with ease, the ceiling perhaps three meters high. The long walls were broken in two places on each side by doors marked by ornamental brass plaques reading "Ye Auld Water Closet." At the far end was another set of stairs, simpler, leading both up and down. All along the corridor, well-framed paintings of several styles were hung decorously — oils, acrylics, even a lush watercolor. Doors to rooms bore carved wooden lettering, some with two such devices, spelling out names — Elfbard, Summerwind, Dreamweaver, Clearwater, Unicorn, Sunrider.

Darkstar bumped gently against a door with his name on it and welcomed me inside. The room was large, a rough guess of six by seven-plus meters on a side, divided into sections by anchored bookcases and wooden dividers that didn't go all the way to the ceiling. In one such self-created area, a work space — desk, chair, computer, printer, wooden trays and shelving, the delightful anachronism of a wooden, two-drawer filing cabinet, and a number of laminated squares being used as whiteboards, covered (at the moment) with a dazzling array of colored notations. In another section, a love seat and chair, the sort that looked like you could fall into them and lose track of time. One window held its own wrought-iron tray of plants; the other, a wide and welcoming bay window, held a seat that could be used to watch the world beyond, at least when the rain and night didn't obscure it.

The lynx padded back to another section of the room where a large bed, closet, and dresser took up a comfortable amount of space. "What's your waist size, Max?"

"Medium-ish," I hedged.

Darkstar chuckled. "I think these will fit. Also medium chest?"

"We could settle on that."

He flowed around the partition, passing over lightweight cotton clothing of a soft sand color, hanging on to another set of dark gray. "Try these, friend. Stay behind the partition, if you'd like a bit of privacy. Bring out those wet clothes when you're done, and I'll take them down to the laundry room for cleaning."

"The jacket isn't wash 'n wear," I cautioned.

He grinned at me, with the full-featured lynx mystique behind it. "We don't toss everything into the washer, Max. In fact, there's one hulking machine down there that claims it can dry clean, on a limited basis. You might guess that we don't have much use for it. The jacket's mostly wet rather than muddy. I thought I'd just block it out on one of the folding tables and let it air dry." He jutted his chin toward the "bedroom" space. "I left out a towel for you; let me know if you need another."

I padded behind the partition — one of the few that didn't have bookshelves in it, I noted — and peeled out of my wet clothes. Stuff from my pants pockets went on the lynx's dresser, since I'd no idea what to do with them otherwise. The warm air blowers in the portico had helped and, after I'd done with it, one very damp towel got added to the wet clothes. As I pulled on the simple clothing, I turned over in my mind what I had learned of the furs I'd met. They were an insanely hospitable crew. I'm not at all sure what I was expecting, either of the individuals or the homestead. The barn was huge, being part stable, part shelter from the weather for however many non-sapients they might have. And this house? I hadn't seen either particularly well from the outside, but I had to imagine that both barn and house must be immense. I started to think of that program with the time-traveling box that's bigger inside than out, and I wondered exactly what I'd found here.

"I'll imagine that your appetite is healthy, after your adventure this evening," Darkstar offered amiably from beyond the partition.

"I hate to be an imposition." I hadn't had to shine up my manners in some time; I hoped I sounded all right.

"Not at all. There's usually plenty, and we enjoy sharing. You'll like the stew, I think. Rainmist has a hunter's sauce that is magnificent."

"A dark-brown mushroom sauce with white wine and spices," I said, finishing my dressing and tending briefly to my fur with casual swipes of my forepaws. "Best with beef, to my mind, especially if she's added some cumin."

"You do know something of the art." Darkstar's words twigged in my brain as a quote from a film, one that I knew was familiar to me, but in my stressed condition, I couldn't place it. He met me as I came around the partition, his own wet clothes in a wicker basket. He grinned at me as I added my sodden goods to his. "Rainmist will be pleased to have such an appreciative audience. I'll go take these down the hall and be back in a moment."

Leaving me alone in his room? Trusting soul. Then again, he didn't know I was a cop. "The laundry's down the hall?"

"No; the dumbwaiter is. The laundry is in the basement, and it's a big house." He turned to leave, adding, "Be right back."

In my solitude, I breathed a low sigh. Taking a look over my garments, I had to admit that they were comfortable. More like wearing pajamas, especially compared to my cop's garb. If I were to be doing undercover work tonight, the costuming would definitely help get me in character. Michael, once his shire's favorite faux-Gypsy fortune teller, would have approved... once he'd stopped laughing his fool head off.

Padding slowly into the more central part of the room, I tried to get a feel of its owner. Darkstar was too young to have been one of the founders of this so-called tribe, but he was clearly a part of it. The lynx's space was warm, welcoming even to me. Glover, who had been known to his tribe as Airdancer, had created a house that was filled with things, all somehow distant and sterile. The kitchen, domain of cook and maid, was more warm than anything I'd seen in the rest of his house. I had the sensation here, in this room, of someone who is comfortable in his own fur, and his living space reflected it well.

The work area had its modern requirements, yet it still felt home-like, even just a little old-fashioned. From the scattered papers "in plain view" (the phrase was not lost on me), I had the impression that Darkstar was a writer. I saw the name Alan Patrick Holloway on a title page; clearly, he hadn't given up his legal identity. I didn't read much — that sort of deep snooping required both time and a level of callous disregard for others that I'd not yet stooped to — but between that introductory page and the notes I saw scribbled on the various squares of whiteboard, I gathered the focus to be a mix of science fiction and fantasy. On the other paw, I saw a stack of paper with a title page that marked it as an academic thesis. The forbidding title was *Speculations on the Bicameral Mind: A Monologue with God*. I had absolutely no idea what that meant.

In wooden trays near a recent-model printer, I saw a small stack of letterhead with the Holloway name on it and a PMB address in the nearby town. The paper appeared to be high quality stock; to my inexperienced eye and pads, I figured the 25% rag content type. I tilted it slightly in the light, and the paper revealed the watermark: a stylized script of a single word — *Darkstar*. No doubt some sort of hidden Satanic message.

The computer itself appeared to be off, or "sleeping," as it had come to be called. I wasn't about to wake it up; you know what they say about sleeping giants. I had no skills as a hacker and no legal authority (much less moral right) to go peeking. I simply noted the happy anachronism of so much simplicity of cotton, wood, natural fibers and environment, all making way for the intrusion of the modern world. It's not something we can avoid, and I wondered if we really needed to.

Another divider wall was bedecked with dozens of pictures on photo paper, different sizes, all neatly arranged, none overlapping. Many showed faces I'd seen tonight, at different ages — the members of Timewind engaged in various acts of revelry. One showed my benefactor in a mighty tug of war between two sets of five furs per side; Oaknail appeared as the anchor of the opposing side, and I wouldn't have cared to place a wager on which side might have won; sheer determination can sometimes overpower even the best anchor. Pictures of individuals, couples, groups of all types and combinations showed smiling and loving faces all around.

One of the larger pictures appeared to be a wedding photograph, although all were in garb similar to what everyone was wearing tonight (what I was wearing, I reminded myself), and all were draped about with flower chains, soft leather tassels, matching waist sashes and headbands. All were smiling, holding forepaws, embracing. It was at least as beautiful as any other wedding photo I'd ever seen. Better than mine. The camera had caught an expression in my new wife's eye that made me wonder later if she, in that moment, had regretted her decision after all.

I shook my head, at that thought and the one that followed. This was the dreaded company of devil-cultists and drug-drenched bacchanalian revelers? The treasonous tribe of pedophilic anarchists, thieving socialists, and morals-destroying atheists? Was this what Eisenhower's "military-industrial complex" was so terrified of that the Fibbies had miles of files on them?

Too much to take in on an empty stomach. I turned back to the door.

Darkstar stood waiting for me, arms loosely at his side, the small smile still present on his lips.

"Just coming," I said, feeling a guilty flush rise under the fur on my cheeks.

The smile grew a little. "I'm flattered," he said softly.

"At my snooping?"

"At your concern."

"Concern?"

"Most furs are brazen about canvassing someone's room, if they have the courage to do it at all. Some try to be subtle about it, but they don't often make it. You actually blushed."

I could feel the blush deepen. "I'm sorry; I'm just a nosy parker by habit."

"It's all right, Max. I have the feeling that you're curious about me, about all of us. You want to know but aren't sure how to ask. Circumstances allowed you to look about my personal habitat to find clues. Did you discover anything?"

"Nothing much."

"You're too modest. Surely some speculation?"

"Perhaps that you're quite a bright fellow. Is that a Master's thesis I saw?"

"Doctoral." The lynx continued to gaze at me with his species' legendary inscrutability. "I felt something as I folded your coat into the hamper. You seem to have forgotten your shield, Detective."

He tossed it to me casually as I made a slow move toward the center of the room. I had no desire to fight anyone, especially not a male maybe twenty years younger and undoubtedly more fit.

"Are you here on official business? If so, you haven't identified yourself as law enforcement yet. That could have some bearing, if you're trying to build a case of some kind."

I blinked at him.

"Philosophy of Law class, and an occasional indulgence in television." His grin became unquestionably, if unexpectedly, friendly. "Is it official?"

"Not exactly. I mean, I'm not here to serve warrants, make an arrest... I'm not even investigating a crime."

"I didn't think so. I won't mention it, then. Your secret is safe. Leave the shield on my dresser, if you'd like; it won't go anywhere." He cocked his head toward the stairs. "Come on; let's get some of that stew before they decide we're not coming."

Again, I blinked. "I thought... well..."

"You'd prefer a scream of 'up against the wall, fascist pig'?" Darkstar chuckled softly. "Max, one thing I've learned in my time with Timewind is to avoid assuming anything. Hypothesis is one thing; it's not a fact until it's proven. In my younger days, when I was in Texas, a trooper pulled me over for driving at 95kph when everyone else on the highway was tooling at about 115, well above the posted limit. I asked him if it was better if I drove with the flow of traffic, driving at 115. He decided I was 'sassing' him, clipped me a sharp one with a baton, and hauled me in. No charges, nothing more than the speeding ticket, the inconvenience, and a headache... but I've grown wary of anyone in a uniform, like a lot of furs, these days. I try to keep myself calm, hoping each one I see is a furson instead of part of the new Reich."

The lynx paused, his face still filled with his soft smile. "You're not here as a cop, so you must be a friend we've not met yet. Besides, you didn't bring your baton."

I felt my stance relax, even as I gave myself permission to breathe again.

"C'mon, Max." Darkstar offered me a forepaw. "If you come in peace, you have come to a peaceful place. You're in no danger. I'll wager you're as hungry as I am, so let's go have dinner as friends."

If nothing else, I thought, it should be a very interesting last meal.

9: Breaking Bread

Darkstar and I padded back to the staircase with no one else in sight. It occurred to me that more than one wicker hamper might be making a trip down the dumbwaiter tonight. I felt as if I should make some sort of conversation, but he didn't start one, and I wasn't sure that I could. Everything I came up with to say felt very lame, so I kept my muzzle shut and followed him to the floor below.

From the landing, I could see into the huge living room that, before, I had merely glimpsed in passing. I took a closer look, feeling drawn into the area by the sheer warmth of the space and its furnishings. The vaulted ceiling rose high on sizeable, rough-hewn wood beams, with large, slowly-turning, bamboo-bladed fans depending from poles attached to the central crossbeam. A fireplace worthy of a British country estate commanded its respect, yet it also welcomed. The thought occurred that it was rather like Oaknail in that regard. I might have expected a display of the tribe's metal handiwork above the great mantlepiece, itself decorated with things ranging from vases bearing decoratively-arranged dried flowers to small ceramic statuary of a variety of subjects. Above these hung not shield and swords but a large circular device with markings and symbols that I did not recognize. Something about it evoked in me a feeling that it belonged in the realm of the indigenous peoples, but I wasn't sure why.

Before the fireplace lay a large sunken space, a square perhaps five meters on a side, with a few chairs, two loveseats, a big sofa, and otherwise festooned with various large pillows and things that looked like velour-covered bean bags. Two shallow steps upward, on three sides, led to more conventional arrangements of furniture, made of a few groupings of love seats, chairs, side tables, and yet more wicker baskets, these containing what appeared to be magazines — an interesting anachronism in this electronic age. The entire area was lit by wall sconces, some with decorative additions above them in which artificial flames danced warmly.

Near the front windows, black with encroaching night and rain, a pair of chairs flanked an end table with a small lamp upon it. From one of these comfortable-looking seats, Rainmist glanced over at me, eyebrows arched in what I took to be pleasant surprise. The otter nodded at me, murmuring, "I approve."

I did my best not to blush, and I felt Darkstar clap me on the shoulder. "I'll go see to our clothes, Max. Back shortly."

Chuckling, the river otter waved me over to her. "I promise not to bite. I won't even qualify it with the usual disclaimer."

Making an exaggerated walk around to her far side and slinking into the chair, I feigned appropriate terror of her female wiles while her chuckle turned into a laugh. I smiled at her, glad for the humor.

"Thank you, Max," she said softly. "I'm a natural coquette, as you may have noticed. Some say it's a species trait, to be playful. I promise it *is* playful, not predatory."

"I could tell that," I offered truthfully. "I'm simply unused to it."

"You aren't flirted with in your daily life?"

"Rarely, and not without some bit of predation." I tried to make my smile less wan than it felt. "From you, it's actually playful, a gentle bit of second nature. Rather like your starting to remove your shirt, upstairs."

I might have caught the faintest hint of blush on the light cinnamon fur of her cheeks. "Sorry," she chittered, her tailtip thapping a little on the side of her chair where she had curled it. "You must think me... what, exhibitionist?"

"No more than Oaknail. Society has decreed that males can parade about with their chests exposed, and females can't. Not entirely logical, is it?"

"Or comfortable. I love being in water, but not in wet clothes. Makes my fur itch." She smiled at me, then looked out at the darkness beyond. "Nights like this are made for stripping furclad and going out for a walk, just to enjoy it." Turning her face back to me, she grinned again. "Not many would agree, I'm sure."

"Wouldn't you prefer a daytime shower?"

"Only if no one minded catching a glimpse of full-frontal otter."

I laughed gently, and she joined in. "Is everyone here so... well, uninhibited?"

"We're reasonably well socialized," she smiled at me. "I simply forgot we had a guest with us. Perhaps it hinges upon what you consider to be uninhibited. On the occasional winter night, some of us may elect to lower the heat in our rooms, bring pillows and blankets down here, and snuggle up for warmth. Clothing is optional; we're usually furclad. It's very warm, comforting. Does that disturb you?"

Considering a moment, thinking of the ages-old ritual Question and Response, I shook my head. "I'm not sure if I could join in readily, but it's not disturbing. It sounds quite cozy indeed."

She leaned forward conspiratorially. "There's one terrible risk in it."

"Which is?"

"Oaknail snores like a jet engine."

I couldn't have stopped my braying laugh if I'd tried. I couldn't even stop when I heard the booming basso saying, "Telling tales on me, Rainmist?"

"Only the true ones, bear," she grinned.

"Then I can't complain, can I?" Oaknail stood near the edge of the living room space, in the general direction that Rainmist had hollered out to when we came in. "And I wouldn't dare risk your denying me your stew which, by the way, we're about ready to serve. If I can pry you away from your beloved rain...?"

"Oh!" the otter cried, melodramatically bringing up a wrist to her forehead. "However shall I bear it!"

"What a place for a pun!" Oaknail laughed.

I rose, still chuckling, finding this bit of interaction confirming my earlier assessment of how well this group had bonded. I once again wondered if she had been one of the founding members. The Fibbies didn't have that information, or at least they didn't share it with me. I remembered that *The Tribal Manifesto* had names in it somewhere; when I was attempting to read it, I skipped over any names, thinking them artificial and trivial. Now, I saw that some of those names might be represented here by real fursons, although you couldn't tell it by their conversation. These folks seemed a lot more sophisticated than what I had seen in that document. Of course, twenty-five-plus years can give a furson room to polish himself up a little.

The great black bear clapped a gentle forepaw to my shoulder as I neared. "Counting you, Max, there's an even dozen of us for dinner tonight.

Unicorn is out of town for the weekend, and Sunrider is taking some newfangled professional credits kind of thing in Las Vegas. We made him promise not to have too much fun, nor gamble away the tribal purse." He smiled at me with great warmth. "You will help to make up for their absence."

"No pressure," I managed to quip.

Oaknail's bellowing laugh was sufficient announcement of our arrival into what could only be called a dining hall. The ceilings here were also high, if not as high as the living room area. I saw six huge oaken tables, each with eight stools just under the tables' edges. All were heavy, sturdy, large slabs of highly polished hand-worked wood. As I watched, Darkstar and the white wolf I'd met in the barn (what was his name again?) were rearranging one table to form a T with the other; stools were arranged around these, with a few displaced seats being set against the walls.

"We're a large tribe, when we're all together," the bear explained, noticing my attempt not to gawk. "When friends and lovers join with us, even this hall isn't enough for all of us. We spill into the den, the hall, wherever we need to."

"Do all of you gather often?"

"Not as often as we'd like. A semi-annual weekend, where we hope to avoid overlapping other familial holidays. We also have a rather open-house sort of time from just before winter solstice to just past the calendar new year. We call it WinterFest, a name borrowed from many sources. It's a fine celebration, encompassing most of the winter rituals and holidays. People come and go as they wish, bunked wherever and with whomever. We have our feasts and fun, various events planned like miniature parties, and yowens dashing up and down the halls..." He heaved a huge and happy sigh. "Perhaps you see why we like the idea of having a guest tonight."

Rainmist was assisting with the general fixing of the area, and others were coming in as if responding to some signal that I had managed to miss. Oaknail took up the host's duties to introduce, or reintroduce, my fellow diners.

Oray, the young red panda I'd seen almost too much of in the barn, appeared before me fully dressed and, on his arm, a comely young female raccoon introduced as Starshine. Neither was particularly embarrassed about the encounter, although the 'coon did blush a bit, flicking her tail gently behind her. Neither mentioned it, beyond asking if I was all right after my accident. The word "uninhibited" crossed my mind again, this time with me wondering what exactly should be inhibited in their behavior.

New to me was Dreamweaver, a lean female black panther whose antique gold cotton garb matched her eyes, in company with a tall mountain lion who, though similarly dressed as the rest (myself included), introduced himself as Frank. I must confess that I blinked, and he chuckled. "I haven't joined the tribe yet," he explained, "so I haven't chosen a tribal name."

"Do you plan to? Join, I mean."

"I would like to." His face held a seriousness that might have suited a young male hoping to become squire to an Arthurian knight. "I like what I've discovered here."

"What might that be?"

He smiled softly at me. "I'd call it a dream."

"As would many of us."

We turned to the voice, I again feeling that strange tug toward the Husky who was rejoining us. I almost didn't see the young doe in her company. It's said that polite males don't try to guess a female's age; if he does, he'd be very wise not to voice it. Being a dick (meaning "detective," but perhaps the other slang meaning would apply), it's an automatic response in me to make an estimate. Mid-20s, I thought, although that could be off; any doe under 50 or so has that sweetly cautious look about her that makes us think of frail youth and innocence.

Lightwing turned her head to the doe. "This is Max," she explained quietly. "His car is stuck on the edge of the road leading to the house. We've invited him to stay until we can extricate it in the morning." The Husky turned her head back to me. "Max, this is Stellamara."

The usual thing would be to step closer, to offer a paw in greeting, but I held back. Something in Lightwing's glance and the gently wary look in the doe's eyes caused me to nod once, slowly, and offer a soft greeting from where I stood. She dipped her muzzle a few centimeters, her gaze still uncertain. With a sensation of backpedaling, I again had the feeling that I was intruding. I felt a slight chill around my shoulders, reminding me of the saying about a non-sapient goose walking over one's grave. I tried to ignore it, but hackles is as hackles does.

The general bustling about the tables included conversation, laughter, finding places in the rearrangement of their usual pattern. No one took a seat yet, as if to make sure everyone would be happy with the seating plan. Darkstar and the white wolf each carried a stack of bowls to a sideboard, chuckling over some comment I hadn't overheard, setting the crockery down carefully. As they turned back toward the kitchen, I called, "Need any help?"

The wolf smiled at me. "I think we've got the fetch 'n carry, thank you for asking. You're our guest tonight."

"Many paws make light work."

"And we appreciate it." Darkstar gave me a fine, lynx-mysterious smile. "We want to offer you some pampering. That's fun for us, also."

"Quite right, too!" Oaknail appeared near me, guiding me toward the crossbar of the T made by the two tables. "I'll commandeer some seats for us and my mate, Moonsong, who should be—"

"Speak the devil's name and see her horns!"

The cheerful alto voice belonged to a buxom brown bear who bore with her a very large crock pot, at least four liters worth, her strong arms more than a match for it. This she set on the sideboard and plugged it into one of the outlets there, as Darkstar and the white wolf returned again, bearing a lacquered wooden platter apiece, one stacked with fresh cornbread, the other a sectioned piece with a variety of oyster crackers, cheese crackers, and other crunchy savories that one might add to a hearty stew, soup, or chili. I was certain that I was drooling. Oaknail was right: The scent of that stew was enough to drive someone mad.

Oaknail's chuckle showed his love for his mate. "I shall refrain from the obvious jokes. Allow me to introduce you to Max."

He waved a generous paw toward me, even as the smiling sow presented to me her own. "Our storm-sent visitor," she grinned at me. "Welcome, Max. What would you care to drink?"

I took the proffered paw, which provided quite a grip. "Some water would be fine, thank you."

"Too easy." With an accompanying chuckle, Rainmist reentered the hall, bearing a large tray with a dozen drinking glasses on it, setting it down further along the sideboard. A wet-bar segment held a sink and, behind a panel, a dispenser for chilled water and ice. The otter turned back to me, grinning, with an explanation at the ready. "Practicality, along with the experience of trotting back and forth to the kitchen. We do have a variety of drinkables."

Chuckling, I said, "No need to break out the Rothschild '58, or whatever it is that's supposed to be rare, famous, and expensive."

"I prefer the Pepsi of recent vintage," Oray laughed, heading in the direction of the kitchen. "Anyone else, while I'm going?"

No other takers, and the firefox padded quickly off with a promise to be "just a sec." I did my best to follow the lead of the rest of the milling bodies, finding myself wondering yet again just what sort of dangerous radicals these folks could be. The feeling was more of family, the house huge yet not ostentatious, as Glover's had been. The hospitality, the camaraderie, the (pardon my dated word) vibe was the antithesis of cultism (or, the ingrained cynic in me piped up, the epitome of it).

"Soup kitchen style!" Moonsong decreed with a wave of her ladle. "Line 'em up!"

"Ma'am, yes, ma'am!" With a grin, Oaknail snapped to attention at the head of the line, taking up a bowl from the stacks. I followed suit with appropriate respect for the gag, and the rest lined up behind me. Rainmist leaned in close to my ear, *sotto voce,* "You don't have to salute."

"Protocol," I whispered back, "protocol!"

The bear presented his bowl with proper deference, and the waves of affection between the two mates was worth ten thousand soppy greeting cards. I emulated my host and, with the amazing efficiency of a well-designed production line, I soon had a bowl of hot, thick, drool-inspiring stew, a large square of cornbread balanced between the lip of the bowl and a spoon, accompanied by a glass of ice water. I then found myself ushered to Oaknail's left at the head of the table. It seemed only moments before all had been served and settled in place around the tables. A simple silence settled, and all put forepaws to either side of their bowls. I did the same and waited.

"We thank you for the gift you have provided us, precious bovine." Oaknail's voice rang softly and sincerely, not merely by rote. "We honor you by sharing with each other, by growing and becoming, by continuing the power of life and love. Thank you."

All around nodded, smiled, and then turned to me as the bear asked, "Do you have a grace before meals, Max?"

"None so eloquent," I replied. "Thank you for that."

With that, all began eating, not quite falling-to in imitation of those who haven't eaten for a week, but instead with slightly more restraint and genuine appreciation of the meal. I did hear Oray, at the base of the T and directly across from Oaknail, make a noise of deep satisfaction in tasting his first spoonful. A few at the table chuckled.

"Glad you like it," Rainmist observed drily. She sat to my left and, opposite her, Lightwing joined in with a chuckle. The otter eyed me with a raised brow. "What's your verdict?"

I held the cornbread in my left forepaw, the better to free my spoon to sample the stew. It was at least as robust as the scent had been declaring for some minutes. My tail expressed itself about the same time as I made my own rendition of Oray's recent song. This brought out a few giggles from around the table.

"A downside of being canine," I admitted. "My tail is an obvious barometer."

"You're not alone," the white wolf down the table offered quietly. "It can be difficult to keep mine still, when I'm happy."

"Which is most of the time," Darkstar observed with a smile. "He's one of the most consistently cheerful fursons I've ever known."

I saluted all with my cornbread. "I try not to be a curmudgeon, and especially not over such wonderful food. Thank you."

Conversation halted for a few moments as we all felt that the stew required our best attention. I took another moment to take little glances at my hosts. The doe sat at the end of the row of bodies in my sight-line, past the mountain lion (Frank — his name was easier for me to remember) and his consort, the black panther. I had an odd feeling about the doe, one that I couldn't quite fathom. I'd attended workshops about autism, as the force tried to appear sympathetic to people who might be "differently-abled," or "emotionally challenged," or whatever other politically correct phrasing was popular that month. It skated over the heads of most of my disinterested colleagues. I listened enough to realize that there are fursons who are just plain wired in ways that affect behavior, that they might not respond well to strong-arm, brute-force tactics (or, in simpler terms, cops being cops).

The doe's behavior could be something as simple as shyness. There was no reason to think it was anything more, except that it really did feel as if I were trespassing somehow. Put a better way, it might not have been that I was unwelcome as much as a surprise, unexpected and of unknown nature. She might simply want to take my measure. Perhaps this wasn't the best time, for either of us.

"Mmm," Oaknail said eloquently. "Too much quiet! Time to slow down and pay attention to one another!"

"The only downside to good food," Darkstar observed. "We tend to forget social niceties."

"So, Max," Lightwing said, preparing a spoonful of cornbread-laced stew for herself. "Tell us something about yourself."

I did my best not to freeze, then I stuck all four paws in it. "You mean, like, what do I do?"

"That always seems like an odd place to start, don't you find?" The white wolf — Heartsinger, I managed finally to remember — smiled at me. "The question, 'What do you do for a living,' as if we are only what we do to make a few dollars."

"True," Moonsong agreed. "Sundrider works as an investment counselor, but if you ask him what he does to live, he'd direct you to the fencing foils."

A healthy bite of cornbread delayed the necessity to respond while I weighed my options.

"I like Quentin Crisp's response," the white wolf smiled. "He said, 'I'm in the profession of being.'"

"Good answer! Good answer!" Oray and his lady raccoon applauded as if on the famous game show. The effect got a few laughs, including from me.

"Let's make it a game, then," I improvised. "I'll bet I'm the oldest furson in the room."

"What do I get if I win?" the otter teased.

"My deepest sympathy."

Some chuckles around the table. Rainmist grinned at Oaknail. "I promised to tell only the truth on you, bear, and I know you're older than I am."

"Guilty," he declared, forepaw to his heart. "I might have you beat, Max. I hit my McGarrett last fall."

The fictional cop reference almost knocked me again, but I let it go. "I'm playing with a full deck," I smiled at him. "Fifty-two."

"Not an issue," Moonsong affirmed. "You're only as old as you feel."

"Or who's feeling you," Oray opined softly. His raccoon lover fetched a slap to his arm for that one, which he giggled off easily.

"Ah, the simple joys of youth," Lightwing observed with a smirk, but not with meanness. She looked down the table toward me, asking, "What else would you like to share, Max? May we ask about family?"

"No wrong answers," Rainmist assured me softly. "We know that not everyone is as uninhibited as we are." The smile on her muzzle was equal parts teasing and reassuring.

"Well," I temporized poorly. "I was married to a lovely female who, I sometimes say, probably deserved someone better than myself." I held up a restraining paw before anyone could speak. "One of those old stories about marrying too young. Our divorce was reasonably amicable. Barbara and I had one pup, Michael, who's now running a tea shop in a small town, a little way up the mountain, one state over. I never had much extended family, so I'm kinda on my own."

The two moments' silence was more awkward than I imagined it would be. I hadn't mean to bring everything to such a grinding halt. I took a spoonful of stew, then heard Heartsinger speak softly.

"A tea shop, you say?"

"It's called Unicorn Keep."

"Unicorn will like hearing that one," Oaknail managed a smile.

"I hope we didn't step in it, Max." It was the first time that I'd heard Rainmist speak so softly.

Drawing an even breath, I shook my head. "I didn't mean to bring everyone down. I haven't been around polite company for a while; I've forgotten what small talk is about."

"It isn't small," the white wolf said, "to talk about your pup." The lupine caught my eyes, and I remembered that feeling I'd had back in the barn, of his wanting to cut past trivial conversation. "He's important to you; I can feel that in the way you speak of him. I'm glad that you told us of him."

"Is he a reader?" Darkstar asked softly, offering a smile. "As a writer, I have a vested interest in knowing."

"Barb read to him." The memory was made less painful as I got a message from the lynx's eyes: *Stay hidden a little longer.* "Got him started. He went from picture books to *The Weatherly Pups* mystery series, to sci-fi, fantasy..."

"Now you're talking!" Darkstar chuckled. "I've been working on some new ideas myself..."

"No spoilers!" Heartsinger admonished gently. "Otherwise, I want to hear all about it."

The lynx took center stage then, all of us enjoying our meals. I caught a glimpse of the doe, far from me, her eyes still curious, cautious, uncertain. As my hackles reminded me, I wasn't entirely off the hook yet.

10: Breaking Down

Darkstar's deft deflection helped to keep the rest of the dinner conversation away from me personally, yet the conversation didn't seem the least bit stilted. I had the impression that my hosts felt that they had made me uncomfortable and, as one, they found ways to take me out of the limelight and into a more balanced (and, as far as I was concerned, more interesting) discussion of topics ranging from books and films to music and wonderfully bad jokes. I hadn't enjoyed such a free-for-all of ideas and views in a very long time. My mind, as well as my belly, was well fed.

When all of us had finished, Oaknail said to me, "You've had quite a day, Max, and we don't wish to overtire you. We have a guest room for you to stay in tonight, and you're welcome to retire whenever you wish. I will admit a selfish desire to keep chatting, if you're up for it."

"Seems rude to leave such good company," I smiled, momentarily forgetting that I was there under false pretenses already. I managed to add, "I'd like to learn more about Timewind, too, if that's all right."

"Glad to oblige," Moonsong affirmed. "We love talking about ourselves!"

Amid general laughter, the tables were quickly cleared, with Oray and Starshine gathering the bowls and utensils, Rainmist looking after what was left of her stew, and Darkstar going off to see to our laundry. Heartsinger took it upon himself to guide me to the den while the rest tended to a few things before their promised return in just a few minutes.

The tall, lean white wolf led me to the large pit before the fireplace, suggesting a chair where I might get a good view of whoever else might join us. For himself, he flowed onto one of the bean-bag seats, folding himself cross-legged in a single motion, like a magic trick. His golden eyes regarded me warmly and his lips curled into a gentle smile. "I hope we don't seem too nosy," he confided, his voice soft, inviting. "I can assure you that our intentions are good, if that counts."

"I think it does, and thank you. I guess I'm not very good at talking about myself."

"You did well, I think. We know a bit about what you like in books and movies. I hadn't heard of the film *Country* before; I think I'd like to go have a look for it. I enjoy a well-told story."

"It's a good one," I agreed, once more feeling lame. "I apologize if I'm staring..." I began.

"Are you wondering about my breed?" he grinned a little. "Many do."

"Again, I apologize..."

"No need. Curiosity is encouraged here. My father is an arctic wolf, with his lineage reaching back to the Western Steppe, down from the Urals. My mother is Borzoi, with her familial roots in Ukraine." He pronounced it oo-KRYN-yeh, and it took me a moment to process it. "The combination became known as 'Borzhvolk,' although the Borzoi lineage already has wolf blood in it."

"Russian wolfhound, if that term isn't offensive somehow."

"Do you mean it to be offensive?" he asked simply.

"No."

"Then I'm not offended." Smiling, the wolfhound added, "Thank you for being concerned. I try not to take offense first. I think that's where the idea of 'political correctness' originally came from. It's good to be sensitive to someone else's ideas and perceptions; being oversensitive, though, seems to cause more trouble than it solves."

I nodded, a soft smile on my lips. "I imagine that's not a popular opinion."

"I suppose it depends on who you ask." He looked up, smiling, as others began to filter in and find places to sit. "It's been part of previous conversations here."

"What has?" Rainmist asked, choosing a seat neither too near nor too far from me, giving me a sly wink as she settled in.

Heartsinger brought her up to speed quickly, and the topic gained some happily-bantered traction as, eventually, everyone joined us. Darkstar padded up closely to whisper in my ear that the clothes were in the dryer, that my jacket appeared to be drying out just fine, and all would be well. I thanked him quietly and waited for a break in the conversation.

"I just wanted to thank everyone for dinner." I cast a glance back to Rainmist. "It was really delicious."

"You're very welcome, good fur," she nodded graciously to me, "but I must imagine you to be the victim of frozen dinners; it was hardly a gourmet recipe."

"If not," I said, "it was certainly carried out with a gourmet's flair."

I have no idea where that came from. Perhaps just being in this atmosphere of camaraderie and good feeling had somehow loosened my tongue a bit.

"Tell me," I tried, "more about Timewind. I know almost nothing, save for some angry local press, years ago."

"Ooo, a torrid scandal from the distant past?" Oray piped up.

"Yes," Moonsong drawled, "long years before you were conceived, yowen. Things *did* happen before the turn of this century!"

The firefox held up peacemaking forepaws, chuckling his surrender. His raccoon lover gave him a low growl, looking unsure if she wanted to tickle him or bite his ear. I tried not to imagine which would actually be a punishment. Maybe neither.

Oaknail smiled at me from the comfort of the loveseat that he and Moonsong snuggled up in. "What flavor of horror did you read, Max? The overtaking of government, the threat of total anarchy, the radical attack on family values, or the poisoning of young minds with our dangerous ideas?"

"Oh, I probably had the whole buffet. I was a kind of news junkie, in my distant youth." *In for a penny...* "I even found a copy of the *Manifesto* you put together in comb binding."

The bear groaned, as did his mate. "That old relic! I beg you not to judge us by that. It was a first attempt and, truth told, a foul one." He managed a chuckle as he looked at me, a wry look on his face. "We were so eager to get our message out that we garbled it up entirely. We've had lots of time to edit and clean it up since then."

"We, meaning 'the founders'?"

"Nine of us, to start," Moonsong put in. "Unicorn, Sunrider, and Rainmist are the only others to stay here; the remaining four have found lives elsewhere."

Or deaths. I felt the vague presence of a shade in the room. "You seem to have grown well over the past years... how long has it been?"

"Depends on how you measure it," Rainmist considered. "We came together in the early spring of 1994, as a band of latter-day dreamers who read about the 1960s, all the manifestos, the history, and wondered why we couldn't dream like that again. We couldn't understand why dreams should have to die."

Oaknail nodded, taking his mate's forepaw into his own. "We found this property in the late summer of that year and discovered that there was a way to acquire it through payment of taxes that were owed on it. 'Fallen into escheat' is the legal phrase. It seemed providential, at the time, and the actual price paid was incredibly low. We asked friends, family, everyone we could; we got the money together, bought the property on..." He shook his head, smiling at the memory. "We claim November 8, 1994, as our official founding day. Election Day, no less! We had created a legal thingummy to buy it, similar to an LLC... it's a long, boring legal trail, never mind. Anyway, that legal thingummy needed a name, and that's when 'Timewind' was born, one week prior. The metaphorical ink was still wet."

"Why that name?" I asked.

"I blame my predecessors," Darkstar chuckled. "I'm considered the author/editor for the tribe, these days, but I've heard the stories about the use of the word 'Zeitenwende,' which can have the meaning of 'a turning point in time,' or 'turn of an era.' Most literally, it's used to refer to year zero of the Christian or Common Era calendar, but it also has that idea of great change, sweeping change."

"I was heavily into the electronic music of Klaus Schulze at that time," Moonsong admitted, a sense of blush rising under her brown cheek fur. "It's the title of one of his albums. I thought it was close to 'Zeitenwende' but easier to pronounce."

"Good idea," I chuckled. "So you came together here and started the commune on this land?"

"More or less," Oaknail agreed, "although I'm going to pick a nit. We're more a community than a commune. It might be splitting philosophical hairs, but we thought from the beginning that we should make the difference. Communism, as a way of living, rests largely on the idea that all that the commune has belongs to everyone, with no individual property. We were all raised in a country that prizes personal ownership and individual expression; there's no way to change that, and no need to. We avoided jealousy over property, money, even other people, simply by letting each be himself, have his own things, his own space, his own privacy."

"We're more like family," Rainmist said, shifting herself upward in her chair. "We share freely, asking, helping where we can, with money, chores, a friendly ear. We sometimes bicker like family, too, but that's only to be expected."

"And all this." I looked around me at the huge house. "I don't imagine this was waiting for you when you arrived."

Everyone laughed at this, with the three founders present braying loudest. "Amazing what you can accomplish in not-quite 30 years, ain't it?" Oaknail laughed. "Our first work here was to establish the perimeter, just to get the lay of the land. We knew that we wanted to move onto the land as soon as we could, if only to stop spending money on apartments and such. We banded together to keep one rental house, the largest of our places, so that we had somewhere to retreat to from time to time. Through the winter, we put up some temporary structures here, and we worked as best we could to make plans for better ones."

I found myself thinking of the squatters on that piece of land that Glover had visited before his death, and I wondered what he had seen, what memories it had brought up for him. "Tents and port-a-potties, maybe?"

"Oh, the good old days," Rainmist groaned. "It was a long process, to put in a proper road, decide how we wanted to make space for structures, gardens, livestock eventually... Oh, the many nights of talk and planning. You'd be amazed how comfortably we managed to outfit some basic storage sheds!"

"Aren't those expensive?"

"They weren't cheap, but something about three meters on a side cost less than one month's rent on an apartment. We swapped one vice for another, for a while."

"We did finally break ground for a general purpose sort of building, one that included showers, storage, and a space that actually had electricity." Moonsong smiled at the memory. "In some ways, a nightmare; in others, some of the best times of our lives. Spring and summer of 1995 were amazing. A lot of sleeping outside, careful campfires, and the slow growth of our tribe."

In less than a year, they had structures to live in, plans made, actual work done. *Dedication* was the word that came to mind. *Obsession* hopped hobo-like onto that train of thought, and I couldn't understand where it had come from.

"I notice the use of the word 'tribe' when you speak of yourselves," I observed. "I think there was an uproar about your falsely claiming status as aboriginals."

Oaknail laughed easily. "The only such claims were by those saying we were making those claims! We asked no special recognition from the government nor any indigenous tribes." With a grin, he nodded toward Darkstar. "I'll let the wordsmythe explain it better."

The lynx chuckled at the acknowledgement. "The term can be used for a group having a common interest, occupation, character... it's just not used as often as it might be. It has a warmer sense to it than, say, 'consortium' or 'association.' I haven't heard tell of a tribe of lawyers yet, although," he added quickly, raising a proper forefinger in the air, smiling, "we do have a tribal lawyer, so anything is possible!"

The ghost, or memory, of Thomas Glover whispered at my ear, a sense of icy air down my neck. Chuckling softly, I tried to shake off the feeling, admitting, "I don't wish to offend the attorney not here to defend himself, but it's easy to make jokes about lawyers who... well, this atmosphere of caring and benevolence wouldn't fit with the popular opinion of attorneys."

"Unicorn would agree with you!" Lightwing piped up, after having been quiet for so long. Her beautiful ice blue eyes held me as surely as they had before. "It's part of why he chose that name: A fair, honest lawyer and a unicorn..."

"Both mythical creatures?"

"Got it first time," the Husky nodded, grinning. "He told me once that he's glad that he doesn't practice 'courtroom law,' because he might not be able to keep a civil tongue in his maw. There are good attorneys, of course, but the bad ones get all the headlines."

"And the money," I agreed, a little too heartily. I hesitated, feeling that I was slipping on the ice a bit. My eyes cut nervously from face to face, yet

I saw only welcoming eyes. "I'm way out of bounds here... You've just come so far from tents and sheds, and I have no idea how you could...?"

"It's no secret at all, Max," Oaknail explained softly. "Everything starts slowly and builds. The land provided some income from trees, taken down to make space for buildings or crops. We found a good land manager who helped us save the best trees, clearing carefully, which is partly why the road to Starhold is long. We invested some of that sale into repayments, more into our building plans..."

"And then came Sunrider," Moonsong chimed in, grinning. "He discovered us quite accidentally, unless you believe in fate. We did some street-level campaigning and fundraising in 1996, for the elections. Along with quite proper campaign materials, we had some copies of the Three Steps to Becoming. We kept the two things entirely separate but, if someone asked about what group we were with, that sort of thing, the whole idea of Timewind came up. The lively fennec fox who became Sunrider joined up with us in February 1997, after he had graduated the previous December with his degree in finance freshly in paw."

"That's the thing about the tribe," Heartsinger put in. "It expands slowly, finding what it needs, as an entity, almost by magic. Each of us brings something special to the tribe, and the tribe gives us something special in return. It's..." The Borzhvolk hesitated, the blush easy to see on his cheeks. "It's a little like falling in love."

"Falling in love with a dream?" I asked, then shook my head. "I'm sorry. Please forgive my cynicism. I must sound insulting to you. I don't mean to be."

"I think I know what you mean, Max." Frank spoke up from his place on the floor, where he lay comfortably with his head resting in his lover's lap. The mountain lion looked softly at me. "It really is a dream, isn't it? And yes, I'm falling in love with it as much as I'm falling in love with this lovely female."

The panther leaned down to bestow a perfectly sweet kiss to his lips. I could have sworn that I caught the soft rumbling of two gentle purrs. The ghost, the memory, the idea (Idea?) of Glover tried to mask the sound.

As the female raised her head, Frank returned his gaze to me. "I'm learning what it means to be a part of this tribe. I want to take it seriously, to make a commitment."

Rainmist drew my attention with a wave of her paw. "No, Max. We don't have entrance exams or ceremonial rites of passage. It's different for everyone. We've had a very few who decided not to stick around for more than a few weeks; some are part of us yet far away; some have joined us after a long period of wondering; some are close yet never joined."

"There's a lot to think about," Frank mused.

His lover spoke softly. "As a tribe, we work together to make each other brilliant. Do you know of the Three Steps to Becoming?"

"You'd mentioned it before," I temporized, glancing at Moonsong. "I may have seen something about it in that comb-bound booklet I found."

"It's been slightly modified since then," Oaknail observed, "but the central idea is the same. First, make of yourself all that you can be. Because that's a lifelong quest, the second step is to ask help of others as you create yourself, as well as help others — as best you can — when they ask you for help in their own creation. Third, take all that you have made of yourself and make it your gift to the world."

"It sounds like an oath of fealty."

"To oneself," the bear noted softly, "and then to everyone else."

"The tribe?"

"The world."

I considered this for a long moment. The whispering tried to be louder, and it interfered with my considerations. It was Frank who drew me back out.

"You can see why I say that I want to think about it more before making the commitment." The mountain lion took his lover's forepaw into his, grinning. "I guess it's a little like marriage. It's about marrying myself, though. About really striving."

"You hadn't done that before now?"

"Kinda sorta," the cat chuckled. "You can have my life story, if you want it, but you've probably heard variations, and I'm not the best storyteller."

The black panther (what was her name again?) tapped Frank's nose with a tender forefinger. "Wanna try again?" she grinned at him.

"Okay, I did say that I wasn't the *best* storyteller." He grinned back up at her, then at me. "I'm trying to learn other ways to say things, to stop making less of myself."

"Words have power," Darkstar murmured.

Thinking for a moment, the mountain lion returned with, "I still feel uncomfortable telling stories, because I worry that I might be boring or burdening someone."

"And he's asked for help with that," the panther said with a touch of pride. "I've asked for help with my own self-doubts. Before I made my commitment to Timewind, I had no idea what asking for help looked like. I didn't know how to feel when someone asked for help, either. It was... eye-opening."

"Heart-opening," Frank murmured, giving her forepaw a squeeze.

The silence that followed was both warming and uncomfortable. This was not expected, not in any form, and I began to feel vaguely threatened. All this really did sound like a cult, like some Manson-family reboot with a bigger budget. I began building up excuses to get to the room they'd prepared for me, wondering if I'd need to barricade the door.

"You're safe."

All eyes, including mine, turned toward the doe at the periphery of the group. She had been almost hidden behind Lightwing, as if using her as a shield against... me? Even now, she huddled close to the Husky, seeming to draw strength. The larger female put an arm around the doe's shoulders, gently, not for restraint but for support. I couldn't speak. Her eyes had the sense of a glow in the black depths of her large pupils, holding my own eyes with a gaze as tender as it was inescapable.

"This is new." The doe's voice was barely above a whisper, yet clear. "You're not familiar with this. Trust that you're safe. The rest is... for tomorrow."

I flicked a glance at Darkstar, who seemed as surprised as I was. Had she learned who I was?

"If we shadows have offended," Oray offered with gentle flair, "think but this, and all is mended — that you have but slumbered here while these visions did appear." The firefox smiled. "I made a decent Robin Goodfellow, back in school."

"It's not midsummer," his raccoon lover observed, "but it's still a dream, if you want it to be."

"What do you mean?" I asked.

"Let's pretend." She smiled at me, quite benevolently. "It's how I think of it sometimes. Imagine the best world that you can, then pretend it's real. How did it get that way? The same way that it got the way it is now: Slowly, with small things adding up to bigger things. Then imagine what small thing you can do, and see what changes. For me, that's the story of the tribe. It's a good story, and I want to keep telling it."

"And every time we tell it," Oray added, "the story gets better. That's how really good stories are built, how they last. Isn't that right, Darkstar?"

"I think you've stolen my playbook," the lynx chuckled.

"Max," Lightwing offered quietly, "you look a little overwhelmed. Was it something we said, something we did?"

I tried to chuckle, and it came out like... something else, whatever it was. The smile on my muzzle felt wooden. The Idea that had ridden in my passenger seat, all the way from my home and my work to this unusual place, had found its way from the car to somewhere just over my shoulder, and I fought the urge to turn my head to look at it squarely, to let it save me from these insane beings who were talking about dreams as if they were creating them. Who does that? How could they, and why? I shouldn't be here. I had to run. I was...

"Maybe a little," I admitted, not entirely sure that I was speaking. "It's a lot to take in. All of this is... well, dreams and all, and all this..." I wave a vague paw at my surroundings.

Rainmist rearranged herself in her chair, as if wanting to reach out to me, then stopping herself. She smiled, that rather sweet, coquettish smile that had warmed me before. I wanted so much for it to work, yet the eyes that I cast on her were still worried. "Max, may I ask you if you found, in those newspaper articles, the word 'cult'?"

I swallowed, more embarrassed than afraid. "I really don't think—"

"Yes, you do." Her voice stayed soft, her eyes as nonpredatory as she could make them. "We sound hypnotized, maybe stoned. I promise you that there was nothing in the stew beyond the usual cooking-type herbs. We do have some homemade sangria, if you want some, but even that is for flavor more than alcohol; the way we make it, it's about six to ten proof. Warming, not actually intoxicating."

"From the outside, any group can look like a cult." Darkstar also spoke softly, his yellow-gold eyes mellowed into something more grayish in the low lights of the den. "A druidic coven gets more bad press than Freemasons, but they have similarities. The Catholic church is a cult, by strict definition, as are Mormons, the Amish, any religious group. Survivalists, the Manson family, any group who slavishly exalts and venerates an individual or ideal. In that sense, Timewind is a cult."

He paused, shifting a little. "Perhaps the negative connotation of the word 'cult' arises when the group isolates, insulates from the world, protects itself, seeing anything outside of itself as evil, degenerate, perhaps even a direct threat. Their thoughts are along the lines of, 'The outsiders tell lies, especially about us, and whatever proof they claim to have must be falsified.' To reinforce that, to make it 'fact,' all that is not part of the cult must be assimilated or destroyed."

Frowning, I asked, "How does the Christian church do that?"

"Ask the pagans, or the indigenous furs around the world." The lynx shook his head sadly. "Please understand. We can point to good things done by the church. We must also acknowledge the bad, the horrors of assimilation, the crusades of death and destruction, so that it can be learned from, redressed, prevented in future."

"None of us is perfect," Lightwing noted. "That's what our Three Steps tries to address. Our goal is not to be perfect; it's to keep trying."

"And to keep dreaming." Frank's panther lover spoke up. "Perhaps that's why I took the name Dreamweaver." She grinned at me. "That, and my skills in textiles. It seemed to fit."

I felt myself nodding a little. The Idea at my shoulder whispered a warning about falling for the shiny-pretties that so often held such disappointment. *Go with the proven thing,* it told me. *Think of the failures. Think of the squatters. Think of Glover. Think of all that's impossible. That's the best bet, isn't it? The surest bet? The proven return? All the things that reaffirm your experience that it's all only going to get worse? Listen to all those who have given up before you...*

"Listen to us."

The young doe once again held my gaze with hers. I had the feeling that she was seeing more than she was telling.

"Listen to our stories," she said. "I promise that they're all true."

Oaknail leaned forward, looking at me carefully. "Max, I hope I don't stick my hindpaws in it... There's a look in your eyes that tells me we really have overstepped. I know we did during dinner, and I'm sorry for that. Is there anything we can do?"

"It's okay, really, I'm okay, it's just stress maybe..." The words bubbled and babbled from me, and I didn't know why. This made no sense. There was no threat here, nothing here to hate, nothing to be afraid of, nothing, just the Idea trying to make me scared, that was—

"Do you want to go rest?" Darkstar asked softly, starting to rise.

"Maybe that's—"

Something broke inside my head. I flinched slightly, sure that I felt Glover's brain matter splatter onto my face, felt my own face disintegrating into a gory spray, one good reason cops have guns, one of the storied ways that they use them...

"—a good idea..."

I felt the young doe's eyes on me, then to something over my shoulder, back to me, then I realized that Oaknail stood before me, helping me onto my hindpaws. I moved under my own power, although I felt the bear's reassuring forepaw on my shoulder. To my other side, Darkstar padded along with us, opening the door to a guestroom the size of a large master bedroom, helping me inside. The covers of the large bed were turned back. I heard soft words around me, pointing out the ensuite, the house phone with a list of numbers, call on any of us, anytime, we're here to help...

I was put carefully, gently, to bed. I remember Darkstar staying for a few moments. Lynx are famous for their enigmatic smiles. He did not smile, neither did his eyes conceal anything. I could see them asking if he could help, wondering why the cop was crying, wondering if he had somehow caused it. Words had already left me, and I was tenderly drowning in something I had no words for anyway. Darkstar left me to my silence and, with a ghost, or an echo, or an Idea my only remaining companion, I gulped a last breath and found the prey's mercy of oblivion.

11: Breaking Through

My eyes opened, not suddenly, not from any stimulus that I was aware of. I had no sense of time, and the quiet seemed absolute. Either the room was very well soundproofed, or the rain had stopped. I became more aware of my body, realizing that I had rolled over onto my side. My long nose stuck out past the quilt that wrapped warmly around me. I could see the bedside table, which held a pitcher and a clean glass. I pushed the cover gently away from me, raising up on an elbow. I saw curtains, a dark color but not black, drawn across a window. The light for the scene came from the ensuite; the door to it had been left open a little for the amber glow of a nightlight to pour in, just bright enough to make sure no one would trip on anything.

Something flickered, just outside my visual range. I sat up, pushing the covers back, looking around the room. An armchair sat near the window, a small table on the far side of it from me; a paperbound volume lay on it, although I couldn't read the title. Across from the foot of the bed, a mesh-backed office chair tucked its seat underneath the lip of a worktable arrangement. To my right, on the wall with the door, a dresser with a mirror above it held a large bowl of water in which floated a flat disc of candle, lit, its flame reflecting warmly in the mirror. It had no scent that I could detect, but its tiny fire brought a warmness, an old-world comfort that pushed away the fear-filled thoughts of the evening before.

I pulled the pillows up, fluffed and plumped them, set them behind me, lay my back to them. I breathed in through the nose, out slowly through the maw, the usual calming trick, except that I wasn't anxious or frightened. I was confused as all hell. I remembered the conversation in the den space, and I remembered the feeling of being frightened, terrified, but I couldn't remember why. Not clearly. I remembered thoughts, fearful images, and I remembered crying. That, in itself, was worrying: I rarely cry, and never in front of strangers.

They had all risen, I remembered, all to their hindpaws as I began crying and saying I needed to get some rest. Only Oaknail and Darkstar actually got me to this room, the others keeping a distance, offering quiet support. My memory skipped a little, remembering bits and pieces, getting here, being brought into the room, guided to the bed, helped out of the cotton shirt and pants, "for comfort's sake," Oaknail said. I was told that there were numbers to other phones in the house, some sort of inside intercom system, the list set next to the phone on the desk. I saw the phone distantly, on the work desk, but I couldn't imagine calling anyone. I couldn't imagine talking with them, not yet. Tomorrow will need... well, something.

The rest is... for tomorrow.

The young doe's words came back to me. I still had no clue what she knew, or how, or why she said those words, and in exactly that way. I looked back at the dresser, wondering all at once where my clothes were... or, perhaps more precisely, where my shield was. Darkstar had seemed surprised at the doe's words; my cop instincts told me that he didn't fake that. My juju ain't infallible, but I believed that he hadn't told anyone about me, unless he'd done it since dinner, since I was brought here. That wouldn't account for what she'd said.

I looked around the darkened bedroom, which was more like a hotel room but with much more home-like accoutrements. For a few moments of wishing, I wanted it to be home — comfortable, close, safe. It was a warm feeling, welcoming, an invitation to give myself over to the relaxation that one could find in the realm of hope. The thought of it stirred something in my belly and, at the same time, something in the room itself. The shadows seemed to shift, subtly, bringing back the space for the Idea to return. Different, now. Almost visible. Almost tangible. A predator, stalking, with the power to make the prey think that succumbing would be a good idea, a welcome outcome.

Was this what Glover felt? In the non-sapient world, a tiger is an apex predator. Even an old dog like myself could hunt, if need be. To feel hunted as well as haunted... Timewind was an idea for him, and Starhold, though not on this grand scale, had been his home. He began with so much hope, and then came the Idea. Suddenly? I thought not. It had to have been there for a while, a long while, working its tendrils into him like some parasite, until he finally succumbed, finally gave up. It was so much easier to give up. So much, for so long, and one grew tired, and hope becomes dangerous, and I would be a fool to think that I —

I blinked. I couldn't give in to that, not now, not here. I tried the calming trick again, and my breath caught. The door to the hall opened inward, slowly, quietly. The light from the hallway was muted, but still brighter than the light in the room. I could make out a general shape, a head that appeared more canine than anything else. Not tall enough for Heartsinger, and this shape was more compact. Could it be...?

"I'm awake," I said softly.

"Sorry, I..." The voice faltered. "I guess I'm checking up on you. May I come in?"

"Yes."

Lightwing opened the door wider and took a cautious step into the room. She still wore cotton pants and shirt, although the sash she'd worn earlier was missing. The garb was casual enough for use in just about any situation, I reasoned. I wasn't at all sure that she slept in them, but...

She turned her face to me and, even in the dim light, I could see clearly by her eyes that she was concerned. "Are you okay? Is there anything you need?"

"I'm okay, or trying to be."

"Do you want me to leave you?"

I took half a moment to see how I felt, or if I felt anything at all. Yes, I felt something. "No," I said.

She paused only a moment, then entered and closed the door behind her. Turning toward the bed, she gestured to the other chairs in the room. "Shall I...?"

Shaking my head gently, I moved my legs a little to one side, my forepaw indicating the large space remaining on the king-sized bed. "If you're comfortable...?"

The Husky smiled softly, padding silently closer and taking up one leg to fold onto the bed, her lush tail giving a brief wag as she sat a short distance from me. "I trust you," she said. Her demeanor sobered a little. "You seemed so upset, earlier."

"I didn't mean to frighten anyone."

"Not frightening, just..." She looked down for a moment, then raised her muzzle to me again. "You looked so hurt. I felt bad. I have the feeling that you really aren't used to being so open."

I hesitated — probably at the openness — then nodded slowly. "You're right."

"Did we hurt you?"

Chuckling softly, I said, "I'm not a Vulcan, I promise."

Lightwing laughed, and I found myself wanting to make her laugh more. The emotion went all the way to her eyes, shining in the candlelight. "Sounds like you've got your humor back."

"As long as it's not hysteria, I'll take it."

She looked at me closely. I felt like an open book, turned to a passage that its reader wanted to study more closely. "Max, who are you?"

Every fiber of my being told me to keep hiding. I had the strong feeling that Darkstar still hadn't told anyone else that I was a cop. *Cop.* I always hated that word. It was a simple shortpaw word, came from *copper,* which had some origin somewhere in Latin or French or something. Darkstar would know, or he'd find out. I just felt it was disrespectful, cheapening. But even "detective" was a word that could alienate me from her, at least now. Tomorrow, maybe, when I could tell them all at the same time, redeem myself somehow.

The rest is... for tomorrow.

I tried part of the truth. "Just an old dog who got caught in a downpour and was rescued by Timewind."

"You were looking for us."

"Yes."

"Why?"

"I thought you might have answers to some mysteries in my life."

The Husky considered this for a very long time. The passage that she was reading in my book must have been very interesting. At length, she said, "She's an empath."

"What?"

"Stellamara is an empath. It's part of why she's here. We provide a safe haven while she learns how to control her gift."

"I'm not sure I understand."

"Few do," Lightwing sighed softly. "She is highly 'sensitive,' to use the common word for it. She has tried to explain it to others, in words, in art. She came to us about four years ago, more by accident than anything else. She, too, was storm-tossed, although it was emotional turmoil more than the weather. Darkstar found her at a 'starving artists' show in the city, commented on her paintings, talked with her, slowly discovering just how damaged she felt. Over a little time, he convinced her to visit here a few times and, finally, to live here with us."

"Didn't she think he was just some guy trying to pick her up?"

"Five things helped." She enumerated them on her fingers. "First, her empathy told her that she was safe with him. Second, part of why she trusted him is because he genuinely is tribal; he has roots in Mi'kmaq, and he has something of 'the Sight' himself. Third, he gave her a copy of *The Tribal Manifesto* — yes, the updated one, like the one on the table over there — and her gift told her that it, and Darkstar, were real. Fourth, she knew that she had to get out of the city, to get away from the crowds of people who seemed to fill her mind with their emotions whether she wanted them or not. Fifth, he's gay, not to mention a gentlefur." The Husky smiled at me. "So no, she didn't think he was trying to pick her up."

I considered a moment before nodding and saying, "Yeah, that might do it."

Lightwing laughed at the joke, as I wanted her to. I chuckled also, fighting strongly against the idiotic concern of stripping down in front of a "gay guy," twice, in fact. I despised myself for even having the thought. It was part of the paranoia of a cop-shop mind — all the guys had to be oh-so-butch, even in these "enlightened" times. I made myself think about Darkstar, made myself try to find the slightest word, gesture, or action that made him even the least bit threatening to me or my alleged masculinity. How masculine could I be if even the mention made me doubt myself?

Her laugh fading softly, the Husky looked at me candidly. "Stellamara told me that she was worried about you, Max. She said that you had a secret that you were afraid to tell."

My blood froze as I tried to control the look on my face, the set of my ears. "Does she think I'm dangerous?"

"No," Lightwing said softly, "certainly not to us. What she feels is that you're in pain. A lot of pain. It's why I came to check on you."

"I see." My hesitation didn't help me, but the Husky was very patient. "I guess that I wasn't expecting all this."

"How can I help you?"

She asked the question without guile or hidden agenda. The look of her, there in the soft candlelight of this midnight room... I felt a sensation of falling. When a female sparks poetry in the patterns of your thinking, you're already in deep kimchi. "Would you tell me what Timewind means to you?"

"I was born to it."

I frowned. "You're not old enough to be one of the founders. Were your sire and dam part of it?"

"No." She brought both legs up onto the bed, crossing them, shifting, getting comfortable. "I found the tribe about eight years ago, but almost from birth, I knew that I was part of it."

"I don't follow you."

"Timewind is more than a group, Max; it's a tribe based on a philosophy, one that binds us, and one that I feel I was born to. When everyone else I knew was learning that their elders were always right; that the world is what it is, and there's not much you can do about it; that church was a place you went to because it was expected of you, and because they told the Only Truth That Matters... in all of that, I was busily questioning, trying to understand why all of this was so damned unquestionable."

I shifted enough to offer her a pillow. "You weren't Catholic, were you?"

"Why do you ask?"

"Because you would have been the Devil Herself, as far as Catholic school teachers were concerned."

Lightwing laughed, placing the pillow on her lap, resting her arms on it. "Bring back the rites of exorcism!" She flashed a wicked grin. "Nope, not Catholic, but I did get my teachers frustrated a lot. I was the pup who asked questions no one had easy answers for."

"Like what?"

She considered, opening up her own self-book. "I wanted to know what happened to the magic. Yowens get to read about magic, elves, unicorns, so-called mythical beasts, and they go looking for them, until they're told to 'grow up' and realize that there's no magic in the 'real' world. I couldn't believe that."

"Did you ever find any magic?"

"All kinds. Rainbows, sunsets, mountains, smiles... the bright eyes of yowens who still believed." Another grin from her. "When I was a yowen, the best magic I found was pizza. You can't stay miserable when the pizza shows up. It's like a ready-made party. Sharing a pizza brings out the jokes, the smiles, the good conversations."

"Bagels," I said. She giggled. "My first bagel with a schmear, I knew I'd found the food of the gods."

"Ever tried sashimi?"

"I prefer my meats cooked, thank you, but you can always count on me for good fish, grilled, baked, or fried." I raised an eyebrow, suspiciously. "Leafy greens?"

"Great for composting; let's put them right into the pile."

"Good answer, good answer!" I echoed the yowens from earlier this evening, applauding softly as Lightwing giggled, clutching the pillow to her chest. All of her joined into the laughter, her body, her bouncing, wagging tail, her smile, her eyes... her beautiful ice-blue eyes...

The feeling washed over me like a wave of... desperate pain. I don't know where those words came from, but they paired together and locked themselves inside me, making a hurt that I thought I would never be able to get over. Somewhere in the shadows, the Idea moved, just a reminder of its presence and its power. I must have done something, made some sound, as Lightwing looked at me with some concern, her eyes holding me even closer than before.

"Max, are you all right?"

"I'm... not sure." The truth came out of me, whether I wanted it to or not. She leaned forward, took up my forepaw in hers, and I felt and heard my breath catch.

"It's so very deep," she said. "I can't help feeling that we did something to you..."

My head shook almost violently to say no. "Not you. Been here. It's been here with me. Brought it in with me—" I heard babbling, not entirely sure it was me talking. "So stupid, so stupid..."

Her forepaw squeezed mine. "What's stupid, Max?"

"Me," I hiccoughed, feeling tears trying to come back again. "Crying."

"I don't think you're stupid for crying, Max. None of us does." She paused, looking, seeing, reading. "Stellamara felt a lot of hurt from you. After he came back into the den, Darkstar said something that I didn't understand; he said that he had underestimated you. We asked what he meant, but all he would say is that he hoped to talk to you in the morning. Thinking about all that made me come down here to talk to you. To listen."

I held her paw, her gaze, and I still felt that I was slipping, that something was falling inside, and that I was going to lose my grip on whatever it was I was trying to hold on to.

"Max?" Lightwing's voice was soft in my ears, in my mind. "Max, listen to me. Would you share your fur with me?"

Swallowing had become difficult. She waited for me, waited through my hesitation. Asking too much, she was, I was, asking is... I finally managed to swallow; the clicking sound was huge in the quiet of the room. Still, she waited. I let the war play out, swiftly, deciding what it was that I wanted, realizing that the Question allowed me to postpone thinking about that too closely. The basis of the ritual protected both parties, gave us the guidelines... Snuffling slightly, I made myself control my maw, my throat, my breathing. It took two tries to give the Response.

"It is warmth to us both."

Giving my forepaw a squeeze, she then released it, returning the pillow, leaning back, moving off of the bed. She began removing her shirt, and I turned away, shifting myself to the left to make room for her, readying the pillow for her. In moments, she raised the quilt and slid into the bed next to me, rearranging the duvet to cover us both. Her body was warm, solid, her fur lush. I looked at her face, close to mine, her smile, her eyes shining from her perfect dark mask. I felt like a department store mannequin, plastic, unyielding, laid out, waiting.

"Max," she whispered to me, "may I hold you?"

I tried to make some sensible word, but I could produce only a soft squeak.

"It's okay, Max. I trust you. Now... will you trust me?"

Closing my eyes, I tried to breathe, tried to remember, to have faith in the Response and all it meant, to believe that I wasn't the scumbag I felt like right now, that I wouldn't do anything I wasn't supposed to, that I wouldn't... ruin it. Like I had ruined so much. Or was that...?

I breathed deeply, opened my eyes, looked into those beautiful eyes, so near to me, and I made myself speak. "I need... to trust. Is... is that okay?"

"Yes." She smiled at me. "It's okay."

"Safe."

"Yes."

One more swallow. "Please... hold me."

So very tenderly, she snaked one arm underneath my pillow, reached across me with the other, pressed herself gently against my side, as I let loose with a sound that could only be described as a whimper. I felt her breasts against my arm, her head upon my shoulder, her leg upon mine, claiming me with compassionate warmth.

"What are they telling you?" she asked softly.

"What?"

"The voices in your head. The ones that are hurting you. The ones that are making you cry. What are they telling you?" She squeezed me gently for just a moment. "They aren't you."

"How can you know that?"

"Because the Max I met doesn't need so much pain."

I managed a brittle smile at the ceiling. "I'd like to meet that guy."

"He's kind. Accepting. Curious. I met him in a barn on a dark and stormy night." Her voice smiled with a gentle tease. "I loaned him my cloak, so that he wouldn't catch a chill. He was very grateful, I think." She paused, and I could feel something shift in her. "I surprised him. When he looked at me, in that first moment, he let me inside. I felt things."

"Are you... like Stellamara?"

"No." I felt her head move gently against my shoulder. "She's far more perceptive than I am. I just listen to what feelings I have. They don't often lie to me."

I shifted my arm, moving my free forepaw to find hers near my belly, and I clasped it gently. "What did you feel?"

"Surprise. A little fear. Something confused, lost." I heard the smile in her voice again. "Some of that might have come from what I've learned of you since. I still think my first impression was the right one."

The quiet wasn't awkward. Me, on the inside, that was awkward. I tried to reconcile the warring thoughts, part of me feeling that I had brought fearsome ghosts into a peaceful place, and I wanted to protect Lightwing from them. How could I let them out of me and still keep her safe?

Will you trust me?

"They..." I faltered and tried again. "The voices. Not real voices. Just feelings. They're telling me not to trust this place. Not to trust what I see here. Not to believe it."

"Do they tell you why?"

"Because the darkness always wins."

She hugged me, her forepaw squeezing my own. "Can you tell me who these voices belong to? Are they specific or generalized?"

"A little of each."

"I see you don't play favorites."

My smile was spontaneous. It was almost like talking with Michael. I had no idea how she knew to treat me with such affectionate humor, but it worked just as well here as it did with him. If she was guessing about me, she showed good intuition. I became aware of her closeness again, and my manners finally kicked in. "How's your arm?"

"Good, actually; how about yours?"

Between my shifting and hers, we rearranged ourselves. My right arm was free to wrap around her, and she pressed closer to me, now laying her head on my chest, her body nearly covering me. She felt familiar, as if we had been this way before. I caught myself wondering if I was trying to think of Barb, but that wasn't the case. This was someone else entirely, and not just anyone else, this was Lightwing, and she was very warm, and comforting, and familiar, even though I knew almost nothing about her.

"Lightwing."

"Hmm?"

"Where did that name come from?"

She chuckled softly. "Doesn't fit a big dog like me, do you mean?"

I gave her a gentle squeeze. "I mean that you're not a butterfly or a hummingbird, and I'm not at all sure either of those would be nearly as warm to cuddle up with."

That earned me a squeeze in return, and I again heard the smile in her voice when she spoke. "What do you know about dragonflies?"

"I know they're beautiful. I don't see them often."

"They always fascinated me, from my earliest days. I remember seeing them, once in a while, in the garden that my dam had made near the edge of the house. She loved black-eyed Susan flowers and something I eventually learned was called giant coneflower. Those looked like black-eyed Susans but with a huge, beehive-shaped thing in the middle. Dragonflies love them, it seems. So I started drawing dragonflies, collecting pictures of them, eventually having a really nice stained-glass panel showing them."

"And you thought of their light wings and speedy flying?"

"You're close," she said, snuggling up with me, the sound of her tail brushing against the quilt. "You remember how I was the pup who questioned everything? I found legends and stories about dragonflies, and I learned how they were thought by First Ones to be guardians of mystical gateways, to other worlds, or other ways of being, other ways of seeing. Darkstar told me that the Mi'kmaq don't have many stories about them, since they're not common in that part of the world; he knew some of the other First Ones' legends, though, and he told me more about them. Dragonflies have beautiful wings, iridescent, some clear, some with markings, and it's like they can change the way light works..."

"Like magic?"

She laughed a little, burying her face into my chest fur, seeming embarrassed. "Maybe, yeah. Harbingers of change, guardians of the gateway... It sounds silly, I guess."

I pet her head gently. "No more silly than a bunch of dreamers trying to change the world."

"Is that silly?"

"I know some voices that would say it's actually damned dangerous."

For a long moment, she said nothing. I was about to ask if I'd said something wrong, when she rearranged herself again, pulling back her lower arm, raising up on her elbow, turning her head to look me in the eyes again. "Max, you truly don't have to tell me about the voices, where they came from. Can you tell me why you're listening to them? Why they have such a hold on you?"

Reaching up to skritch behind her ears, I let myself trust her, trust that she didn't yet have to know what had brought me here, what was dragging at me with such black, poison-tipped claws. "I don't know if I have the right words. I've seen so much ugliness, lately, maybe over the past several years. Sometimes, it becomes all I can see, and I start feeling that it's all there is. Makes me into a vastly different Max. Not a nice one. Maybe that's the one that Barbara saw."

"That's your mate? Or... excuse me, former mate?" After I nodded, she gave me one of her gentle smiles. "You call her by her name, instead of some neutral term. She's still real to you. You show respect. That's positive."

"It's taken a while."

"How long has it been since you've had someone to hold?"

I gazed at her, trying to disguise a sense of desperation. "A long time."

"Has no one asked to share your fur? Haven't you asked?"

"No, and no."

"Can you tell me why?"

"Too much darkness."

"In the world?"

"There too."

For a long moment, she simply looked at me. "I'm going to take the chance of sticking all four paws in my maw." She took a breath and said, "What you're afraid of is that you're going to ask too much."

I said nothing.

"Because you need too much."

I said nothing.

"You're safe here, Max. Especially right here. C'mere."

She rolled onto her back, then waved, pulled me to her, reversing our positions. I lay on my side, one arm under the pillows, the other across her stomach, my muzzle at the ruff of fur at her neck, indelicately sniffing the warm scent of her. She pet my back so gently yet firmly, rubbing my back as much as smoothing my fur. No words from her, yet I knew what she was asking of me, what she wanted of me. I wasn't sure, I was afraid, I couldn't ask this of her. The emotions churned within, and something rose through them that was determined to prove them wrong.

My body jerked a little as a sound came from my maw. I felt her nod, and she shifted her hold of me slightly. I knew that I wasn't going to be able to stop myself, and her only response was to whisper my name so very softly, then to say, "Yes."

The dam burst, and I wept against her as if I hadn't cried for years... and perhaps I hadn't.

12: Morning

The precinct had been making changes, although no one knew where the money was coming from. I didn't bother challenging it, since I'd finally been given an office of my own. It reminded me a lot of Chelsea Watson's claustrophobic office at LK&M, because it was absolutely too damned small to take care of everything I needed to get my job done. The desk was a heavy, metal, military cast-off whose idea of having seen better days had to have been on the front lines. Metal filing cabinets, nearly bursting, proved that the Paperless Era had yet to happen, and yet more paper was stacked in piles all around me, almost enough to block the keyboard and monitor. The room was a wreck, four solid walls with a door in it, but it was mine. Mine, dammit.

"Hey, Dad."

I turned to find Michael at the door to the office, a grin on his muzzle, his forepaws bearing a paper bag and a brightly-colored thermos, a blister of color in the otherwise bland surroundings of my daily life. I grinned back at him. "Tell me that's a bagel and schmear, and that it's all for me."

He passed the bag over to me, laughing gently. "You own it," he said, then brandished the thermos at me. "I bring to you the very best hemlock, Hippocrates. Brewed it myself."

"You never really know what's in your food, do you?" I watched as he filled a ceramic mug bearing some comment that I couldn't read clearly. Probably something about Mondays. Of all the days of the week, Monday always catches the most flack.

"Nothing bad for you, I promise. This blend has a lot of healing properties. It's got—"

He told me ingredients that I didn't recognize, a list of things that he clearly thought made the brew better than anything else. He knew his teas, so he was probably right. Steam rose up to my nose, and I sniffed. The scent was fruity, pleasant enough, and the temperature wasn't too hot. I took a sip of it, sighing a little. "This is good."

"I thought you might like it. It helps."

"What does it help?" I set the mug on my desk, glad that there weren't any papers in the way. The computer showed its screen saver, and I wondered why Barb's picture was on it. I jiggled the mouse; the image stayed. Perhaps it needed to, or maybe it was just stuck. Some things stick, even when you try to unstick 'em. As if that idea made sense.

"Like they say, it's good for what ails ya."

"I'd better have more then." Another sip went down well, reminding me of some flavor I'd had before, but I didn't know from where. I glanced at the window, glad that I got the office that faced the meadow. Spring had arrived, and it was going to be a beautiful one. I glanced at the wood filing cabinets, free of the piles that usually covered them, happy to see that the paperwork was finally caught up.

"How're you doing, Dad?"

"Just keeping going. Some cases are tougher than others, take a little legwork. Can't stop halfway, right? One paw in front of the other. Just gotta keep the routine going." I raised my cup to my pup, who nodded back at me, a happy smile on his muzzle. He still looked good in his MedSoc gear, or at least something like it. It felt familiar. I tried to remember the name that he had chosen for his Romany-like character. He read Tarot, I remembered, and the name was something to do with that, it seemed to me, but I couldn't recall it clearly. I knew that he was good at his readings; never had a customer complain. He told stories more than fortunes. It went over well.

Another sip of the tea, and I perhaps rudely closed my eyes to relax. I felt the sun on my face, not sure when I'd felt it last. The softest of breezes came in through the window. I'd thought it was closed. I turned my head toward the light, opened my eyes carefully. The picture windows that took up the entire meadows-facing wall were clear as crystal, and the sliding glass door was wide open. I turned back to my pup, who was sitting on a tree stump on the other side of my wooden desk. His smile never wavered, was still warm as the sunlight that poured into what was left of my office.

"Something's wrong," I said.

"What do you mean?"

"I had the case file here a moment ago."

"Which one?"

"The suicide." The computer was gone, and my smooth wooden desk looked like it hadn't seen a day's work before. I could see myself in its polished surface. I saw a collie who had shadows around his sunken eyes, whose face looked drawn and haggard, who had the black shape of a tiger hovering behind him, somewhere near his shoulder.

"Drink your tea, Dad."

My forepaw shook a little as I took another sip of the brew. I had the strange sensation of it flowing through me rather than down my gullet. Shaking my head a little, I blinked hard, found the desk replaced by something like an end table, my chair more like a wingback, the space around me filled with sunlight pouring into the large, comfortable living space to one side. It was a familiar space, although it had been seen at night, and that was what finally made me figure out that I really was dreaming and that I was becoming aware of it.

Sitting in the other chair, my pup... my son still smiled, as if he had known where I was, what I was doing there. The images had already begun to slither away as I said, "Wait, Michael, what do I..."

"Dream, my sire," he said.

I reached the edge of consciousness, that point where enough of the brain is awake to log as much of the dream as it's going to, and I slipped back down again.

* * * * *

Morning.

I sensed it before I opened my eyes. My mind pulled up the dream as best it could, and I tried holding on to the essence of it before waking up fully. I thought about tea that could erase my office, about my son who told me in my dream to dream, about how beautiful that picture window was, even when I knew there wasn't a meadow within (at best) three kilometers of the precinct, probably closer to twenty or more. The sunlight, though, that was something to remember. Warm, like the tea. Like the dream.

Holding myself quietly, I closed my eyes again, wondering if I could have just a few more minutes of just being Max instead of Detective Luton. That moment was inevitable, once we got the car pulled out of the ditch.

I would find the wooden box and the items it contained, and everything would have to be told, and I wasn't looking forward to it. I wondered how they'd treat me when they found out. I wondered if there really would be a few renditions of *"Up against the wall, fascist pig!"* after all.

That wasn't what I was, though, was it? Did I really belong to that unhappy idea? What if there were something else? The tea seemed to erase so much pain, so much of "It Is What It Is," and I wondered if there might be some sort of dreamer in me after all. I thought about this tribe, and I wondered if I could be part of it. That was less drinking some tea than drinking the Kool-Aid. I was no artisan. The best I could hope for would be to help them with their gardens, or their livestock, or something else. That would mean leaving what I'd been used to for so very long, the stuff I'd accumulated, whether physical things or otherwise. I thought of baggage that I would drag along, realizing there was no place for it here. The same was true of me.

I opened my eyes again as I felt Lightwing stirring beside me. She lay on her side, facing away from me. We had spooned for a long time, talked, eventually fallen asleep. I suppose the lust-filled monsters from my id had behaved themselves after all. After a few moments, she looked back over her shoulder, moving carefully to see if I'd woken up yet.

"G'morning," I whispered softly.

She slowly rolled her body back toward me, stretching out enough to pop a few joints in the process, smiling at me. "Hi there."

"Sleep?"

"Good. You?"

"Good," I nodded. "Thank you."

Lightwing reached up to pet my chest, and I stroked her headfur gently. "You see?" she grinned. "You were a perfect gentlefur."

"You're very warm, and... yeah, I guess I needed to let that out." I smiled at her. "Modern male, attempting to get in touch with his feelings, speaks some measure of truth."

She tapped my muzzle playfully with a finger. "And doing better than he thinks." She raised up on one elbow and looked at me affectionately. "Crying is an act of courage, Max. I don't remember where I heard that. It means letting yourself be vulnerable. Crying with someone else takes trust. Thank you for trusting me."

For a moment, I just looked at her, my smile still real yet not quite sure of itself. "Thank you for trusting a stranger, especially one with a secret."

Inwardly, I cringed at my words; I had let too much of the truth out, saying that. Her forepaw reached out to caress my cheek. "Is it a secret, or something private?"

I had to think about the difference for a moment, then decide which it was. "It's a copout to say 'both,' so let me try something else. It's a secret that is connected to something private." I touched her cheek softly, my smile melting into something more somber. "I want to tell you them both. I think..." I swallowed. "I think both will happen later this morning. When it does, I hope you'll still want to know me."

"That bad?" she asked quietly, her voice carrying no judgment.

"It feels that way. Perhaps it won't be."

Pausing for a moment, the Husky considered me carefully. "Can you tell me the reason for keeping this secret? Is it selfish, dangerous...?"

"A little bit selfish. A lot about not wanting to hurt others."

Light rose in her eyes. "You really were looking for us."

"Not to hurt you." I reached out to clasp her shoulder gently. "I really did come here to look for answers. That's the selfish part of it. I think you've all given me some answers, and I hope to be gentle with you all." I shook my head. "Lightwing, I need your help. The more I have to talk in circles about this, the more frightening it must seem. When the car is pulled out of the ditch, I'll tell everything. All of you will hear everything. Is that enough? Is it okay?"

She took my forepaw and placed flat to her breastbone, holding my eyes with hers. "I want you to swear on my heart that you won't hurt us."

I felt tears trying to form again, knowing that the truth would make me say more. "My secret concerns news that may be painful to hear. It is not something that I bring to hurt you, any of you... most of all, you."

After a moment, she raised my forepaw to her lips and kissed my palm tenderly. "It's hurting you to keep it. So let's get started. Get dressed, we'll get breakfast, and we'll find out how to get that car out. After that, you can finally drop that burden. I will be here, Max. I promise you."

She hesitated only a moment before leaning in to press her closed lips to mine, a promise and a benediction of peace. It lasted only a few seconds, during which my heart tried to explode out of my chest. She pulled away, moved slowly out of bed, and got dressed. I found it difficult to say anything. After she had assembled herself, she leaned over the bed to touch my face once more.

"Better hurry," she smiled softly. "I hate suspense."

And she was gone.

* * * * *

As I tended to my morning needs, my mind decided to take a romp around its own playground, just to make me completely nuts. I tried to guess Lightwing's age, compared to my own 52 years, and concluded that we didn't belong sharing a bed together, even though "nothing happened." Of course, something happened, and it was both terrifying and liberating. I couldn't remember ever having broken down like that, especially not with someone there to witness it, much less *share* it. That's the part that was really doing a number on my head, when I looked at those moments through that lens. Lightwing wasn't just in the room like a casual observer; she held me, shivering a little, like she was feeling it too, like she dared to be a part of what was happening to me. It helped me, and I couldn't have imagined how much it would help, how good it would feel to let go of all that.

Fragments of the dream tried to resurface in my mind, and all I could remember fully was drinking tea, sitting in beams of sunshine streaming in through a big window. There was a feeling of release, of relief, that I was somehow letting go of... I shook my head. Not "life." It wasn't about dying, although there was some of that in there, too.

I dressed, feeling unready to face the day, feeling also that the anticipation of pain is usually more painful than the event itself. I found myself unsure what it was that was going to hurt, and in what way it would hurt. A sensation from the dream, rather than the memory of the dream, came back to me — something about erasing things, familiar things, important things... they seemed important, anyway. What was it that was so frightening?

The face in the ensuite mirror looked back at me. He was confused, not sure what about, and he was wondering what had happened in the last twelve or so hours. Dinner, conversation, tears, uncertainties. The body seen in that mirror was recovered in the cotton garments borrowed from Darkstar. They looked less foreign on me today, felt more comfortable. That was probably a sign or some horrible portent. That nagging idea of wondering if I had any dreams left, if I could dare to try something new. But no matter how much pain it might carry, the old life was still familiar, like a car that didn't run well but at least was still running, no matter how much money, stress, and energy it took to keep it going. I guess it's true what they say: The only person who welcomes change is a wet baby.

Ah... that's more like the old Max.

That thought didn't comfort me. Perhaps breakfast would.

* * * * *

As I exited the hallway toward the den and dining hall, the stillness of the house struck me as odd. I couldn't be the first to leave his room...? That made no sense, for any reason. Besides, the aromas in the air told me that someone had been doing a bit of cooking already.

The tables had been returned to their original positions, and I found some small warming dishes on the sideboard, which surprised but delighted me with their contents. I found scrambled eggs far more orange-yellow than store-bought eggs would provide, some Canadian-style rashers of bacon, multigrain toast (homemade, I shouldn't wonder), marmalade-style cranberry preserves in a crockery pot nearby, and a carafe containing warm, rich cocoa. I tried not to be immodest with my portions, not sure how many others would be coming down and when. Enough was missing from each warming dish to tell me that I was most certainly not the first, and perhaps I wouldn't be the last.

A grand, leonine yawn turned my attention back toward the entranceway. Darkstar padded in wearing a rather grand robe, hanging down to mid-calf, which surprised me only a moment. I found the cotton pants and shirt amazingly comfortable, but when it's one's daily wear, one might want to be casual in other ways. I wondered if those fur-clad cuddle-piles ended with equally fur-clad breakfasts, and I thought probably not. I might have to ask, though. It would make a morning meal interesting, wouldn't it?

The lynx made a line directly for the warming trays, serving himself a portion of everything about the size of my own. I put my guilt on hold and smiled at him. "G'morning."

"G'morning to you, Max." He returned my smile generously. "Did you sleep well?"

"Yes," I managed to mumble through a bit of egg. "You?"

"Fine." He set his plate down at a place opposite me and sat himself on a stool. He took a long sip of the cocoa in his mug, and it seemed to revive him like coffee. "Ahh," he sighed, setting the mug down. "I could almost feel awake now." His eyes held a twinkle of mischief as he said, "Should I mention that I saw Lightwing this morning?"

"Don't you see her every morning?"

Darkstar chuckled softly. "No presumptions, just well-wishes. Timewind seems to agree with you, Max."

"I wouldn't have imagined it before, but perhaps I agree with Timewind."

He paused before eating, forepaws on either side of his plate, eyes closed — a silent, personal grace. I'd neglected my own but paused during his, sharing it maybe. He breathed deeply, took up his fork, and dug in. I joined him, privately chastened, giving in to my hunger. As with the night before, conversation took a backseat to stuffing our maws for a good minute or so. After that, Darkstar looked around and leaned forward as he spoke softly. "I still don't know what you're here for."

"I know."

"You said it wasn't an official matter, or at least you weren't here to serve papers or whatnot. What really brought you here?"

"I told Lightwing that I thought you might have the answers to some mysteries in my life. It was after that that she told me about Stellamara."

The lynx nodded somberly. "There's no question that she knows you're concealing something."

"Yet she trusted me."

"You cried. You became vulnerable. She must have felt that the secret was hurting you more than anyone else." He paused, then added, "Whatever it is, Max, I think you'll need to tell us. All of us. We keep private things private, but we don't keep secrets."

"You kept mine."

"Yours could be considered a private matter, unless it affects us directly; as a secret, it needed to be kept, for a short time, anyway."

There was no malice in his voice. I sighed a little, trying to make a decision. "Oaknail is your leader, isn't he?"

Darkstar let out a small snort of mirth. "In a way. We call him 'Chief' once in a while. When Timewind was created as a legal entity, he became its representative, like a CEO. We're a pretty democratically socialist bunch, overall; we manage to work out our differences without resorting to a strict chain of command. The bear will kick some tail when necessary, but not out of a position of absolute power. It's usually because we're letting ourselves down, and he motivates us."

"He's the founder, then?"

"He's *a* founder, yes. He doesn't lord it over us, if that's what you mean. I came along later, about twelve years ago." He regarded me over his mug of cocoa. "This is to do with one of the founders?"

"Does the name 'Airdancer' mean anything to you?"

"Thomas." The young fur's voice held a touch of awe. "I never had the chance to meet him; he hasn't been here for years. He's part of the history of the tribe, which I've been trying to compile. A lot of stories about him."

I decorated a bit of toast with cranberry marmalade, hoping I wasn't going to drop some onto my fur; the urge to lick it off might overcome accepted social graces. "What sort of stories?"

"He was the wielder of the sword of justice, called Albion. He would cut through the red tape and unnecessary bureaucracy that might hinder Timewind's growth. The tribe helped to put him through law school, and then he went into the public defender's office in upstate New York, taking the cases brought by furs who couldn't afford the big lawyers for themselves. After that, he went to a firm specializing in real estate law, which would really have helped us. I have the feeling, from the histories, that he was going to do exactly that, but..."

"He never came back?"

"Not as far as I know, and definitely not since I've been with the tribe. The early stories about him always seem to paint him a little larger than life. A powerhouse in law school — bold as brass, said what he thought, pissed off his professors, too good to get flunked out. Politically active, fighting for the best causes... He was 'born with the knack,' as Oaknail put it."

"You admire him."

"What I know of him, yes. I like dreamers, and Airdancer was one of those. One of the founders. Maybe a bit of halo effect, but all I've learned of him tells me a lot about him."

I looked down, realizing that I was about to destroy that picture. I remembered all the things that I'd learned, the things that defined the life of Thomas Glover, from being too unimportant to merit being murdered to the wholly pedestrian, wealthy-life activities that were so inconsequential as to be considered ordinary to those with such incomes. Nice to the staff, nice to his kits, supportive to his wife, and yet lost to those who still dreamed. The idealist went to law school, then became a lawyer, then became little more than a shyster, a cog in a wheel, a tiger de-fanged and de-clawed in every important sense.

"Max?"

The words refused to stay caged any longer. "Thomas Glover is dead."

Darkstar paused for a long moment, then asked softly, "How?"

"Shot through the head."

Turning his head away, the lynx physically winced. Another brief pause before he said, "You're a homicide detective."

"Yes."

"He was murdered?"

"That's what my superiors wanted to believe. Glover was monied, part of a crowd that simply doesn't commit suicide, so they sent me to make sure that it really was murder."

"And it wasn't."

"No."

Another deep, steadying breath before he said, "You came all this way to tell us?"

"Partly," I admitted. "The rest was to try to understand why he did it."

"You think we caused him to—"

"I think," I raised my forepaws placatingly, "that he may have realized what he had lost. That's only a guess."

He nodded a little. "I see why you were hiding." He sat back and regarded me steadily, without judgment. "I won't say anything until you talk to Oaknail."

"I'm sorry for the secrecy, Darkstar."

Smiling softly, he said, "That's the first time you've used my name, Max. Thank you."

"I didn't realize," I said. "Sorry for being so late."

"Late for what?"

The lynx and I turned toward the voice. Seeing our faces, Lightwing's happy demeanor shifted to one of concern. Darkstar rose from his place and went to hug her. She seemed instantly aware that he needed it, and she held him for a moment. That, I realized, was what this tribal family was about. More than friends, less than lovers. That feeling that asking for help didn't even need words or reasons, just someone who would be able to understand without them, or at least be patient enough to wait for the words, the answer to the "why" of the request... if there was one.

The Husky couldn't quite see over his shoulder to look at me while I was still sitting. Remembering my manners, I stood so that she could see me, and her expression remained concerned. When Darkstar gently released her, he kept a forepaw to her shoulder as he turned to me. "I'll fix a plate. I think she needs to know now instead of later."

I nodded, padding around the table to give Lightwing a hug of my own before sitting her down on one of the stools. "Everyone else will hear this soon; will you keep my secret for just a few more hours?"

"Of course."

The decision to reveal myself as a cop took only a few seconds; I still felt the cocoon that she had made for me last night, and I let myself continue to trust. I explained quickly that I had told Darkstar because he had found my shield the night before, and I apologized for telling him first. She was surprised, but not offended, especially not after I told her the reason for my visit to Timewind. She took the news of Glover's death only slightly better than did the tribal historian, as she was less familiar with the lawyer's legend. She still registered the hurt, as I explained to her the same details that I'd just given to Darkstar. The lynx brought a plate of food to her, as well as a mug of cocoa. She looked at me, her ice blue eyes filled with a different type of pain.

"No wonder you were hurting. Oh, Max..."

A saw a tear form and run down her cheek. I nearly had one myself. The morning, I remembered, had started off a lot nicer than this.

13: Recovery

Several minutes had passed as the three of us tried to regain our composure. Lightwing managed to eat, joking weakly that she was rarely so upset that she'd ever miss a meal. We had agreed quickly enough that we needed to keep my bomb from going off quite yet. Getting the car out of the ditch still seemed the best start. I didn't tell them that the metaphorical pin to my information grenade was in the back seat of the vehicle. Next steps, I told myself. Just next steps.

We were finishing the meal when Heartsinger rounded the corner from the kitchen, a full chef's apron covering his daily garb. He seemed to be in good spirits, softening his mood very slightly when he saw me, his golden eyes regarding me with warmth. "How are you, Max?" His rich velvet baritone made it clear that he wasn't being merely polite; he really wanted to know.

I smiled softly at him. "I'm doing better, thank you. I think the sleep helped a lot." I nodded at the chafing dishes. "Do I have you to thank for that?"

The white wolf seemed to blush a little, his tail trying not to show its usual exuberance, for fear of looking immodest. "I volunteered for the kitchen this morning, yes."

"He has a genius for making the most of scrambled eggs," Lightwing allowed, "even when in bunches."

Nodding my agreement, I said, "Thank you, Heartsinger. It was truly delicious."

He was unable to control his tail at that point, and I realized that, as with Darkstar, I hadn't used his name until now. My own tail returned a few wags to him; my smile was genuine and, for just a moment, the morning held some better promise.

I insisted on helping to carry plates and glasses to the kitchen and, with Lightwing to assist me, Darkstar was freed to go change into something more like everyday workwear. Following Heartsinger into the kitchen, with the comely Husky just behind us, I found myself dazzled by a huge, modern, restaurant-outfitted kitchen that also held beautiful wood cabinetry and artisan touches in several places. It was an updated version of the mansion kitchens seen in those British shows I'm so fond of, bringing in the conveniences and functionality without losing the warmth.

The white wolf guided me to the sink and sideboard, where I set my burdens down with others left before us. "It occurs to me that you might likely be able to produce nearly all of your breakfast foods from resources here on the land. The only thing you'd need to get from the store would be Pop-Tarts."

"We do *not* keep Pop-Tarts in the tribal kitchen!" Lightwing huffed impressively. Then, grinning, she added, "They're in the tribal larder, next to the Sugar Pops."

"Cheetos are one shelf over," Heartsinger laughed heartily, the warm baritone voice adding richness to the sound. "We're not entirely self-sufficient, Max. And besides, a little 'junk food' now and then makes a treat."

"No argument there," I grinned at him. "My downfall is..."

The hesitation went unnoticed, as I quickly censored my usual line of *donuts... occupational hazard.* I found a rapid substitute.

"...cookies. Oatmeal raisin, soft, heavy on the raisins." I patted my stomach self-consciously. "Good to keep things moving."

Another laugh from the wolf. "Moonsong is the bakery chef of Starhold. I might mention it to her, now you've sparked a craving."

"Fresh, warm, with ice cream?" Lightwing's eyes practically shone with begging. A thumbs-up from the lupine got her to wag her tail and clap her forepaws with glee, making Heartsinger laugh and wag more. The cynic in me tried to claim that it was all just to help my cover. Something else in me really hoped that the response was true. Her gesture was innocent, puplike, and I thought about a young Husky who looked for magic. There was part of me that wanted to see through those eyes, even if just for a moment.

"Something to look forward to." The Husky turned her gaze to me, still sincere, still as uplifting as she could make it. "Well, Max, shall we see if we can locate Oaknail?"

I caught something in her gaze that asked me to trust her, as I had before. I brought up a smile from somewhere. "Good plan. Where shall we start?"

"Try the barn."

We turned to the new voice, to see Rainmist enter from the dining hall. The smile on her muzzle was soft and concerned as she approached me. She paused a short distance away, spreading her arms, her face a gentle question. I let myself accept her offer and embraced her warmly.

"You look better, Max," she murmured in my ear.

"Getting there," I replied, giving her a squeeze and releasing her gently. "Did you get your walk in the rain last night?"

"For a little while. I splashed in a few puddles, finding my way by the light from some of the downstairs windows. I was going to sit in the creek for a bit, but that water was colder than the rain, for some reason." Her smirk was friendly, self-cajoling. "Icy tushy not fun."

I felt my tail bob lower for a moment, just in sympathy. It made her chuckle as I said, "Another reason I prefer a walk in warm sun."

"You'll have that today," she grinned. "Which also means that we're likely to have more customers."

I blinked, having forgotten the sign at the base of the long drive until Lightwing filled in, "The store will be open later. We'll want to get your car out of the ditch before then." She gave a teasing jerk of her head in a *let's get on with it* gesture. I nodded and followed her out of the kitchen, waving at the otter and wolf, both of whom smiled benevolently. Rainmist's eyes held a twinkle that I tried not to notice too closely.

The Husky led me to the stairs, explaining, "I'd just like to get something out of my room. Want to come up?"

Hoping that I was reading the look in her eyes correctly, I answered, "Sure."

We made the upstairs landing in time to see Darkstar coming out of his room, dressed for the occasion. In one forepaw, he brandished my keys, which I had pocketed out of habit when I left the car behind last night. Lightwing was slightly ahead of me, so perhaps he caught some look in her eye. He glanced down the hall past us, then waved us back into his room and closed the door after us. I could hear all three of us expelling sighs of relief, having escaped detection. Turning to look at one another, we all had the same embarrassed reaction and promptly cracked up. We managed to contain our laughter enough not to be heard outside of his walls.

"What the hell are we doing?" Lightwing managed through a giggle. "And why are we laughing?"

"We'd make lousy spies," the lynx observed, grinning.

"Thank the gods for that," I nodded, unable to keep my tail from wagging in anxious mirth. "It's nerves. It's part of what keeping secrets does to us." I felt myself sobering all too quickly. "I hate it. I'm so sorry to have dragged you two into it like this."

Darkstar put a forepaw to my shoulder briefly. "We're almost done with it, Max. How are we going to tell the others, and when?"

I realized quickly that it was time for these two, at least, to know it all. They'd earned the right. "It will start just about the time that we open the car doors. I've brought Albion back home."

"It's real?" the lynx asked, a little pop-eyed.

"Very."

The lynx briefly explained to Lightwing what that meant. After taking a moment to absorb the information, she turned to me and hugged me tightly, whispering, "Thank you. Thank you for having the strength to do this."

Her response surprised me, and I returned the hug awkwardly. After a moment, she pulled gently away from me and said, "Time for us to return that favor. Let's get this done."

* * * * *

I appreciated the sweet air and clear skies that I found waiting for us outside. I wasn't quite ready believe in omens, but I'd take what I could get. The walk to the barn/stable was shorter than it had seemed las night; it was certainly more comfortable, since I didn't have to run through the rain toward an unknown destination. Casting a look back over my shoulder, I realized that my sense of the house being more like a castle was well-founded, partly due to its size, partly to its façade. The exterior had been sculpted to look like stonework, probably using prefabricated sections, as genuine stonework would have been an enormous undertaking and prohibitively expensive. Even so, it was impressive.

The barn structure, seen in daylight, also seemed imposing. I'd not exactly been around barns or stables much in my life (as close to "never" as made no odds), so I had nothing to compare it to. There was certainly some activity going on, however. I heard occasional bumps and banging further down the central aisle of the structure, noting that the large doors on that side were also open. My guides led me toward it, past the empty stalls for non-sapient horses. I wondered aloud where they'd got to.

"In the fenced-in area, grazing," Darkstar supplied. "They're turned out each morning so that we can muck out the stalls. I was given today off, to sleep in a bit. Oaknail and Oray took over for me and Heartsinger. We rotate out, just so we don't all get tired of it at the same time."

"Good plan," I smiled.

"That banging," Lightwing suggested, "is probably the two of them readying harnesses for the horses to pull out the car."

"Plural?" I asked. "More than one horse to pull out a car? I guess I never thought about it, but it seems..."

It took me a moment for me to realize that something had changed in the atmosphere around me. I turned to find Darkstar bearing his species' trademark smile and Lightwing reaching out a forepaw toward me, a grin on her own muzzle.

"I'll stop it," she said, touching my arm tenderly. "I was trying to lighten the mood."

"We're not entirely agrarian," the lynx explained. "I think those bangs might be work under the hood of one of the ATVs or a small tractor."

Making a snort through my nose, just to express a little annoyance, I noted, "I was taken here in a horse-drawn cart. It seemed reasonable."

"A question of need," Darkstar explained. "Last night, Oaknail and I were looking for Ginger, as well as seeing what we could of what the storm might have been doing to the road and the fencing, in case she'd managed to get out. A simple cart was all we needed, and Clipper actually likes the rain. Besides giving him something of a treat, we also avoided putting more gas fumes into the atmosphere." He paused and smiled. "Besides, with the horrifying price of gas these days, it's cheaper!"

"No argument there."

We had crossed the interior of the barn/stable/whatsit and padded into the sunlight beyond. My eyes traveled to a large open field, a fenced-in area where several horses appeared to be grazing and wandering comfortably. Darkstar led us around to another building near which several cars were parked under covering that was created with both efficiency and aesthetics clearly in mind. It's not easy to make a carport look good; they managed by using paints, tinted plastic roofing, and some hardy trees nearby to help provide shade as well as the feeling that Detroit hadn't yet forced unnecessary intrusions into this natural place.

On the side of the building just beyond the carport, we found Oaknail and Frank closing up the hood of a large dark brown 4x4 truck with an extended cab. The cop in me did its best to make a guess as to the year and make of the beast, and he got as far as guessing that it was about ten years old and was a domestic make before I told the little bastard to shut up. Frank's first glance at me showed discomfort before he managed a weak smile. Oaknail came over to me slowly, standing before me with his arms to his sides, a warm, caring look on his face.

"Good morning, Max. How are you?"

I offered as much smile as I had in me, perhaps getting used to the question by now. "Better, thank you. A good night's sleep helped."

The bear nodded, happy with the response. "We're readying to rescue your car. Frank's lending us the power of his truck."

Chuckling, the tall mountain lion padded into view, retrieving his shirt from the front seat of the vehicle. I tried not to notice how well-formed he was, to keep me from remembering yet again how I had voluntarily let my gym membership lapse. "The Beast should have enough power to get you unstuck. We can help push, to control the recovery. Did you bring your keys?"

I patted the pocket of my pants, making the keys jingle, then remembered something that Michael had told me about his garb for MedSoc. "I'd taken pockets for granted. I thought period garb prohibited those?"

Lightwing looked at me as if I'd grown another limb. "Were you in a ren faire?"

"My pup, Michael. He had a Romany-like character who read Tarot at various faires and gatherings. He told me about the lack of pockets."

The grinning bear chuckled deep in his large chest. "We make pants and shirts in various styles; our preference for daily wear includes pockets. They're just too useful."

"All in favor?" Darkstar raised his forepaw formally.

Viewing the raised paws, Oaknail proclaimed, "Motion carried unanimously!"

I chuckled along with the others. "I like the voting system here."

"And you didn't even have to register." Lightwing patted my arm teasingly. "I vouched for you."

"Enough!" Oaknail's friendly bellow ended the caucus. "Who's going with us?"

"I'm going to beg off," the Husky said with what felt like a forced good humor. "You know how us females are so useless at the mechanical stuff." She raised her forepaws to fend off comments. "Let me get a few things done at the house, and I'll see you all when you get back there."

"We shouldn't be long," Frank assured her. "We'll have everything taken care of long before the store opens."

"When will that be?" I asked.

"Doors open at noon," Oaknail told me, "although a few folks sometimes show up early. We've got a few hours at least."

My stomach sank even as Frank waved us to "the Beast." Darkstar and I got into the spacious back seat as Frank took the wheel and the bear took shotgun without even having to call it. The mountain lion made a slow turn to aim us back toward the main road on the grounds (or, perhaps, just "the driveway," as far as the residents might be concerned). We took a graceful curve that I didn't remember from the night before, but I was at a considerable disadvantage in terms of my sense of direction during my time under the tarp. I saw a small building set to one side, with a particularly nice metal-worked sign spelling out *The Artisanry*.

"The shop, I take it?"

"Got it in one," the bear chuckled. "We hope you'll stay long enough to have a look around, if you'd care to."

"It'd be a shame to have come all this way and miss the sights. Frank," I added, "I hope this doesn't come out wrong... you've done this before, right?"

The mountain lion laughed heartily. "Once or twice. Part of the price of driving a 4x4; everyone wants a little help with something. I first learned about recovery points and kinetic ropes from an online video. Don't panic! I also got some help from tow truck drivers over the past few years, so I know what I'm doing."

"Sorry," I grinned at him. "It ain't much, but it's what I got."

"All TLC here."

It took us only seconds to reach the car. I shouldn't have been surprised, as a truck in clear daylight can travel more quickly than a horse-drawn cart in a rainstorm-blackened night. The sinking feeling in my stomach turned into a knot, but only until I opened the door and put my hindpaws back on the ground. Moving forward is the only direction, after all. As Lightwing had said: *Let's get this done.*

Unseen by the other two, Darkstar put a forepaw to my shoulder and let his eyes ask the question. *Yes,* I nodded, *I'm okay.* I patted his forepaw with my own, thanking him for his strength. Forward. Only forward.

In daylight, it didn't look nearly as bad. On an angle, yes, and the side of the poor thing seemed to be partly in the way of rushing water. The creek did, after all, rise a bit after last night. Other than that, rescue seemed possible. I looked to Frank. "What do you think?"

"I think you did good, given the surprise on the road." He looked to and fro, assessing the vehicle and what it might need, then nodded. "We can do this."

The mountain lion set to work, making a quick job of it, while I tried not to feel too much like I was just along because I had the keys. He explained how it would work, with the kinetic rope that, in a way, was like a specialized bungee cord. He also suggested that we assist matters, carefully, by putting some muscle behind it.

"Put 'er in neutral," Frank requested.

Oaknail held the driver's side door open for me as I managed to get back in, put a hindpaw on the break, put in the key, turn it, find neutral... I heard some pings, so the battery and electrical seemed unfazed. Nice beginning. The passenger-side window stayed closed, just in case, but I tried the switch to lower the driver's side window, and it opened fully without complaint.

"Good sign," the bear echoed my thoughts. His eyes scanned the interior briefly, assessing the situation inside. "Looks more just wet than actually damaged. Let's hope we're lucky."

"We'll know more once it's out," Frank called. "Let's get into position."

My stereotyping waited for Darkstar to make some joke about that, then realized that it was my own expectation that brought that one up. I wasn't sure what to make of that.

The bear and lynx got behind the car, ready to add some push if need be. I was to push on the frame and stay near to the driver's door, to hop in and press the brake if the car started rolling when it was back on level ground. Oaknail shouted the signal, the mountain lion fired up his mechanical horses, and the kinetic rope pulled taut, then stretched a little. That was when I felt the car start to move. Frank's Beast was pulling at something of an angle, the idea being to help get wheels onto the level road, rather than pulling straight, which would likely keep the passenger-side wheels in the ditch. This is how he explained it to me, or at least how I remember it. I was just following orders.

Movement was caused less by the mountain lion's Beast and more by the kinetic rope trying to reduce its own stretch. The 4x4 was still, yet my own car was trying to move, helped along by the three of us offering assistance to the "rubber band." The front wheels came out on the first push, and the rest in only two more tries. The effort was gentle enough that I didn't have to rush into the vehicle to apply the brake. Happily, the seat itself was dry. The carpeting, the bits of detritus on the floors, and whatever else had landed on them was now under an inch or two of water.

"Yick," I articulated as I got back out of the car.

"And what would you have said if you'd not gone to college?" Darkstar chuckled, dusting off his forepaws. The lower ends of his pants and his hindpaws were wet but not muddy. It would appear that the stream did some good after all.

Frank joined us, glancing over the partially-soaked interior. "Let's get 'er into the garage. I can vacuum that out, and I can check the engine while I'm at it."

"I feel like I'm being a bother."

"Hey, I volunteered." The mountain lion's grin was entirely disarming.

"Besides that," Oaknail added, "it's our cow that got you into this situation anyway, so we owe at least that. Anything you need from in there?"

"I'll do a quick inventory." I first saw my SuperWonderThing in the corner of the passenger side paw-well and leaned in to fetch it. I brought it out carefully, unsure if water was dripping from outside or inside. "Is that thing about rice a myth?"

"Not necessarily," Darkstar said, taking the device carefully and fitting it into a shirt pocket. "We can always give it a try."

"If not, we'll see to replacing it," the bear added.

"Thank you," I said, meaning it. "I'll check with the insurance on it first. I'm such a klutz that I was afraid of dropping it. Maybe 'accidental drowning' is covered, too."

My assembled companions chuckled softly at that one. I looked around, realizing that there was only one thing left to rescue. I breathed as evenly as I could, reached into the back seat and brought forth the box that I had come to deliver.

"Lovely woodworking," Oaknail observed. I wasn't sure if his voice held a note of recognition. Probably my imagination.

Setting the box onto the trunk of the car, I moved to open it. Darkstar kept my secret all the way to this point, not crowding me to get a look at what he knew had to have lain within. I opened the lid, observing that the box wasn't waterproof but that very little water had gotten inside; the copy of *The Tribal Manifesto* was only a little soaked. I moved it to one side, withdrew Albion, and turned to face the rest of the party.

Oaknail knew his work at once; Darkstar had been told what it was, and his first glimpse of it caused a reaction just short of awestruck. Frank appeared not to know if perhaps he should be readying for one devil of a knife fight.

The bear spoke without accusation. "Where did you get that?"

"From a tiger once known as Airdancer."

A flicker of recognition from Frank. Perhaps he knew of the founders through his study of Timewind.

Once again, the bear spoke softly, padding toward me. "Did he sell this to you?"

"I wouldn't have thought it was his to sell."

"It isn't. It belongs to Timewind. He was the Defender of Albion, a title he created for himself. We all agreed that it was fitting." He drew a deep breath, still calm, not at all intimidating. "How do you come by it?"

"There's no easy way to say it. Thomas Glover is dead."

The information sank in, painfully. At last, he nodded. "Who are you, then? Why have you come?"

"I'm a homicide detective from the city. My bosses were convinced that it was homicide staged as a suicide, but forensics proved otherwise. I wanted to know why he did it. I found you by digging into his past." I looked down. "One thing wasn't a lie: I came looking for answers."

"Have you found them, Max?"

"Some of them."

"Do you accuse us of something?"

"No." I looked back into the bear's eyes. "I have felt his ghost, Oaknail. I have felt a sense of the thing that made him do it. I think it wants me to do the same." I reoriented the blade and held it out to him. "I ask for your help. For answers."

Oaknail took the sword from me gently, looking into my eyes. "Let's get your car towed up to the garage. If we have answers, you're welcome to them."

Darkstar put a forepaw to my shoulder. "Yes, Max. Welcome."

Setting about readying the car for more ordinary towing, Frank said nothing.

14: Disclosure

When Oaknail had said "garage," he wasn't kidding. Just off the extended carport and its modest collection of vehicles, a small building stood, looking equally modest. From the outside, it appeared to be a large two-car garage that might be found in many a suburban neighborhood. The bear entered a side door and found the control to raise the door for one of the bays. After Frank had left the car in position to be pushed in, if needed, we took the chance of trying to turn over the engine. The electrical seemed to have worked earlier, and the poor baby had drip-dried for the few minutes of time to get this far. I slid into the driver's seat, put in my key, crossed my fingers, and cranked. It fired up as quickly as it usually did, given its age and overall condition. With Darkstar's help as a spotter, I backed into the spacious bay with greater ease than I would have ordinarily. Backing up a car into any spot, even a spacious one, is not in my skill set.

Exiting the vehicle (how quickly the cop had returned to my vocabulary), I saw that the second space, currently empty, had a service pit dug into it and, at the far end of the garage, stairs to get down into the pit. The set-up would have looked at home in any speedy oil change place, right down to the retractable safety mesh of thick cloth bands that covered the hazardous hole in the floor. I nodded at it as I spoke to the lynx. "That looks handy."

"One or two of us actually have enough skill to use it. Oray has been known to get his paws dirty, sometimes, and Frank is a veritable wizard."

I smiled at the mountain lion. "Thank you for your help."

"Welcome." His tone was clipped, almost rude. He turned away and padded toward a shop-vac near the far wall.

Head down, I padded silently out of the garage and toward Oaknail, who carried the wooden box with Albion back inside it. His expression was serious but not hostile. "We'll need to assemble everyone, tell them what's happened. Are you up to telling the tale?"

"As best I can." I looked into the bear's eyes, trying to understand what I was seeing, confused by the sense that his emotion was one made more of compassion than anything else. It seemed that he really was waiting to hear the entire tale. I found myself wondering what he would make of it. I almost flinched as he held out his forepaw to me. I took hold of it in my own, and he squeezed very gently, his eyes still holding mine.

"Your name is Max, isn't it?" The hint of a smile on his muzzle was amplified in his gaze.

"Yes. I hid rather than lied about..." I stopped, making a rueful snort. "Yes. My name is Max Luton. I usually have to say 'Detective Max Luton,' so much that I'm afraid of 'Detective' becoming my first name."

The bear released my forepaw as gently as he had held it. "Perhaps you just needed time to be 'Max' first." He nodded once. "Come on. Soonest begun, soonest done. I, for one, need to hear this story."

"Hey."

Oaknail and I turned toward the voice. Frank, with an ashamed glance at Darkstar's dark countenance, tried hailing me again.

"One of the reasons I'm not sure I'm ready to join the tribe."

I let my eyes ask the question.

Shifting from one hindpaw to the other, the mountain lion continued to look uncomfortable. "Darkstar's been trying to help me stop being so judgmental, or... Okay, look, I gotta knee-jerk reaction toward cops." He exhaled sharply, regained himself, made himself look me in the eye. "Ain't proud of it, but it's there, and finding out you were... I mean, I was getting to know you last night, like the rest of us, and it feels like maybe you were just lying about everything, and you were just spying on us." His shoulders were down, resigned, or simply tired. "I don't know what you're really here for, and I got..."

None of us moved. "Will you come in with us?" I asked him. "Listen to my story? I want to think Max is still in here, somewhere."

"I should vac out those carpets before they mildew."

"They'll wait. This is more important."

When the cat hesitated, Oaknail spoke up. "That thing'll shampoo as well as just vac. Come with us, Frank."

"Please," I added, then smiled a little. "No sense my having to tell it twice."

After a moment, he nodded.

"Quickly, then," Oaknail said, getting us moving. "We've got to prep the store in an hour."

* * * * *

We assembled everyone into what was essentially a modern conference room, a space meant to hold perhaps eight to ten comfortably, so the dozen of us were very slightly crowded. Oaknail explained that it was a space where business was conducted, to let the rest of the house be home. "It's like any proper office space. It's important that work and home be kept separate." He rested a compassionate forepaw on my shoulder at that point. "I'm not trying to make telling your story into 'work,' Max. Truth is, the room is equipped for teleconferencing. I think we need to have as many of the tribe here as possible."

I nodded, swallowing past the horrible, necessary cliché of a lump in my throat. The bear gave my shoulder a reassuring squeeze, then set to work getting everything ready. The box containing Albion lay near to his paws, and although its presence caught the attention of a few in the room, no one commented on it. I tried to... I think the term is "take the temperature" of the others. Darkstar and Lightwing sat near me, the Husky with a forepaw discreetly on my own, under the table. Frank sat furthest away from me, the look on his face working hard to be as neutral as possible; his tail had other opinions. His lady Dreamweaver felt his discomfort, and she looked worried; did she think this might be about Frank? Rainmist looked concerned but otherwise okay. Heartsinger looked faintly confused, as if calling the conclave was a mystery to him. Oray and Starshine, youngest and likely newest to the tribe, were equally puzzled. They sat cuddled, the 'coon in the firefox's lap, no doubt to conserve space. Moonsong entered with Stellamara, the lady bear faintly grim, but the doe...

This surprised me. Stellamara was so calm as to appear more brave than her family. She looked at me softly, letting me feel her heart through her glance. I felt sure that she knew what was happening — not the specifics, not about Albion or even about Glover. Her empathy, her differently-wired brain (there's a term for that, they used it in that training seminar that most cops slept through), her sensitivity to others... to me... she knew the general shape of what was happening. She said it last night. *Trust that you are safe. The rest is for tomorrow.*

Today.

I heard voices through the speaker on the table in front of me, although none was introduced, at least not yet. After all were assembled, near and far, Oaknail announced, "We have a guest with us. Max Luton has brought news that I felt we must all hear together." He then nodded to me.

"Hello," I said, out of reflex. "Let me introduce myself more formally. I'm Detective Max Luton, a homicide detective from the city. I must tell you that Thomas Christian Thaddeus Glover, the tiger and co-founder you knew as Airdancer, is dead."

Those who did not know before had sharp reactions, even those who had never met Glover; he had lived on in the history and legend of Timewind. Moonsong and Rainmist both fought tears; Heartsinger leaned on Darkstar for support; Dreamweaver sought Frank's forepaw with her own; even the youngest couple seemed quiet, perhaps confused, as if this were something that simply couldn't happen.

"I am Unicorn," one voice said through the speaker. "My given name is Ezequiel Jeffries, and I'm the tribal attorney. I must ask if you are here on some official business."

"I'm not. In fact, counselor, I will tell you that I arrived last night, and I haven't identified myself as a police detective until this morning. There is no legal component to my presence."

"Thank you for your candor, Detective. Why did you come here?"

"In part, to tell you this news; in part, to find answers for my own questions."

No one spoke for a bit. At length, Unicorn asked, "Let me first ask: How did Thomas die?"

"He was shot through the head, in an apparent suicide." I saw many cringe. "The gun was found in his left forepaw."

"Wait a minute," Rainmist said, leaning forward. "Airdancer is right-pawed. Could someone else have—"

"That's why the brass sent a homicide detective. On arriving at the scene — a large, ornate study in his mansion — I found that he had apparently shot himself with his left forepaw. It was easy to see, from the placement of various items on his desk, that he was right-paw dominant, and his mate later confirmed it. The immediate idea was of someone trying to disguise murder as suicide."

As I spoke, I saw reactions to a few words — *mansion* and *mate* in particular. They had no idea of these things. This was not the tiger and tribe member that they remembered. He had not been in touch with them in quite a long time.

"Several things didn't fit. Both his mate and his senior law partner could not imagine Glover being a target for homicide; as the law partner put it, Glover 'didn't have the right temperament,' that he wasn't aggressive enough to make enemies who would want to single him out to be 'worth' killing. The house and grounds were undisturbed, nothing was taken or left behind. His mate had no motive for killing him; facts suggested that his death actually might have harmed her. So then... If not murder, then suicide, right? But that couldn't be, my own bosses assured me, since very wealthy people simply don't kill themselves. There was no suicide note, they persisted. All that was left was a scratching of weird runes on a desk blotter. What I noticed was that his dominant paw held not the gun but a sword."

"Albion!" came another voice from the speaker. "He still had Albion."

Oaknail opened the wooden box and withdrew the sword carefully. "I'm holding it now. Max brought it back to us."

"I don't understand, Detective." Unicorn's voice had a slight edge to it. "What brought you here?"

"A ghost."

All eyes in the room turned to Stellamara, including mine.

"I saw it riding on your shoulder. Last night. When you were fighting it."

"Stellamara," a female's voice on the speaker asked gently, "can you tell us what you saw?"

The doe gathered herself a little, then continued. "Max found us last night. His car got stuck in the ditch, and we couldn't get it out in the storm, so he agreed to stay the night. He had dinner with us, and we all talked. We didn't know about Airdancer last night, but I felt... I was sure that something was haunting Max. I saw something on his shoulder, something trying to whisper to him. Lies. Pain. That was what brought him here."

In the resulting silence, I nodded. "You're right. You see, forensics confirmed that the death was suicide. I couldn't understand why he had done it. He had the whole millionaire's package: Solid income, a mate, dutiful kits in good private academies, all the house and possessions anyone could want. What had made him do this, and especially like that? What was the 'why' behind the sword?"

I shook my head. "My cap'n told me to forget it, that 'why' isn't our department, unless it's motive for a crime, to hunt down a perp. That wasn't the case here, but I just couldn't let it go. I had to know why he did it. I had to know... why I *didn't* do it."

Stellamara's eyes welled with tears, and I felt Lightwing's forepaw on my arm, gripping lightly. I covered it with my other forepaw, not concerning myself with who might notice.

"Two things happened. One is that, in Glover's study, I eventually found the lined wooden box that would have held Albion and, inside that, I found the comb-bound volume of *The Tribal Manifesto*. I tried reading it..."

"My deepest sympathies," Rainmist managed a small smile.

I reciprocated the smile, softly. "I'm told that I would do far better with a revised edition. That old volume at least led me to Timewind. The other thing that got me here was the sword itself. A young officer saw the sword for the first time only yesterday and, having been part of the Medieval Society for a time, he recognized the runes."

"Tolkien," Darkstar noted.

"Exactly. He was able to read the name of the sword, as well as the inscription on it." I looked to Oaknail, and he obliged me by reciting it more from memory than from reading it.

"Justice by word and need; honor by loving deed."

"I mentioned a scratching of weird runes on his desk blotter. I can remember the translation pretty well. 'No justice by words, no honor in my deeds. I have betrayed us. Albion, forgive me.' He signed it, using the runes, with the name Airdancer."

After a long pause, the female voice on the phone spoke again. "Do you think we somehow caused him to kill himself?"

"He has said not, Stormsinger," Oaknail replied softly. "I believe him. And I believe Stellamara. Max has the sense about him of someone haunted."

I lowered my head. "I think Glover... Airdancer... had the ghost first. You see, when I finally had to admit that it really was suicide, I couldn't understand it, until I connected that note with the last case that he worked on. In a way, I think the case killed him."

"Was it that serious?" Unicorn asked.

"Not in the grand scheme of things, probably. It was a fairly simple real estate case. He seemed to have a special knack for that area of law."

"He was damned good at it," Oaknail noted with a tone sharper than I'd have expected. "He was the one who researched our initial legal issues in getting Timewind established as its own entity, in securing the property we now own. He had a solid feel for vagaries and intricacies, and he began to speak it, like a new language. We all agreed to put him through law school, and he'd take over all our legal work."

"He didn't, though."

"An overlooked part of the legend," Darkstar observed softly, without rancor. "He took some time in the Public Defender's office first. The tribe backed him up, as it was part of tribal idealism to fight for those who couldn't fight for themselves."

"Not quite that simple," Rainmist countered, her tail-tip thapping a tattoo on the floor behind her.

The lynx's ears folded back. "I didn't mean it like that."

The otter nodded, sighing. "He was a good defender, and he helped us with ordinary stuff when he could. Unicorn, what's it called?"

"Conveyance," the voice on the phone explained. "Transferring legal title. He helped me get through my own first year law courses. In a way, he was responsible for my becoming a lawyer."

"Because he left?" I asked.

"I prefer to think of it as being because I stayed." The lawyer's voice was soft. "It's not easy to speak ill of a mentor."

"I apologize for presuming." I couldn't help but notice Frank's surprise at my being polite; that was Max, not "the cop" Detective Luton. "Did he stay in touch with you?"

"I think he wandered away from us all, bit by bit." Rainmist sighed heavily. "The ideals were powerful, to start with. It's how Albion was born."

"The sword of justice." Oaknail had brought in a cloth to dry and polish the blade, and he tended it with great care. "He told us that he wanted to carry the torch of Timewind to the people, becoming the best PD he could. I crafted the blade myself, blending his description of what he wanted with some historical nods and my own vision."

"He was a defender for I don't know how many years," Unicorn put in. "His caseload was huge, right from the start, and he was... unable to do as much for his clients as he'd hoped. His correspondence with me became more and more sparse, more tired, more... despairing. He went from frustrated, to angry, to talking of quitting, in only four, maybe five years. I remember him creating a personal scoreboard, but the 'wins' were plea bargains rather than defenses, arranged between counsels to clear the court calendars, and the losses consisted of being unable to make proper defenses in court, unable to sway juries. It was a meat-grinder, to him. In the end, he had to give it up."

"He lasted for eight years," I took up the tale. "He eventually went back to real estate law, started doing well working at a small firm in Massachusetts. He was there for seven more years, amassing the beginnings of a fortune and attracting the attention of Langston, Kilgallen, and Mondekirke."

The frowns and angry faces appeared everywhere, to some degree or other. Whether or not Timewind hoped to be as non-judgmental as possible, their group opinion of the law firm was clearly evident, and it was certainly in alignment with my own. Frank seemed unable to restrain from voicing his views. "Langston is the greediest land-grabber in the state. He's bought up rental properties, forced out old tenants, and put in new ones at three times the rent. He bleeds people and places dry! Why would a member of Timewind go to work for him?"

"A member of Timewind wouldn't." I looked back to Oaknail. "That was the problem. Airdancer was a product of Timewind, whose back was broken by the so-called 'criminal justice system.'"

"Quite possibly the greatest oxymoron in the world," Darkstar observed.

I nodded sadly. "As you might guess, I've seen too much of it myself."

Movement from across the room. I paused, seeing Frank wanting to speak, but he kept his maw shut. I gave him a slight nod before I continued.

"Airdancer, whose idealism was all but drained from him, tried going back to something he was good at, perhaps to take a step back. With neither salary nor safety net, it was Glover who had to practice real estate law. He got in over his head, that 'idyllic' rich life that I described. He immersed himself in it, not letting himself take that optimistic long view that had helped him to fashion Timewind with the rest of the founders. It, the *Manifesto,* the sword, all hid inside a wooden box that he probably hadn't even thought about for years. His conscience didn't have a chance to bother him... until recently."

I drew a deep breath and plunged in. "Glover's last case involved evicting squatters from a parcel of pine forest downstate. It didn't push any buttons for him, at first; he filed papers and took details without actually visiting the encampment itself. Just routine, distant, intangible. That changed when his senior partner told him to serve papers personally, perhaps to intimidate the squatters with the sheer 'shock and awe' of such an almighty behemoth as LK&M. Glover went there last week, and that seems to be where it started.

"I visited the place myself a few days ago. I found a new definition of squalor. A half-dozen tents, two toilet sheds, a large army camp tent for cooking and taking meals. The small group there — I saw five, although I'm sure there were more, somewhere — weren't terribly well-nourished, with poor clothing besides. They had taken up residence there sometime late last fall, so say five, six months ago. What I described to you is all that there was there, save for a couple of older-model cars, like mine, and a plot of ground barely the size of the living room here, set with seedlings for their crops."

"That won't feed them," Heartsinger considered softly. "They couldn't grow enough to..."

Darkstar put an arm around him, then looked to Oaknail. "How did that compare with Timewind's origins?"

The bear shook his head. "We didn't plant until spring, of course, but we had a couple of sheds, at least, within the first month. I have to think we had more money behind us than they do. We bought the land; we didn't squat. We worked to improve..." He paused, hanging his head. "What went through his head? What did he see?"

"I can only guess," I said softly. "He had lost touch with you. He would remember what the founders had done in that short time. Even so, he might also have thought that the dream had died. It had died within him, and he saw it reflected in this image of failure, or that's what I imagine. It's a feeling, rather than anything I could prove. This group of squatters..." I took a moment just to breathe. "They weren't anything like Timewind's beginnings, but maybe he didn't remember it anymore. Maybe he only saw what appeared to be a complete failure of hope. Maybe that was the ghost, the dark spirit that pestered him, haunted him to death."

"And it frightened you, too."

All eyes turned to Stellamara.

"It's why you were so surprised by all this. It's why you were afraid of us. I understand now. I understand that black shape that I saw on your shoulder. I could almost hear it whispering to you."

I heard sounds around me and on the phone, and I raised a paw to forestall them. "She's right." I looked into her eyes, understanding for the first time. "It really was like a voice, something whispering to me, telling me not to trust this illusion of love and acceptance, because the world is only made to hurt and destroy all such dreams."

A pause before the voice of Stormsinger rose from the speaker. "Is that what you meant, when you said that you were looking for answers?"

"Yes. It was too easy for me to see and believe in Glover's despair. The one thing that drove me to keep looking past the obvious was the sword. Albion. It was more important to him than the weapon that he killed himself with. Paradoxically, the very symbol of the dream was the key to what drove him to destroy himself."

"And that paradox became your ghost."

All eyes, including mine, went again to Stellamara. "Yes. I kept pushing, searching, until the clues sent me to find you. Timewind. Starhold. To see if I could find out why. Or maybe to find out why not."

"Did you find your answers?"

"Some of them."

"Stay, then," Lightwing told me. "Stay until you find them all."

"We'll help," Darkstar added.

"We have lost one to the Void," Oaknail spoke solemnly. "Let us pledge to lose no other."

"May I suggest," Unicorn made himself known again, "that Detective Luton be set aside for another day, so that Max may find his answers?"

Voices on the phone and around the table assented. Like last night, I was welcomed. This time, however, there were no masks; I was welcomed. All of me.

Something at my shoulder whispered darkly, *That's what HE thought.*

15: Tea and Empathy

My impulse, at that point, was to go back to my room and hide away from everything and everyone. I felt more tired than anything else, although I also felt uncertain of how everyone really felt about... No. That wasn't true. The welcome was real. I was the one who didn't know how I felt. I was the one who still felt alienated, but not by the tribe. My paranoia was entirely personal.

I stayed in my seat as I watched them file out, trying to reconnect myself with the rest of them, the way it was last night, before I fell apart. I couldn't do it. The thing that whispered to me slithered more of itself into my mind, and my eyes changed to obey its vision. I saw Frank looking belligerent, and Dreamweaver angry at me for making her worry about him. I saw Moonsong plotting to poison my food, and Stellamara using her mind to direct the others into an attack on me. Rainmist would probably try to drown me. Heartsinger and Darkstar would plot some strange fetishistic torture, while Oaknail readied Albion to slay me by a thousand razor-sharp slashes. Oray and Starshine would help make sure that my car was never again found, and Unicorn would help everyone coordinate alibis to keep them all out of court.

"Max?"

Lightwing's voice was soft, and I turned toward her. Those beautiful blue eyes held me as they had before, offering only help and care, if I could trust her. Or trust myself.

The breath I'd held captive finally escaped. "I guess it's over, huh?"

"The call is over, Max. Are you okay?"

Before I could answer, I felt Darkstar's forepaw to my shoulder. "I'm going to help get the shop set up. *Are* you okay, Max?"

"Not sure." The room had emptied out by now, save for the three of us. "I was really..." I took in a deep breath and let it out slowly, finally starting to nod. "Yeah, I'll be okay. Nothing that some really heavy drugs and a few years in a psych ward wouldn't cure."

The lynx smiled softly at me. "I'd kiss you to make it better, but I have the feeling you might freak out worse."

My laugh wasn't entirely forced. "Sorry. Guess I'm not as cool as the rest of you."

"The hope was to make you laugh."

"Worked."

"I'll leave you in good paws then." He got to his hindpaws, glancing at Lightwing. "I'll see you both later, eh?"

I nodded once more, then looked back to the Husky. "I think I must really be crazy."

"Why?"

"Promise you won't laugh?"

"I won't laugh."

Another deep breath, and I told her as much as I could about my brief descent into PsychoLand. Her expression didn't change, unless it was to look somewhat more serious than before.

"Nope. Not laughing." She stood, offering her forepaws. "Let's get you out of this room."

Without another word, she led me back down the hall, past the guest rooms, past the living room, through the dining hall and kitchen, to a bricked back porch area of wooden deck chairs, tables, tall overhanging trees, and a very welcome amount of soft breezes and quiet. She sat me down and then, cupping my face in her forepaws, she kissed me. With her closed lips against my own, I felt a tender yet powerful emotion, a willing of strength and comfort, a sense of the deepest trust and affection. I think I made some little grunt of surprise, or perhaps pain, or confusion. When she broke the kiss, she again focused her eyes on me, holding me there for several seconds.

"Max," she said softly, as if tasting my name, "I want you to stay here, close your eyes, take slow, deep breaths, and try to count how many birdsongs you hear. Any of them, all of them. Keep breathing and counting, while I go make tea. Then, I'm going to bring it back here, and I'm going to find whatever it is that is hurting you so badly, and I'm going to yank it out of you, and I'm going to kick its fucking ass." She left another short kiss on my lips. "Start counting."

Amazing how many different sounds can be heard, even in the supposed quiet of a forested area, and even by the ears of a collie my age (measured more by mileage than years). I was intent enough on the task that I almost didn't hear the Husky padding up to me and setting something down on the nearby table.

"Is it safe for me to open my eyes now?"

"It'll probably help you to drink your tea without spilling it."

I silently conceded the point. On the table lay a small tray with two steaming mugs, a honey pot with dipper, and a small shallow bowl with some lemon wedges. "That tea isn't going to start melting my reality, is it?"

"Max, what—"

I waved a forepaw at her. "Part of a dream I had before waking this morning."

She looked at me for a long moment. "This thing has really put you through the wringer."

"Been a long time coming."

"Why do you say that?"

Reaching for a mug, I thought about it. "I'm not sure. It just seemed to be what I'm feeling." I hesitated, feeling foolish. "I don't get tea very often. Is there etiquette to this kind of thing?"

"How did you take reality-melting tea in your dream?"

"My son prepared it for me. He had also brought me a bagel and a schmear."

"Did you eat it?"

"No. I think it melted with everything else."

"Dreams are like that." She gave me a gentle smirk and began handling the honey dipper quite deftly. "What else are they like?"

"You really want to know?"

"If it was anything like what you told me in the conference room, I'd probably better hear about it. Melting reality, you say? I know Rainmist didn't put any of that type of mushroom into the stew." She added honey to both mugs, squeezed a lemon wedge into each, stirred them, set down the spoon, and handed a cup to me. In case I ever needed to fix a cup of tea, I'd now learned at least one method. "So tell me how to go about melting reality."

"First, I'd have to find a working definition for reality. I'm not even sure I can see it from here." I sniffed at the tea, finding a sweet, fruity blend, with honey and lemon (obviously). A little too warm to sip, so I couldn't use that to avoid answering. "Okay," I said at last. "I'll try to piece it together."

Lightwing was very patient with me, waiting for me to fill gaps in the images. I had no idea how much of it might have been the dream, imagination, or some peculiar mixture of the two. It didn't matter, of course, since the imagery was the same and, let's face it, obvious. I was curious to know whether the taste of the tea in my dream presaged the flavor that I was drinking now, or if I had conveniently overwritten the flavor to match what I was drinking now. That, at least, could have been interesting.

"I don't need to bring out Sigmund Freud or anyone, right?" the Husky teased me.

"Not unless you want to make something out of the term 'wood'."

She smiled. "Welcome back, Max."

Shaking my head gently, I said, "I have no idea where all this paranoia comes from."

"Maybe something really is after you. Just not what you think, or the way you think."

"That wants some explanation."

The Husky sniffed the tea, also seeming to find it too warm to drink just yet. Moving the mug away from her muzzle, she regarded me with something that my poisoned mind tried to label as irritation or disgust. It was probably more like her trying to make up her mind exactly how to give me the explanation I'd asked for.

"Not everything in your life is what you think it is," she began. "At least, that's what I discovered for myself. Magic is everything it seems; I still believe that. Not everything is as magical as it seems."

Waving a paw, shaking her head, she sighed an apology. "Short form: I was deceived by someone who used my way of looking at things — thinking of things as being magical — as a weapon against me. Do you remember me telling you that Darkstar told me of the stories of Dragonfly, how they weren't really part of Mi'kmaq Medicine Stories, but that other tribes had them? My paranoia, my tormentor, was a male who used my interests, my magical beliefs, as a way of getting into my head and my heart, and he turned everything against me."

It's not an exaggeration to say that my heart hurt at those words. Even the black, twisted shape of Glover's shroud sat up to take notice, perhaps trying to discover a new weapon to use. I wanted to reach out to her, but the darkness stayed my paw. I raised my cup to my lips, finding the liquid still hot but not too hot. The flavors reawakened my tired palate, and the honeyed warmth felt good on my throat. More than that, my actions caused Lightwing to sample her own brew. After a small but apparently fortifying sip, she began again.

"He claimed to be a Cheyenne Medicine Man, and perhaps he was. He certainly had a backward charm to him that made it easy for me to believe his stories, his claims to being ostracized royalty, meaning clan-based royalty, and maybe even his lies about thinking that I might have Cheyenne blood in me somewhere. That, he said, is what gave me my 'Medicine Power' abilities — intuition, speaking with my Spirit Guides, my vested interest in what is magical in the world." Another headshake. "I ate up every word."

After she had paused for a time again, I managed to ask, "What happened?"

"For everything in the world, he proselytized, there is a light and dark side, whether it's magic, the Force, or duct tape. He began to warn me about the dark, the evil things, things that were trying to hurt me, because I was more powerful than I thought, and that made me interesting to The Dark Forces." Her voice emphasized capital letters in her words. "I began worrying about anything that might possibly be unusual, strange. My world of magical things began to feel threatening, even genuinely dangerous. Certain furs seemed suspect, and I avoided them. I wore a talisman on a thin hemp strap around my neck, to emphasize my connection to my Spirit Guides; even though it was under my shirt, it represented a kind of mental warding, like a cross against vampires is supposed to be. I started thinking that it was dangerous to believe in magical things, or to see too much beauty in a world that was filled with things that might kill you... or worse, claim your soul and doom you for all eternity."

She turned her magnificent blue eyes back toward me, a crooked smile on her muzzle. "That old line about 'which is the greater fool' comes to mind, doesn't it?"

"When did all this happen?"

"It started late in my college years, and it continued for a time after them." She sipped at her tea, but not out of any delaying tactic. She was back to herself, and the tale was once again a story for her. "I backed out of grad school, lost a promising job, lost a promising relationship... What's that song lyric about 'paranoia strikes deep'?"

"He really did a number on you."

"It took a few years to figure that out. Just glad that I finally did."

I turned my body toward her. Glover's shade followed me. "How? What happened?"

"It wasn't some grand revelation that made me all better, like swallowing a magic potion." She managed to smile at me. "Or drinking the Kool-Aid. I've been part of Timewind for eight years now, and I learned from them before that, and I was working on myself even before that, and the biggest break between me and the alleged Medicine Man actually came from him. I figured out that he was lying to me, and I tried to get in touch with some of the people he had told me were part of his life. One of these was a Catholic priest who, according to my Pseudo-Shaman, had succumbed to his sexual wiles and worried what would happen if his — the lying Medicine Man's — mother were to find out."

She held up a finger, shaking it gently in the air. "I forgot an important part of this story. We had met through a third party, who was online with me and knew this guy through having met him at some gathering or other. This Medicine Man... oh, hell, who knows what name he's using now, but let's call him by something distinctly non-First-Ones. How about Bert?"

"I like it. Rhymes with 'perp.'"

This got a chuckle out of her, and she continued. "Bert never got much into technology beyond a phone and a land line, or so he claimed. I wrote paper letters to him, although I doubt there's anything in them more incriminating than my own ignorance. The point of that is that I never met him in fur and bone, just as a voice; he was some distance away, and we never seemed to find a way to meet."

"That didn't make you suspicious?"

"Not at first. There must be a point where trust and naivete share similar ground." Another head-shake. "He was a skilled huckster, until some of his stories started having little holes in them. The priest was one of those. Supposedly, Bert lived with his aging mother, and the small-town priest would come by to look in on her, just to be neighborly. After, Bert would seduce the priest, as if to prove that his magic could control even a God-botherer."

I sensed something trying to settle on my shoulders again. I tried to ward it off with some more tea.

"Somewhere between kindness and deviousness, I cooked up a plan. I found the number for the only Catholic church in the rural area, introduced myself to the only priest there, and said that I wanted to make an offering in the name of Bert's mother, to thank him for looking after her." She smiled wryly. "Guess who'd never heard of her?"

"Nice. Did you confront Bert?"

Lightwing shrugged. "Not right away. That particular story had been so outrageous that I sniffed it out fairly easily. I took some time to see what else I could think of that I could catch him out on. He was slippery but, ultimately, I was able to confront him with several at once. I saved the story of the priest for last, and he tried playing the moral outrage card — how dare I endanger him by violating his trust, all of that crap. He the set about cutting me off, forbidding me to have any further contact with him, effectively 'disowning' me, refusing to help me find my Cheyenne roots... By the way, those DNA testing kits are worth the money." Another wry smile. "Bang goes another illusion."

Another sip of tea as I considered. "You had to have been very strong to get through all that."

"Strong or stubborn, depending on your definition. I was pretty aimless for a few years after Bert. I was still feeling paranoid, but for other reasons. I no longer worried that I was being pursued by evil forces, but I wasn't sure I could feel the happily magical aspects of the world anymore either. Things began feeling neither bright nor dark but just... gray. The magic that we talked about last night? It was still there, waiting for me to see it again. It was me who still felt haunted, or hunted, or that something was after me. Or maybe nothing."

"How did you come to find Timewind?"

The Husky managed a smile much more like the one that I'd first seen in the barn last night. "The usual thing is to say that Timewind finds those who need the tribe as much as the tribe needs them. That gets back to the feelings of magic that I love, and it helps me rewrite my personal history with practical optimism." Her soft chuckle made me smile back at her. "You'll find those two words used prominently in the newer editions of the *Manifesto,* along with other attempts to think positively without resorting to empty slogans and vapid affirmations."

I set my mug down, nodding. "I thumbed through Glover's comb-bound copy"

"Oaknail is right: The original edition is not the best introduction to the tribe. I read the edition prior to this one."

"Updating the dream?"

"More like providing observations about more recent happenings in the world, applying the tribe's collected wisdom in the form of support for dreamers who are starting to lose the dream." She smiled again, her eyes so inviting that even Glover's shade retreated a little, in fear of being permanently banished by them. "It was Rainmist who found me first, actually. Some time shared at a co-op near the city, random conversations, some coffee meets. She sussed me out pretty neatly, and she found the right time to offer me a copy of the *Manifesto,* explaining that she'd helped to write it, so she wanted my opinion of the work."

"Sneaky."

"You hadn't guessed that about her already?"

"Now that you mention it..."

Another chuckle from the Husky. "I read it, and I was lucky enough to start remembering what the magic was like back when it was real for me. I still didn't really believe it all; as I said, I wasn't going to drink any new Kool-Aid after the garbage that Bert pulled on me. As you might imagine, I didn't meet 'Rainmist' first. Her given name is no secret, but I'll let her decide if she wants to tell you. For myself, I go by Troi Knowlton when I'm out in the world."

She watched me closely at that point, and I gave myself an even-money bet that she could read my expression like a book. "Okay," I admitted, "that phrase does start to sound like something cultish. I think I get the context, but maybe you'd better explain it to me."

"Think of Starhold like a retreat, a sanctuary from the rest of the world. Part of what makes it so rejuvenating is our camaraderie, our sense of family, along with our sense of being wholly ourselves here. I can be 'Troi' to everyone, just as Ezequiel is Ezequiel. When we call him Unicorn, when they call me Lightwing, it's like another level of intimacy between us. Choosing the tribal name is about giving yourself a name that might feel more true to you than the one that you were given at birth. There are things that Troi has to deal with, that she has to be, 'out there in the world'; Lightwing can set those things aside and use the time to reflect upon herself, perhaps to help Troi know how she feels about things. Ezequiel can set aside some of the persona he presents as a lawyer and let Unicorn come out to play."

"You make it sound like you're pretending to be someone else when you're away from Starhold. Like you have more than one self."

"Don't you? You were Detective Luton an hour ago, but yesterday, you were Max." She seemed to blush a little under the black-brown fur of her mask. "You were Max last night. 'Detective Luton' is an official sort of figure, someone who follows 'rules and regs,' right? Max is who you are when you take off your badge."

I had no means to disagree, nor did I want to. I didn't want to be "Detective Luton" right now, and I thought how good I felt last night when I wasn't having to be "official." Maybe the tea was melting some of my reality after all.

She set her mug down and turned to look at me directly, her ice blue eyes warmer than ever toward me. "Max, you feel like something is after you, that this fear has been a long time coming. Maybe it's more real than you think, but it's not like evil things trying to grab at you. It's that sense of nothing, made worse by the way you discovered Airdancer. Let me ask you outright: When Stellamara said that she saw something on your shoulder, something telling you lies, what did you think? No, change that... what did you *feel*?"

It was there. I felt it last night, this morning, even now. Something slithering around my shoulders, something with a voice that wasn't sound, wasn't even words. It was, as my mind had labeled it, an Idea. It was after me, had been for a long time, but now it was where I could really tell that it existed, that it wanted me to give myself over to it. How do I talk about that kind of crap without sounding completely crazy?

"Max?" Lightwing took my forepaw into her own, squeezed. "What did you feel? Look at the feeling, give it a word."

The more I looked into her eyes, the more I had the sensation of that thing, that Idea, that tiger-shaped shade, slinking around my shoulders. I felt myself starting to shake, and I couldn't understand why. This was all so stupid, so crazy, this doesn't happen, normal furs don't feel like this, ordinary furs don't have things on their shoulders, or think that something is after them, not normal, not sane...

"Max! Word!"

"Terrified."

She leaned over quickly, her arms moving to grip my shoulders, and my own forepaws shot up to grip hers just as closely. I closed my eyes tightly, and I heard a high yipping sound, a whine, like a yowen scared of the dark, imagining terrors that couldn't possibly be there, because bogeys and monsters and demons are all fiction, all tales made up to scare us, like that fake shaman did to Lightwing, and she deserves so much better than that, and we're not yowens after all, and what am I doing holding her and trembling so much, and why was I...

The whispering now in my ear was real, and it was soft, consoling, bringing me back to myself. Where had I been? That was a ridiculous thing to think. I was right here, sitting on this large porch, with Lightwing, sharing tea, talking... I hadn't been anywhere, had I?

"Ledge," I heard myself say.

Lightwing did not reply, just held me, her strong forepaws still gripping me tightly. My nose was at the ruff of her neck, and the scent of her helped to calm me. I thought of last night, when she held me, pet me, let me cry. I didn't think that I wanted to cry now. I just wanted to stop feeling like I was so... so very...

Terrified.

I gave Lightwing a squeeze, which she returned, and slowly extricated myself from the embrace. She pulled back, but she took hold of my forepaw with hers, clasping gently. She seemed in no rush, and I let myself fall back into my chair, eyes still closed, listening to birdsongs, counting them, feeling what was around me. I still felt something at my back, my shoulders, but I tried to explain to it that Max wasn't at home to anything that Detective Luton might have been working on last week. I might have to deal with it on Monday, but not now, not today... and not here. Not in this place.

Giving her forepaw a little shake, I gathered up enough breath to say, "Okay. I think I'm back now."

"How can I help, Max?"

I managed a smile. "It seems like all I'm doing is asking for help."

"Shall I remind you of the Three Steps to Becoming?"

"But I'm not a member of the tribe."

"Why should that stop you from Becoming?"

I opened my eyes, finding myself looking at the bright sky, a lush forested area not far beyond me, and the sense that I could almost forget about anything beyond the boundaries of these many hectares of land. It was, as Lightwing had called it, a retreat from the world. Or, perhaps, just a place where someone could let a good cup of tea erase what hurts. A place where...

"A place where you can dream," I said softly to the sky. I felt Lightwing squeeze my forepaw with her own.

"I think you're getting the idea," she said. "How're you feeling?"

"Like maybe drinking the tea isn't the same as drinking the Kool-Aid." I turned to look at her, the beautiful mask on her face, and those amazing eyes within. A smile appeared on my muzzle. "Maybe, like Starshine said, we can just pretend."

"Pretend what?"

"That I'm just Max."

"One change," the Husky told me. "You're not 'just' Max. You're Max. There's a lot involved in being Max, and I've enjoyed getting to know him. Now..." She rose from her chair, getting me up on my hindpaws as well. "Let's get these tea cups back into the house, and then I'll show you what dreaming can be like."

As she led me back to the kitchen, I felt something on my shoulders, realizing that it was the faint touch of breeze whispering through the trees. I wasn't sure what it said. Maybe I would hear it better later.

16: Artisanry

We stayed in the kitchen long enough to tend to the mugs and accoutrements that Lightwing had brought outside, then padded our way back through the dining hall, past the living room, and out the front doors. Back in the sunshine, I quickly reoriented myself to the property in general. Pointing down the road/driveway, I said, "Your shop is down that way?"

"We call it The Artisanry, where we show our talents and wares." Lightwing grinned at me. "I think you'll find the place interesting. You haven't had much chance to see it."

"Just the passing glance." We continued toward the bend in the road, keeping an easy pace that seemed to suit us both well. "I did notice the name, over the entrance. Who does the signage? Is it one of the tribe?"

"In this case, yes. The metal sign outside is Oaknail's work; inside is another sign wrought in wood, which is Redlance's specialty. He is amazing at woodworking. I sometimes tease him by calling him 'the tree whisperer.' He is quite literally a tree-hugger. I have found him with his arms wrapped around one of the pines here, eyes closed, seeming to want to melt into the trunk. He makes it look like a loving gesture between friends instead of something comical or political."

"It sounds almost paradoxical that he could use parts of a tree for his work."

"Pardon me sounding mystical again, but I think it's because the wood trusts him. Yeah, I know, New Age bunkum, but..." She shook her head gently. "He seems to be able to coax designs and finished work from all manner of woods, and he has a special love for his work. He began his artistry long before he joined the tribe, selling his work at craft fairs and ren faires. He jokes that he only joined so that he could have his work in a proper store."

"Is that true? Would he not be able to have his work there without joining?"

The Husky cast me a sideways glance and laughed briefly. "What part of 'democratic socialism' did you miss?"

"Oops," I grinned at her. "Do I lose points for being an unenlightened member of the bourgeoisie?"

"I don't imagine that..." She paused, rethinking her comment, and patted my shoulder. "In the land of 'Let's Pretend,' let me say that I suspect that Detective Luton probably has a salary that makes him firmly part of the proletariat."

"Thank you," I said, nodding. "Yes, I can safely say that he does."

Picking up her original thread, Lightwing explained, "The Artisanry will accept good work from anyone, if they agree to the same terms that we all accept. Whether part of the tribe or not, an artist tithes ten percent of the sale to Timewind. We take care of the sales tax receipts and payments, and we make sure the inventory is correct; that's easier for us than for most of our artists, because we're already set up for it. It seems to be a good arrangement for everyone."

"Only ten percent? That seems..."

"Too low for common capitalism?" She grinned at me. "Welcome to the tribe, Max."

I had more questions, dredging themselves up from somewhere, but I elected to suspend my disbelief while I took a closer look at the shop building and its surroundings.

The Artisanry was set a perhaps a hundred meters from the main house, around a bend in the drive, with the beauty of trees and the nearby creek to make a setting almost incongruous to the presence of a building for trade or commerce. The secret, I discovered, was that the building looked more like a house than a store. I'm not all that good at estimating the relative sizes of houses, so I let myself stop at the notion that the building looked like a "large" house, one level, with a very homey front door, which stood open, a screen door in good repair keeping out any bugs and small critters that might be about. Three cars parked properly in front of the place, despite there being no formally marked spaces. I could only think that the tribe attracted far nicer customers than, say, "WalWorld."

Enough of my cynicism returned to remind me that that wasn't too high a bar.

"I take it this building wasn't waiting for you, either?"

Another laugh from the Husky. "It's been here for about six years. Before that, Timewind rented space in the town nearby, with a limited amount of stock on display. We made it possible for customers to order more and then pick up the goods there."

"Owning is better than renting, but how did you afford to create this place?"

"You'll have to ask Sunrider how he does it. I got about as far as the ideas of increasing the value of the land and something about business advantages of improvements and attracting new customers to a specialized location. After that, it was some mystical intangibles concerning taxes, write-offs, and mini-max solutions that took into account our tribal values. Those last two words, I understand, the same way that I understand what I can see of the benefits we bestow and reap." She grinned at me. "I told you that I believe in magic."

Lightwing and I padded to the screen door, which she opened and held out for me. Entering, I found myself in the front room of the house, which featured mostly jewelry, with the gold and silver in cases and ceramic medallions and semi-precious crystals hanging from leather-looking cords on posts on the wall. I noticed a pair of young females interested in those, a Shiba and a poodle, high school age; they were chatting softly about which might look best for some event that they were looking forward to. I thought of my high school days in one of those fleeting moments that is like sneaking the fastest possible peek at the scary monster on the movie screen before closing your eyes again.

"Max!"

I turned to see Darkstar behind a cashier's station, perched on a stool, his smile warm and welcoming, not at all enigmatic. I wondered if he were violating some species-trait contract by being so open. I also resolved that I'd never report him for it.

"Getting the nickel tour?" he asked.

"I left my change at the house," I smiled back at him. "Think I'm good for it?"

"I'm willing to take a chance."

I glanced at the laptop on the desk, thinking it almost out of place, yet necessary; I could see that it was hooked into the peculiar device that could accept plastic in one form or another, including from a phone, which still confused me a bit. I'm enough luddite that I still preferred cash whenever possible. What surprised me was that I might not have been alone in the idea. When the yowens went to pay for their purchases, purses opened to reveal small pouches which contained bills and coins, the trousers being a bit too tight to allow easy access to the pockets. From below the desk, Darkstar pulled up a small chest made from beautifully polished California buckeye. Inside, wooden troughs separated bills and coins, no doubt with checks (if those are still used) placed underneath the money tray. It was like any other cash box, save for the sheer beauty of it.

After the two young females had left, Lightwing motioned for the lynx to keep the box out a little longer. "Redlance has made five of these, including this one, and there's a clamoring for him to build more, in spite of the cashless society."

"A bit much for a yard sale, but yeah, I can see a small business wanting one. Would they be expensive to make?"

"Depends on the wood, naturally." The feline stroked the box with an appreciative forepaw. "This buckeye makes it pretty pricey, but that fox can make even plain woods glow from deep within."

"Did he make the box for Albion?"

"I don't know, but I think it's a good bet."

Nodding, I said, "I'd like to meet him."

"He travels a lot, between specialized craft shows and teaching his skills in woodworking." Darkstar's smile was larger than regulations should permit. "You'll have to come back sometime."

"Sneaky."

"C'mon." Lightwing turned me further toward the back of the shop. "Let me give you the rest of the tour. We've got six rooms to go through."

On the wall that served as a bridge for the two open doorways leading to the rest of the rooms, I saw the sign that the Husky had mentioned: a large, beautifully shaped carving of wood spelling out *Artisanry,* the rich darkness of mahogany offsetting the lighter color of the walls. The fox who called himself Redlance (I would have to ask him the origin of his name, if I had the chance) was indeed quite the woodworker.

The next room, maybe eight or so meters on a side, was filled with a wide variety of mugs and steins, ceramic and glass, ranging from the sublime to the silly; some of the hand-painted work comprised outstanding reproductions of German biergarten designs, while others asked such probing questions as "Is there life before coffee?" Also here were the knives, forks, and accessories from metalworkers, and platters, plates, bowls, Lazy Susan's, and other eating-related items from ceramic and woodworkers.

"The Dining Room," my guide told me without undue pride. "Look here."

She gestured toward a shelf of steins, and I saw a 10x15cm placard with a familiar face on it, along with the Borzhvolk's name and some background about his work in ceramics. As I looked, I noticed that other shelves, with the work of other artisans, also carried similar credits and information. "Some of these contain contact information," I noticed. "Do folks come through and pinch your artisans away from you?"

Chuckling, the Husky observed, "More capitalism. Abandon it!" She teasingly punched my shoulder. "Placing work with us is entirely voluntary, and we hope that they get some good exposure as well as a few shekels. If they get commissions on their own, it means that they're getting recognition for their work which, I think, is what we all want. They might continue to place works with us, or they might not. A few have tithed ten percent of their independent commissions, as thanks for helping to get them started. We don't require it of anyone."

"Do you ever get any of the really ungrateful types?"

"Who's asking?"

I looked at her sharply. Her gaze was soft, but it held the message just fine. After a few seconds, the penny dropped. A moment of breath, in through the nose, out through the maw, then I nodded. "Never mind that last question."

"I don't mind answering, as long as I know who's asking. The truth is, Max, most furs in the world are pretty decent about things. They have to learn how to become ungrateful types. Unfortunately, a lot of schooling and experience in this world today is rife with ingratitude." She smiled wanly. "Even those who believe in magic can be led astray."

"And sometimes, they can be led back."

The wan smile regained its warmth. Less than a day, and I knew that I wanted to see that smile more often. I was about to tell myself all the reasons why that was a bad idea when I felt her forepaw on my shoulder, gently tuning me to the next room. Clearly, she wasn't done showing me things.

* * * * *

The third room, the same size as the first, contained paintings and, to make vertical space to contain them, two movable partitions stood parallel in the middle of the room. The subject matter seemed to run the gamut from reproductions of real life to depictions of greatest fantasy. One showed a pair of dancers, clearly Darkstar and Heartsinger, stripped to the waist and engaging in a display of great physical prowess, whether of ballet, acrobatics, jigs, or just plain enthusiasm. It was a night scene; they were lit by torches around them, perhaps part of one of the ren faires, and the swirling of color and feeling of motion made me think of Van Gogh's later works.

"Stellamara's?" I asked.

"Many of them, yes. We're still getting other artists involved. Frank is a very good photographer. We'll be displaying some of his work before long, and he has also suggested that we photograph the finest examples of the artwork, to send them to galleries across the country for their consideration."

"And Stellamara is hesitating."

Lightwing paused only a moment. "Yes. She's worried about the demands of the publicity. She doesn't want her work to become popularized, production-line material."

"I have to imagine that she must be getting some recognition through her local exposure, here and from those starving artist shows. Is it possible that she's going to have to face the problem sooner than she thinks?"

"None of us is sure. We don't have the answers yet."

I put a forepaw to her arm gently. "If I find any, I'll let you know right away."

Another of those lovely smiles. "Already sounding better, Max. Good for you."

Lightwing let me linger for a while as I took in the full scope of Stellamara's work. Imagining her being consigned to "starving artists" shows made me wonder if she were, in some ways, even more similar to Van Gogh than anyone had thought. The Dutch artist sold almost none of his many works during his lifetime, and his own physical and psychological issues led ultimately to his suicide. I came to realize that Timewind might well have saved the young doe's life. She was protected here, nurtured, given a safe place to grow.

Telling all this to Lightwing surprised her only a little. "Do you give credit to psychic phenomena, Max? Telepathy, precognition, that sort of thing?"

I paused, looking at a painting depicting Heartsinger tending to, grooming, a non-sapient horse; I remembered the name "Clipper" from this morning, and let the picture complete itself in my mind. "I'm not sure," I said truthfully. "I've had my share of intuition, I suppose. Why do you ask?"

The Husky shrugged gently, her eyes flickering with mischief. "Some of us have the feeling that, when we really connect with someone, we are actually sharing something more than mere words. The sensation is like knowing something beyond the words you've shared, reaching some subconscious level that makes a mutual joining. Tough to describe, but the emotion is there. It's particularly strong with Stellamara. Her intuition about you was very strong, and it seems now that you are have some insight into her as well."

"Are you suggesting that our souls have touched?"

"No, but I think you just did."

My smile was soft. "Have I already drunk the Kool-Aid?"

"Just the tea," she assured me. "But it seems to be working. C'mon," she said, cocking her head toward the back of the store, "there's a surprise in the next room."

* * * * *

It was definitely a surprise. The fourth room ran the width of the building (perhaps 17 or so meters), a good bit deeper than the front room, and was decked out like a small, comfortable café from the days when such places had poetry readings and acoustic music. This room was too small to accommodate such crowds, but the feeling was similar. Much of the light came through the skylights a respectable distance above, room enough there for a few more ceiling fans to turn lazily in the warm air of the cozy space. The chairs were a happy mish-mash of styles and designs, with a half-dozen tables nearby them. At one of these sat a pair of older males who were engaged in an animated conversation about something I couldn't quite catch.

"Hello again, Max."

I returned Moonsong's hail with a smile and a wave. The big brown bear wore a long apron over her usual garb, and she rose from her chair, indicating the small but well-equipped coffee bar near her (including the fancy machines, bean grinder, and a variety of syrups to add), and a small glass case with plastic-wrapped samples of her baked goods.

"What can I fix for you?"

"I'm still enjoying the mellowness of Lightwing's tea. I didn't know that you had a café on site."

"We sort of don't." The sow grinned and pointed to a sign next to a wide-mouthed ceramic mug. The sign read, *Complimentary Beverages (your generosity is much appreciated)*. "We avoid some of the health code requirements, although we use their guidelines to keep things up to snuff. This just takes the red tape out of it."

"Nice sidestepping," I grinned. "Does it work?"

"It's amazing how generosity supersedes mere greed, in both directions. This wouldn't work almost anywhere else, but here, it works out very well indeed."

Nodding, I observed, "Considering you have a captive audience — this being the only place to offer food or drink for kilometers around — the usual tendency would be to charge as much as you could milk out of your visitors."

"This bit of indulgence isn't meant to be our main business, so it's not make-or-break for us. Besides, offering some free coffee and cookies might get folks to linger a bit and loosen them up for more purchases on their way out." She grinned at me. "We're not entirely innocent."

Lightwing chuckled. "Besides, it made a great excuse for us to get this wonderful machinery for our own caffeine indulgences." She flashed that beautiful smile at me again. "Another term you'll find in the *Manifesto*: 'Enlightened Self-Interest.'"

* * * * *

The opening to the fifth room (a duplicate size as the other side of house) lay at the far end of the café, thus making a clockwise loop the best course to visit all of the spaces in turn. This particular space was almost frightening to me. "I'm not sure I should be in here," I told Lightwing. "I have eleven brown thumbs."

From her stool at the side of what I could only describe as a barely-restrained jungle, Starshine made a sweet giggle. "No such thing," she declared. "A little instruction and a good hardy ivy can make believers out of anyone."

I'm not sure if the various potted plants I saw here would actually produce enough oxygen to make a difference to the air in the room, but it felt like it. Greenhouses always strike me that way. Maybe it's just the sensation of so much life, and the smells from some of the potted herb plants, and the headiness of the scent of moist soil. It's not something I get regularly in the city, and I found myself pushing that "city" part of me away again, just for now, there you go, take a seat in the next compartment in my mind for a while, and if you're very good, I'll bring you some fresh coffee later; right now, I'm busy enjoying the local flora.

"Are you the gardener, then?" I asked the young raccoon.

She giggled again. "More like an apprentice. Unicorn is the real gardener."

"A lawyer who is also a gardener?" I couldn't suppress a grin. "It seems an unlikely combination."

Lightwing explained, "He will counter with Nero Wolfe, the great fictional detective who cultivated orchids."

"Point taken. He certainly has done well, if this room is anything to go by. What's his secret? Talking to them? Special lights? Soil from a secret forest somewhere?"

"Getting warmer." The 'coon waved a forepaw at three stacks of flat bags (plastic?) in the corner of the room. "We compost and process manure to use as fertilizer. It's easiest for us to get the horse dung, when we muck out the stables. Our cows are also indoors at night, so we can get flops from those stalls." She wrinkled her nose. "Pigs are the worst, as far as I'm concerned; I love 'em, but their poo reeks. But it's a great cost-to-profit ratio, huh?"

I had to laugh. "Okay... manure, in connection with the practice of law... that part I can believe."

Lightwing fetched me a playful slap to my arm. She did not, however, disagree with me.

* * * * *

The sixth area was clearly Dreamweaver's domain. Although the black panther wasn't here at the moment, everything in the room was about fabric —shirts, skirts, pants, caftans, vests, coats, pouches, bags, serapes, capes, and anything else that you could think of. The selection was modest, with small cards describing each offering, perhaps because it might not be in stock, or perhaps to offer the shopper an opportunity to special-order something. I hoped that the feline wasn't swamped with orders from around the world. The downside of what used to be called a "cottage industry" was that careful, individualized offerings took a lot of time to make.

I looked at some of the shirts and pants that were like the ones that Darkstar had loaned to me, that the tribe wore almost as a uniform (begone, suspicious shade). I wasn't naïve enough to think that they were paw-cut and paw-stitched, not in these quantities and with this much continuity in the seams. There still felt to be something personal about them, as if any machine-processing had somehow managed to retain the original intent of the designer, like the clothing equivalent of heredity, bringing the panther's heart down through the lineage of the cloth itself.

...and where in hell did that idea come from?

"You know, those do look well on you."

Lightwing's soft observation floated gently into my thoughts. I felt my ears twitch with a sense of embarrassment. "Thank you, I think."

"You think? What's wrong?"

Those amazing eyes helped me see myself through them. "I'm still trying to be Max instead of all that other stuff. Telling me that you like me in this rather simple costuming is a different thing for me to think about."

"Costuming?"

I smiled at her. "What I wore yesterday, when I came here, was costuming, too. I'm expected to dress a certain way as 'Detective Luton.' Now, I'm 'Max,' in a different costume, in different clothing. And you said it looks well on me. Perhaps it suits Max after all."

"Is that a bad thing?"

"For my bank account, yes, if I buy everything I want from here." The laugh wasn't forced, but it didn't last long. "Maybe I don't know where Max would wear it."

The Husky moved close to me and hugged me warmly. "Right now, Max is wearing some borrowed clothes and rediscovering himself. Let that take a little time. It'll be okay."

Returning the hug was easy; controlling my tail wasn't. Happily, the room wasn't cramped, or she and I might have knocked over a great deal of merchandise. The most interesting thing was that I don't think either of us would have cared all that much.

* * * * *

When we had finished stirring up as much air as we cared to, we returned to the front room of the store, on the side away from the cashier's station. The area was, in its way, a seventh room, considering the items it featured. I hardly noticed Darkstar padding his way toward us, as my eyes were fixed on the various pewter and silver tankards which lined three shelves. Several of the handles were in the shapes of dragons, lions, unicorns, and other creatures of fact and fantasy, and the sides of the flagons were beautifully polished and delicately etched. A few pewter holders held glass containers, a style I had always associated with a proper Russian tea service described in works of Dostoevsky. Also of interest was the collection of blades: swords, rapiers, and daggers, each polished to a brilliant sheen and, I had no doubt, quite able to hold an edge.

"I have the feeling," I said softly, "that this is Oaknail's domain."

"Full marks," the lynx observed with the slightest bit of snark.

"These are items made singly and with dedication," I continued. "I have to imagine that the clothing is made more in batches."

"The way of progress, perhaps," Darkstar agreed.

"And yet they too still have the sense of being unique. The heart that created the first of them is still in all of them."

In the somewhat surprised silence, I turned to the feline, holding out my arms. "Permission to hug?"

Darkstar moved close and held me, and I returned the embrace warmly. Detective Luton, who was neither a prude nor a rampant homophobe, probably still couldn't let himself be this vulnerable. Max could do this. Max could let himself feel things that he... I... hadn't felt in years.

Gently, the lynx pulled away from me, looking me in the eyes. "Less than twenty-four hours, and you're starting to get free with your hugs."

I plucked at my shirt. "Yeah, I borrowed these duds from a guy who seemed like a huggy sort of feller. I must have picked up the vibe or something."

"At least you didn't say 'cooties,'" the feline laughed, then sobered softly. "I still don't think you're ready for a kiss."

I managed a chuckle, feeling my ears and tail do an uncertain dance.

"I'm not asking for one, Max. I hope I'm not that much of a jerk. I'm trying to thank you for letting your guard down."

"Does Max have guards?" Lightwing wondered.

Ruefully, I nodded. "Probably. But maybe, just maybe, he's not as haunted as the homicide detective."

"I could see why a homicide detective would have reason to be haunted," Darkstar noted. "I have a question for you, Max. Do you think that healing one could heal the other?"

"Okay, maybe I'm not a split personality, or whatever it's called these days."

"I didn't mean it like that. You're one being, one collie who has had to put on different faces for different situations, like all of us. This Max, standing before me, is a face that hasn't been allowed to come out to play for a while. I like him."

"Me, too," Lightwing admitted.

"So my question might be better phrased as, can this face, this Max, help Detective Luton to get rid of the ghosts that are haunting him?"

For what felt like a long moment, I simply looked at the two of them. Then I reached a forepaw to each, and they took mine in theirs. "If I can learn to ask for help, then yes, maybe I can."

They both squeezed my forepaws warmly, both smiled, both said the same thing without saying a word: *Welcome, Max. Welcome to Timewind.*

17: A Short Walk to the Past

The sound of new shoppers at the door convinced me to withdraw my forepaws, but not too swiftly. I tried telling myself that it was in order to let Darkstar move to greet them, welcome them, ask if he could help them find anything, rather than that I was embarrassed to be found by strangers, holding forepaws with two other fursons who were (for all the strangers knew) just standing there, with no other purpose than to be a tableau of some kind. I was able to split the difference a bit, and my slightly splayed ears and gently drooping tail signaled to Lightwing that my pretense was entirely in my head and not the least necessary. I managed to smile at her as she drew a little closer to me, putting her arm around my waist.

"How about we blow this pop stand?" She did a pretty good imitation of Humphrey Bogart, and it surprised me as much as the line itself.

"What movie is that from?"

"I have no idea, or even if it really is from a movie." She grinned at me. "Darkstar informs me that later generations turned it into 'popsicle stand' because they didn't know what 'soda pop' was. Supposedly, the original is from a Bogart movie."

"You do him credit," I said, returning the grin. "What next?"

"Come with me."

Taking my forepaw firmly into her own, she led me to the front door as Darkstar escorted the new visitors further into the shop. He cast me a glance as we passed him, and again I had that feeling of benevolence in his presumably enigmatic smile. I still felt the warmth of his hug as I reflected the smile to him. Somewhere over my shoulder, I had the sense of a black tiger-like shade hissing at the lynx like an angry housecat. The image made me want to chuckle, and the shadowy spirt cowered from my amusement.

Back outside, the fresh air felt bracing, and I took in an especially large quantity of it. Lightwing looked at me in gentle amusement.

"You look as if you're starved for oxygen."

"I don't get this fine quality of air in the city." I released her forepaw and made a show of patting my chest in a reenactment of the old cliché. I stopped short of actual chest-beating like a non-sapient mountain gorilla, if only because I saw a car approaching slowly, looking for space to park near the other cars, and I didn't want just anyone to see me being so exuberant. *Still some restraints,* I thought, *but better than yesterday.*

The Husky looked me over and seemed to like what she saw. It should have been no surprise to me that I enjoyed having her look at me that way. That cop, the one I was trying to set aside for a little while, really did feel like a weight on me, and I felt free here. More Kool-Aid, maybe? With another chest-full of crisp, clean air, I pushed aside the thought, envisioning it as a load of bricks toppling on that dark Idea that was still trying to crowd me. It was a very pleasant image, and it let me regain my smile.

"Where to?" I asked.

"Back toward the garage," she informed me, waving an arm expansively back up the road.

"Excuse me."

We turned toward the voice to see a casually-dressed young cheetah smiling at us, his wolf companion looking on. "Hi," Lightwing offered lightly, "welcome to Starhold. How can we help?"

Coming astride the cheetah, the wolf blinked at us. "This isn't Timewind?"

"It is," the Husky chuckled softly. "Starhold refers to the land and holdings; Timewind is our tribe. The sign at the road describes us more than the land, so..."

A soft, nervous chuckle from the wolf. "I guess I get that," he said.

The cheetah appeared embarrassed as he said, "I read about this place on line, and it's only a short detour on our trip, so I wanted to see it for myself. I'm an artist."

"Welcome to The Artisanry," Lightwing gestured to the building, still smiling. "I think you'll find it worth the side quest."

"I don't understand what is meant by 'tribe,'" the wolf continued. "It sounds sort of weird to me."

The cheetah nudged him with an elbow. "Galen, don't be rude."

"It's not rude at all," the Husky assured them. "The concept is unusual to many. It's also a lot to explain, and we have some business elsewhere. You're very welcome to ask some of the tribal members in the shop. Darkstar is just inside, Starshine in our greenhouse section, and Moonsong is in the back. She'd be glad to make a beverage for you while she talks about the tribe. She's one of the founding members, in fact."

"I've read a little of your *Tribal Manifesto* online," the cheetah continued. "It was really interesting. I've thought about it a lot, and I..." The fur on his cheeks colored a little. "I'm sorry. We're keeping you from your business. We'll talk to the others."

"It's quite all right. Thank you for your kindness," Lightwing acknowledged with a smile and a nod of her head. She then took up my arm again and led me back toward the garage.

We kept quiet for a little while, partly to make sure that the young males were out of earshot. I thought about the exchange and wondered why I thought it awkward. Everyone was reasonable, soft-spoken, yet something bothered me. It took very little time for the Husky to catch the whiff of confusion about me.

"Something bothering you, Max?"

I breathed sweet air softly, getting rid of glib answers. "Yes, although I don't know what. Or maybe..." She gave me several seconds to work it out. "I keep coming back to the use of the word 'rude.'"

"The wolf was calling it as he saw it, and I eased it back a notch. Is that what's bothering you, Max?" When I didn't answer after several seconds, she asked, "Did you think I was rude?"

Frankly, it felt like biting the paw that was feeding me; I also knew that she was going to get the truth out of me. "I've always felt that it was rude not to give others what they ask of you. The boss asks, so you do it; the spouse asks, so you do it; if you don't, in either situation, there's likely to be consequences." I could sense the heat of an embarrassed blush on my cheeks. "I feel like, if I hadn't been there, you'd have given all the time they needed to answer their questions."

She bumped up against me in comradely fashion. "That's two things, Max, but they're linked. The first is that it's not rude to tell someone that, in this instance, I have something else to do, but that there are others here who can help them. I get to go on my way, and they get the help they're looking for. That's a win-win.

"The other point is that you *were* there, and my first duty was to you. To us, if you want to make it out that way. If it had been just me, perhaps

I'd have given them a tour myself. It would be a pleasure to provide it, because I'm sort of wired that way. In this case, I am giving you the more personal tour of Starhold, telling you of Timewind, and that means I think of you first today. So I found another way to help them and, as I said, it's a win-win."

The argument was simple, sound, absolutely sensible. A thought occurred to me, and I smiled as I found myself taking a page from *The Tribal Manifesto*. "I'm going to ask for help. Can you help me understand why I think it's rude?"

Lightwing smiled one of those smiles that I'd grown so quickly to love from her. "Taking a clue from what you said a moment ago, I'd say that you'd been told that it's 'rude' to put your own needs above someone else's. You can always choose to put someone else's needs first, if you think it is beneficial to both of you, or even if you simply want to. If you *never* put your own needs first, you're making yourself a slave, without recourse, without getting your own needs met."

She stopped us, turned me toward her, placing a forepaw to my shoulder. "I'm gonna take a chance here, Max. In my experience, when I gave away all of my own power, my own needs, in favor of always putting others first, I was furious with my own life, angry at myself for letting others control me. I could never get anything done, never feel like I had time to make my life work. It was all about whatever I could do for others. It was all that made me feel valuable, because I didn't have a Me to value."

My eyes looked into hers, and that shade at my shoulder tried to make me turn away. It was no match for the connection I was feeling in that moment. "Bert. The would-be Medicine Worker."

"He was the worst of the batch, yes." She nodded. "Others can be more insidious — family, spouses, bosses, friends, neighbors, just about anyone." The Husky gave my shoulder a quick squeeze. "Remember that the opposite tack — thinking only of yourself — can cause even more grief and pain to the world and, ultimately, to yourself."

It was all too easy to think of examples of narcissists in history and in recent headlines; that point needed no hammering. "Finding a balance is, I take it, what you're suggesting."

"You learn quickly, Grasshopper." Her smile became a grin. "Not that I suggest you take that as your tribal name, if you want one."

"It would be a tough act to follow." I breathed more of the sweet air. "Any tips on how to figure out the balance point?"

She released my shoulder in favor of taking up my arm and continuing our walk toward the garage. "Calling it 'gut feelings' sounds too vague, but it's an indicator. How do you feel when someone asks you to do something? When you say, 'I don't mind,' do you feel that is true? If you feel taken advantage of, that's a good indicator that something's wrong. There are those people who seem to assume that you never have anything better to do than to cart them around, or listen to them complain, or just plain take up your time. Drawing your boundaries, finding the place where you get 'you time' instead of giving it all up to others... all are lessons from that non-existent Adulting 101 manual that none of us ever got a copy of."

"Is that what *The Tribal Manifesto* is? Adulting 101?"

Lightwing laughed loudly at that one, her ears up, her tail wagging with mirth. "Dreaming 101, maybe! Oh, we do toss in our bits of how we hope to treat one another. You may end up having to read it for yourself. The new edition is quite good, if we do say so ourselves. We took the focus back to the Three Steps to Becoming, with some of our personal stories about how we took our own first steps on that long, never-ending road."

"You forgot 'winding'," I smiled at her.

"I think McCartney and Lennon will forgive me." She shook her head gently. "No, there's no way to define 'adulting' accurately, like steps in a process. I think Starshine's idea might be the best of all: Let's Pretend. We can do it in both directions — imagine a perfect world, figure out how it got there, and take an action toward that goal; or look at the action you are considering taking now, and imagine the consequences down the line, for your own future and for world that it might build."

"Every choice making a different world, that sort of thing?"

"You've read your science fiction."

"Sliding Doors."

"Great movie. I love a good rom-com." The lovely Husky graced me with another smile. "A circumstance — whether or not you catch a particular train — might be called 'passive,' while making a choice is 'active.'

We don't always get much time to make a choice, like a few minutes ago. My choice was to follow the guides and ideas that I've already set for myself. I chose to help those two visitors, as best I could; I chose to be my best self by caring for myself and for you. I found the answer that made the win-win." She bumped me gently once again. "Shall I quit yammering and give you no more than fifteen seconds to reflect on all those choices that have made you feel bad over the years?"

I made a short, sharp bark of surprise over that one. "You'd make a great therapist."

"No. It's just that that's what I would probably do, and I have a feeling we're a lot alike."

"I'll take that as a compliment."

Even though I wasn't looking directly at her, the way that she lowered her head a little made me imagine that she was blushing. It was when I started to turn my thoughts back to those things she had suggested I'd probably think about that I became aware of a certain lightness around me. The sun was warm, the air crisp, the trees providing shade and that sense of sweet strength that forested areas seemed to exude... and no trace of that blackness that had been haunting me so persistently. The realization was as good as calling for a loyal non-sapient dog to come running up to meet me. With a genuinely benevolent dog, I would welcome him with open arms and joyful petting. With this black "dog," I made it sit a short distance from me and told it to stay there. I had no idea if it would work, but it was worth a try.

The deadline had narrowed to less than ten seconds, by my reckoning. I didn't even need that much time to find a good number of examples. I had long since been taught that growing older meant having more things to regret. The list of poor decisions seemed endless, and their sheer weight only added to the weight of that thing that had followed me here. With less than five seconds left, a few pawsful of incidents had risen to the surface of my mind, each fighting for the right to be called "worst" or "most dangerous," as if being singled out that way made them the Alpha of this pack of rabid creatures.

"Time's up," I heard her say, her grin taking any sting from it.

"Oh, poo; it was just getting into the big fight scene at the end."

"Too late; we're almost there."

I had thought we were already there. I heard movement in the garage, first seeing that all the windows of my car had been opened, then catching sight of Frank at the rear of the car. The tall mountain lion stood up at our approach and, after seeing who it was, seemed to steel himself to pad forward to meet us.

Doing my best to appear un-cop-like, I said, "Thanks again for the vacuuming out. I hope it wasn't too big a mess."

"Some wrappers and stuff went into the trash, but the seats and carpet seemed to shampoo fine. I can check the trunk, too, if that's okay."

"Only if you don't make fun of me for leaving the spare just laying there instead of being bolted down."

"I might even bolt it down for you." The big cat managed a smile. "Do I need a warrant to open it up?"

It felt good to smile back. "I consented. You're good." Extending a forepaw to him felt like a risk; I was glad to feel him shake it warmly. "Thank you, Frank."

"You're welcome, Max."

Lightwing took me gently by the shoulders and made to excuse us. "I thought I'd show him the Bunkhouse."

"Going back in time?" the mountain lion chided gently.

"It's good to know your roots, even though I wasn't there for the origins."

"I think it's good for Max to have the full tour." Frank's smile faltered for just a moment, and he looked away again for a moment before returning his eyes to mine. "Sorry about that," he said softly.

Equally softly, I asked, "Were you about to have a different opinion about Detective Luton?" Raising a forepaw gently toward him, I cut off his response by saying, "Truth told, Frank, maybe I'd have the same opinion about him. I hope I'm learning how to be Max again, and... well, thank you for giving me the chance."

His smile returned, more warmly, as he said, "Back atcha. Enjoy the tour."

"Thank you."

Lightwing nodded. "I'm going to take a moment to be proud of both of you." When the feline and I both turned blank expressions toward the Husky, her smile widened. "Give help, accept help? You two are becoming your best selves right before my eyes. As a Yorkshireman I knew once put it, 'Good on ye.'"

* * * * *

My guide led me past the garage and further down a graveled track into a small clearing. The "Bunkhouse," as she had called it, wasn't a rustic structure that might have featured in some film of the Old West. A Quonset hut can rarely be called "beautiful," but it can be immensely practical. The most familiar shape is half a tube cut longways and set on the ground; to prevent the edge areas from being nearly useless, this half-tube was set on walls not quite as high as my shoulders. It gave the rounded shape the feeling of a vaulted roof, and the double doors facing us seemed friendly, even more than merely practical.

Saving me from having to calculate distances, Lightwing provided details. "This is the structure that Rainmist was talking about last night. The building is 12x18 meters, and the kit for the exterior cost $12,000, at the time. To hear Oaknail tell it, he put in all the sweat equity by himself!"

"Does he really?"

"Only until Unicorn throws a pillow at him and talks about being the strong young stallion who was all but enslaved to do the heavy lifting. About that time, Moonsong and Rainmist start threatening head slaps all around, and everyone breaks down laughing."

I laughed as well, if only because I could envision it so easily. The entire scene was familial in the very best sense. I had to admit to feelings of envy and, breathing evenly for a moment, I put a gentle forepaw to Lightwing's arm. She turned her beautiful blue orbs to me and let them ask the question for her.

"Would you think it foolish of me to wish that I could have been there, to be part of an undertaking that created such a... well, family?"

"Oh, *hells* no!" she barked a laugh. "If I could have been there, at that age, with those amazing dreamers, to find out what it would be like to have built these first incredible pieces of the dream itself? Sign me up!" Her laughter mellowed a bit, and she held my gaze benevolently. "Instead, I found the tribe about ten years ago, then joined them properly about eight years ago, and I've been helping the dream grow in every way that I can ever since."

"You became part of the family."

"I did. They welcomed me, and I welcomed them, and there are plenty of stories that we've created together, and plenty more that they've told me about." She considered me again. "There's a quote I heard somewhere, and I'll mess it up... Something like, 'If you keep trying to face down the past, the future will sneak up behind you.' I think of it more on the lines of a really good book: There are chapters you'll want to reread, even share with others, but new chapters are always being created, so be sure to give them proper attention, too."

A smile crept onto my muzzle. "Darkstar would probably agree."

She nodded and turned toward the door, entering a code into the touchpad near it. A few beeps sounded, and she swung the door gently inward.

"Did the security system come with the kit?"

"Hardly!" Lightwing chuckled softly. "In those first days, I'm told, it was enough to have keys and a simple deadbolt, if necessary. It would have taken a pretty dedicated crook to track the tribe members down and penetrate this far into the woods. As the tribe grew larger, and tech grew cheaper and easier to put together, Firecat figured out how to wire it up so that we didn't have to carry sets of keys all over Starhold."

"Firecat?"

"Our electronics wizard. He joined us about the time that Darkstar did. The shared joke with those two is that they dragged the founders, kicking and screaming, the rest of the way into the 21st century."

"No 'Founders Pride' to fight back against that one?"

"Rainmist boasts that she joined when she was still finishing her high school classes, and that she was programming in C, whatever that means." The Husky smiled, shaking her head. "That's one area that I seem to have little head for. I'm fine using a program or an app; as for understanding how it works or how to crate something from scratch, I'm completely lost."

I looked at her blankly. "What's an 'app'?"

She blinked, until I let the smile start to grow. I was treated to a fine raspberry before she escorted me inside.

The space was hardly palatial, but it was big enough to make a good-sized dormitory for the newborn tribe. Things had to be different now than they were then; if nothing else, I had the feeling that some of the fixtures and furnishings I saw were too modern to have been part of the original configuration. The structure itself, however, was impressive enough. Horizontal casement windows were spaced along the length of the curved roof structure, just above the concrete wall; other windows were set into the ceiling to provide light from above. Between those, some built-in shelving made for storage of less-used items. The overall effect was something that felt spacious rather than cramped. I made a bet with myself that you could fit maybe five of Darkstar's room into this place; it would easily hold nine founding members, if they were the least bit friendly. With all that I'd seen, I took that as a given.

"I love visiting out here," Lightwing told me. "Almost the first thing that they installed was the indoor plumbing."

"No one would blame them. Actual showers, sinks, and toilets make any living situation more livable. Not to mention less stinky."

"A vital point."

"Was this here before as well?" I patted the door to a small, fully-enclosed space that had its own keypad, a small red light blinking periodically.

"Trust me; it wasn't."

Lightwing and I both turned toward the new voice. I recognized it from this morning, on the teleconference call that we all shared. The phone speaker robbed the hide-and-bone speaker of certain subtleties in timbre that filled in the cultured, even precise, speech. The stallion who stood before me needed no formal introduction, and my Husky guide did not provide one. I put forth a forepaw in greeting. "You are Unicorn, I presume."

"If you can see the horn already, perhaps you're more tribal than you think, Max." He took my paw in his own and held it rather than shook it. The smile on his muzzle was worthy of a benevolent mythical creature, and he had greeted me as Max, not as That Other Guy. I looked up into his eyes (he stood as close to 2m as made no odds), and they were a soft, reassuring amber that would set any client at ease. I'm not as good at identifying genetics of equines as I am of canines (Heartsinger notwithstanding), but I'd have bet on palomino, given the cream of his coat and his amazing white-gold mane. His clothing was contemporary casual, and it was clear that he'd just arrived back home. I imagine that he had his own tribal garb that he would likely feel more comfortable in.

"Lightwing was showing me what she called the Bunkhouse."

"And so it is. Has she told you the tall tales of our beginnings with this building?"

"We'd only just arrived."

His smile grew larger. "Then allow me the privilege of escorting you back in time." He leaned forward, conspiratorially. "It's my favorite magical power."

18: Bunkhouse Stories

"I thought you were out of town for the weekend," I said, "not that it's not good to meet you."

The stallion's smile never wavered. "Not that far out of town, and I very much wanted to meet you as well. After I parked my car, I saw Frank in the garage, and he told me that you two had headed in this direction, so I followed on."

"I'm glad you did," Lightwing told him. "You can tell the stories better than I can."

"The advantages of having lived through them, treasured them, and embellished them so lovingly over the years."

"Stories need time to marinate properly, seems to me," I said. "After all these years, I can revamp my high school days into something survivable."

"Good stories?"

"You wouldn't believe who I asked out for prom night."

"How did that story turn out?"

"In my revised version, she still didn't go out with me, but at least she didn't laugh in my face." I held up a placating forepaw. "Not a good example; sorry. My insecurities showing through."

"You weren't the only one, Max." The stallion actually enacted the cliché of rubbing the back of his long neck. "High school is its own morass of class systems. In fact..." He paused and shook his head. "Remind me later. Let's go back to a time just past my own high school years, and I'll tell you about a group of crazies who actually decided to make a dream happen."

Unicorn waved us toward a comfortable sitting area about halfway down the length of the building. I took up part of the sofa, Lightwing a discreet distance from me, and the stallion himself in a large recliner that he kicked up to its first position, to put his hooves up. He smiled at me again. "No, this wasn't here in the beginning, either!"

Chuckling, I said, "I get the idea that the first thing to be installed was the plumbing."

"A complete accounting would get boring quickly, so let me offer a few highlights. Running rural electric out here cost a packet, as did the costs of finding an artesian well we were assured lay under here somewhere. It did, at exactly 114.6 meters down. We kept a small sample of the gravel and stones brought up from that depth, so when you see the jar marked '114.6', you'll know what it is!

"Once we had water and electric ready to go, we were able to start bidding for the Quonset hut design and kit. Don't ask about the financing; that's a headache for another discussion. Anyway, we worked out where to put everything, got basic pipes and a septic tank in, had the slab poured, got the concrete walls set up, put the cap on the beastie, yadda yadda yadda, and we eventually got potties." His grin widened. "See how much smoother that tale has become over time?"

"Perfect," I grinned back. "What was it like, having reasonable comforts at long last?"

"We celebrated with a ceremonial First Flush, one for each toilet. After that, we chivalrous males let the females get first call. After all, we could still go out and mark the bushes more easily than they could."

"Honorable knights, one and all!" I cheered. "Moonsong was saying that was, what, summer of 1995?"

The palomino nodded. "We satisfied the legalities for the tribe by November 1994, planned studiously through the winter, got started in the early spring, built up each step over the summer. By late autumn, we had a good chunk of this place year-round livable. It took a little while for us to learn various cold-proofing secrets, but by the second winter here, the only real issues we had were accommodations for our various vehicles. We learned the hard way about getting stuck up here, about provisions, keeping the pipes warm, being careful with use of butane... we had a tank for emergencies, if the electric went out. There are a few permanently-fitted camp lanterns here, for light, and a small furnace for some heat. It was a gamble at every level, and we dedicated ourselves to seeing it through."

He gestured in various directions as he spoke. "We had everything from camp cots to futons, to start with. Camp kitchen over there, a nearby cold chest, pantry. We rigged partitions to help keep heat in sleeping areas, in the winters, taking them down to get the best cross-breezes for the other seasons. In some ways, it was luxurious; in other ways, more like roughing it as we got other things together. We still kept that one rental house in town, and we rented another space to sell what goods we could put together — ceramics, metalwork, textiles, and so forth. None of it happened overnight. It sometimes feels like it."

"Is there a history of the tribe's progress? Seems like it would make some fascinating and entertaining reading."

"Darkstar has taken it on himself to get as much oral history as he can piece together. He's good at getting us to talk, pick our brain for memories. Some of it would make great melodrama, like the time that we got ourselves stuck up here during a big snow, that first winter in the bunkhouse. That would have been late February 1996. We were lucky to keep the power going, and Oaknail had the foresight to learn how to work a ham radio. This was before cell phones were so easily affordable, and anyway, there wasn't a decently-working tower out here until maybe fifteen years ago. We ran a land line to the bunkhouse, but even that failed us during that winter storm.

"It was me, Oaknail, Moonsong, and Rainmist, unable to get a car down the drive and to the main road. Airdancer was in his second semester at law school, and Stormsinger, Riverrunner, Quicksilver, and Phoenix were all safely in the rental house. It was sort of an experiment, with the four of us here to see how well the place would hold up during a winter storm; we just had no idea how bad the storm would be."

"Clearly, you all survived," I observed, feeling slightly feverish in spite of what had to have been a good outcome.

"We had a few safeguards in place, including regular check-ins by radio. We figured out that, given the vehicles we had at the time, a good 25-30cm of snow would pretty well keep us stuck up here. We got just shy of 50cm during that storm." The stallion smiled ruefully. "It got us thinking about reallocating some funds pretty quickly, just to have at least one vehicle to get us out of here, if needed. Happily, the snowfall doesn't usually get so high. We probably would have made it without help, but the four of us were grateful to get a respite after only three days. Phoenix knew someone with a sturdy ATV, and the two of them brought supplies and some goodies for us. Rainmist had gotten more cabin-feverish than the rest of us, so Phoenix let her go back with the guy in the ATV. After another two days, the weather shifted enough for us to hire someone who had a good 4x4 truck with a snow plow on it. We won the record for the longest drive he'd ever cleared."

"No argument!" Chuckling softly, I said, "Tell me one good memory and one bad memory from that experience."

Unicorn raised an eyebrow at me. "What made you come up with that?"

"*Same Time Next Year.* Great movie."

"Not bad! Something to put into the history." The stallion considered for a moment, then nodded, smiling. "A good memory would have to be the furpiles, especially with Phoenix in the mix. He's a panda, and he's a great cuddler. We joked that, with Oaknail and Moonsong, and the color of my mane, we were role-playing 'Goldilocks and the Three Bears.' The warmth of those winter evenings was juuuuust right."

Lightwing must not have heard that story before; she was laughing as much as I was. "And the bad memory?"

"Let's just say that it was years before I ever wanted to play Monopoly again."

The Husky barked another laugh. "That was the only game you had up here?"

"Something else we fixed! Phoenix brought up Pente, some dice to play Farkle with, and a few decks of cards, which helped a lot. After that, the cupboards got filled with all kinds of games."

I jerked a chin toward the locked space near the front of the bunkhouse. "Is that what's in there?"

"No," the stallion said softly. "That's where my private files are kept. I trust everyone here, and they also know that the rest of the world would want tangible reassurances that confidential material is kept confidential. I have a desk there," he nodded toward the space this side of the enclosure, "so that I don't have to work in the dark. It helps to keep workspace and homespace separate."

"Like that conference room in the house," I nodded. "Do you work from here, then?"

"I have a small office in town, with hours by appointment. I don't put on much of a front. I don't work in that sort of law."

"Conveyance work?"

"That, and other things that don't require a courtroom."

That brought a chuckle out of me. "Lightwing said that you're afraid you might not be able to keep a civil tone when needed."

"Too true!" Unicorn offered a self-deprecating laugh. "I'm not always successful at keeping my tongue behind my teeth when I need to. Paperwork doesn't talk back."

"Not until another attorney does."

"Point taken."

He paused then, regarding me carefully. I didn't feel scrutinized, despite that general sense of paranoia that had plagued me earlier. Something more like "considered," perhaps. I wasn't sure just what he was looking at, what he was considering. I wasn't even sure if it made me uncomfortable. So much about me had been changing that I couldn't be sure how to react. I didn't have much time to wonder, as he was quiet only for a few seconds that felt much longer.

"Max, I'd said on the phone that I wanted you to have time to discover yourself, not to have to deal with Detective Luton for another day or so. I don't want to go back on my word..."

I nodded slowly. "There's something you need to ask him."

"Yes."

Breathing in carefully, I exhaled slowly before saying, "Who's asking?"

His eyes asked the question, and Lightwing spoke up. "Is it Unicorn who's asking, or is it Ezequiel?"

He took a moment to get the idea clear in his head, then said, "A little of both, but mostly Unicorn. I don't think that there's anything that has any legal bearing. I knew Airdancer, or I thought I did. He was a mentor, and he and I were founders of this tribe, yet he..." The stallion paused, regaining himself. "I feel that I need to know what happened, what you saw, everything you put together. That means I need to hear from Detective Luton... and that feels like I'm betraying your trust, when we've only just met one another."

Words new to me until this weekend came bubbling up without effort. "Help others, as best you can, in their work to be their best selves." I smiled ruefully. "I may have garbled that a bit."

Lightwing gave me the barest punch to my upper arm. "No need for perfection. You have the spirit of it, and in record time."

Unicorn's gaze became warmer. "How may I help you in return, Max?"

"By listening, maybe hearing something that I'm not telling myself, helping me face it."

He nodded. "I can do that."

I turned to the Husky, not quite daring to reach out for her forepaw. "It's not a pretty story. Would you rather not stay for it?"

"Four ears are better than two. And I still owe that soul-consuming thing inside you a proper ass-kicking."

"As you have no doubt discovered," the stallion observed quietly, "Lightwing is not easily deterred."

"Or frightened." I regarded each with a soft smile. "Okay. Once more, from the top."

* * * * *

The telling took quite a while. Unlike the famous "just the facts" detective, my narrative was filled with recollections of details and emotions, which was exactly what Unicorn said he wanted. He didn't intrude so much as guide my recollections, my impressions, getting me to reveal more about the scene, about Glover's life, about what had happened to Airdancer, and what all this meant to me and my own journey to Timewind. The stallion only made the suggestions a few times, at the beginning, and the rest came forth as if I were actually a storyteller instead of a tired old cop. Maybe that was more Max coming out, as if I were recounting the tale from somewhere outside of Detective Luton. It didn't hurt, which surprised me. It was actually more of a relief than anything else.

Although the assembled tribe had heard the essential information, only these two had followed me down those twisting mental corridors that had actually brought me here. Lightwing had shed a tear, and even Unicorn was clearly moved. I wasn't able to let go, not that far, but it was a near thing.

Several moments of quiet lay between us before I asked, "Did you find the answers you were looking for?"

Another pause, and he nodded. The stallion returned the chair to its ordinary position, leaned forward, arms on his knees. "You saw Thomas clearly, even sympathetically. He let go of the dream. Given what he went through, I'm not all that surprised. Perhaps if we had been there to help him..." He sighed, raised a forepaw. "And he could have reached out to us. If we're looking for blame, there's plenty to go around."

"Don't do that to yourself," Lightwing chastised softly. "It's not about placing blame."

Unicorn acknowledged her with a smile. "Causes are factual; blame is about guilt, whether real or imagined. And it's why we keep reminding each other. Thank you, Lightwing."

"Am I hearing something from the Manifesto?" I asked.

"Part of why we call it a dream." The Husky favored me with a smile of her own. "So-called 'reality' keeps intruding. We're taught blame and guilt from an early age. How young were you when someone told you that something was 'your fault,' and inflicted all the shame that went along with that judgment?"

The idea was all too easily relatable. It was, to make an ironic observation, our collective "default" mode. Any issue is treated less as something to be rectified and more as a way to find a scapegoat and avoid responsibility. To be *responsible* was to invite punishment; the problem itself might never be fixed, but at least the *responsible party* was made to suffer, and everyone else gets to feel the self-righteous satisfaction that they weren't *at fault*.

"Does that mean..." I began.

"It only means," Unicorn interrupted me gently, "that I can accept what I did or didn't do, in this instance, and not wallow in guilt or self-recrimination. I can't change the past, and there's little I can do to make amends; I can only learn from it and move on."

"Is it really that easy?"

"Oh, *hells* no!" He offered a weak smile. "But I can keep trying. That's all any of us can do, and that's why it takes so many of us to create one of us."

"By reminding each other." I felt myself understanding the idea more clearly. "The path to Becoming can't be made alone."

"It really can't," Lightwing said. "We need others to help us remember the best of us, or we'll get mired in the worst of us."

"That's what your journey here has told me of Thomas." Unicorn's eyes were thanking me. "His time in the public defender's office worked against him. He went in, alive with the dream, with hope in his heart, with the sword of justice in his forepaw, and then everything started falling in on itself. He began to see the worst of himself reflected in others, whether it be the clients who the police insist must be guilty, or the prosecutors who reduce justice to a bidding war. The failure of that system became all that he could see, until he broke away into something else, hoping to find himself there. His strength in understanding real estate gave him a different focus. He created a version of himself that he could live with, insulated from everything else, and he surrounded himself with others who reflected that back to him — work, spouse, family, acquaintances, in a nicely-arranged package."

"He forgot you," I said. "He forgot all of this."

"He never *saw* all of this. He had visited the bunkhouse that summer, had even helped to build it, before his law school days, and then never came back, pleading trying to get the degree done quickly, working through summers, pushing ever forward. He fell out of regular communication, eventually, and we became a dangerous group of optimists, out of touch with the Real World. We're still on government watch lists, the type that people in his brave new real estate world would consider suspicious if not criminal. It's part of how you found us, after all." The stallion sat back in his chair. "Ultimately, he found himself at that squatters' campsite, and that was what finally broke through those false mirrors that he had been staring into. Except that he didn't really see the squatters at all."

"What he saw..."

"...was what he expected to see." Unicorn nodded at me. "You were right, Max: He saw the squatters, saw what they had failed to accomplish, and he found himself fearing that the dream he had helped to found had failed as well. At the very least, he felt that he had lost the dream."

"He never contacted any of you?"

"It would have been easy for him to find us, through our given names, through Timewind's website or social media pages... but no, he never contacted us."

"He felt that he couldn't come back, even though it was here. He..." The suicide note blossomed in my mind. "I have betrayed us," I quoted.

"And he took the blame for it," Lightwing whispered into the quiet. "He took on the guilt, and he punished himself."

"Max," the stallion said softly, "you asked me to tell you what I might hear in your narrative. Tell me first what you hear."

"I think you know."

"Tell us. Tell yourself."

For a moment, I had a sense of that damnable spook or whatever it was, hovering somewhere near the sofa, or poking into other places in the bunkhouse, as if looking for somewhere to call home. I had called it an Idea, or Glover's shade, or anything else to make it as distant from me as possible. It wasn't part of me, not my idea or my Idea, and I didn't want it, and I wanted to yell at it, scream curses at it, throw grenades at it, whatever it took to destroy it, to destroy it utterly...

As if of its own accord, my forepaw reached out to find Lightwing's, and she didn't hesitate. I felt her squeeze me, and it helped to push down the sense of panic but not the thing itself, that black thing. It was still there.

"Max." Unicorn was leaning toward me again, his voice low and quiet. "It's not an illusion, not a fantasy. It's also not what you think it is. I trust Stellamara's intuition, because she's seen it before. I want you to trust us. Can you do that?"

Slowly, I nodded. "What do you want me to do?"

"No mystic rituals or spellcasting." The stallion smiled with great affection. "More like dubious psychotherapy, but it will at least help. What does it feel like?"

"Lightwing asked me to name the feeling when we had tea this morning. 'Terrified.'"

"That's what it makes you feel. What does this thing actually feel like? Can you describe it?"

Hovering. Slithering. Grasping. Clinging. "It's like a physical thing, sometimes. A weight, or something shifting around my shoulders." I felt my fur bristle, not quite settling down afterward. "It... sneaks. I don't notice it until it's... well, there, like it's in front of me, or slithering around me. Then it won't go away."

"This isn't a new feeling, is it?"

"Not really. It keeps sneaking in, once in a while. Keeps trying to come back."

"What keeps it down?"

"Yelling at it. Cursing it. Putting up blocks against it."

"Does that stop it?"

"For a while."

"Does yelling at it keep it in your head?"

My brow furrowed enough to feel painful. "What do you mean?"

"Using up all that energy. The feeling stays with you. It's feeding on that negativity and sticks around."

"What..."

"Breathe," said Lightwing.

I knew what she meant, and I took a good solid breath. I gave her forepaw a grateful squeeze.

"It was worse this time," Unicorn said. "Can you tell me what made it worse?"

"Glover," I replied, almost without having to think about it. "The more I learned about him, his life, the sense of hopelessness that led to him killing himself... and the sword. Albion. From the start, I knew it was a symbol, something so intensely important that he held on to it even as he ended his life. It felt as if..." I turned to look at the Husky who still held my forepaw so strongly. "You said it. Taking on the guilt. Punishing himself."

She nodded. "You felt that about him."

"Yes, I could feel it. See it. All around him was wealth and status, the trappings of success in all areas of his life, but he still killed himself."

I took another breath, pushing down the fear as best I could, because I was safe here, Lightwing made it safe, Unicorn made it safe, and maybe even Max made it safe. In a swift recounting, I watched Detective Luton working through the crime scene, through interviews, through clues and reports.

"I had to know why."

"Why he killed himself?" the stallion asked softly.

"Why I didn't. If everything wasn't enough, how could nothing make up for it?"

"What does 'nothing' mean here, Max?" His warm amber eyes held me gently, not accusing, just asking to understand. "Can you tell us?"

"Feels like nothing."

He nodded. "Tell us what feels like nothing."

I felt my own head bobbing, following his lead. "The work, the hours, the relentlessness of it. Always more cases, more bodies, so meaningless. The endless stream of death and destruction, for stupid reasons, or no reason at all. Loneliness. Empty house, empty life. No one there. No one home."

"No one?"

That wasn't true. "Michael."

"His pup," Lightwing supplied.

"He's his own dog now," I told them. "He used to think I called him 'pup' to belittle him. I didn't mean it that way. Finally understood it, worked that out with him."

"You're close."

"Well... maybe."

I told them about his youth, his growing, his making something of himself that he's proud of. I told them about his tea shop, and Unicorn smiled at the name of it. I told them of the phone call, how he worried that this case might be too much for me, even though I didn't go into too much detail about it. I told them that he wanted me to come visit, get a good cup of tea, to relax a while.

Lightwing gave my forepaw a squeeze, a soft smile on her sweet muzzle. "At least you got some tea here."

"More than that." The smile that I returned to her wasn't exactly discreet, and I started blushing. I looked guiltily to Unicorn, whose benevolent gaze didn't falter for a moment.

"Keep going, Max," he said softly. "Look at Thomas' life again. He had everything, you said?"

The sword, I thought strangely. In his final moment, he had gripped Albion with his right paw, his true paw, as if to find strength... to kill himself? That didn't feel right. The note. *I have betrayed us.* Death was his atonement, his payment of the capital crime of betraying...

I breathed again and, heedless of my own inhibitions, I raised Lightwing's forepaw to my lips and kissed it. Turning back to the stallion, I favored him with as warm a smile as I knew how to give.

"He didn't have this. Someone to help him become."

"He became someone, though, didn't he?"

That was not the response I had expected. I blinked, and that specter tried to make itself known again. It was smaller than I remembered, not as close to me now. It was a more strange, less frightening form, like a lost child, if demons ever lost their children. The darkness of it was a feeling, not something I could actually see. Something about it was familiar, yet not something I could identify.

"I'm going to invoke a little hoodoo on you, Max." Unicorn smiled at me. "There's a psychological and metaphysical truism that says that your reality is what you think it is. If you're in a bad mood, everything seems to go wrong; if you're in a good mood, things aren't so bad. Nothing has changed other than your perception. If you keep seeing that specter, it stays with you."

"I keep trying to battle it, hurt it, get rid of it!"

"That's another form of giving it your attention. It's still there. That's how it works, how it keeps you trapped. You become what you focus on."

Another breath gave me time to think about what the stallion had said. "That sounds really simplistic."

"It is, my friend. So simple that it's overlooked, or else it's turned into some New Age 'secret' cure-all that will actually solve problems. Trust me: It won't solve them. With support, though, it will probably help you find solutions."

"Support?"

"Yes." Lightwing squeezed my forepaw again. "We're back to the Three Steps to Becoming. I truly feel that it's impossible for someone to become her best self on her own; it's far more likely to happen with the support of others."

"So," the stallion leaned toward me, "choose those others wisely. If you don't know who you want to become, you'll probably become someone else."

The breath I took came out as more of a sigh than I had intended it to, but my companions didn't seem to mind. They both smiled at me. I had the feeling that they understood what my sigh had been about.

"Ain't cured, am I?"

"Nope," Unicorn agreed, his amber eyes giving me all their warmth. "That's gonna take a while, and a lot of work. You don't have to do it alone. Probably better if you don't. The good news? You get to be Max again."

"For today, at least."

"That's the day that matters. Another cliché, that 'one day at a time' thing. Trite, but true." The stallion clapped his forepaws and rubbed them together, grinning. "Okay then. Enough work for the morning. Anyone want lunch? I'm starved."

"You should have enjoyed Heartsinger's breakfast." I grinned a little at the horse's groan. He clearly knew what he had missed.

"Meanwhile," Lightwing announced, rising, "I propose we go raid the kitchen. Lunch is 'catch as catch can' around here," she explained.

"That can be fun," I allowed. Unicorn and I stood with her, making our way toward the door. "Afterward, we can play Monopoly."

I think the sound the stallion made is called a "horse laugh," but it didn't sound like laughing to me.

19: Watercourse Way

As the three of us moved toward the front door, I took long, lingering looks at the bunkhouse, wondering, dreaming, thinking of what it might have been like, perhaps even wondering what it might be like now. The main house seemed palatial by comparison; was it better? I paused near the door, taking in the size of this place, its limitations along with its sense of closeness. I noticed for the first time that a ladder had been constructed near the door, leading to a loft, fashioned as an oversized safety-railed bed, where one might curl up with a good book or a friend who's read one.

"Max?" Lightwing moved quietly to my side. "Anything wrong?"

"I think I'm feeling a little overwhelmed. This place..." I shook my head gently. "You know the expression, 'If these walls could talk'? Maybe they can, or maybe it's just my own sense of..." Whatever the word was, it wasn't making itself known.

"What is it that you imagine, Max?" Unicorn had also come back for me, and his voice and manner was soft, caring.

"That winter that you described. That's part of it, anyway. Imagining this space being the entire world for four young dreamers who had committed themselves to making those dreams happen, and those days and nights in summer, where everything began to grow, literally and figuratively. It's all so very..." Slowly, a word rose in my throat, along with what could have been a sob. "...connected."

The stallion had placed a forepaw to my shoulder, gently, but he said nothing, giving me time to breathe, no demands on me.

Until his stomach rumbled.

All three of us laughed, me loudest of all. He tried to apologize through his chuckling, but I waved him off. "Greetings from the Department of the Interior," I quipped, wiping away a tear from the sheer perfection of the moment.

"Are you okay, Max?"

"We can talk while we lunch," I said. "And yes, I think I'm okay."

"I think you're doing just fine." Lightwing smiled at me and again took my arm, leading me outside. Unicorn closed the door to the bunkhouse, and I took another moment to appreciate the air. The stallion smiled at me.

"You look like someone who hasn't breathed before."

"Maybe I just haven't appreciated it. It's always nice, in a forested area. That whole thing about trees making oxygen. I have a second-grader's understanding of it, but I've always felt that there's better air in the country."

"The rain helped, too. Everything's freshened today."

He offered a smile that included Lightwing, and I felt myself starting to blush again. That was all on me. The look was not leering, not suggestive, just happy, companionable. There was another emotion there as well, but I couldn't quite put my finger on it. In truth, there were any number of emotions roiling in me in those moments, and I didn't know how to handle them all, what to think of them all. I didn't feel overwhelmed, exactly, but... was "whelmed" a word? Maybe I wasn't overly-whelmed, just sort of whelmed? It was a question for Darkstar, if I could remember to ask it.

Frank had apparently left the garage while we were in the bunkhouse. I had thought that we might invite him to join us for lunch. I told Unicorn about the mountain lion's help in getting my car cared for after its time in the water, and about my attempts at détente. The stallion nodded at my description of the feline as "passionate."

"It's his strength and his curse, I think." Unicorn had slowed his pace a bit for me, as his long legs could outwalk me at any distance. "I've gotten to know him during his time here with Dreamweaver. She met him sometime last year, in the spring, I think, and he came to meet us at our Thanksgiving dinner. He was nervous, somewhere between the 'meeting the family' and 'date for the event' kind of thing." The horse smiled, again with fondness more than anything else. "The kit was worried what we'd think of him staying the night with Dreamweaver, and he was surprised at our being so accepting. We seem to be winning him over, bit by bit.

"His reaction to you being a police detective is not surprising. He's had his share of being hassled, and he even once was falsely arrested, which has caused him no end of problems. Because of that incident, he has a record, technically speaking, even though everything was dropped."

Another head-shake from me. "Computers are lightning fast; the people who use them aren't always so quick, nor thorough. Any record, even a false one, is seen as leverage, something to be kept back and used if they need information. Even those who aren't part of that element get hassled. I've seen it happen too many times."

My moments of quiet caused Lightwing to say, "You're not like that, Max."

"I hope I'm not," I said. "I can see why Frank is still angry. Job applications, loans, insurance, housing... any blip on capitalist radar can shut you out from the start." I glanced at Unicorn. "Anything you can do?"

"Any member of the bar can make enquiries on behalf of a client, and the titles look good on a letterhead. So far, the letters seem to fall on deaf ears. Forgive me if I sound bitter: It's something Thomas would have had better luck with, when he was still a public defender. He would be known in the courts and official offices, including police departments. I'm more of an outsider, with no particular reputation in those circles."

I looked to him, then Nightwing, then simply nodded. For once, I didn't feel that I had to state the obvious.

* * * * *

Back at the house, I made the late discovery that there were no clocks that I could see in the common areas. My stomach told me that it was half-past hungry, but I had no idea what time it was. The notion disturbed me. The world is run by clocks, for everyone to be on the same schedule, for jobs, for meetings, for everything. Even the Artisanry had posted hours, somewhere, and there had to be some way of keeping track of when to be there, when to close. No one wore watches, not that I'd noticed. Did Timewind not keep time?

The three of us had trooped into the kitchen, at this point, and I noticed the most universal clock of modern times. The readout on the microwave oven read 1:27, which certainly explained why I was so hungry. I had spent more time talking, back at the bunkhouse, than I had realized.

Lightwing waved her arms around the space. "Who wants what? Max, I can suggest anything from soup and sandwich to convenience foods nuked to your preference."

"I don't mean to be greedy, but is there any of Rainmist's stew left?"

Unicorn turned wide eyes to me and the Husky. "Rainmist made stew?"

Chuckling, Lightwing moved toward the refrigerator. "I think we have a winner!"

We kept the conversation simple as Lightwing prepared a generous amount of the stew in a pot and Unicorn fetched bowls and spoons. With a bit of guidance, I found glasses for us, and all elected for water, to keep things simple. In little time, we took our steaming repast back into the dining hall, a space that once again felt warm to me. Perhaps it was the stew, linking me back to the camaraderie of the night before, or simply that I had gotten past the morning's revelations and yet was still welcomed by the tribe. The sensation continued to feel new to me — welcomed, accepted, even wanted. I couldn't remember the last time I'd felt this way, and it was strangely intoxicating.

I wondered (this time, with an inner smile) if Lightwing had doctored the tea after all.

By the time we'd transferred the contents of the bowls safely to our bellies, I pondered what we might do with the rest of the day, discovering that I didn't much care, as long as I could continue sharing this wonderful company.

"Isn't there a word for that feeling of being sleepy after a good meal?" I asked.

"I'm sure Darkstar could tell you," Unicorn chuckled softly. "He is quite the word maven. I'm sure that lawyers are considered word-stretchers, but I do try not to make my words contort themselves too much."

"You are as rare as your horn, good sir."

Our laughter was joined by one more, as I noticed Heartsinger had come into the hall. The tall Borzhvolk seemed to tower over us, from our sitting positions yet, as before, he remained a gentle and comforting presence. It would be cliché to equate his white fur with depictions of angels in white robes, but I did have that fleeting comparison cross my mind.

"Have you had lunch?" Lightwing asked, with a smile. "We just might have some stew left."

"I've had something light," he replied, the faint hint of a blush showing at the tops of his cheeks. "I ate a good bit of my own cooking this morning."

"And why shouldn't you?" the stallion asked, grinning. "I'm sorry I missed it."

"The perils of leaving home," the Husky chuckled as she rose from her seat. "I don't think these dishes will wash themselves."

"Let me help," I offered, gathering the various paraphernalia into stacks. "Many paws, after all."

"Actually..." Heartsinger paused, the blush increasing beyond the level of mere hint. "Max, may I talk with you?"

Unicorn rose and nodded. "Lightwing and I can take care of these. You two go ahead."

I stood, looking into the wolf's golden eyes, feeling again that sense of welcome, of openness, and of that desire I first felt from him in the barn last night, to bypass the trivial and talk of things that are important, between friends. I still mistrusted the word "intimacy," because that only means sex, right? The dictionary and my experience were probably at odds with each other. I hesitated just long enough that I had the clear sense of Heartsinger's eyes begging me. I had no idea what could have caused the intensity of emotion that I sensed, but the message wasn't lost. I pulled up a smile from somewhere, finding it as sincere as the words I spoke.

"I'd like that."

* * * * *

Out through the front doors, the white wolf led me around the side of the house again, toward the barn. I had first thought that he might be taking me to meet some of the non-sapient horses that he took such good care of; it would be familiar territory for him, physically and emotionally, which might make it easier for him to talk. However, we veered away from it, down a rough-hewn path through the trees and into the deep quiet of the forest. Not paved (that, I felt, would be a sacrilege to this beautiful land), the path bore the marks of many hindpaws, and the edges along the way appeared to have been carefully cleared and tended. It was a delicate sort of surgery, creating a space where one could pad through single-file without feeling cramped or lost. The local wildlife would not have been greatly disturbed. The word *cooperation* floated gently in my head as I followed Heartsinger through the trees in silence.

Lightwing's instructions from this morning returned to me, this time with gentle amusement. Birdsong was prevalent here too, along with the occasional rustlings in the distant wood. Non-sapient squirrels, foxes, deer, and other beings did not seem to mind sharing their space with the inhabitants of Starhold. From what I could estimate, some huge amount of the land was still unaffected by change or development. Now, *sanctuary* came to mind, and not just for the wildlife.

The path ended in a small space cleared mostly by the creek that ran through the property and partially by more of the careful clearing like that I'd already seen. It was unlikely that the logs I saw nearby had fallen there naturally, especially not with such neatly sawn-off edges. The effect was to make these natural benches for two-legged beasties like ourselves as unobtrusive to the setting as possible. Heartsinger stopped and turned toward me, his arms at his side, the look in his golden eyes still warm, yet now the warmth was tinged with pain.

My experience was telling me to say something, perhaps about the beauty of this place, or even something like, *So, what did you want to talk about?* The old formulas didn't work, the usual ways of interacting didn't feel right. I waited.

"Max," the Borzhvolk's voice a shaky imitation of itself, "may I hug you?"

Spreading my arms toward him, I replied, "I think you need to."

He was too graceful for me to say that he collided into me, yet he had himself pressed up against me so rapidly that I felt no intervening time at all. He rested his chin on my shoulder, holding me close, and I wrapped my arms around him and held him as tightly as he held me. Parts of my mind tried to bring up the fear of catching the gay, even as other parts tried to insist that I didn't even know if he was gay, and yet more parts insisting that

I shouldn't take the chance. All were pushed aside when I heard the soft sobbing in my ear, felt the hitching in his chest. I sensed something from him, like a wave of emotion, wondering how that was even possible. How could I feel someone else's emotions? What was going on?

A memory of Lightwing, of her letting me cry last night, stilled all other thoughts, and I let myself just hold him, waiting until he was ready to talk.

It didn't take long, perhaps a minute, no more. I just held him, waiting patiently, occasionally petting the thick ruff of his headfur, feeling fraternal, or paternal, or something that let me feel "properly" connected to him. I was still unsure about all this, but I did feel sure that he needed to cry, for whatever reason, and he had chosen me to help him. He regained his breathing and pulled a little distance away from me, his tear-filled eyes looking at me. For a moment, I had the feeling that he wanted to kiss me, and I tensed a bit. The slightest smile appeared on his muzzle as he shook his head gently. He lowered his forehead down to rest it upon my chest, just below the shoulder. I reached up to pet the back of his neck, wondering if I had hurt him.

When he raised his head, he looked at me again, his eyes more clear, his smile the very smallest bit larger. "Come sit with me," he said indicating one of the logs.

Straddling it, we faced each other, and he reached out a forepaw to me. I took it, and he squeezed mine gently. "I'm sorry, Max."

"For crying?"

"For your pain."

I felt my eyebrows try yet again to take residence in my headfur. "What..." I began. Another squeeze from his forepaw signaled me to let him speak.

"Stellamara came to see me, a few hours ago. She is far more sensitive than I am, but I share with her a milder version of her gift. We find comfort with each other, sharing our fur sometimes, just to take moments of quiet with someone who can sense these things." His laugh was shy, a little self-deprecating. "I'm not sure if I'm being clear. I only mean to say that she and I sometimes communicate with emotions more than words, and we can still understand each other. It's its own language, in a way.

"The point is that we both felt how much it hurt you, to tell us everything this morning. Stellamara saw how it affected me, and she told me to come find you, to talk to you, to ask if I could help you." Again, the shy smile. "The *Manifesto* strikes again."

It was my turn to chuckle. "It does keep coming back to that. Maybe that's a good thing." I returned the squeeze of his forepaw, hesitating, avoiding. Looking around, I brought out the words that would give me just a little more time. "It's beautiful here."

"One of my favorite places on the whole property. The trees, the space, the sound of the creek. It's why I wanted to share it with you, Max. The flow of the creek helps to quiet the mind and open up the heart. I find it cleansing. Reminds me to go with the flow." The Borzhvolk's chuckle even sounded like the creek. "I'm trying too hard, aren't I?"

I laughed softly, giving his forepaw a little shake with my own. "I probably need it. I'm still learning, Heartsinger, and I'm not sure what to do. You've said something huge: You were crying because of my pain. Do you mean I have hurt you? I certainly didn't mean to..."

He shook his head quickly. "No. It means that I felt your pain. I felt how much it's hurt you — finding Airdancer, finding us, finding how much the darkness has been affecting you. Through all of this, you have come to us with only the best of intentions, the best of yourself that you could offer us. You told us that you were fighting that darkness." He paused, looking deep into my eyes. "I share that emotion with you."

My understanding did not come from my brain, but from my gut. "Would you tell me?" When he hesitated, I said, "If it will help you... tell me."

Gently, he released my forepaw and hunched over, as if protecting himself. "I am never quite sure how or where to begin with a story like this. In my 34 years, I've gone through a lot. To me, of course, all of it is important, relevant. Trying to get to the points that will help you understand what I think we share, that's difficult to summarize. Darkstar is better with words, and he..."

The wolf nodded then. "He's where to start. We found each other about ten years ago, and it didn't take me long to realize that Timewind would... I hate to say 'save me,' because that sounds so melodramatic. It's also more true than not." He offered a self-deprecating little snort. "Okay. I'll tell it, and you decide.

"My journey here began with meeting Darkstar at a small independent coffee house not all that far from here. We had seen each other there several times, each of us usually with his muzzle in a book. He asked me what I was reading, explained that it was because he was a writer, and conversation started. We started making actual coffee dates, and our friendship grew from there. He learned about my work in ceramics, and he asked to see it. I took him to a small shop where I had several pieces on display, and he began to speak of the Artisanry. At that time, Timewind had a shop space in town, open for short bursts during the week, longer on weekends. I'd seen the shop, but I'd thought that it was only for members of Timewind, so I didn't ask to put my work there."

"And Darkstar told you differently?"

"Yes. He introduced me to Rainmist and Oaknail, who often ran the store on weekends. A few others of the tribe were there. I could give you names; they no longer live in the area, but they are still with us in spirit, and there are always reunions... Anyway, Darkstar and I grew close, and I began to trust him. He let me be open with him, tell him things that had been bottled up for so long..." The Borzhvolk looked down for a moment before raising his eyes to me again. "I need to tell you this too, Max, if you'll let me."

Feeling the heavy burden of his words, I felt too choked up to speak, so I simply nodded.

"I've been raped, Max. Twice. One of those was by someone who had used the Question and Response with me, then turned on me. I have also been suicidal, with only one attempt in my checkered past." He looked at me, his eyes revealing everything. "I know those ghosts that brought you here. Stellamara saw them clearly; I only knew about them because she told us all that they were there. When she and I talked, a few hours ago... We held each other and let the emotions flow between us, because she knew of the ghosts I've had to fight, the ones that still try to haunt me from time to time. It's why she suggested I find you and talk with you.

"Darkstar was the first sapient being that I came to trust enough to hold again. He honored the Question and Response with me, gave me someone to help me ground myself. He held me, let me talk, let me cry, and he began telling me more about the tribe. It sounded nearly impossible that such people could exist, much less that they could welcome an unknown artist into their shop and a broken pup into their hearts." He smiled wanly. "I can say that, because it was true of me, then."

"And you've come so far," I said, "or so it seems to me." A thought occurred to me, the way he had phrased something, and the memory of him with Clipper, last night and in that painting in the Artisanry. "Sapient beings. You trusted non-sapient beings, but not beings on two legs."

Heartsinger nodded, smiling. "I've always felt comfortable with non-sapients, or most of them anyway. It felt easier for me to relate to them than to sapients. I was smart enough to learn about them in books as well as in the fur. I don't think I could be a doctor, but I'm good at reading various signs and mannerisms of non-sapients."

"Especially horses."

His smile broke into a small laugh. "Yes. That was something else that Timewind gave to me. Darkstar had invited me here for a weekend, to show me everything. The Artisanry, here on the property, was still being planned out. The barn and stables were here, although only three horses, at that time. I'd not had a chance to meet non-sapient horses, and the experience was amazing. I wanted to stay and never go back home. I did go back home, of course. I also read up on grooming, maintenance, taking care of non-sapient horses, then asked Darkstar if he would teach me more. He said that he'd help, but I would be taught by the best."

Laughter threatened to bubble out of me, as the obvious answer came to mind.

Heartsinger nodded, grinning. "Takes one to know one."

I practically fell over laughing, and the wolf caught my shoulders and laughed with me. When I finally got my breath back, I clasped his arms as best I could, given that his reach was longer than mine. "You came back, to learn, to share, to stay. I'd say that was a good choice, for you and for the tribe."

"Yes," he said simply. He squeezed my shoulders with soft affection. "Max, I'm not trying to sell you on the idea of being part of the tribe. I'm telling you that I think I understand your ghosts, your demons, whatever you want to call them. I've had my own, and they almost won. Timewind did save me, if only by showing to me that there is still a dream, that there are still good fursons in the world, and that they are family to me, helping me to Become, just as I'm helping them."

He slid his forepaws down my arms, ending with clasping my forepaws gently. His eyes still held mine, and I found myself saying, "That explains something to me."

"Which is?"

"Last night, in the barn." I took a breath and continued. "I had this feeling that you really wanted to talk, to get past the so-called polite conversation and really connect, communicate."

On his cheeks, that sense of blush showed yet again as he said, "Yeah, I'm not very subtle. I think that's what happened to me, all those years ago. I think I was too... emotional? Not quite what I mean. I kept my emotions very near the surface, always very open, no shields or pretenses. Maybe some others thought that I was trying to be sexual, but that wasn't on my mind."

"Heartsinger, I want to ask something; tell me if I'm putting my nose where it doesn't belong."

"You probably won't," he smiled at me, "but thank you for caring."

Another few seconds of hesitation, and I finally found my voice. "I think I understand better, from your descriptions, the difference between sex and intimacy. I'd like to think that we furs had grown past all that nonsense, mixing them up all the time, but it's still with us, or maybe just me. I just mean to say... to ask you... you're more interested in intimacy than sex, aren't you?"

Nodding, he added, "Not that I don't enjoy being sexual, but I do so much enjoy the conversation, the cuddle, the sharing of fur and warmth and feelings and words." He shook our clasped forepaws gently. "Thank you for letting me touch you so much. I think that you may not be used to it, and I realize that I can be overwhelming."

"In my opinion, Heartsinger, it's the world that is lacking." I gave a rueful snort. "I need to ask Darkstar if 'whelmed' is a word, so that I can say that I'm not overly whelmed, just whelmed. All this is a lot for me to take in. I can tell you one important thing." I gave his paws a squeeze, tried to open my feelings, to open my eyes to his and let him in. "You have told me something very important, very deep, and I thank you for helping me see... me, I guess. I don't know that I'd ever really try to kill myself, unless..."

The pause was significant, and the Borzhvolk let me work it out on my own. I had the sense that he knew what I wanted to say; there was pain in his eyes, but the source of that pain was within me. Was that the answer? I didn't want to keep hurting him because of the hurt inside me. To help him not be hurt, I had to find out how not to hurt, to tell him, to ask his help, to take that step toward Becoming. After all this long journey, would it be so hard to take one more step?

Around us, the day lay cool, the creek trickled and chuckled softly, the sounds of birds, perhaps something in the undergrowth moving somewhere just beyond. What I saw most was him, this passionate wolf who waited, open, caring, making a safe space for me, holding my paws to help me know that it would be okay to take one more step.

I felt my jaw move, my lips, tongue, breath moving, and I took the step. "...unless I already have."

20: Homicide Detective

My next genuinely aware thought was that I was being held and rocked, not quite in Heartsinger's lap, still there on the log, the creek and forest still keeping us safe from the rest of the world. I hadn't truly lost consciousness; it was more like I had scared myself into a moment of not being able to think coherently. I was slowly becoming more aware, and I gave the Borzhvolk a squeeze to let him know that I had more or less returned.

"How can I help, Max?" he whispered into my ear.

I chuckled softly. "The question of the day, it seems."

"Every day." His voice held a smile.

Giving him another brief squeeze, I pulled back from his embrace to look once more into his warm golden eyes. "Maybe I'm more Vulcan than I thought."

"What does that mean?"

"Something I said to Lightwing. She had asked me if you — the tribe — had hurt me by being too open, or bringing up to much of my emotions. I told her that it was okay, that I wasn't a Vulcan after all."

He nodded at me, smiling. "I don't know the franchise as well as I might, but I think I get the idea. For some reason, it was supposed to be bad for a Vulcan to get emotional. There's something in the canon about it, I'm sure."

"The connection in my head said that it was because Vulcans are supposed to be so completely ruled by logic that being emotional was bad form, at the least, and maybe even dangerous, at worst. I thought of it like that because I was afraid of how much emotion I was feeling last night. This morning." I swallowed. "Now."

"Are you okay, Max?" His eyes searched mine. "Can you tell me what you're feeling?"

Shocked, I realized that the first answer was, *I feel like I want to kiss you.* What the hell was that? Too much emotion turns you gay? Heartsinger didn't seem to help matters much when he reached up to pet my headfur with amazing tenderness. I closed my eyes, almost whined, felt my tail wagging uncontrollably.

"Listen to me, Max." His crushed-velvet baritone became another caress to my system. "New term for you: Emotional overload. If I'm sensing you right, you're feeling way too vulnerable. You've opened up a huge cache of emotions, and words are getting kinda crazy right now. Can you hear me?"

I was able to nod but not much more. Some part of me tried to focus on breathing while another part of me wondered about the kiss, the kiss that couldn't happen, that mustn't happen, that seemed like it *should* happen, and the sheer shock and fear that whole idea was causing in me.

Heartsinger hugged me again, then helped me to my hindpaws. "Let's get you back to the house, Max. There's someone else you need to talk to. More than one, I expect. C'mon. It's not far."

All but tugging me away from the clearing, the Borzhvolk held my forepaw in his. It was no trouble, keeping up with his pace, but I still felt mightily confused. Moving helped. As I padded along with him, slightly behind and on his left, I began to use my breathing technique to better advantage. The trail wasn't physically challenging; I wasn't panting from exercise, just taking more breaths, trying to deepen them. He complimented me from time to time, encouraged me, seeming to understand something that, so far, I absolutely did not. When we got to the head of the trail, not quite at the barn, he turned to me, speaking softly again.

"Max, do you still want to hold my paw?"

Yes, my mind or heart or whatever wanted to shout. I had the crazy idea that I needed to be tethered to the ground, that I might run away or start screaming if I didn't keep hold of something, someone, and it frightened me to think that I would have to start doing things for myself. I had to have Heartsinger's warmth, his strength, his connection. Did he not want me?

I blinked and looked at him again. Not want me for what? He looked at me with so much compassion and patience that I felt embarrassed all over again. Through all this, he simply smiled, so very softly. I managed to croak out, "I guess you've seen this before."

"Lived it, Max." He gave my forepaw a squeeze before we mutually let go of each other. "Emotional overload. It makes you wonder about... everything. It's why it's best to get through it with one or two trusted friends, to help you. It changes you, but it takes a while to figure out just how, and how you want to show those changes to the rest of the world. So, in case anyone's around..."

A soft bark accompanied a smirk that probably said volumes about my confusion. "What would they think?"

"In truth," the white wolf smiled, "they wouldn't think anything the least bit negative. The problem is more what you're afraid they might think. That's what would hurt you, Max, and I don't want you to hurt."

His compassion flowed out from him in waves, even though I wasn't sure what it meant to me. That was the point that finally started getting through my numbed brain: I was putting my interpretation on things. I was judging, not everyone else. I managed to regain myself a little and, nodding, I returned his smile. "Thank you, Heartsinger. I think I can make it to the house."

"Of course you can." He gave my shoulder a squeeze. "Let's get inside."

The rest of the walk was fully under my own power, although I still felt disconnected from things, or perhaps from myself, or both. There was a fair bit of afternoon left, and the day was still beautiful; it surprised me that we didn't find anyone else enjoying it, on our way back to the house. I supposed there was no one there to notice if I was still holding Heartsinger's paw and, like he said, they wouldn't have thought badly of me for it. For my own part, I still couldn't understand why I wanted to, why it felt so reassuring to be tethered. I wasn't floating away (and if I ate much more cooking like I'd experienced in the past day, I would be firmly anchored by the kilos added to my weight from sheer overindulgence). I tried to order my mind enough to get some idea of whether I had felt like this before, or at least something similar. If so, I couldn't recall it.

For that matter, I couldn't remember exactly what caused it. Something I said, I think, something I felt. I remembered talking with Heartsinger, remembered his story, and I felt so deeply with him that I... No. I couldn't catch it. The thought floated somewhere just beyond me, like that eerie sensation of worrying that I needed some means of holding myself to the Earth before I lifted away and became lost, gone from everything that I'd known.

Once we were inside the house again, I no longer felt like I was going to fly away into outer space; the ceilings here should stop that. I found myself looking at the thought from an entirely sensible standpoint. I knew that I wouldn't literally float away, that I was not literally in danger of losing my body or even my spirit (whatever that was) to some kind of weird antigravity effect. I also knew that I was feeling *something,* and the way that I was interpreting that feeling was being afraid of letting go, being lost, separating from myself, or from my life...

Heartsinger had his arm around me even before I was fully aware that I had staggered where I stood. I felt light-headed as well as momentarily disoriented. Part of my mind tried to diagnose something physical, anything from tripping (while standing still — good trick) to some sort of small stroke or an issue why my heart. My physical heart. It wasn't that. The rest of my mind, the part of me that somehow knew to come find the tribe, told me that it wasn't a physical condition at all. It was the words that I had spoken, back at the creek, the words about not wanting to kill myself.

Unless I already had.

"It feels physical."

I blinked. The voice had come from in front of me. I saw the young doe standing before me, her black eyes as tender and open as they had been last night and this morning. Stellamara was alone, standing quietly, her russet-colored clothing setting off the light tan of her hide. She had been more hidden before, half-cowering behind others, mostly Lightwing, but always with someone nearby. As I learned more about her, I could understand why, just as I understood that her standing here before me was an act of trust.

"Are you okay, Max?" she asked me softly.

"Maybe I should sit down."

Heartsinger guided me toward the chairs in the pit area before the fireplace, reminding me of the shallow steps leading down, holding onto me. The feeling was a bit like being drunk, although I was starting to come out of it now. With the white wolf's help, I seated myself in the chair I had sat in only last night. He once again folded himself onto one of the bean bags, pulling up another for the doe to use. She sat near to me, closer than she had been during my entire visit here, and she continued looking at me with her comforting gaze. It was so easy to imagine that she was looking into my heart, my mind, my spirit, looking at everything that made me who I am, and that look was so complete that she could somehow rip me apart, if she wanted to... and I knew that she wouldn't. No judgment, no violence, nothing but understanding, caring, support, because...

"You've been hurt enough."

I did not know if she read my mind and completed the thought, or if I had heard her words and coupled them with my thoughts. It was easy for me to believe either one. "Thank you," I said softly. My own voice sounded distant to me, as if I actually had become as separate as I was afraid of becoming earlier.

"Have you found your answers yet?"

"I think I have more questions."

The doe nodded slowly. I had the strange feeling that she was trying not to frighten me. "That's part of finding the answers. I have to imagine that your work has shown that to you, Max. I'm not a big fan of television, but there are some tropes that filter through even to those of us who prefer a more sheltered life." She smiled at her own words. "The tropes are fiction, but I have to imagine that there's at least a grain of truth in them."

"Some," I admitted. "You might like the British detective shows better; they don't rely on violence and gore. Even I prefer those."

"Because they use intelligence more than brawn," Heartsinger observed. "I have a few favorites on my own lists."

"You use words, too," the doe ventured. "You investigate. You ask questions."

"Yes. A lot of questions."

"Do you get answers?"

"Eventually."

"Why does it take so long?"

Before the answer reached my maw, my brain finally kicked in enough to bring understanding to the party. "Because I don't always know what questions will bring me the answers that I need."

Stellamara nodded again, slowly. "What questions would you like to try? There's time to ask as many as you need."

I smiled softly at her. "I think I need an answer to this one first. Can you read my mind?"

Her laugh was beautiful, tender, genuine amusement rather than derision. I realized then that she was, finally, truly comfortable with me. Real laughter doesn't happen without trust. "No," she assured me. "I can't pull words or thoughts from you. I am empathic, like Heartsinger."

The Borzhvolk shook his head gently. "You're much stronger than I am, lovely star. I wear my openness in order to invite others in. I seem to have developed stronger shields and resistance to negativity than Stellamara has. I also prefer life in the safety of Starhold, but it's easier for me to venture out more often."

Looking at the doe, I asked gently, "Do you ever feel trapped?"

"No," she answered simply. "I feel safe. When I do venture out, someone goes with me. I never learned to drive, so it's a given. Everyone here is good at helping me ground myself, if I get overloaded. It's probably easier for me to be overwhelmed; like Heartsinger said, I never really learned how to shield myself."

"What were you feeling from me last night? You seemed so frightened of me."

"Not of you. Your ghosts." With a gentle smile, she raised a slender forepaw to forestall my follow-up question. "When I sense things, I don't always get an easy way to interpret them. You were a stranger, in my home — in our home — and inside my safe place, so I felt nervous. What I sensed was something I had felt before, from someone who described himself as haunted by things in his past."

She paused, looking to the white wolf, the question in her black eyes. He nodded. "Yes, I told him. Thank you."

Returning her soft gaze to me, she said, "You seemed haunted in the same way. It's why I asked Heartsinger to talk to you about it."

I took a breath and nodded. "I've been battling with Airdancer's ghost. It's why I asked if you could read my mind. Your description of that ghost, that feeling, was exactly the way it felt to me. Unicorn asked me to imagine what that ghost felt like. Words like 'slithering' and 'grasping' came to mind. It feels like a weight, something tangible, pressing down on my shoulders."

"Trying to make you collapse, to make you small."

"Yes."

"To make you less than yourself."

"Yes."

"To destroy you."

"Stop," I pleaded, and I felt them reach out to me, to hold me. I returned the touch, my forepaws to their arms, and I made myself breathe. Something was happening, in my mind, in my heart, somewhere inside me, I didn't know where. A connection, like a battery, an electric circuit, draining off power, the excess energy, the fear... Words left me briefly, and I let the sensation flow through me, less electric, more like water, still no words...

Sounds. Voice. Words? Are those words?

"How are you feeling, Max?"

I swallowed, tried to get some words of my own. "What," I managed to eke out, "happened?"

"Grounding." Heartsinger's voice was close to my ear. "It's a word we all throw around, yet there seems to be a genuinely physical component to it, like grounding an electrical circuit. I don't know if it's actually scientific or logical; it's something Stellamara and I do automatically."

"You did something."

"Touch. Hold. Help you feel safe."

I shook my head slowly. "Something else."

"What did you feel?" Stellamara asked softly, not quite a whisper.

"So much pain, and then... something like having water flow through me, draining off the pain, the fear..." I looked into her eyes. "Is that the grounding you mean? Did you take it from me?"

"It depends on how much science you believe, or what type." Her smile was almost as enigmatic as one of Darkstar's. "In one sense, everything is energy, and consciousness channels energy. That's my cop-out nod to science. The mystical hoodoo version is that we opened our hearts to you, letting the emotions flow between us, to try to heal your pain."

"And you thought we *weren't* some bunch of flakes," Heartsinger grinned.

Laughing, I said, "Whatever it is, I'll take it. Thank you."

"It's all communication," the Borzhvolk continued. "Words, yes, but there is communication through touch, through sight, sound, scent, taste, and even communication that is somehow outside of all that."

"The sixth sense." I nodded. "Intuition, gut feelings. I guess nobody really knows what it is, how it works. You two seem to know more than most."

"It's more a part of us than most, perhaps." The doe's cheeks reddened slightly. "It's not something that's easily explained. We're usually just thought of as crazy. It's easier for most fursons to keep things in mental boxes. Things they call 'normal,' not always able to explain what that means." After a pause, she added, "I hope that doesn't sound cynical."

I shook my head. "It sounds true. Even my experience agrees with you, and I don't have your gifts. Or perhaps they aren't gifts...?"

"Sometimes. Like a lot of things, it has good points and bad."

"Max," Heartsinger squeezed my forepaw gently. "Do you feel up to looking at the words you said to me, down by the creek?"

A jolt of fear would have been expected; I'd been cowering like a whipped pup all day, or so it felt to me now. What I felt instead was my forepaws held by two fursons who were connected to me, plugged into me, as crazy as that sounded. A physical analogy might be that they were on either side of me as I took my first steps after some accident had taken away my ability to walk. Physical therapy, translated into something emotional, spiritual. I had absolutely no understanding of what that all meant, but it felt right. Feelings, it would seem, are important after all.

So much for being Vulcan.

"One more breath," I said, suiting actions to words, in through the nose, out through the maw. I squeezed their forepaws once, then recounted the essence of my and Heartsinger's talk for Stellamara's benefit, ending with those strange words: *unless I already had.*

The doe's soft voice asked, "Can you tell me what that means?"

"Can I get Darkstar's help with that?" My smile felt weak, but it was there. "It's some sort of poetic conundrum, or something like that. It's not literally true, of course; I mean, I'm still here and breathing. I guess... I'm not very good at existential thinking."

"But you're a good detective." The white wolf spoke gently but earnestly. "Where does an investigation start?"

"Crime scene," I said automatically. "Called in to view the crime scene. Look at the body. Look for the cause of death. Look for anything that might be motive, any evidence that lets you pursue whatever leads you can track down."

"There's no physical body, no physical crime scene. Maybe work backward. What evidence do you have that the crime has taken place? What leads can you find?"

Whatever else the Borzhvolk was, he was also a good therapist. He had hit on exactly the right formula. "Max," I said. "Max is the evidence. The dog who came here for answers, the dog I've been while I've been here. Max is different from Detective Luton."

"Why? In what way?"

"Max has been listening, learning, opening himself. Feeling. Crying." I squeezed their forepaws. "Touching. Reaching out."

"Detective Luton doesn't do that?"

"It's been such a long time. Even Lightwing teased me about it last night." I felt myself flinch, realizing suddenly that I'd said too much. Instead of any rebuke, both of them squeezed my forepaws at almost the same time.

"No judgments, Max," the doe soothed. "No shame. Sharing fur is a special joy, an important one. We trust you, and we trust Lightwing. Whatever you shared with her is private; we won't pry."

Heartsinger added, "Is it a lead, Max? Something about your not having shared your fur with anyone in so long?"

"Yes," I admitted. "Something else that you and I talked about, Heartsinger. The idea of intimacy and sex being one thing. I am going to take a chance that Lightwing won't mind if I talk about myself, in connection with last night. I resisted sharing our fur because I was afraid that I wanted too much of her. We talked, and we held each other, and I cried still more." Another headshake seemed both cliché and necessary. "I haven't cried so much in years."

"Detective Luton probably can't afford to cry. He sees too much pain in his world."

"Was it always like that, Max?" Stellamara wanted to know.

"Honestly, I don't... well, no, maybe it's just that I can't be sure." I tried to remember what I was like when I started. Is it why the yappy Labrador, Parsons, irritated me? Was I like that as a newbie? I didn't think so. I was intense, not bouncing off the walls. I wanted to learn everything, to find out the secrets that the TV shows didn't reveal, the tricks, the wiles, the way to get to the bottom of any mystery.

"I think I started out okay. Learning the job, the techniques, the procedures. I had friends, on the force and off. I met Barbara, and we married, and Michael came along..." I thought about it now, the beginning, the various points where I had hit some new self along the way. "Further back," I told myself, bringing them with me. "High school diploma or certification would have been enough to get me into the police academy, but I had to be 21, so I whiled some time taking courses at a junior college. Barb and I met there, in fact. She encouraged me to become a cop, get on the detective track. That's where the college classes came in handy after all."

"You were a policeman first?"

"Ten years. It's where you learn the ropes," I explained. "The academy teaches a lot; experience and mentoring does the rest."

"You had a good mentor," the Borzhvolk said rather than asked.

"Moshe," I nodded. "Moshe Gillette. Homicide detective. He became my rabbi, in the cop sense. He was Jewish too, so it was a joke between us."

"He was a rabbi and a police detective?"

My chuckle made me realize that the term wasn't as popular now as it used to be. "No. To cops, a 'rabbi' is a higher-up on the force who helps pave the way for a good career. Moshe had influence, but he only used it to make sure that his protégés learned and kept on the straight and narrow. No short cuts, no mavericks, just good detectives. I practically worshipped that mastiff."

"What happened to him?" Stellamara asked.

"Retirement. He didn't have to take it, but he felt it was time. He told me..."

The thought welled up so fully that I could almost relive the scene. It happened at his home, his small, well-kept house, where he lived alone, his wife gone, his two pups grown and married, a few grandpups to visit from time to time. He was ready for the quiet, ready to listen to the peacefulness of his later years. He made tea for us, in the days before I knew much about what tea was supposed to be for, long before Michael tried to teach me, in real life or in dreams. He told me he had one last bit of wisdom to impart to me. What got him to "last this long," was how he described it. Holding my gaze with his insightful eyes, he said that there was one thing, one vital point, that I had to remember above everything else.

"He told me, 'Learn to recognize what to let go of and what to keep, or you might get them mixed up. Don't ever mix 'em up, Max. You can't always make it right.'"

"Did you, Max?" The doe's voice was nearly a whisper. "Did you mix them up?"

Memories can be brought forth individually, or in groups, or in hordes, or not at all, depending upon what it is that you want of them. Generally, they choose the least helpful form in any given moment. Right then, they elected to appear as a deluge of impressions and fragments that let me see myself in every possible form of horror that one could imagine. I was always wrong, always incompetent, always inept, always inadequate, a complete waste of fur...

I squeezed their forepaws, made myself look at them both, made myself speak. "Help. Me. Please."

"We will, Max." Heartsinger leaned closer to me. "Listen to us. Focus on us. Let go of the voices, let go of the fear. Keep hold of us."

Nodding vigorously, I tried to breathe more slowly, looking to each of them in turn, the wolf, the doe, Heartsinger, Stellamara, letting go of everything but them. "Working," I managed.

"Emotional overload, Max," the Borzhvolk reminded me. "Your mind will return."

"Our voices," the doe murmured. "Let us help ground you. Let yourself trust us again. You're safe here, Max. More than that — you're a far better dog than you're telling yourself."

My exhale let itself turn into a laugh. "I thought you said that you couldn't read my mind."

"More like reading mine," Heartsinger explained. "You have to hate yourself a lot to try to kill yourself."

"That." I said, my eyes growing wide with realization. "What I said before, about looking for leads, for evidence... for motive."

"Tell us." The Borzhvolk's crushed-velvet baritone seemed to hold me as he had done before. "Tell us what you've found."

"More like what I see." I swallowed hard. "Detective Luton. I think he's my murderer."

21: The North Tower

I listened to my own words, having to fight the mad desire to laugh at how stupid it sounded. Detective Luton, in the study, with the Sword of Justice. To my own credit, I didn't say that out loud; to their credit, they didn't laugh at the stupid words I *had* said out loud. For a moment, I wondered why they didn't laugh. It was ridiculous. I killed me, but I'm still here to tell the tale. I'm some kind of split personality, with each half fighting for dominance. Yeah, I've seen that movie, too, several of them; it's a popular idea, beginning (for me) with Norman Bates. How far down that crazy-trail did I want to run?

After a few more seconds of wallowing in that idea, I realized that my companions even now hadn't laughed, not even chuckled. Heartsinger and Stellamara still held my forepaws, still gazed at me steadily, warmly, openly. I came slowly to understand that they were waiting for me to say something so, naturally, I couldn't think of anything at all to say.

I still felt somehow outside myself, remembering something from before, that feeling of being tethered, grounded, connected. I tried to find that feeling again, and I couldn't quite do it. I didn't think that I was going to fly away, so that part of the crazy wasn't hanging around. This was the more ordinary crazy, the kind that gets treated with lots of really good drugs, the ones that go along with making potholders and playing with modeling clay in a room with a lot of other people who get the same sort of drugs.

"Can you say something?" I blurted out. My voice sounded unreal to me. Maybe I wasn't real after all.

"We're here, Max." The Borzhvolk's soft baritone was real, familiar, very calming. "I'm here. Do you remember me telling you about emotional overloads? And how I said that I'd lived them?"

"Yes."

"This is part of that." He leaned closer still, and I again had that feeling that he was going to kiss me, or that I wanted him to, or that I didn't. "You have to hate yourself a lot to try to kill yourself."

He'd said that a moment ago, and then I'd said... I'd said...

"We're here." Stellamara squeezed my forepaw, and I shifted my gaze to her. "That's a very big secret you've been keeping."

"I told you everything this morning."

"Except for this last part. I didn't know it last night."

"Know...?"

"That this was the secret that was hurting you so much." The doe nodded her head once. "Keeping back the rest was hurting you also, but this last piece, this last clue... this is what you have been fighting all this time. This is the murder that you've been trying to solve."

I felt my head shaking, denying. "That makes no sense..."

Again, even as I said the words, I knew that they were crazy but, this time, from the other direction. Denying it was the crazy part. Not looking at the evidence was crazy. Not paying attention to the clues, the very reason for so much of my life... yeah, that was crazy.

Heartsinger released my forepaw, putting his to my shoulder briefly. "Stay here with Stellamara for a moment. I'm going to find someone I think you need to talk with." He unfolded himself and rose in a single fluid motion, then padded off to the stairs.

The quiet stretched. I felt the doe's forepaw holding my own, inviting my trust, but it took several seconds for me to look into her face again. She was calm, radiating gentle confidence. I wished that I could know how she did that, how she appeared to be so at ease with herself. She was so withdrawn last night, hiding from me, until she saw my ghosts and named them, and then this morning, listening to my story with what could be called "poise" if not outright bravery. And now, so centered, so strong, how did she...

The rueful smile flashed across my muzzle. "I think I need to ask for some more help."

Her own smile was warm, genuinely understanding. "I'm glad you can ask, Max. How can I help?"

"I was just thinking how calm you look, how accepting you are. I'm not sure I can say this right. We both know it's not about me being 'dangerous' or something. It's more like being an unknown quantity. I don't even know what I am right now, but you seem to be handling it as if this isn't new."

Her right forepaw joined her left, holding mine in both of hers. "It's new to you; it's not new to me. I've seen this before."

"Heartsinger."

She shook her head. "Not the ghosts. Not even the idea of suicide." The doe's smile became even warmer than before. "It's not about death, Max. It's not even about the deep hate that Heartsinger experienced, hating yourself enough to want to kill yourself. That may have been what sparked this in him, even in you, but it's not where that discovery took him, nor where it will take you. Not hate and death, Max. Love and birth, rebirth, rediscovering."

My face must have made some interesting change, because she chuckled softly.

"That part really does make us sound like a cult, doesn't it? 'Be reborn with us, brother; you are born again in our spirit!' Or something like that. That's not what I mean, not even what Timewind means. Remember the Three Steps to Becoming? The first step isn't to belong to something outside of yourself, like a group, a religion, a country; it's to belong to yourself. Your commitment is to make yourself into the best You that you can. Then comes giving and accepting help with that commitment, and then comes giving your best self to all the world."

Her eyes held mine carefully. "That takes love, Max. It takes a commitment to your own life, your best life. That's what I've seen before. Dreamweaver found Timewind, as well as herself, about the same time that I did. I'm watching Frank go through this same process. I've heard the stories of others, like Darkstar, Rainmist, Unicorn, Stormsinger, Summerwind, Clearwater... all amazing stories, so filled with life and hope. They all began with something like what you're going through now."

I breathed evenly for a few moments, looking into her eyes, feeling my forepaw in hers. "I'm trying to reach out again," I said, "to feel that connection I felt before. Is that okay?"

"Absolutely. Let me help."

This time, I didn't close my eyes, and the feeling was somehow mutual, less like her taking away that sensation of overload, more like something flowing between us, back and forth, commingling. I still didn't understand it, but that didn't stop it from helping, so I didn't question or analyze it. Wanting it, letting it happen, helping it happen... that's what was working.

"Better?" she asked softly.

"Yes." My voice sounded calm again. Judgment, perhaps even reason, suspended. I just let it happen. "Can you tell me more about those stories?"

Stellamara nodded. "They have many things in common. The most important one is the change of direction. Embracing a better self, a better way of living. There is an interesting lesson that non-sapients can teach us: They never travel quickly when they aren't sure which way they should go. They move slowly, carefully, until they find something that feels right to them, perhaps something that they choose to move forward into, something that they choose move away from. When they find a path that works, they move quickly again, following that inner certainty.

"We sapient beings have forgotten that simple truth. We rationalize that, if a path feels wrong, it's because we're not trying hard enough, or that it doesn't matter because we think we have no choice. It's more difficult for us to find a right path, because we keep clinging to a wrong one. It's not the path that's at fault, we tell ourselves... or others tell us."

The feeling between us put the gentle emphasis on her words. "It's too easy for us to believe in our failure instead of our success."

For once in all this craziness, I didn't feel like crying. The feeling was more like the realization of a basic, powerful truth. The thought that came along with it seemed somehow obvious, after all this time. "Airdancer saw only failure."

Another nod from the doe. "I didn't know him; I know his legend, and what you described this morning. His story seems to be centered on running. He didn't realize how trapped he was, in his career paths, his life paths... As you told us, how he seemed to have everything, yet he had nothing that would sustain him." She paused, speaking softly, shielding any sting from her words. "You said that you have nothing."

Considering a moment, I then said, "It *feels* like I have nothing. Nothing is what I keep seeing, like Airdancer did."

"That's why his shade haunts you."

"Yes." I kept breathing, looking into her eyes. "Maybe I have something, if I can figure out how to get myself to find it, accept it."

"Your pup."

"Michael. Yes. He's still in my life, and we've been trying to talk more."

"That's a good start, don't you think?"

"I certainly do."

We both turned to look toward the speaker. Lightwing smiled gently at me; Heartsinger, at her side, seemed also to beam at me. Under so much affectionate attention, my usual response would be to cower, hide, get away from it, probably with a self-deprecating comment, or even with anger. I saw myself doing it, images in my head of me doing those things, whether in past situations or as something I needed to do now. That's the thing: I saw it, as if looking at myself doing it, or watching someone who looked like me doing it, and I didn't understand why that person would do that. It was like feeling separate from myself again, or like maybe Detective Luton was doing those things...

A different instinct took over in me, and I stood up, gently releasing Stellamara's paw and padding over to the Husky to take her into my arms for a firm hug that she returned even more tightly. I felt something like relief, gratitude, affection, lightness, other words that I couldn't catch clearly. It was good and right that I held her close, my tail wagging, my nose catching whiffs of her scent from her neck fur. It was several seconds before I remembered that others were in the room with us, and my old patterns tried to kick in again. This time, though, that first inclination toward embarrassment lasted only for a moment. I pulled away from her enough to look into her lovely ice blue eyes, smiling at her as she did me.

"I hear you're looking for me," she said.

"Heartsinger wouldn't mislead you," I told her. Extending an arm toward the Borzhvolk, I was glad to feel him take my forepaw into his and return the squeeze I gave him. "Good intuition."

"If nothing else, she makes tea better than I do." His smile encompassed us both. "Lightwing, perhaps you'd like to show Max the North Tower? I think he'd like the view." He chuckled softly. "I promise that not a euphemism."

My laugh was soft and sincere, even as part of me tried to make me cower, ashamed at being so open and vulnerable. That was my exact thought — I could see it clearly enough to speak it — and I felt the confusion of being separate from that emotion, again as if I were somehow two beings. I asked, "What is the North Tower?"

"You may not have noticed that the house has two turrets on it, one to the north, one to the south." The Husky smiled at me. "They aren't just decorative. Here, I'll take you."

I clasped her offered forepaw gently in my own, then turned to Stellamara. "Thank you," I said quietly. "I will see you later, I hope?"

She nodded, her smile warm and reassuring. "I would like that."

"Me as well," Heartsinger assured me. "I have reason to believe that dinner will be quite good tonight."

"The food has been exceptional already."

He placed a forepaw to my shoulder. "I was thinking of the company."

Just let it happen, something inside me said. A much nicer voice than the ones I'd been hearing. "I look forward to it," I assured him.

Still holding my forepaw in hers, Lightwing led me down the length of the ground floor, past the guest rooms, past the conference room with its telecom system and its revelations of this morning, and to a staircase just beyond. Wide, though not as wide as the main staircase to the upper level, this flight of steps had an interesting feature that the Husky pointed out to me. "These windows run the height of the entire stairwell, on both sides," she explained as we climbed upward. "Sometimes, when it rains, we'll find Darkstar sitting on the second or third floor landing, just watching the drops fall. There's a very peaceful feeling in this stairwell, and I've never figured out why. And I've never been sorry that it's here."

"What makes a big house beautiful is the secret that you never see," I paraphrased. Lightwing glanced at me quizzically. "From *The Little Prince,* sort of. I'm taking liberties."

She smiled at me. "When did you read that?"

"About a thousand years ago, it seems." I shook my head, wondering. "I'm surprised that I remembered even that much of it."

"Memories get triggered by all kinds of things. Scent is a big trigger, for most of us, and maybe canines in particular; other things trigger by association of words, ideas, physical sensations." The Husky paused in her ascent, turning back to look into my eyes. "Can you tell me what brought that idea up in your head?"

"I'm not sure." I stood with her on the landing between the second and third floors, looking away through the windows at what seemed an enormous, unbroken vista of forest and landscape. If my sense of direction wasn't failing me, this landing faced west. I could see the drive leading toward the Artisanry, and the sun lowering from its earlier zenith. The peacefulness of this land, this space, came through to me with a sense of comfort, of safety, just as the tribe had been providing to me. A flicker of that old pain tried to seep in, to tell me not to trust it, but it really was a ghost now, a phantom. "Something about this place."

"The staircase?"

"Everything. Starhold. The tribe. The sense of being safe." I turned back to look at her again. "I keep wanting to ask if it's real. How is it possible to keep dreaming? How do you keep a dream alive?"

"By working at it. Remembering to keep dreaming."

"Something about the price of liberty being eternal vigilance?" I asked. "That sounds paranoid."

"It is." The look on her face showed genuine pain. "I think that quote isn't correct anyway, but it's been used to justify acts that are supposed to preserve liberty by taking it away from just about everyone. You can't protect something by destroying it."

I took her into my arms and hugged her tightly. She put her arms around me and shuddered once through before regaining herself.

"Sorry," she mumbled against my chest.

"*I'm* sorry; I think I stepped on a corn."

"You couldn't know." A squeeze, and she pulled gently away from me. "One of my own ghosts, I suppose. Some people I knew, when I was first considering joining the tribe, they gave me a lot of grief over it. Timewind was a 'cult of dangerous subversives,' or words to that effect. It's why I understood your comments about pain and failure being the only real path, that the darkness always wins. It felt very dark when they pulled away from me. Shunned me." She offered me a wan smile. "You see? You aren't the only one who is having to face down the darkness."

"And this 'cult' of Timewind offered you light?"

"Support for finding my own light. Becoming me. We cherish our differences instead of trying to make us all into cookie-cutter 'good citizens.' It's why I say we remember to dream rather than that we fight for the dream. Even fighting *for* something feels violent, to me. Timewind isn't about violence."

I smiled softly at her. "Although I do seem to remember a certain Husky telling me that she was going to rip a demon out of me and kick its fucking ass."

"A momentary lapse."

We laughed softly together and, before anything in me could think of a good reason not to, I leaned forward to kiss her gently on her lips. I heard her quiet intake of breath, felt something shift gently inside me, as if to get more comfortable. When we separated from the kiss, the smile on her face was much warmer.

"Just showing my age," I told her. Her eyebrows drew together, and I answered, "I'm old enough to remember the slogan, 'Make love, not war.'"

"A saying that should never grow old," she chuckled. Offering me another quick kiss to my lips, she turned us toward the last set of steps. "Let me show you part of how we keep the dream alive."

At the head of the stairs, I found a stretch of hallway perhaps a quarter the length of the house. Near the stairs was another water closet, which told me that the tribe did indeed plan both for contingencies and comforts; no sense dashing down the stairs in a case of need. Lightwing stood near a door bearing a wood-carved plaque reading *Areopagus* in a lovely script. "I have no idea what that means," I admitted.

"I had to get Darkstar to give me the background of it all, but it was the founders' idea, part of the original concepts for the tribe. The name comes from the Greek Hill of Ares, located in Athens, where the Athenian tribunal met for council."

My turn to frown. "I thought that a tribunal was a court of justice or of decision-makers. Timewind is more democratic than that, isn't it?"

"Absolutely!" the Husky assured me. "This is the conference room for what became known as the Prime Council, mostly because the other usage of the initials 'PC' is its own travesty." She grinned. "I don't suppose you're a fan of the Arthurian legends?"

"Does it count that Michael and I have watched *Excalibur* about a dozen times?"

She giggled sweetly. "Addicts, like the rest of us. Allow me to show you Timewind's own version of the Table Round."

I padded through the open door into a room with about the same dimensions as Darkstar's room, dominated by a large round table, surrounded by particularly comfortable-looking office chairs. The table was inlaid with seven wedges of color: a rich antique gold; royal blue; forest green; a gently understated purple; a warm, passionate, yet not garish red; a soft white; and a clean yet subtle sun-like yellow. Each of these held what appeared to be gold leaf inscriptions: Chieftain, Household Advisor, Financial Advisor, Projects Advisor, Legal Advisor, "MOOR," and Keeper of Time. Below the MOOR inscription, the words *Siege Perilous* appeared in a sweeping script.

"You're going to have to explain this to me," I told her softly.

"This is the boardroom of the corporation-thingummy that is Timewind." She grinned at me. "Just because it's legal doesn't mean it has to be dull."

"When did paradise have to be so regimented?"

She nodded, still smiling. "This is why I say that I dislike saying that we 'fight' for the dream. We work for it, build it, maintain it. Part of this is to fulfill the legal requirements that protect us as a group; the rest is our combined effort to keep us going." Her smile faltered for a moment. "Airdancer set it all up, originally; Unicorn has tweaked and maintained it since. I don't understand all of it, even though I'm part of it... Here, let me explain what I know."

Moving to the table, she waved me toward the chairs, inviting me to take one. I sat at the Siege Perilous, wondering what a "MOOR" was, as well as what it had to do with Sir Percival.

"As I understand it," the Husky began, "the legal setup needs only a President, Secretary, and Treasurer. As a practical matter, the tribe developed the idea of divvying up the business of running this dream into specific areas. Each member of the Council has the power to act autonomously, generally speaking, like departmental managers of a business. We all come together here, compare notes, make sure we're on track." She nodded, again smiling. "Sounds ridiculously complicated, but we're used to it by now. The tribe in general has been working this out since they started."

"Practice makes, as they say. Is it? Perfect, I mean?"

"Hardly! But it works." She again gestured to the table. "Oaknail is the corporate President, although he thought 'Chieftain' was a better title for the liege lord of the land and tribe." Lightwing chuckled. "It's very tongue-in-cheek. He never takes it any more seriously than his duties actually require of him. You'll notice that his chair is one of the largest; he insists that it's because of his physical size and not because he wanted a throne. We still tease him about it.

"The Household Advisor position covers all aspects of running the household and grounds, including purchases of food, overseeing the overall groundskeeping, arranging seeing to the needs of our non-sapient animals, and so forth. A rough job, since it includes all the buildings on the property, including the Artisanry. Moonsong is our overseer, and I sometimes think she handles it with one paw.

"Sunrider is our Financial Advisor, the accountant and Treasurer for Timewind. He handles all the taxes, financial income and outgo, and overall budgeting. Anything that requires money in any way has to be worked through with him, and that includes household, projects, and everything else. It might interest you to know that there are currently eleven separate bank accounts for Timewind, simply to keep all of the accounting separate."

"My head is already swimming," I smiled at her.

"Hang on; four more positions to go!" Another game show hostess wave as she indicated the purple wedge. "The Projects Advisor is Summerwind; she's doing some consulting work in Houston and should be back next weekend. For us, she oversees the big projects, like the construction of the Artisanry. Her 'skill set,' as they say, includes everything from subcontracting negotiations and project management to something called Critical Path Method, which I don't pretend to understand. My tease for her is, if they want to build it, she will come."

"Good movie," I acknowledged.

She pointed to the purple wedge next to the place where I sat. "Legal Advisor — Unicorn, of course." Another brief pause before she observed, "I wonder what Airdancer would have made of this."

I kept my muzzle shut, letting the emotions of the moment be whatever they needed to be. It occurred to me only briefly that Glover's shade didn't seem to be there at all. Perhaps there was too much of the dream here for it to tolerate.

"This space is next," I said, indicating the soft white wedge where I sat. "What exactly is 'MOOR' when it's at home?"

"Another tongue-in-cheek title: Minister Of Outworld Relations."

"Okay, so what does 'Outworld' mean?"

"Remember our discussion during tea this morning, about how Starhold is a sanctuary, and Timewind is a safe group, good folk to be together with?" The Husky's ice blue eyes shone warmly. "We use 'Outworld' in the ironic sense. You see, Timewind and its concepts are still largely thought of an experiment in being a commune, or a throwback to the sixties, or maybe even a bunch of weirdoes who are trying to subvert Our Great and Sacred Way Of Life. The MOOR keeps tabs on all aspects of Timewind as it relates to the public, both as a source of information for the curious as well as the monitor of our own safety, especially in these modern times of suspicion of anything that's too... well, 'generous' is the word I'd use. We dad-gum commie hippie pre-verts are gonna ruin This Great Nation."

I considered the words, sighing softly. "I don't remember if I mentioned it... Part of how I found you was a phone call I received from the FBI."

She nodded softly. "Yeah, we're still on their watchlists. That's one part of what I have to deal with."

"You?"

"Yep." She grinned at me. "You're sitting in my chair."

"It was the 'Siege Perilous' that caught my eye. I can see why this place at the table would be labeled with that. How can you find the Holy Grail? What is the Grail, for Timewind?"

Lightwing sat next to me, sighing softly. "The sacred chalice is a symbol. Some think it's one of sacrifice, of the pain of the crucifixion. I think it in terms of love. Remember in the film, how Arthur sips from it and exclaims how filled he was, how his spirit was renewed? That's what love does." Her eyes again regarded me with their special warmth. "That Grail is always worth pursuing, and we sip from it whenever we can. We share it whenever we can."

"What does that look like?"

"Each of us gives of ourselves to the world, in various ways. The tribe, as a group, also gives of itself. That's the other part of my job. I oversee donations of time, goods, services, or even money to our nearby communities, in times of need. With Sunrider, I oversee the tribal scholarship funds; some of that is for the yowens of our own members, but there are also a few that are available to others who show both an interest in higher education and in our own precepts. Oray is one of those, in fact."

"You mean he doesn't spend all of his time in the hayloft with Starshine?" I grinned.

"Not *all* of it, no," she chuckled. "He studies things other than Procyon anatomy."

"Perhaps not with as much ardor." I glanced at the soft yellow wedge where she sat. "I think the Keeper of Time is the last position here."

She nodded. "Currently Darkstar's domain. The position has several functions in terms of time. First, he is the Secretary of record for the corporation-thingummy, as well as being the secretary for the meetings, keeping minutes and records of the Council. As you already know, he is also the chronicler of the history of Timewind, in all its aspects. He keeps the calendars, including the timing of plantings and harvests, the animals' reproductive cycles as they bear their young, and anything else to do with time and schedules.

"There is one thing that is, to me, more important than all of that. He is the keeper of the future as well. Darkstar has a need for the dream of Timewind that is greater than any of us, I think; it is his passion that always renews us when we feel slowed down in our progress. He draws the future for us, predicting activities that we might have decades from now."

"He seems so quiet," I said, hearing a touch of wonder in my voice, "at least in my conversations with him. You're describing a level of passion that I feel more from Heartsinger than Darkstar."

"Heartsinger wears it openly. He'll tell you that he can't help it, but it's more like he finally feels safe enough to set those feelings free. Darkstar is..." Her pause was reflective, her face showing many emotions, settling on a powerful affection. "Remember me saying that I'll find him watching the rain from one of these landings? That's who he is, Max. He's the one who sees through the veil of time. He is bringing our future home to us."

22: The South Tower

I was reluctant to break the spell that Lightwing had woven, as it appeared to affect us both so deeply. It felt good to let the dream wrap around me, to give myself the chance to feel it, to see it through her eyes, to believe in it. That was easier to do now than before, if only because I could see the Table Round, see the place where dreams met practicality... what had she called it? "Practical optimism." I had the feeling that I might need to read this *Manifesto* for myself. Perhaps it was more Kool-Aid. Perhaps it was just more tea, which I would prefer; the flavors are much better, more individualized, when the tea is prepared properly.

"Well," the Husky exhaled softly. "You've now seen the furson behind the curtain, so to speak."

"This is no illusion, Lightwing." I reached for her forepaw again; she took mine gently. "None of you is trying to manipulate or deceive, all for your own ends. You're right: This is how a dream is built, created. How it's maintained." I smiled at my own words. "Who am I, and what have you done with Detective Luton?"

"It's okay, Max. Don't be afraid of it."

Nodding, I breathed in deeply before speaking. "You're right: It's frightening to me. I think I'm getting some idea of what Stellamara was going through with me. She wasn't afraid of Detective Luton, because she didn't know that's who I was, last night. What frightened her was sensing my deception."

"Not of hiding the detective," Lightwing whispered.

"No. I was deceiving myself."

"Yes." She brushed a thumb over the back of my paw, as if exploring the fur there. "She felt your conflict, your ghosts, and she knew that she couldn't help you until you let yourself ask for the help. That's what she spoke to me about last night. I guess that's part of the reason that I came by your room."

"Part?" I smiled at her, finding myself enjoying the sense of blush rising up on her cheeks, faintly visible underneath the fur of her mask, and the way it made her gaze so tender.

She squeezed my forepaw and got to her hindpaws. "C'mon," she tugged at me. "Let me show you a bit more. Or a bit MOOR, to make a joke."

It took me a moment to hear the emphasis in the word. It helped that she flicked a glance at her spot on the table. "This, I gotta hear."

As we padded out of the room, I noticed a door that had a security lock on it. "Tribal papers," she explained. "As Unicorn said, we trust each other just fine. If any representative from the IRS or some other government group comes to visit, we can show that we keep the physical records secure." She grinned at me. "Unicorn calls it the Hemorrhoid Requirement."

Laughing, I raised my forepaws in a gesture of surrender. "I promise that I am not part of any such governmental agency! I will not ask for a tour of what's behind locked doors." I paused, considering. "Come to think of it, I've not seen too many of those in this house."

"We're a courteous bunch; if a door is closed, we knock on it. We avoid going into each other's rooms without permission and, as you may have noticed, we're reasonably casual about our personal space in our shared areas. Common courtesy rules, generally speaking."

"Common courtesy isn't all that common anymore."

"Another reason why Starhold is such a safe haven."

I nodded my agreement. "Where to? Back downstairs?"

"Nope. This way."

With a gesture displaying just the right amount of flourish, she led me away from the stairs, passing another door ("More storage," she explained; "can never have too much") and to a sturdy door at the end of the short hallway. This, she opened, and waved me out onto the roof. A wide, flat space with decorative waist-high walls to either side, the space was clearly meant to be used.

"I'm glad the weather is so nice today," she said, joining me. "I'd swear that you can see for 50 klicks from up here."

Not that far, I was reasonably certain, if only because of the tall trees that remained of the forested area around us. When Timewind had made space for themselves and harvested trees to help support themselves, they had not clear-cut the majority of the forest; they left the slender trees to grow larger and taller over the years. From this vantage point, it was easy to see the area to the west, the curving drive, the Artisanry, the swath of state road, and the roof was high enough to see maybe a dozen klicks to the horizon, if unobstructed. The illusion of greater distance was there, though, and I enjoyed indulging in it. At the very least, it was a quiet adventure in clean air, soft breezes, the sweetness of country life... all the clichés that a city-dweller like me would come up with. I crossed to the opposite side of the roof, looking east, and I saw a large section of plowed land.

"How big is that plot?" I asked, gesturing toward the field.

"Only about 600 square meters. It feels huge, when you're working it, but it's really very small. Preparing the land with a tractor takes only a few hours, even with our modest equipment. It's the planting, tending, and harvesting that takes up the time."

"A lot of yield?"

"Enough to sustain about 30 fursons, according to the math. We do go through much of it, but we give away any excess. The local food bank loves us; they even lend us a few volunteers at harvest time, and they never go home empty-pawed." She paused, looking at me slyly.

I laughed. "Okay, yes, I was going to make some snide comment about their taking the whole harvest as their due, either from manipulating you with guilt or by the sheer greed of capitalism. I guess old habits die hard."

"They've been reinforced for years, Max. I'm not surprised, nor am I judging you for it. After all, I have to deal with the Outworlders, too, and I am wise enough to be cautious when dealing with unknown fursons. My goal is to avoid judging them, and to be cautious rather than suspicious."

"Sounds like a challenge."

"There are days when it's almost impossible," she chuckled. "You know the saying, 'No good deed goes unpunished'? It's all too easy to find examples to prove it rather than ones that refute it. That, too, is part of modern culture: Negativity is reinforced."

"That sounds harsh," I admitted.

"Here's a statistic for you. The average satisfied customer of a business tells eight others of his good experience; the average dissatisfied customer tells 23."

I thought about the penchant of online reviews to be negative more often than positive, as well as the "up-votes" for that negativity, and I had to concede the point. I felt the hint of the Idea trying to come back, to remind me that the darkness always wins. Looking to Lightwing, I could tell that my face must have expressed that thought, because she put a forepaw to my arm.

"A friend of mine explained it with an example from his own life. He heard some music, an instrumental ballad, by a group called Mannheim Steamroller... and no, they're not a punk band. More like classical jazz. Anyway, my friend felt moved by the music and set out to write lyrics for it. He had no idea of trying to sell the lyrics, or lay claim to the music, nothing like that; he simply wanted to express his appreciation of the music by being creative with it. He sent the lyrics to the record label, saying all of that, how he enjoyed the ballad, felt a desire to show the group how much the music meant to him."

The Husky sighed softly into the gentle air around us. "He never heard from them. He had wished for little more than a simple acknowledgement, a 'thank you for sharing, and we're glad you liked it' kind of thing, nothing more than that. It was only years later that he realized: The band could not acknowledge even having received his letter, for fear of being sued over the lyrics. My friend had no such intention..."

"...but the world has to base its actions on the lowest common denominator." I nodded. "There are jerks out there who *would* do that, and this group couldn't take the risk that your friend wasn't one of those." It was my turn to sigh, which I realized was a frequent response to the world at large, these days. "Is it just me, or is that 'lowest common denominator' becoming lower every day?"

"Easy to make a case for that, isn't it?" She gave my arm a gentle squeeze. "That's what those ghosts in your head were trying to tell you, isn't it? That the dark always wins. That it's easier just to accept how bad everything is, because it can't be fixed."

"Is that what the MOOR is? The furson trying to fix it?"

"Not on your sweet life," she chuckled. "Ain't nobody gonna 'fix' that stuff. We can work to change some of the systemic issues — providing help in general ways, moving to change bad laws, working to promote good laws, voting for good lawmakers... and yes, there are still a few of those out there. What needs to shift is perception, and that has to be done one furson at a time." She hugged me, her cheek to my shoulder. "Each one becomes, so that all may rise."

I held her close, happy for any excuse to do so, some part of my mind wondering if I really needed an excuse. "Is that part of the *Manifesto,* too?"

"Not sure," she chuckled softly. "I was thinking of the old adage, 'A rising tide lifts all boats,' and it kind of morphed into that."

"Then you may have created something new for the Tribe. For each of us."

Once more, the moment stretched, comfortably, sweetly, and I felt in no hurry for us to leave it. Was this what all those "Be Here Now" mantras were all about? The insipid "Mindfulness Movement," as I had dismissively labeled it? Maybe. That was me, trying to quantify everything, to be able to account for it all somehow. Like filling in a time card, proving that what I was doing was valuable to the bosses and overseers, that I was worth my paycheck. Right now, I was worth Lightwing's time, at least. That word, "worth," had so much baggage. Where had I heard a certain dessert being described as being "worth getting fat on?" Is everything a zero-sum game? Will I have to pay for this moment of joy with an equal moment of suffering or, worse, multiple moments of suffering, to appease the all-grasping darkness that I had been sensing?

I felt her give me a squeeze and pull gently away from the embrace. "Come on," she said, taking my forepaw into her own once more. "The South Tower awaits."

We crossed the roof to another outer door, and she entered a code on the keypad next to it. Casting a glance behind me, I saw that the door to the North Tower also had a keypad to one side. That idea of the "lowest common denominator" tried to creep in again, and I dismissed it as best I could. A lock on the door doesn't mean that you're imprisoned or under siege. If I bothered to look, there were probably smoke alarms in the house, perhaps even phone links to call the fire department automatically, in the event of a blaze. Was this another side of "practical optimism" — perhaps something like "reasonable pessimism?" The worst probably won't happen, but simple safeguards are still sensible.

It would be nice to live in a world where they weren't needed. Until then, let the keypads do their jobs without giving into the fear, the paranoia slinking like some terrible shade behind their presence. Keep living in the light.

Be the light, some long ago saying teased at the back of my mind.

Lightwing held the door for me, and we entered a small vestibule that led into a hallway running perpendicular to the house's usual hallways. We turned right, which would lead to the front side of the house, then through a curtained archway to reveal a single room of huge proportions. At the far end, a stage area stood raised to about a half-meter high, with steps at the front and either side. Chairs and folding tables were stacked to one side of the space, and I could see a small lighting and sound control setup in sight of the stage but otherwise unobtrusive to audience or performers.

"Do you put on plays here?" I asked.

"Readings of new material, sometimes," the Husky explained, her gesture inviting me to look around. "We have musical performances, some improvisation, the occasional guest speaker. This is part of our outreach program. We do a lot more with a similar space in the town proper — a little theater space, about 80 seats, that we also rent out for other shows — but we have smaller gatherings here."

"I'm not sure I understand."

"We invite a modest number of guests, a few times a year, to stay and learn from us and learn with us. A week in the country, spending time with a few of us who lead classes in areas that are their expertise. Oaknail finds a few metal workers; Dreamweaver attracts a few who are interested in textiles and clothing design; Darkstar and Heartsinger mentor writers of all kinds; Redlance sometimes finds fursons who are interested in woodworking; Stormsinger works with musicians and singers, as you might guess; and Rainmist has been an actor and performer, in her day, and she teaches improvisation to any who might want to join in and play the games. The space in town is where she gives improv classes regularly, with a show as the 'graduation' exercise for her attendees. Here, it's more like a 'side quest,' so to speak."

I whistled softly. "Sounds like quite a crowd. How many show up for these gatherings?"

"Usually, no more than 12 to 15 at a time. We spread out the students between the guest rooms and the Bunkhouse, with at least one of us out there with them, just to make sure they don't get lost. Some of our younger students will bring camping gear, if the weather's going to be good. There's a list of 'how to camp here' sort of rules; most are pretty good about it." She smiled at me. "After all, we're picking the best and brightest."

"I assume each gets a copy of *The Tribal Manifesto*?" I teased.

"Yes, if they ask for one. We do mentor in life as well as in our various areas of expertise. That's what it says on the sign, after all."

"So it does." I paused, absorbing what that had meant for me as well. "A week, you said? Days filled with classes?"

"Not filled. Usually, some time in the morning, with the rest of the day given to enjoying the grounds, practicing their various crafts, talking, sharing, discovering. They arrive on the afternoon and evening of a Sunday and stay the week. On Saturday evening, we all gather here to share what the week has given us. We set up tables and chairs, the dumb waiter brings up food, and it's an evening of happy revelry for all. We film the readings and performances, and the participants all get access to it on private pages of our website. Each one who gives us permission has his or her work put into the public pages of the site. That becomes our best advertising for these mentoring weeks."

"Which lets them show their talents to the world, and it gives good credit for Timewind's relation with the Outworld." I nodded slowly. "Sounds like a win-win. Do your students ever worry about being targeted by the Fibbies?"

Lightwing laughed gently. "Our mentoring doesn't come with a warning label, and most of our guests aren't even aware of it. I remember one young stoat who had heard the rumors and, with a grin, told us that the government probably knows everything about him anyway. It didn't seem to bother anyone else either, and no one has ever come back to tell us that they've been somehow targeted or scrutinized. With the weird mix of social and political stuff going on these days, I can't even begin to guess what's going to happen in the future. I keep tabs on it, because of my Council position, and everyone has his ear to the ground as best he can without becoming mired in it."

"That's the danger." I looked around the room, wondering what a Saturday revelry might be like among masters and apprentices, mentors and students, new friends gathered to celebrate their learning and becoming. The Steps to Becoming begins with the self, and these students — "guests," as Lightwing called them — come here to learn more about their Selves, becoming more, taking that with them back into the world. That had to count for something.

"Your Ministry also includes how the tribe presents itself," I continued, smiling softly at the use of her official title. "Tell me a little more about that."

The Husky nodded, gladly taking up the description. "All kinds of examples, there. I mentioned the local food bank getting some of our harvest, and that we have a few scholarships that are awarded outside of the tribe itself. We offer some assistance to various other 'local good works' when we can. Thanksgiving and Christmas will find us volunteering at food kitchens; Heartsinger and Moonsong love to cook, and they will usually provide a bit of flair to one or two dishes, just to have something different. Most guests of a food kitchen want good, basic food, but the spices tend to make things interesting for a few of them."

"Sounds like it would be a treat," I agreed.

"We also help at the library in Green Town. You probably drove through the town on your way here." I nodded, and she continued. "With the governmental budget cuts, as well as so much complaint that a physical building 'just isn't needed anymore'..." The derision dripped from her voice as she said it. "The truth is that a well-funded and fully-functional library still serves a huge and valuable purpose. Our local library provides a yowens' summer reading program, internet connections and computer terminals for people who can't otherwise afford them, helps families save money by checking out books and DVDs instead of buying or renting them, an after-school program for yowens, study space for adult literacy tutoring... The head librarian is particularly good at genealogy searches, and she has coordinated a group at the town's retirement home who might otherwise have trouble trying to navigate the internet for information."

She smiled. "We're even helping them with a bit of expansion. The library obtained a grant to build an extension to their main building. Redlance is donating time and talent to make a new checkout desk, creating a surface with an inlay made from California buckeye, like the cash chest that you saw in the Artisanry. The rest of us mere mortals will be helping to build shelves and various bits of interior finishing. A little sweat equity, as it were." The Husky grinned at me. "Oaknail and Unicorn are happily grousing that they're back in the days of building the Bunkhouse, with the stereotyping of being just brawny males to be used as slave labor."

"I'll bet that goes over well," I snerked at her.

"Better than you think. The head librarian I mentioned? Mrs. Sudbury is a feisty kinkajou with a wicked wit. She's planning to challenge them to a trivia contest while they're there, forcing them to prove that they have both brawn *and* brains. They'll have their work cut out for them on both fronts!"

My laugh was loud and long, and some part of my brain allowed my ears to make note of the acoustics of the space. For performance, dining, gatherings of whatever kind, it was a good room. I could imagine the place ringing with song, conversation, laughter. There was a good feeling here, and I once again had that feeling of appreciating that it felt... well, it just felt *good* here, like that space in the north staircase, like the Bunkhouse, like the house and grounds. I was not like Stellamara, with her sensitivity, her empathy, yet even I could sense the feelings of this place. Yes, it was a dream, but it was a substantial one. Maybe I was looking for the word *workable*.

Lightwing was chuckling with me, her whole face joining in with joy and warmth, her ears twitching slightly, her tail wagging with undisguised mirth. I felt my heart swell, and I followed my new instinct yet again, leaning forward to kiss her lips, gently, chastely, but unquestionably mirroring the warmth that I saw and felt from her. I felt it in the way that she returned the kiss, and my heart filled still further, as if I had drunk from Percival's chalice as well. My thoughts crashed in around me, not dark thoughts (for a welcome change), but enough for me to let my wits return.

Breaking the kiss as tenderly as I had begun it, I reached a forepaw to cup her cheek softly. I hoped that my breath didn't sound as short as it felt to me. "Lightwing," I tasted her name, so sweet on my tongue. "I want to ask for your help."

"Of course, Max."

Was her breath as quick as my own? Was she feeling...? *Words, Max,* I heard me tell myself. *Use your words, like a grown-up dog.* "I have taken to heart Heartsinger's words about an emotional overload. I don't think that's what this is... I hope it isn't..." I felt the blush rise like a burning on my cheeks, and I wondered briefly if that explained the sense that the entire room was suffused with a faintly rose-colored tint.

For her part, Lightwing smiled at me with great affection. I was sure that's what it was (wasn't I?). "Thank you, Max," she acknowledged softly. "You're showing that you care about me by asking me to help you with your feelings. I'm very glad to help you in every way that I can."

I have to imagine that some expression on my face registered a bit more than I'd intended it to. She did not laugh; the smile she gave to me was not mocking, not suggestive, just understanding.

"What would you say to nice hot cup of tea?"

Grinning, I replied, "Hello, cup of tea; how nice and hot you are."

"Good answer." She turned her head and kissed my palm briefly before taking it in to her forepaw. "The dumb waiter is a little too small to ride in. Stairs okay?"

"Down is always easier than up."

This time, she did chuckle a little. "Max, it's okay if you're worried about how much it sounds like double-entendre. I'm doing it, too."

"Then we're doing it together?"

I swear that it wasn't intentional. I was just glad that we both were able to laugh about it. Something else that's fun to do together.

Yep, I can stop. I can stop anytime I want. No, really, I can...

23: Rooibos and Reflection

The stairs from the South Tower weren't as grand as the central stairs up to the living quarters, nor as beautiful as the stairs on the north side, with its warm display of windows. This staircase was as wide as the stairwell on the north, but the decorations were more like windows onto Timewind itself. The walls were festooned with simply-framed photos, each with a small caption at the bottom, showing members of Timewind as well as group pictures of (as Lightwing explained) their various guests, students, even some celebrities that I recognized.

"Experts in their fields," Lightwing answered my unasked question. "A few actors, some writers you might know from dustjacket covers, professors whose reputations may have gotten them into the news a few times, and yes, that fur," she pointed to one of the pictures, "is the Congressional Representative for this district. He was not here to stump for votes; no press, no handlers, and the only photographer present was whoever was taking the pictures for the particular gathering. He supports our mentoring work and came by as a sort of before-and-during dinner speaker. He took about five minutes before the meal to explain that he had no speech, that he wanted to talk about how dreams are unknown in lawmaking but that he'd be damned if he'd stop trying, and asked for help, from our guests, in his own Becoming. It might win him some votes, but not because of stumping and publicity. He really wants to listen, and we gave him a great chance to do it."

"Forgive my cynicism," I said, "but it might have cost him votes, if that got out."

"He addressed that idea by asking all of us for help in deciding what to do it. A conspiracy of silence? An opportunity for blackmail? Coming out of the tribal closet? He got a good laugh for that one."

"What did you all decide?"

Lightwing smiled. "That there is a difference between 'secret' and 'private.' Furs in the public eye are constantly scrutinized, as if they are not permitted even the semblance of privacy; it is assumed that they should answer questions that most of us are offended even by the asking. There was no reason why the Congressman should be asked where he spent that Saturday evening; he could answer, truthfully, that he spent it with friends. What friends? Constituents. Why no press coverage? It was a dinner, not an event." The Husky shrugged her shoulders. "It could get as nasty as anything else, but the consensus was that it wouldn't be an issue. If the press really got nasty, the Congressman has thirty or so witnesses to the fact that he was invited to speak, privately, at a dinner of students who had been instructed here at Starhold. We would rightly wonder what the big deal was, and it would wash out of the next news cycle."

I shook my head. "Why does it have to be this way? Why do we always have to be on our guard against the rest of the world?"

She put a forepaw to my shoulder. "It's okay, Max. That's actually what the discussion was about. Our student guests began to understand that the Congressman was making that very point. There's a lot of negativity out there, and a great many furs who seem to revel in the destruction of anything or anyone good. A wise philosopher once said that our society tends to put people on pedestals, then take pot-shots at them."

"Did you come up with an answer?"

"It comes back to Becoming. Give your best self to the world, always. Keep your private life private, do your best, and don't let the haters win."

"If he gets chased out of office, though, then the haters will have won."

"Only if he lets them. His supporters know that he does good work in Congress, and if he's not allowed to do it there, he'll find other ways to do it. He is not a member of Timewind, but he's definitely tribal. He'll keep on doing good, as best he can, whatever he's doing."

The point needed no driving home, because even a comparative dolt like me can see analogies, similarities, parallels. I felt no "wave of fear" crash over me; more like a "lapping of unease," which is a phrase that I thought Darkstar would smack me for coming up with. I'm no writer, but even I could figure out that I was really pushing it, with inner dialog like that.

"Hey." Lightwing squeezed my shoulder gently. "I get the feeling that it's definitely time for tea. Let's go."

We continued down the stairs, past more and more pictures of smiling furs, all of whom shared a dream-filled moment. Each photo captured a single moment, and I guessed at 70 or 80 of them here, perhaps a hundred.

Maybe there were other photos, in other places, that captured yet more moments. Photos capture moments, and yes, some could be horrifying, or sad, or devastating. Not all moments are like that. Here's proof. *So obvious, Max.*

Then why do I never think about it?

* * * * *

Back in the kitchen, the microwave clock told us that it was indeed "tea time," or as near to 4:00pm as made no odds. Lightwing again did the honors, this time with something she described as a "blackberry roo-ee-boss," which certainly tasted of blackberries (she'd added some honey, no lemon), so I just enjoyed it and decided I'd ask her more about it another time. We chatted idly at a table tucked into a nook space there in the kitchen that, she explained, was often used for those who wanted to make a quick meal or snack without trucking back and forth into the dining hall. I think Lightwing sensed a change in my mood.

"This space," I explained, leaning back in the padded bench seat. "There was something like it in the kitchen of Glover's house. It was where I interviewed the maid and the cook — the only inside staff. The cook told me that Glover would pad his way to the kitchen rather than use the buzzer to call up for some tea or cocoa. He would sit in that nook, chatting with the cook while she prepared the drink for him. She said that he treated her like a cook, not a slave." I paused, considering. "Some part of Airdancer was still in him, at least enough to be civil."

"That's good to know." The Husky leaned a little closer to me, her voice soft. "His name hasn't come up in a little while. How are you feeling, Max?"

I looked into her eyes, those beautiful ice-blue eyes, and I was still smart enough not to be glib with my answer. Nodding, smiling a little, I breathed in and really tried to put words to it. "Bringing him up doesn't hurt, or at least it doesn't right now. Remembering that bit of what I was told about him... I'm not quite sure what words come up. Makes him seem more real to me, somehow, instead of some restless, malevolent ghost. Helps me feel like there's really some good left in the world, even in his world."

Smiling warmly, her tail softly thapping the seat behind her, Lightwing patted my forepaw. "It would be good to bring that story up at dinner tonight. I think the others would like to hear it as well."

My attempt at agreement was interrupted by a yawn that demanded my full and immediate attention. I was absolutely certain that my host could count, if not outright inspect, every tooth in my maw. My eyes screwed themselves shut as if to concentrate on the sheer power of it. I brought up a forepaw to cover as much of it as I could, managed to keep a soft whine from escaping my throat, and eventually brought my face back under my control. I opened my eyes and was about to offer a proper apology when I noticed Lightwing's seemingly knowing smile.

"I was waiting for that."

"I hope you don't mean that you think I find you boring," I half-mumbled.

"No," she chuckled at me. "You've been through a lot this morning. Emotional work can be as exhausting as physical work, and by my rough guess, you've done the equivalent of chopping a couple of cords of firewood. C'mon." She rose and extended a forepaw toward me. "You need a nap."

Getting to my hindpaws, I found myself not entirely sure how to take that, although I felt sure that many of my not-entirely-innocent interpretations showed on my face, if not during the few moments that it took for me to get my tail to stop being obvious. All the while, even as she took my forepaw and gave it a gentle squeeze, her smile radiated nothing but benevolence. We did take a moment to wash out the mugs before she led me back to my guest suite. No one was in the halls as we went through, which suited me just fine. I felt a burning on my cheeks just realizing how much I was reading into her comment. I felt like I was back in high school, a foolish pup still trying to find out if what some of the jocks had bragged about was true, not knowing what love and sex had to do with each other, what the Question and Response was really for, since yowens weren't supposed to do that kind of thing, and oh my furry tail, we were at the room...

With slightly exaggerated patience, Lightwing guided me toward the bed, spun me around, and pushed me down to sit on it. I looked up into her eyes, a lump in my throat making it impossible to speak. She bowed toward me, smiling tenderly, then leaned in to whisper into my ear...

"Nap, Max. You need the rest. I'll be back to get you for dinner."

I hadn't felt so embarrassed since those horrible high school days. Like then, I wanted the earth to swallow me up; also like then, the earth stubbornly refused.

As she began to pull away from me, the Husky turned her muzzle toward mine, offering a brief, warm kiss to my lips before she straightened up and pet my headfur tenderly. Hesitation? Pity? What was she...?

"See you in a few hours."

With that, she turned and padded to the door, closing it quietly as she left.

Letting out a slow breath, I tried to deal with a frenzy of emotions. How could I have thought... Maybe I shouldn't have... Would she really have... I wasn't sure what I was feeling, I told her about that... Better that we don't... She is so beautiful... What was I thinking... *Was* I thinking? Could she have...

I shook my head and lay back on the bed, letting my crazed brain run around like a pup with a sugar high. No way I was gonna fall asleep with this going on...

* * * * *

Slowly opening my eyes, it quickly became obvious to me that I was waking from my nap. Recovering from that chagrin was the first of many, as I tried hard to keep from beating myself up over the racing thoughts of earlier. I was certain that Lightwing thought a lot less of me, after that little episode. I had probably screwed up my welcome here, which would make dinner more than a little awkward.

Rolling onto my side, away from the door, I considered my options. If I could find Darkstar, I could discreetly ask for my clothes, find my car, drive off. Maybe I could make up some sort of emergency, or...

I sighed heavily. I didn't think that I could get away with lying to this bunch, not with Stellamara and Heartsinger in the mix. It would only make things worse. That old phrase "laugh and lump it" came to mind, although I didn't feel like laughing. There was nothing pressuring me to leave the room, not before Lightwing arrived to get me. I guessed I could find something to do, to bide my time until then. Give me a chance to hide a little longer.

Raising my eyes a little, I looked over at the chair and table near the window. The book still lay there — a copy of *The Tribal Manifesto*, as Lightwing had told me last night. Seeing it seemed to still my thoughts, making a space for me remember what the day had shown me. I remembered how motels used to have a copy of Gideon's bible in a drawer somewhere, presumably to offer comfort to weary travelers. Where that particular book had failed me, perhaps this one might help.

Further scootching and rolling got me to the far side of the bed, and I made my way to the comfortable armchair in short order. Taking the book into my forepaws, my first observation was that the cover wasn't what I had anticipated. Instead of the house, or the Bunkhouse, or even the Artisanry, it was a montage of pictures, as if a photo album had been spilled and pictures went every which way. I saw a lot of familiar faces, some unfamiliar ones, in singles, pairs, and groups, all happy and sharing whatever moment might have been going on at the time. Superimposed, in modest font, was the title and, near the bottom, the attribution of *Timewind*. The authorship belonged to the tribe, as it had on the original volume.

Inside, the title page offered a bit more elaboration: *The Tribal Manifesto, Being Our Attempt to Share Our Dreams With the World, by the Members of the Tribe of Timewind*. Next, a table of contents offered section or chapter titles and names of individual authors — again, some names I knew, some I didn't, and titles that covered many topics and ideas. It seemed to me that I would benefit from reading the whole thing, although certain section titles jumped out at me, including *Dreaming Awake* and *Dreaming Well With Others*. Leafing through the pages, I had the impression that the "chapters" were more like essays, portions of journals or diaries, or simply the reflections of individual members upon their experiences with "being tribal."

The differences between this and that comb-bound original that I had tried to suffer through a few nights ago were substantial. This was a book, a regular 15x25cm sized paperback, 185 pages, and the contents were better presented. Just skimming a few of the entries told me that the language was more uniform, in the same font and size, and looked to be better edited. I'm no expert in that kind of thing, but I know when a sentence feels smooth and when it doesn't. I sensed Darkstar's paw in this edition.

As for actual reading, it seemed sensible to start at the beginning, which happened to be Oaknail's introduction.

Welcome [it read] *to the sharing of a dream. That may already sound a little crazy to you. It did to all of us, when we first started talking about it in the early months of 1994. Nine of us, young, idealistic, and maybe more than a little crazy, wondered what would happen if we banded together to forge a life based on our dreams, with values built on mutual support and trust. Yup, definitely crazy.*

The funny thing is, it worked.

As I write these opening notes, our tribe has been together for 25 years, and we're still dreaming, and we're bringing as much of the dream back out into the world that we can. You can read about current projects, scholarships, mentoring, any number of our ways of bringing forth and sharing our dreams, on our website; the URL and QR code is on the back cover. This book is about the background to all that, the things we've learned along the way, presented with a view to explaining how we brought all this about, and how we hope that you, too, will be able to find your own dreams and make them happen.

We've all been asked about the title of this book. Why The Tribal Manifesto? *Our statements are a manifesto, meaning "a public declaration of policy and aims" (yes, I looked it up). Most furs hear the echo of Engels and Marx's* The Communist Manifesto, *and they're meant to. The irony is intentional. We've been called "commies," even though we really aren't a commune or collective, nor do we insist that all the world adhere to the ideas we manifest here. This book is about what we did, how we did it, and most importantly, why we did it. Let's start with this...*

The next page was devoted to a large and beautiful rendering of the Three Steps to Becoming (numbering corrected).

This sounds [Oaknail continued on the next page] *like the oft-heard phrase, "Be the change that you want to see in the world." Research tells us that this phrase, although attributed to the Mahatma Gandhi, was not what he actually said. We discovered that Gandhi's words were, "We but mirror the world. All the tendencies present in the outer world are to be found in the world of our body. If we could change ourselves, the tendencies in the world would also change. As one changes his own nature, so does the attitude of the world change towards him. This is the divine mystery supreme. A wonderful thing it is and the source of our happiness. We need not wait to see what others do."*

Our version of this idea took on the form of the *Three Steps to Becoming.* None of us would claim to be wiser than the Great Soul Gandhi, least of all this bear! It was through our talks that we, the nine founders of Timewind and all who have joined with us over the years, realized that changing ourselves is a huge project and, ironically, not one to be undertaken alone. Although each furson must do the work him/herself, and although s/he must begin the work individually, the task of continuing the work is benefitted by having others around who are also doing their own work. It's why "gym buddies," dieting clubs, support groups, and recovering addicts groups exist: It helps to have sympathetic fursons around you, fursons who are going through the same (or at least similar) challenges.

More than that, however, it is important to be able to get help from others. For some, this means reading self-help books or attending seminars. What we have discovered, in our many late-night talks, is that asking for help and giving help are both — to overuse the word — helpful. The give-and-take of discussion, of working out ideas with each other, often brings out things that we hadn't considered before. (I salute Darkstar, our writer and philosopher in residence, for pointing out that this is essentially the "Socratic method" of learning.) We run the risk of stepping on toes, bruising egos, dredging up old memories that we'd rather have left buried; we also are there to apologize, to build back up, to comfort each other through the reconstruction of ourselves. This is part of the pledge to ask for and give help. It means to take care with one another, to be responsible to each other in our journey to make ourselves the best that we can be.

The Mahatma's urging to "change ourselves" so that "the tendencies in the world would also change" is the third step of our Becoming. We give ourselves to the world, each of us, every day. What we do, say, accomplish, offer, every action that we take, that's what we give to our world. We strive to give our best, *to share kindness, to be helpful, thoughtful, gentle in our interactions. Short form: We try to give a damn.*

That can take a lot out of a furson, and we need to regain our strength and focus. This is also what the tribe is for. We call on one another, as friends, as family, to lean on each other, talk out the issues, reinforce our commitment to being our best selves. Cheaper than therapy! It's also <u>community</u>, *not in the socio-political sense of communism, but in the sense of* <u>communing</u>, *of sharing intimate thoughts or feelings. For some, the word is related to prayer, and some of our tribal members have described the act of sharing our thoughts and feelings with each other to be akin to one of the ancient meanings of the word* <u>namaste</u>, *"The divine in me honors [bows to] the divine in you."*

So I, and the tribe, bow to you, to honor the divine in you by sharing this glimpse into our crazy dream for a better self and, through that, a better Us, and thus a better world. Welcome to our continuing journey and, perhaps, to yours as well.

I closed the book and set it back on the table, giving myself a few moments to breathe and let the words sink in. The line about "bruised egos" rang truest for me, and I let the idea run through my mind to collect evidence, like a certain detective dog would do. This time, the search wasn't cold and calculating; strangely, it felt rational yet emotionally connected, sympathetic. That sort of emotion wasn't helpful in the Homicide Cop line of work, or so the world tried to tell me. Moshe told me otherwise without ever actually saying it. The idea of "what to let go of and what to keep" pertained to evidence and clues as much as to the rest of my life, and it required a sense of listening to the gut as well the head.

The knock at my door was almost too soft to hear. "Come in."

Lightwing entered, her gaze first toward the bed, then the chair where I sat. "You're vertical," she smiled at me.

"Not disappointed, I hope?"

Her tail wagged gently as she chuckled. "I take it you're feeling better?"

"Yes," I said, rising to meet her. "I do have something to ask you, though."

"What's that?"

I took her forepaws in mine. "I'm not quite sure how to phrase it. Something like, 'Do I have something to apologize for' comes to mind."

"You don't. Will you tell me why you feel that you do?"

"You mean, aside from acting like an inexperienced adolescent who was hoping that 'IT' was really about to happen, regardless of any reasons why it shouldn't?"

The Husky nodded once, a twinkle in her ice blue eyes. "It's good to know that I haven't lost my touch," she grinned at me. "You had asked me if what you were feeling was just the emotional overload. Most of it wasn't. That last bit, though, the part you described as being like an adolescent... yes, that was the overload, coupled with your needing a nap."

I looked down, laughing a little, feeling the blush on my cheeks, feeling my tail giving some nervous wags. Her forepaws gave mine a little squeeze, and she bent forward quickly to give my burning cheek a brief kiss.

"C'mon." She tugged my forepaws gently. "There's still a little time before dinner, and we can wait in the den for a while."

"Afraid to be alone with me?" I tried to make the joke. I gave her forepaws a squeeze, then released them. "A good idea. Let's go see who else is lining up for the grub."

To my surprise, she didn't move. She stood, looking at me, and I wondered what had changed. After a long moment, she asked, "Do you really think I'd be afraid to be alone with you?"

I blinked. "No."

"Then why did you say it?"

"Just a joke."

"Deflection." She put a forepaw to my shoulder, giving me a wan yet sympathetic smile. "Blame my time on the therapist's couch. And, if you want, blame it on my wanting to look out for you. Max, you're free to tell me if I'm wrong. It feels like you want to talk more, and I didn't want to just cut you off."

For a long moment, I had the feeling that she was speaking in a foreign language. It was the look in her eyes, the warmth there, the entirety of her face, of her presence, that made me look at myself the way she was seeing me, hearing me. *Reflecting me.* I didn't have time to wonder where that notion came from; Lightwing was waiting for me to speak.

"I'm not gonna get away with anything with you, am I?" I asked with a self-deprecating smile.

"Nope. Not if I can help it. And I want you to do the same for me. It works both ways, Max."

"Yes," I said, then swallowed. "I do want to talk. Is it okay to say that I still have that feeling about you?"

Her smile warmed, and she brushed her forepaw against my cheek. "It's always okay to be in touch with what you feel, and I thank you for sharing it with me. Do you want to talk now or after dinner?"

The feeling swirled in me, brought up all the double-entendres, and I finally settled on a guilty chuckle. "It's a lot to talk about before dinner."

"Then we'll talk tonight, shall we?"

"Yes, please." Imitating her move from earlier, I turned my muzzle to kiss her open palm. "Thank you for your patience."

"Thank you for your respect and trust."

I smiled gently at her. "Is that from the time on the couch, too?"

"Maybe," she allowed. "Still true. Thank you, Max." Patting my shoulder gently, she added, "Let's go see who's going to join us."

The ornery teenager in my brain tried to stir up a series of naughty images. I told the pup to sit in a corner and shut up. I'd have sent him to bed without dinner, but that had connotations that he wanted to pounce on, and I wouldn't give him the satisfaction.

24: Visitor's Vita

When Lightwing and I got to the den, I half expected to see Rainmist in the same chair I'd seen her in last night, gazing out the window. Tonight, there was no rain to attract her attention, so I wasn't all that surprised to see her in one of the chairs of the sunken area I'd come to think of as "the pit," in an entirely cozy sense. She glanced up from the book that she was reading and gave me one of her warm and slightly coquettish smiles. "Hello, Max," she greeted me. "How's your day been?"

"We've been giving him the nickel tour," Lightwing smiled.

"More like the fifty-cent tour, at the very least!" I laughed softly. "I think I've seen pretty well everything of the house and grounds."

"And what do you think?" the otter asked, rising from her place.

"I'm amazed that you've all managed to do so much in so little time. Less than three decades, and you have the Bunkhouse, this house, the store and, what's more important, the scholarships, the mentoring weeks, the help with the community... It's all just..." I shook my head, then realized that the otter and Husky were looking at me with equally admiring expressions. All that could come out of my maw, at that moment, was a simple and genuinely confused, "What?"

"We have succeeded in corrupting you, Max," Rainmist giggled. "You mentioned the property development, but you also said that the outreach was more important."

"It is," I mumbled, trying not to blush. I have no idea why I felt that I should apologize, or be embarrassed, or ashamed, or anything like that, but that's what I was feeling. Lightwing gave me a side-to-side hug, and Rainmist rose and did the same. Sandwiched between them, I managed a laugh that was unquestionably from the "embarrassed" side of the laughter collection.

"Sorry, Max," the otter chittered gently. "Wasn't trying to put you on the spot."

"Wish I knew why it felt that way. I mean," I added quickly, "why I should feel that I was put on the spot, not that you..." I stopped when I felt her gentle squeeze.

"You've been through a lot of change in a very short time," Rainmist said softly. "Even before you got here last night, there have been changes happening. We accelerated it. Maybe we even foisted our ways of thinking on you when you were vulnerable. Are we moving too fast?"

I returned a squeeze to both of the flanking females, the smile on my muzzle feeling more comfortable. "Fast, but not too fast. Maybe I just surprised myself."

"You did just fine."

"Hey, is this a private hug, or can anyone join in?"

We all turned to see Darkstar grinning at us, his arms slightly outspread. The otter and Husky released me to take up the lynx's offer. I was fully aware that my tail was wagging, and I didn't care who noticed. "Are you violating some Oath of Inscrutability, smiling this much?"

"What happens at Starhold stays at Starhold," he quipped, chuckling softly. Releasing me from our tight hug, the lynx looked at me with an unstinted glint in his eye. "Is it okay for me to say that you look... well, different?"

"Better, I hope?"

He nodded. "Funny for a writer to say that he can't choose a good word. 'Better' is a definitely good word. Maybe 'more whole' is what I'm looking for."

"I'll take it." My laugh felt nervous. "When I had an awkward moment like this, earlier, I was saved by Unicorn's stomach gurgles."

"Did I miss my cue?"

There was no mistaking that fine, cultured voice, and we all turned toward it. The stallion, now clothed in "proper" tribal garb, swooped in upon Rainmist, providing her with a warm kiss and an even warmer hug. The otter seemed almost lost in the embrace, and her delighted chitter made us all smile. The rest of the tribe, meaning those present at Starhold this weekend, joined us over the next several minutes. Casual chatting, some of it concerning my opinions of the Grand Tour (I could hear the gentle jibe of capital letters), until someone pointed out that we had 13 at dinner. Rainmist noted that it was the title of an Agatha Christie mystery, and I observed that it was the same number as the legendary Last Supper.

"Depends on who you ask," Darkstar observed, this smile a bit more representative of the enigmatic variety that lynx are known for. "You probably know the infamous theory that Mary Magdalene was also in attendance, and that DaVinci's painting was altered?" He chuckled. "Fact or fiction, it's still an amusing idea."

"Enough theorizing!" Moonsong's voice called to us from the dining hall. "Dinner's on!"

Heartsinger and Darkstar once again made the tables ready, as the rest of us pitched in to set up the stools. The issue of the odd number at table was dealt with when Oray and Starshine volunteered to sit closer together.

"Oh, such sacrifice!" Unicorn observed drily. "I'm deeply moved."

The yowens at the table provided proper raspberries for that remark.

Dinner proved to be an exercise in the finest of comfort foods: spaghetti topped with what I announced, without exaggeration, to be the best tomato and meat sauce I'd ever had. The dish was filled with sausage, finely-diced pepperoni, chopped onion, and red, yellow, and green bell pepper. Moonsong jested that it was her "Traffic Light" pasta sauce.

"I hope that won't merit a ticket," Frank observed, his eyes gently hoping that I didn't mind the joke.

Grinning at him, I replied, "Hey, do I look like a beat cop to you?"

The group laughed well, and Frank and I saluted one another with our glasses of root beer (what else do you have with spaghetti or pizza?). The mountain lion had taken a risk, had tested the trust between us, and I rewarded that trust. I think I had that right — the words, I mean. I was paraphrasing some of the things that Lightwing had been talking about, as well as things I'd heard in those half-remembered police training sessions, the ones about trying to understand and deal with furs whose brains are differently wired. I made a note to myself to ask Darkstar if he knew the right word for that. It might help my learning to know the vocabulary better.

Conversation ranged across several topics, and the feeling was friendly, maybe even familial. I felt welcomed again, and yes, it was because I was Max and not Detective Luton. What Frank made me realize, though, was that there was at least some aspect of the "cop" that was welcome, too. I didn't have to live separate lives, even though being here gave me a chance to find the "me" that I'd let the "Detective" cover up for so long. (That phrasing, in my head, did not escape my attention.)

Portions had been generous with both sauce and pasta, enough to feel comfortable but not over-full. Talk around the table had been winding down a bit, when Heartsinger suddenly called out, "Visitor's Vita!"

This phrase received a round of applause and gentle cheering, and Oaknail put a reinforcing forepaw to my shoulder, smiling at me. "It's something that we've come up with, to ask our guests to share their lives with us, just a little."

"We stole the term from 'curriculum vita," Darkstar explained, "which literally means 'course of life."

"That's what a 'CV' is, isn't it?" I asked. "I thought that was for academics, professors, something to do with schools. The rest of us mere mortals use résumés."

"Same thing, even for mere mortals," the lynx chuckled softly.

"For us," Oaknail continued, "we hope that our visitors will tell us about themselves — nothing too revealing, just to give us an idea of what their paths have been like."

"Max," Lightwing offered, "this might be a good time to share that story you told me earlier, about Airdancer."

Nodding, I said, "A good point." I paused, feeling all eyes on me. "I can tell you more about me by starting with something about Airdancer that will give you the same sort of hope that brought me to Starhold, to find you all. To find me."

I told the tale of the breakfast nook, here and at Glover's mansion, telling them (as I told Lightwing) that the tiger hadn't lost all of his goodness to his lifestyle. That led to my talking about my own beginnings, my growing up (if I really did), my meeting and marrying Barbara, Michael's birth, and the origins of Detective Luton. I told them about Moshe, about things that Stellamara and Heartsinger helped me remember about him. I left out the idea of having been murdered by Detective Luton; this rendition, which went on for about twenty minutes, focused on more positive aspects, as much as I could make it.

"That's a good slice of my life. I have only a couple more things, if you don't mind." Heads all around the table nodded and smiled encouragingly.

I cleared my throat softly. "I'd like to thank Frank for his joking tonight. He's helped me feel less... well, trapped in that 'cop' identity." I nodded to the mountain lion, as his lover Dreamweaver put an arm around him. He smiled at me, and I was fairly sure that he blushed a little.

"I guess the other thing is an extension of that. Much of my life, in recent years, has been about that 'cop self.' I used it to wrap myself up in, to push away and keep away anything that might hurt. What happened between me and Barbara was more complicated, but it was essentially the same thing. Michael worked on me, kept me from withdrawing entirely. The rest of the world..." I looked to Darkstar, who I figured might well know. "What was that line in *A Christmas Carol*, about Scrooge keeping the world away from him?"

"But what did Scrooge care!" Oray piped up, as if in performance. All eyes turned to him, as he delivered the rest. "It was the very thing he liked. To edge his way along the crowded paths of life, warning all warmth and sympathy to keep its distance." The firefox smiled at me. "I'm partial to that dramatic reading."

Smiling at him, I nodded. "That's exactly the quote. 'Keep its distance.' My suit became armor; in cold weather, the trench coat was a cliché that let people see a character, a function, instead of a furson. And then came a case that pierced through that armor, and a rainstorm that drenched it, and a houseful of dreamers who stripped me to the fur and put me into clothing that is just too soft and free to be used as armor."

"You're welcome," Dreamweaver chuckled, "although it was Quicksilver who made the original designs and the first cloth that was used."

"And don't forget to give them back," Darkstar chuckled.

I plucked at the shirt. "You mean, right now?"

Oaknail laughed along with the others. "A little early in the evening to call for a furpile!" the bear opined.

"Who says?" Oray piped up. Starshine gave his arm a playful slap, but he didn't seem the least dissuaded.

"Don't think I'm quite ready for a furpile," I laughed gently. "There's something else, though. Something that I've shared with only a few of you so far." Standing, stepping slightly away from the table, I said, "I want hugs, and I'm not gonna let any of you go until I've gotten one from each of you."

"DIBS!" hollered Moonsong, as she jumped up and almost tackled me where I stood. The phrase "bear hug" is sometimes called speciesist; I think the only ones who claim that are just jealous of those of us who have experienced one. I had both arms full of warm ursine, in the sense of body heat and of her huge heart. I almost didn't want to let go. Two things fixed that: The others were already lining up to fulfill their part of the bargain, and I knew that Moonsong would gladly hug me more, as much and as often as we both would want.

I found myself wondering who would ever think it would be boring to "just hug." Oray's youthful enthusiasm made me wonder for a moment if he was going to try to climb me, and Starshine very nearly did. Rainmist cuddled up close to me, almost disappearing into the embrace, and then wiggled happily against me. Frank was a happy back-pounder, and I returned the same, and we fake-rassled for a few seconds, laughing the whole time. When Stellamara had her turn with me, I held her gently as she seemed to float in my arms. Oaknail put his arms around me and lifted me into the air briefly before returning me safely to the ground again. As if well aware of his stallion size, Unicorn held me powerfully yet tenderly, an amazing combination that surprised me greatly and happily. Every one of them hugged me... another bit of Dickens floated into my brain, "anyhow and everyhow." I had no words to describe how wonderful that felt, and I somehow had discovered enough sense to let myself just enjoy it for itself.

We tended to the dishes, yet again proving the old adage of "many paws make light work." When everything was taken care of, Moonsong shooed us out of the kitchen, telling us to "go play a game or something for a while." Lightwing and I glanced at one another, grinning with our shared secret from this morning. It wasn't a certainty, but we could at least hope.

Although I teased Unicorn about starting up a round of Monopoly (Oaknail and Rainmist had a good laugh over that one), the game that was brought out was called *Taboo*. The object was to describe to your teammates someone or something without using any of five words listed on the card; how many cards can you get through in 60 seconds, with someone looking over your shoulder, wielding a buzzer, to make sure you follow the rules?

Trying to describe a giraffe without using "long" and "neck" (plus three other words) would have stumped me but, happily, it had come up during Darkstar's turn; he opted for "a fur with a hyperextended esophagus," and his team got it fast. It was a challenge, especially to my underworked brain, but I did get a few good clues out here and there. Hilarity ensued when some of the guesses got a bit bawdy — nothing actually crude, but it made for giggles and laughter. I couldn't remember the last time I had been to a party, much less played a party game. A dog could get used to this sort of thing.

There were six to a side, in this particular game, so twelve total rounds. Given the shifting and readying between one-minute rounds, it provided precisely enough time for the slowly-growing scents of molasses, cinnamon, and that sweet aroma that happens when sugar is an ingredient in baking. When I caught Heartsinger's eye, he grinned at me, his barely-controlled tail only slightly more subtle than the nod he gave me. Lightwing had caught it, too — our Borzhvolk had made his request of Moonsong, and the absolute joys of dessert were in our very near future.

"Okay," Oray said after the game had ended. "My nose is better than some, but I'm pretty sure everyone is catching a whiff from the kitchen by now."

"Patience, yowen," Oaknail admonished. "She'll call us when she's ready." The bear took an exaggerated sniff and whined softly. "Hope it's soon...!"

While we all pretended to wait, like civilized furs, instead of descending on the kitchen in a mob, I marveled at the realization that I actually looked forward to the dessert. After such a happily filling meal of fine spaghetti, I didn't think that I'd have had room for it; instead, an indulgence in a night of comfort food seemed to be an absolutely perfect way to cap off the week.

"Okay, you lot," Moonsong eventually hollered at us. "I want an orderly, single-file line through the kitchen. Frank, you're at the front."

"How come?" Oray pouted, presumably as a jest, although it sounded quite serious.

"Because I need his arm muscles to scoop ice cream. C'mon, no pushing, shoving, tripping, or any other activity subject to the punishment of being denied dessert."

It was amazing how quiet and cooperative we became.

Another soup-kitchen line-up (this time, actually in the kitchen) got each of us a shallow bowl, a spoon, a very large and freshly-baked oatmeal raisin cookie (soft, warm, with extra raisins), topped with a large scoop of rich French vanilla ice cream, the kind whose velvety texture and color inspired that pale yellow shade that some interior designers and second-wedding brides used to great success. We all returned to the dining hall, resumed our respective seats, and waited not even a moment before diving in. I wasn't the only one who made "yummy sounds" over the amazing dessert, and a few others chuckled.

"Is it bad manners to enjoy this magnificent dessert too much?" I asked.

"Only if you're shy," Rainmist affirmed.

Turned out none of us was. The word "ecstasy" has more than one definition, or at least more than one cause, and everyone at the table got into the act. There were giggles, laughs, deep grunts, outright moaning, the occasional banging of a spoon handle on the table, even Unicorn belting out, "Ooo, yeah, baby, that's what I'm talkin' about!" At one point, Oaknail offered a rousing, "Moonsong, my honeybear, you do it sooooo good!" An audio recording of those moments might have sold well on some sort of audio-porn site. I had no idea if such a thing existed, but Rule 34 being what it is, I wouldn't be the least surprised.

Maybe the best joke of the evening was the general consensus that washing the dishes seemed almost unnecessary, given how all of us had been even less shy about licking the bowls clean. I even managed to joke that I hadn't used my tongue that thoroughly in a very long time. Oray, naturally, bellowed at the obvious joke, but at least he had enough tact not to elaborate on the idea.

Dishes stacked, spoons gathered, Darkstar and Heartsinger took them all back to the kitchen while the rest of us waddled back into the den to find spaces to collapse onto. There was still a lot of chuckling going on, comments about just how silly we all were, and idle conversation starters that felt a lot like the parties I used to go to, years ago. Back then, we still wanted to be together physically, to talk, to laugh, to be together. When did "party" start to mean having a few furs physically in the same room, with everyone making calls and texts, or online gaming with people down the street or across an ocean, instead of interacting with each other? Was I just "being an old fart," wanting things "the way they used to be," or is it that relationships in this 21st century have become electronic-only? Intimacy seems to exist only through texts and video, rather than really being together. That time spent in the Bunkhouse, that Unicorn had described, really hit home with me (emphasis on "home"). This evening, too, with its familial feel, also felt like...

Home? Yeah, that word kept coming up way too much. That's a big jump, I told myself. Maybe it's just a good weekend's relaxation. Not good to drink too much Kool-Aid, or tea, or even slurp down French vanilla ice cream, too often. It might spoil me for everything else. I might not want to go back out there, into that cold world that could turn even colder with absurd and terrible ease... and often did.

In the middle of listening to the conversation around me, I quietly took a breath and released it. No fear tonight. No second-guessing. No matter how foreign it was to me, that idea of just letting the moment be what it is, I made myself do exactly that and let the evening be whatever it wanted to be. The rest, that coldness I was afraid of, belonged to the nasty shadow that I would not allow back into my thoughts. It had no place here. In this moment, at least, I did.

There was no sense of time, of hurry, of anything but anecdotes and discussions and jokes and the thousand random things that great gatherings are made of. It was only after a happily long period of this that we all started to notice that the talk was lagging a bit. Even I, despite my nap, was wondering if it was time to call it a night. Before I had the chance to raise the question, I was one of a dozen witnesses to the most powerful yawn I'd ever heard. When he had finished it, Oaknail asked the assembled company, "Anyone have a differing opinion, or is it just gonna be me blaming it on my age?"

I started to reply when I rediscovered the truism that yawns are contagious. This one wasn't as bad as the one I'd had earlier, but it was enthusiastic enough. I wasn't the only fur infected, and more than a few chuckles accompanied the shuffling of otherwise-tired bodies getting out of chairs.

"I know some non-sapient horses who are expecting me to greet the dawn with them," Darkstar allowed, rising to his hindpaws. "Anyone joining me?"

"Count me in," Unicorn raised a forepaw. "I'm usually on the roster for the weekends."

"Your cousins have missed you already," the lynx quipped.

The stallion produced that "laugh" again and, since I was looking at him, I was able to see that he definitely used his tongue; that, then, was unquestionably a raspberry. He then turned to me and set a large and gentle forepaw to my shoulder. "You are hereby enjoined not to leave tomorrow without a proper send-off. At the least, stay for lunch. We'll arrange for as many of us to join as possible."

"I never argue with a lawyer," I quipped, smiling. "Besides, being ordered to stay for lunch is an offer I can't refuse."

"First one with a Brando imitation," Oaknail bellowed, "gets a headslap!"

Starshine clapped a forepaw over Oray's muzzle and started maneuvering him toward the stairs, offering "good night" wishes on their mutual behalf. We all took this as our cue to take ourselves away to our respective rooms. Lightwing wrapped up my arm in hers and escorted me quietly to the guest room. At the door, I turned to her, giving her forepaw a gentle squeeze.

"That was the finest evening I've had in a long time," I told her. "A fine day. Thank you, Lightwing. It's truly wonderful."

"Max," she asked softly, "weren't we going to talk for a little while?"

"Yes, of course. Did you want to go back to the den, or...?"

The Husky silenced me with a tender, chaste kiss, sending my brain reeling. My earlier thoughts and hopes rekindled with that same adolescent-crush feeling that I'd had earlier. As she pulled gently away from me, I was certain that she could see that response in my eyes, and the blush on my cheeks felt like twin flames.

"I do want to talk, Max. Just the two of us." She took my cheeks in her forepaws and looked deeply into my eyes. "Max, would you share your fur with me?"

Before my less-evolved emotions ran away with me, I breathed softly and felt the power of the Question, promised myself to honor it, and her. Gently, intoning the words, putting all of my best self into them, I Responded, "It is warmth to us both."

We entered the guest room, closing the door gently behind us. I turned to her, finding that she was already beginning to remove her shirt. I chuckled softly, and she stopped, looking at me.

"I was just remembering last night, with Rainmist."

Lightwing laughed as well. She readjusted her shirt and padded over to give me a hug. "I didn't mean to be so quick."

"Me, either," assured her. "I'm making myself slow down. You want to talk, and I want to be sure I'm really listening."

"Thank you for helping me be my best self," she offered, with a chuckle. "We must sound like twelve-steppers, in a way; we use phrases like that to help us remember, to focus on our goals."

"That's what the Twelve Step phrases are for, aren't they?"

She nodded. "That's what I understand. There's a tendency, in our modern times, to make fun of affirmations, positive thinking, all of that. It's not *The Great And Final Secret That Will Save Your Life!* or whatever it's being billed as these days." She laughed at the words, and I joined her.

"It's what Unicorn said, what you both were telling me, back in the Bunkhouse. We keep reminding ourselves, and each other, to keep the dream going. Taking those moments to remember, to recommit." Shaking my head a little, I asked, "Is it politically incorrect to say that we're in recovery? We're recovering from... what, lousy realities?"

"Maybe it's just that we're addicted to believing that our realities are so terrible. It's so easy to believe in, to accept, terrible things. The news focuses on horrors, evils, atrocities; it's the 'If it bleeds, it leads' philosophy. That's what we think is 'normal,' or 'ordinary,' or 'the usual.' It's difficult to remember how to be happy."

"'It is what it is,'" I intoned with the sense of a mindless mantra, which it was. "I genuinely hate that phrase. When I was growing up, I heard 'It's

God's will', with that same sense of helplessness, the sense of... abdicating responsibility. 'Oh, look; the baby's diaper is full of pee and poop. Well, it is what it is.'"

"That's not supposed to be what that phrase means. It's supposed to be about accepting a thing for itself, but..." She shook her head. "They stop there. There's a phrase that my therapist used on me: 'Radical acceptance.' The idea of accepting that you don't have all that you need, or all that you want, or even that you're not able to be what you truly are. Accept it all." She looked at me, a terrible truth in her eyes. "For me, that would have meant accepting that there truly is no reason for me to have lived. The truly radical part of that 'radical acceptance' is to give up all hope, all faith, all responsibility, and just end your life, because there's no reason to continue."

I pulled her tightly to me, holding back most of the whine that boiled up from inside me. "I'm so very, very glad that you didn't end your life."

"Because I didn't stop there, Max. I didn't accept that there was nothing left to do. I didn't 'radically accept' nothingness. I found the tribe, and I found the rest of that misunderstood phrase." She pulled away from me to look into my eyes. "It is what it is... and here's what I'm going to do next."

"Here is where I will begin making myself all that I can be." I smiled at her. "And I will ask for and give help, because 'what it is' doesn't have to stop there. We don't have to accept helplessness. We *must not* accept that. We have ourselves; we have each other."

"Yes, Max. Yes, we do." She reached up to caress my cheek softly. "That's part of what I want to talk about."

I turned my muzzle to kiss her palm, and then we separated to take off our clothes. We moved slowly, calmly, caring for our shirts and pants, laying them on the chair. Furclad, we padded to the bed and slipped under the sheets, finding a comfortable shape to melt into and taking a little time simply to hold each other. When she spoke, it was more or less to the air, her tone a tender murmur.

"This sounds a little like a confession, perhaps," she began. "I have spent a lot of time with you in the past 24 hours, and we have shared some secrets and some insights, some joys and sorrows, tears and laughs... During your time with Heartsinger, and while you took your nap, I had some to think, jot a few things in my diary."

"Anything about me?" I asked just as quietly, the smile in my voice seeming to color it just fine.

"Quite a lot, actually." I could tell that she, too, was smiling. "It's been a long time since I've found time to really look at myself through someone else's eyes, and you gave me that opportunity today. In talking to you about Timewind, I was able to get an even deeper look into it, into what it means to me."

"What did you find?"

"All of the best reasons to renew my commitments, to myself and to the tribe. Being the MOOR can be a tough job, but it's also one that I love. I'm good at it, and I'm supported in it."

"You're also good at being yourself, and you get support for that, too."

She shifted in our embrace, raised herself on her elbow and looked at me. The ambient light in the room, from the nightlight in the ensuite, was plenty for me to see the soft flames of her Self in her eyes. "Max, you and I have given ourselves to each other a lot today. I want to stay with you tonight, as I did last night." She rested her forepaw on my chest, the gesture intimate yet not forward. "I am happy to let us enjoy this closeness as it is."

I felt the thudding of my heart, felt my maw go suddenly dry. "I can honor that, and I am very happy to be with you, just like this." I made an attempt at swallowing. "I'm also feeling a very strong desire for you, for more." I managed to chuckle. "And no, I don't think it's the overstimulated adolescent talking."

"Not the emotional overload, either, is it?"

Shaking my head gently, I paid very close attention to what I was feeling. "Not that good with words," I said. "Out of practice, maybe. Yes, it's been a long time since I've... It's not something I can really enjoy with a stranger or a casual acquaintance. I've tried, and it just..." I sighed softly, covering her forepaw with my own. "It takes more for it to be of real value."

"May I offer my take on it?"

I nodded, smiling gently.

"For me, there are four parts to it — a physical connection, a mental one, an emotional one, and a spiritual one. Body, mind, heart, and soul. When that all merges, it makes lovemaking... well, the word Darkstar used was 'transcendent,' and that's the best word I've ever heard for it."

The moment stretched gently as I looked into her eyes. "That might take a lifetime."

"Or a moment."

"Or twenty-four hours?"

She pet my chest gently, warmly, not suggestively. I felt something like what I felt with Stellamara, that sense of deeper connection. Empathy. "We have shared a lot in that time," she said. "If you wish, I would like to share more."

"Yes, if you will help me."

The blink of her eyes and her mildly surprised expression made the moment perfect. I chuckled as I pet her headfur.

"Help me experience this in a way I may not have experienced it before. I've never talked so much before... well, beginning. This is not some casual seduction. It's sudden, yes, but it's also... Lightwing, it's the emotion, the sense of bonding, that's what I want to hold on to, as much as I want to hold you. Help me to love you with my best self."

Moving closer her muzzle closer to mine, she whispered, "You're doing just fine, Max."

The kiss, the warm embers growing warmer, the most tender of beginnings, showed me that I could believe in me as much as she did, as much as I believed in her. The night held us as sweetly as we held each other. We made the dream real.

25: Leaving Starhold

I woke slowly to a sweet, soft, hazy quiet. Sunday mornings have a particular quietness about them. Unless I'm on a case that can't wait (not many of those, contrary to television cop shows), my alarm is off, no church to go to, no friends for brunch. I usually just wake when I wake, do whatever the day might require of me, and try not to think too much until Monday rears its ugly head once more. The usual pattern for an old dog trapped in a life he no longer truly recognizes.

This Sunday morning was different in so many ways. Country quiet, large room, soft pillows and comforter, big warm bed, warmer companion who still dozed beside me. My nose was pleasantly overloaded with scents that brought back some intensely beautiful memories, and my mind swam through a private lagoon of recalled sensation, only some of it physical. What I remembered most were words, sounds, emotions, a merging that was enhanced through the physicality. I wasn't so maudlin as to think I'd never experienced it before; the truth was that I'd never paid this much attention before.

Beside me, a shifting, a gentle stirring. I smiled, waiting to see if she might be still asleep or if she might be waking. We had not fallen asleep in each other's arms; as romantic as that sounds, such a sleeping position all too often led to someone getting the circulation cramped in one or more limbs. Lightwing and I had fallen asleep on our backs, close enough to be near without infringing on each other's personal sleeping space. It was a companionable arrangement that had allowed us both to sleep... after we had exhausted ourselves, quite blissfully, somewhere in the wee hours of the morning.

Taking the chance, I moved my arm a little, finding her forepaw with mine, touching gently. She moved her fingers, interlacing them with mine, making a soft murring sigh. She turned her muzzle toward me, her eyes lazily half-lidded. "G'morning," she whispered gently.

"Very good," I agreed, giving her muzzle a gentle kiss.

Smiling, the Husky rolled onto her side, half-covering me, an arm across my chest, a leg over mine. I arranged the pillow under her head, my arm under the pillow to hold her, my other forepaw reaching up to touch hers, my tongue giving slow little licks to her muzzle as she offered soft whines and whimpers of affection and appreciation at me. We eventually returned to the sweetness of just holding each other, saying nothing for a long moment.

"Is it cliché," I asked softly, "to ask how you're feeling?"

"Maybe," she smiled, "if it's just you doing what's expected. If you really want to know, it means that you care about me. It means you're listening."

"It means I care. It means I'm still feeling our connection from last night, and I want to know how you feel."

She provided a sweetly chaste kiss to my lips, and her smile grew wider. "I'm feeling warm, connected, and very well-loved, thank you for asking."

"Good answer," I grinned. My hesitation didn't go unnoticed by either of us; it didn't last long. "I'm feeling that I never want this moment to end. I'm pretty sure I'm welcome to come back..."

That earned me something like a raspberry, followed by a growl and some particularly sharp-looking fangs headed toward my laughing muzzle. She mock-snapped her jaws, then said, "You'd damned-well *better* come back, you mangey cur!"

I held her close, laughing a little more before the sound became something more like a sob. She pulled away from me, a concerned look in her eyes, and I shook my head. "Lots of emotions, Lightwing. I really don't want to leave Starhold, much less this bed. I know that you want me to come back, and I imagine that the others will, too."

"Fair assumption," she smiled at me.

My voice sounded like a whelp's whimper. "I don't want to put that suit on again. I don't want to be that dog again."

Lightwing took my head into her forepaws, made me look at her closely. "You won't be. Not ever again. I have an idea, how to prove it to you, but it will have to happen later. How can I help in the meantime?"

"Keep on believing." I cupped her forepaws with my own, looked into her eyes. "I'll get there, eventually. Or I'll keep on working at it, like an addict in recovery. Hey, only three steps instead of twelve? It's a bargain!"

We both chuckled, then I sobered again.

"Not politically correct, I suppose."

"Your audience understands. There might be some in recovery who would appreciate it. You didn't say it to be mean."

"That's what Heartsinger said," I realized aloud. "I had asked about his breed, mentioning Russian wolfhound. I was afraid it might be considered offensive or insensitive or something, and he just asked if I meant it to be."

She nodded, gracing my lips with a quick kiss before giving me back my head. "You didn't, and you understood each other. That's called 'communication.'"

"Is that what it's called?" I smiled at her. "I'll bear that in mind."

Giving my nose a playful tap, she said, "Are you up for breakfast?"

Realizing the mistake in her phrasing, she joined me in a laugh. "Do you think we missed breakfast this morning?" I asked.

"Hey, I'm a half-decent cook, on a small scale. No need to worry."

"We might want to shower."

"Good idea."

"You want to go first?"

She blinked at me. "Oh, you meant separately?"

* * * * *

By the time that we emerged from the guest room, freshly showered and suitably clothed (these cotton garments wore beautifully), it was well past any usual time for breakfast yet far enough away from lunch as to merit some sort of stop-gap. We had the kitchen nook to ourselves as Lightwing introduced me to a stout Earl Gray (the company that made this hardy variety called it "Earl Grayer"). The tea was made famous by a certain starship captain, and my fine Husky hostess used steamed milk and vanilla to make it into something called a London Fog. It was an interesting brew with an aroma that, I admitted with a blush, reminded me of her. She combined this enticing brew with some hearty, thick-cut oat bread slices, perfectly toasted, with butter and blueberry jelly, all made here at Starhold.

"Just so you know," the Husky told me, "we don't have a full processing system for milk cows. Only two of ours produce milk, and a bearcat from a nearby farm brings a portable system each morning and evening. He processes the milk, and we get some of that back for our own use."

"That still must be a lot of milk...?"

"We don't take it all; anything more than what we really need, we donate to the shelter, food bank, whoever might need it."

I nodded and, with a smile, raised my mug to her. "The MOOR at work, with a win-win for all sides, from what I can see."

She blushed cutely under her dark mask. "It's just a question of acknowledging that there are other fursons in the world."

"Just that?"

"Probably a lot more than that, although that's where to start." The Husky sipped a bit of her Fog, then said, "Did you ever see a shopping cart corral, at a grocery store parking lot, and there are maybe five or six carts shoved in at every which angle, so that there's almost nowhere to put your own cart?"

My soft groaning affirmed my agreement. "I try to tell myself that at least they didn't just leave the carts in the middle of the parking spaces, but it still ticks me off. If the carts are lined up and nested properly, the corral could hold maybe 20 or 30 carts."

"Easily! And it would be very little effort on each furson's part, not to mention a small help to the poor fur who has to gather them up and haul the bunch of them back inside. It's one of those small things that will help everyone in small ways. It's a little like the 'pay it forward' idea — a kindness that is given to someone you probably won't even meet."

Considering a moment, I offered, "That would be part of the third step, I imagine. Part of giving yourself to the world would be to acknowledge that there's a world to give yourself to."

Lightwing chuckled. "Not everything grows out of the three steps."

"Maybe not... but it's a good place to start."

* * * * *

We had been chatting idly for several minutes, when Unicorn entered the kitchen with a large smile on his muzzle. "Just the furson I was looking for," he said to me. "I have a surprise for you."

The stallion waved both of us toward himself, glancing at his watch. As I rose, I asked him, "What's happening?"

"Just a little impromptu meeting I've managed to get together. Come along now." He spoke with the unassailable attitude of a kindergarten teacher, and I resisted a pup-like urge to ask if it was time for recess on the playground.

Lightwing delayed matters long enough for us to put our plates and cups through a rinse, put away the butter and jelly, and generally clean up after ourselves. After our conversation, we weren't about to leave our shipping carts in the parking lot. Unicorn made a happily exaggerated show of impatience at our "shillyshallying" (a term I hadn't heard in years, which made it all the more fun), until we finally left the kitchen and went back down the length of ground floor hall, to the conference room I'd been in perhaps 24 hours prior.

The palomino sensed my discomfort. "Easy, Max. It's a good surprise, I promise. I've a few more tribal members I'd like for you to meet."

"We won't bite," a playful male voice on the conference phone speaker promised. "At least not today."

"Riverrunner, hush," a rich alto voice admonished gently. "Let's at least introduce ourselves first."

Closing the door quietly behind us, Unicorn explained, "I called each of them yesterday, told them the story; you don't have to go through that again. I managed to get them to call in now, so that you could meet them. Max, meet Riverrunner, Quicksilver, and Phoenix."

"Founders." My voice sounded the slightest bit awestruck to my ears.

"We want to meet you in the fur-and-bone, one fine day," added another male voice. "Until then, we want to thank you for bringing the news in furson."

"I get the feeling that it's been a very difficult journey for you," the female offered softly. "Unicorn has been discreet, don't worry. He's only said that... finding Airdancer brought up a lot of emotions in you, and that you've been asking for help from us."

"He's right; I have." I grinned. "I did, however, hear that certain winter furpiles in the Bunkhouse were juuuuuuust right."

The laughter rang freely between us, particularly from Phoenix, who declared that I was in danger of being quite thoroughly hugged at the soonest opportunity. We all passed a great half hour or so, as I got to tell

Quicksilver how I still felt her spirit in her clothing design, to hear how Riverrunner was a very successful architect who had designed everything from the Bunkhouse to the palatial home of Timewind itself, and to learn how Phoenix had gone from planning and laying out the first few hundred square meters of garden to degrees in agriculture and land management. All three were still tied closely to their tribal roots, despite not living on the grounds. They "tithed" actively, and I was discreet enough not to ask for any numbers. Any percentage of income from the talents that these three commanded would be substantial. Sunrider would invest it well, and Lightwing would help find projects and fund grants in her position as MOOR. The next general gathering of the tribe was to be in late June, and I was instructed quite sternly to be in attendance. My Husky (if she wouldn't mind me calling her that) assured everyone, including me, that she would enforce the attendance by any means necessary. The benefit of the voice-only connection was that only she and Unicorn saw me blush.

Less than a minute after the call had ended, a polite knock at the door turned out to be Darkstar informing us that lunch was ready, if we were. It seemed that the lunchtime "catch as catch can" rule had been suspended in my honor. The Artisanry was open, and Oray, Heartsinger, and Rainmist were taking their turns at holding down that particular fort; the remaining ten of us made sandwiches from a fine array of meats, cheese, and trimmings and gathered at the tables for more conversation. Oaknail and Moonsong, in particular, were amused by my descriptions of the call.

"I didn't get to hear from... I'm sorry, I can't recall the name from yesterday's call? Another founder..."

"Stormsinger," Unicorn supplied.

"Yes, thank you. I hope to get a chance to talk with her more, to learn still more of the tribe's origins."

"We'll make sure you have a copy of the *Manifesto* to take with you," Darkstar offered. "That will help tell more of the stories."

"That would be wonderful. I feel honored that I've met all of the founders now."

It took me a moment to realize just how badly I'd stepped in it. I started to apologize, but Oaknail put a forepaw to my shoulder.

"We know what you meant," he said softly. "There is also some truth to the idea that Airdancer introduced you to us."

After a pause, I said, "Then I owe him a debt of gratitude."

"We all do," Moonsong added. "I think we're all very glad to have met you."

Unicorn's *Hear! Hear!* was the loudest of the affirmations around the tables, but it was far from the only one. With the soft patters of applause settling around me, I felt myself blushing. I was doing that a lot during this weekend.

* * * * *

Lunch included more camaraderie and conversation, reminding me of that song with "another Thanksgiving dinner that couldn't be beat." After a long and happy time of this, there came a moment of restlessness that surprised me, until I realized that it was more from me than my hosts. It didn't take long for me to figure it out, and I voiced it ahead of the rest of them.

"It's probably about time for me to get back to my house." I looked around at the sympathetic faces in the dining hall. "It may sound silly of me to say that I'm not exactly anxious to leave."

"May I be a little unsubtle, Max?" Lightwing asked.

"You? Unsubtle? Never!"

Everyone chuckled, the Husky most of all. "Maybe it's not so much that you want to leave as you don't want to go back to being Detective Luton."

"Kinda obvious," I admitted. I didn't physically shrink, but it felt like it. "Makes me want to burn that jacket."

"Waste of a good jacket," Darkstar observed.

"You will always be welcome here, Max," Lightwing promised.

"And you don't have to put the armor back on," the lynx added. "That's the part that's in your mind. I'm not saying that'll be easy. I am saying that it's doable."

I nodded, trying to convince myself more than anyone else. "I'll probably be asking you for a lot of help."

"You'll have it," Oaknail affirmed, then looked around the tables. "You have helped us already, in many ways. I think you can call on any of us."

Murmurs, confirmations, nods, invitations to return anytime, to telephone anytime. As I rose from the table, everyone followed suit. "I guess I'd better get ready to go. I'll drive back, arrive before sunset, get myself ready to face Monday." I grinned at Darkstar. "Gonna invite me up to your room?"

The lynx laughed. "Are you inviting me to get you out of my clothes?"

Several double entendre comments and *bow-chikka-wow-wow* noises took much of the hurt out of my impending departure.

* * * * *

As expected, Darkstar was the perfect gentlefur, once more giving me the privacy of the bedroom section of his room as I took off his clothes and put on mine. I had been right: They felt foreign to me. They were clean, and the jacket was in fine shape. I put away the wallet, change, pen, notebook, phone (the rice appeared to have worked), and the shield into their proper pockets. The shield felt heaviest, familiar in a horrible sort of way, like a weight that I had been carrying for too long, been free of for a while, now returned. I wondered briefly if a probationer's ankle bracelet felt like this, physically, psychologically, or both.

I bodily steeled myself for my reappearance around the partition. Darkstar's expression was no different than it had been before. I realized that, in some way, I was disappointed by that. After all, I was dressed like the enemy again.

"Everything looks clean enough. How does it feel?"

My hesitation told him more than I wanted to express out loud.

Without a word, he padded close and embraced me. I put my arms around him as well, the shape of him familiar from other hugs, save for the sensation of this button-down shirt and jacket being like a barrier between us. He held me for a very long moment, then moved his muzzle to whisper into my ear.

"Tell me your middle name, if you have one."

"John. Well... Johnathan."

"Maxwell Johnathan Luton. One of the finest males I've met. I'm glad to know you."

I gave him a gentle squeeze. "Thank you for helping me to become my best self."

"Anytime."

We separated slowly, looked each other in the eyes, and smiled. "Still not ready for a kiss," I quipped.

He gave me his best lynx smile. "Give it time."

* * * * *

We were met at Darkstar's door by Lightwing, who asked me to accompany her a few doors down. Her name, in the form of a lovely wood rendering by Firecat, adorned the door that stood ajar. "I wanted to speak with you for a moment, in my capacity as the MOOR."

Her room was the same general size as the lynx's, differently furnished and differently divided. Each room, I realized, would have a great capacity for individualization as the occupant took it from empty space to living space. This room would give me a great many insights into the Husky's mind and heart, if I were allowed time and leave to explore it. As it was, I simply had the unshakable feeling that this was, indeed, her room. It felt like her.

"And how may I serve the Minister Of Outworld Relations?"

She didn't let her grin run away with her, but it was a near thing. "I think I spoke to you about our assistance with the county library?" After I nodded, she continued. "I wish to recruit you for some shelf-building and other general maintenance work on that project. We're going to be starting our prep work this next weekend, in fact. Feel like visiting and putting in some work with the tribe?"

"I'm hearing something about whitewashing a fence." I smiled at her and said, "That includes room and board, I take it?"

"Absolutely."

"May I have the guest room again?"

"No."

I blinked.

"You'd stay here." She looked into my eyes and spoke softly. "Remember that I told you I had a way of proving to you that you're still Max?"

"Yes."

She reached up to pull my head gently to hers, providing a particularly passionate kiss that brought back a great many warm memories from the previous night. When she broke the kiss, my toes finally stopped curling, and I began to get my breath back. The smile on her lips, in her eyes, in the sound of her voice, told me what her words confirmed.

"Still Max. Without a doubt."

* * * * *

Each of the tribe who was in the house managed to take me aside for a moment, for a hug, for some kind words, even some cell phone numbers and email addresses written on cards. I was reminded that I must stop by the Artisanry on my way out, or the three who were working there would have to track me down separately and hug me where I stood. I wondered how any of that could remotely be considered a threat, but I also was smart enough not to chance it.

They gathered as a group at the front of the house to bid me a final farewell. Oaknail took my forepaws into his and spoke warmly. "There is an old pagan saying: 'Merry meet, merry part, merry meet again.' We come together in joy, and we part in joy, not in sadness, because we will meet again." He leaned a little closer, and his grip became a little tighter. "The tribal Chieftain insists upon it."

"No Brando imitations," I chuckled. "And since I don't have any sunglasses, I won't do any imitations when I say 'I'll be back.'"

Frank had brought my car around, and I spoke softly to him as he handed me the keys.

"First of all, thank you for your work in cleaning out the mess."

"Glad to help. And by the way, I think you're about due for an oil change and tune up." He grinned at me. "I'll give you the tribal discount."

I chuckled softly with him, then sobered gently. "Frank, I hope I'm not telling tales out of school. Unicorn told me about the issues with getting your record cleared."

The look on the mountain lion's face darkened, more with sadness than anger. His ears and tail spoke quietly, without accusation, to a weight I could empathize with. I placed a forepaw to his shoulder.

"I'm not exactly sure what I can do, but I'm actually in the cop shop. I can check records, get specifics, maybe convince someone to get rid of it entirely. If I can't get that far, I'll find out what I *can* do and make it happen. Unicorn knows the law, and I can help him get what he needs to move forward."

His thanks started as a pawshake, and I turned it into a hug. I was getting more comfortable doing that, even in the police detective costuming. Lightwing was right: Max was still here after all.

* * * * *

The short drive to the Artisanry was oddly punctuated by seeing the entire group of tribal members (save three) waving at me in my rearview mirror. The mixture of emotions was profound yet not painful. The surprise, for me, was discovering that I could feel so much and so deeply. It was unlike anything that I'd felt in months, years. It was raw, powerful, real. *Connected* was the word that sprang up. *Unarmored* clamored for attention as well.

I parked in front of the store, alongside two other cars. I left my jacket in the back seat, partly to feel less formal, partly to enjoy the day, and partly to conceal the parcel. I didn't really imagine anyone would steal it, not out here, but I didn't want to take the chance. I guess that much of the cop, or the city-dweller, remained.

Holding the door open for a couple whose arms were filled with parcels of their own, I waited to make sure that they were okay getting to their car before going inside. Heartsinger was at the front, and he enveloped me in a warm hug as soon as I reached him at the counter. His height made it easy for him to rest his chin on my head, and I lay my cheek to his chest, enjoying the brief cuddle. Both of our tails were wagging up a small windstorm; if we'd been feline, we'd have been purring. Yesterday, about this time, I had found myself wondering if I wanted to kiss him, because of the emotional overload. Now, I realized that we were expressing our emotions toward one another just fine.

The other customers in the store were ready to pay for their goods, including one of Stellamara's paintings. They seemed a little confused at our display of affection.

"Are we intruding?" the vixen asked tentatively.

"Just bidding a fond goodbye to our visiting family member," the Borzhvolk smiled. "We don't get to see him nearly enough."

I excused myself and headed to the back of the store. *Family member.* Not tribal member? No, I realized. Heartsinger had given me a title of warmest affection without assuming too much too fast. Smiling to myself, I realized that the thinking was definitely tribal. I would have to mull over that idea, along with a good many others that had come up over the last hour or so.

I had guessed right that Rainmist was tending the coffee bar, and that she wanted a hug of her own. I provided one with a teasing nibble at the otter's neck that caused a truly delightful chittering and a quick thapping of her tailtip against the floor.

"Flirt!" she giggled.

"Guilty as charged," I grinned at her. "Shall I arrest myself?"

"I never do handcuffs on a first date."

She caught me out, and she knew it, laughing and hugging me again. "Now you know how dangerous it is to make such jokes with me," she said.

"Worth it," I acknowledged, this time providing a chaste and very sincere kiss to her cheek.

"Hey," a young voice called in, "are you two gonna make out right here in the store?"

"You're right," I agreed. "The hayloft is better."

"Oh, *hells* yes!" the young firefox agreed and hugged me warmly.

While Rainmist prepared a fancy coffee for me to take with me on my trip back, she and Oray made me repeat my promise to return soon. I noted that I had been more or less commanded by the MOOR to help build things at the library this upcoming weekend.

"Is that the only thing you're going to be erecting?" the yowen asked.

"Hush, before I box your ears, stripling!" Rainmist warned.

The red panda took a half-step backward and looked at me with a soft smile and perhaps the most earnest look in his eyes that I'd seen all weekend. "Too far, Max?"

A breath gave me time to really look at my emotions. "Okay, maybe a little. I don't what to step on your enthusiasm."

"I go a little too far, sometimes. I'm sorry."

"Starshine seems to keep a pretty good leash on you." I raised a forepaw quickly. "Don't go there!"

Oray laughed. "Okay. We'll find a balance somewhere, yes?"

"Yes." I provided him a classic "Dutch rub" on his head, just to prove it.

Back at the front of the shop, Heartsinger gave me a chance to set down my coffee before giving me one last hug "for the road."

"I haven't been hugged this much in all my life," I told him.

"Too much?"

"Not that long ago, I might have said so. Now..."

The Borzhvolk grinned at me. "You know you can always come back for more."

"Count on it."

Padding back out to the car, I got behind the steering wheel and debated asking the phone for directions back home. End of the drive, turn left, about ten klicks back to the northeastern edge of Green Town, connect to roads I knew well enough to get back to the house. Maybe 280 klicks all told; what took time was the back roads where the limit was maybe 70kph, or the few towns to drive through instead of around. Not something I could complain about; it's part of what gave Starhold its peace and quiet, as well as what had given them so many hectares of land for such a low price, all those years ago.

I let the phone sleep in my jacket pocket. It was a quiet Sunday mid-afternoon, with very pretty weather, and I wasn't in too much of a hurry anyway. I had a lot to think about. Things to tell Michael, when I got home, especially about that word *family*. Consideration of the offer that Unicorn had made to me. Turning over the comments that Oaknail had made to me. Feeling the emotions and possibilities that Lightwing had explored with me. And feeling the curious spiritual pull of the parcel under my jacket, there in the back seat.

Driving to meet Timewind, I had an Idea riding with me, something that Stellamara called a ghost or a shadow. Now, on the return trip, I had a different passenger, and the contemplation that it was causing was far brighter, which made it a much more welcome companion. I saluted it with a sip of my coffee and got on the road.

26: Will You Serve?

The drive back to my house — I still couldn't quite call it "home," for so many reasons — was calming, thoughtful... thought-full. I didn't feel burdened or depressed in any way. I wasn't even whelmed (Darkstar assured me that it really was a word). More like I was finding whole new ways to imagine myself, or reimagine, or whatever the life-coaching gurus called it this year. I felt a strange combination of exhausted and exhilarated. Lightwing had told me that my mental and emotional work had been equivalent to several hours of chopping wood, and the analogy held true in odd ways. I couldn't really explain it, but I felt it. I was beginning to see how that — feeling it — was actually more important. The experience may not need explanation so much as acceptance, at least at first.

Upon my arrival, I didn't even get out of the car before I called Lightwing's cell number. She answered quickly, and I felt my heart do that cliché thing.

"Home again, home again, jiggety-jig," I told her.

"Goooood evening, J.F.," she rejoined with a chuckle.

I laughed. "We share movie references. Now we're in trouble."

"Only now?" Her voice smiled at me. "How are you feeling, Max?"

"Lonesome."

"Good answer. How else?"

"Excited, scared, curious... very different. A lot more alive than I've been in a long time. Confused, maybe. I'm organizing my thoughts so that I can call Michael. I've got a lot to tell him."

"Does that include me?"

"Absolutely." My voice warmed for her. "I'll be discreet, of course, but I can't promise that he won't take a guess."

"Sometimes, when one dog meets another dog, there's this thing that happens..."

Her laugh told me that my raspberry had been received loud and clear. She promised to let everyone else know that I was back safely, and we reaffirmed our promised meeting this next weekend. Saying goodbye was so romantically bittersweet that I silently laughed at myself. There are reasons for those clichés to exist, after all.

I made sure to get the parcel out of the back seat, taking it into the house and setting it on the living room table. The jacket was returned to its proper hanger in the closet, if only to respect Darkstar's care of it. The brand new copy of *The Tribal Manifesto,* in its 25th anniversary glory, was set next to my chair in the living room. I glanced over the cover again, smiling at the various faces that I now had names for, and at the other faces that I might yet get to meet. Dreamweaver was there; Frank was not. They had met a few years after the book came out, but I had the mountain lion's information on a card in my wallet. Unicorn had given it to me during our last conversation...

* * * * *

"Thank you for your offer to help," the stallion told me.

I looked at his business card, which included his personal cell number written on the front, and Frank's full name and birthdate on the back. I made sure that they were safely in my wallet before I answered, "He's a good kit, seems to me. I'm not sure what I can do directly, but between you and me, we should be able to make something happen."

"Nothing too sneaky."

"Don't tempt me." We grinned at each other. "I'll get the file, all the ID numbers, records, whatever I can find. We'll see what you and I can do from there."

"That'll be further than I've been able to get." He studied me for a long moment, and I wondered if perhaps my fur had changed color. "Max, there's something I'd like to talk over with you, but it's quite a can of worms to get into just before your going home."

"Try me."

"I'm thinking about the trench coat. I wonder how long you want to go on wearing it."

Sighing heavily, I said, "Can open; worms everywhere."

He set his large forepaw gently on my shoulder. "This would require a helluva lot of conversation," Unicorn said softly. "I want to talk to you about some alternatives, some ideas that you could think about."

"Law school?" I made an attempt at a laugh.

"You already know a lot about the law; that's not what I meant. We certainly don't need more lawyers in the world." He paused, then asked, "Have you ever considered getting a PI license?"

"Paul Drake to your Perry Mason?" I shook my head. "You're too young to know that reference."

"I saw them in reruns, the same way you did." The palomino smiled. "And no, I don't do courtroom law, especially not murder cases. What I'm talking about is better defined by the term they're known by in England: private enquiry agents. The license gives a little privilege, especially in terms of allowing me to bring you in as a confidential consultant. Serving papers, some due diligence efforts for certain conveyance work, getting information... you know, making enquiries."

"Do you handle divorce?"

"Only rarely, and then with a strong pair of tongs."

The chuckle came quite naturally. "I can't see myself as one of those stalker-types, snapping photos of cheating spouses."

"Not what I had in mind. It's as I said, Max: You know the law, or at least much of it. You know what a PI can and can't do. You're good with details, you're observant, make good notes, and you solve puzzles when something doesn't add up. That's someone I could work with."

I blinked. "Are you offering me a job?"

"I'm offering you the opportunity to think about an alternative to what you're doing now, and I'm pointing out traits that would make you a good fit for that sort of work. I want to talk to you more about it. We can consider it together, if you've any interest."

Silence stretched, but not for too long. "I'm still a little dense, I think."

"Yeah, lotta worms." Unicorn chuckled softly. "You've got my number, if you want to talk before your return. In the meantime, just give yourself the benefit of knowing that you really do have some other options available."

Nodding, I asked, "Is research part of that job description?"

"Might do. Why do you ask?"

"Just figured it wouldn't hurt me to find out the process of getting a PI license."

The stallion grinned. "Add 'initiative' to your list of qualifications."

* * * * *

Sunday evening lay quietly around me, for a change. I wasn't entirely sure that I was looking forward to Monday — in this crazy modern world, few of us do — but I didn't dread it as much as I usually did. Early April weather is fickle, in this part of the world; that rainstorm that caught me at Starhold (was that really only 48 hours ago?) might make me consider keeping the trench coat handy. The jacket was considered a requirement, but I might be able to keep the coat in the closet for now. I snorted quietly at a misuse of the expression, wondering if it was about the coat in my front closet or me being in a sort of tribal closet. I'd have to ask Lightwing about that.

The lovely Husky had insisted that take along some of the leftover spaghetti sauce, after making sure that I knew how to boil pasta. I threatened her with a tickling, but I didn't follow through, since she still held the container of sauce in her forepaws; the possibility of her dropping it was simply not to be risked. I now set a pot to boiling, taking some of the bow-tie style pasta that she also provided to me ("Not taking the chance that your cupboard is bare, poor dog!") and measuring out a reasonable amount for a "single serving" rather than the meager quantity that the box suggested. A little oil to prevent boiling over, a pinch of salt to the boiling water (putting it into the cold water lets it sit on the bottom too long and might cause a little damage to the non-stick surface), and I let myself pretend that I was my own best chef, for tonight, at least.

While the microwave timer counted out the minutes for the pasta to become *al dente,* it also warmed up the sauce on low power. The timing was my best guess; cooking is more art than science, right? I comforted myself with that idea while I took another cursory glance through my copy of *The Tribal Manifesto.* Darkstar was putting together a historical narrative of Timewind, from its beginnings to the present day. This volume was more about the theories, philosophies, thoughts, impressions, memories, and experiences of individual members about what "being tribal" means to them. The pasta would take 11 minutes to boil, and I'd spent some of that time prepping the sauce, so I didn't have a whole lot of time to read. I noticed an entry by Phoenix and had a chance to read some of it.

I've always had a knack for growing things [he wrote]. *I don't mean to brag about it; it's simply to explain how I found myself so attracted to tribal life. They're intertwined, you see.*

When I was young, my parents — we used some of the "cutesy" terms that seem universal across species, so my Mom and Pop — were surprised at how quickly I learned how to help them tend our little garden. I learned to recognize the sprouts we wanted rather than the weeds that we didn't, and Mom got to where she set aside a small area of garden, to let me do the cultivating of that space entirely on my own. I got to ask questions, of course, but the decision-making was mine.

I didn't grow a hectare's worth of vegetables in a dozen square meters or something. I like to make up stories, especially those with a folktale feel to them, but that's not what this book is for. What I wanted to tell you about is a story that Mom always told on me, to anyone who would listen. The thing is, I would sing while I worked my garden, and also when I had finished gardening for the day. I would sit and sing to the garden, and I'd talk to it. I'd heard that talking to your plants and flowers was good for them, that they responded well to it. My garden wasn't perfect, but it did pretty well. Mom always said that it was because I loved my garden, and it loved me back.

Easy to see the analogy, so I won't beat you over the head with it. We, as a tribe, developed the Three Steps, which is based on the same idea. If you talk, encourage, share, believe in something or someone, you will get that back. My plants didn't speak in words, of course, but they did seem to thrive more, and more easily. I'm guilty of anthropomorphizing, science would say. Some might point toward Peter Wohlleben's book The Secret Life of Trees. *Me, I just shrug and offer them a very healthy head of lettuce. Unicorn, who you'll also meet in this book, would probably offer you a fine phalaenopsis from his greenhouse. You just have to look and to appreciate. It's not that difficult.*

We seem to forget that.

Beeps and boings tore me away from the writing. The sieve was ready in the sink; in went the pasta, drain, rinse, yadda yadda yadda, and I had my shallow bowl of dinner ready very quickly. I indulged in a healthy sprinkle of parmesan, romano, and asiago cheese (a lovely combo), then sat myself at the kitchen table. As I said my grace, to thank once again the non-sapient animals who had given themselves to my nourishment, the feeling came over me that there was something new at this lonely table. I was new, or better, or at least different. Dinner was less lonely, although I was the only one in the house. I didn't even have the *Manifesto* to keep me company, since I didn't want to risk getting sauce on it. Perhaps the sauce itself linked my emotions back to the tribe of dreamers I had supped with this weekend, or perhaps there was something more. I glanced at the parcel on the living room table and remembered my last conversation with Oaknail...

* * * * *

We sat in the small conference room again, "just for a bit of privacy," he had said. "I want you all to myself for a moment."

"What will Moonsong say?" I chuckled.

The bear raised an eyebrow at me, smirking. "You're sounding better and better, Max. I'm glad of it. No, I think it's that we all want to be able to say our goodbyes, and I have something to say that I thought best to keep just between us for a while."

Maneuvering myself into a chair, I said, "That sounds a trifle ominous."

Oaknail shook his large head. "Just private." He sat as well and looked at me, a warm yet frank expression on his face. "It's about Albion."

"What in particular?"

"Its status. Is the sword still considered evidence?"

My cheeks puffed out with a sigh. "Technically, it's not evidence of a crime, although it was found at a crime scene. It was first thought of as evidence, in the sense that the victim was right-pawed, yet the gun was in his left, making the suicide idea look suspicious. After the ME confirmed that the cause of death was suicide, the sword was not evidence of the death itself. On that technicality, I brought it with me, to return to you, maybe to make it easier, somehow, to break the news."

"Are you saying that we could keep it now?"

"Probably," I hedged. "There might be an argument to the effect that it belonged to him, is part of his estate. I don't think his mate would want it, truth told, and his kits might never hear anything of the story. Was there ever anything to prove that it belongs to the tribe, rather than a gift to him?"

"Nothing in writing. We didn't think it necessary, of course. The founders can affirm the intent, maybe make the case without other evidence."

"A question for Unicorn."

The tribal chieftain nodded slowly. "I want you to take it back with you, for now." He raised a forepaw. "Several reasons, but the main one is to cover your tail, in case anyone asks about it. If they don't, maybe you can bring it back to us then." He paused for a long moment. "Or perhaps you'll want to keep it."

"Me? Why me?"

"Why not you, Max?"

"You made it as a symbol of the tribe, for the defender of the tribe. That would be Unicorn now. By my thinking, he should have had the sword for a long time."

"Perhaps," the bear admitted. "He is a founder, part of the Areopagus, and he is an attorney, as Airdancer was." His smile was just a little rueful. "I spoke with Unicorn about this. He mentioned that he was wondering if you might want to make a bit of a job change."

I chuckled softly. "You could make me into a conspiracy theorist."

"Sorry, Max. I'm not trying to force you into anything."

"But you are trying to make it more attractive."

"Again, perhaps." Oaknail smiled fondly at me. "You're going to take the sword back with you anyway, just to make sure everything is in order. Personally, I'd keep it quiet unless someone or, as you say, some technicality makes you take it back. Unicorn can wrangle up whatever legal jiggery-pokery might be needed; we'll tackle that when we get to it. Eventually, Albion will return. I promise that I'm not trying to push you into any decisions, but I have to tell you that I hope you'll be back."

"I'll be back on Friday, at least. The MOOR has recruited me."

"So it would seem." His smile grew warmer. "She has good taste."

My face felt hot, although the source of my embarrassment could have been one or more of many reasons.

"Take Albion with you, for your own protection. Once in a while, perhaps, listen to it." His smile became a grin. "Yeah, more mystical hoodoo poopoo, I know. Hear me out. Redlance knows wood; Phoenix knows gardens; Unicorn knows plants; Quicksilver and Dreamweaver know textiles and design; Stellamara knows pigments and colors; Heartsinger knows ceramics; I know metal. Ask each of us about our work, and we'll probably say similar things about *how* we know our art, our craft. We've gotten to know you too, Max. As a result of this visit, Stellamara could probably pick one of her paintings that you would find particularly attractive; Dreamweaver will find clothing colors to compliment your fur and your personality; Heartsinger might have, or create, a ceramic piece for you, perhaps a mug, perhaps a statuette, but it will truly suit you."

He put a tender forepaw to the wooden box that held the sword within. "My metals speak to me, to help me to know what they are, who they are for. Albion tells me that you might be its champion now."

"Again, why me?"

"You brought it home. You found its home because it told you. You reunited it with the tribe it was made to defend. You forged a connection, with the blade, with us. The runes spoke to you, once you discovered what they meant. The sword itself may speak to you as well, if you listen."

I paused for a long moment before saying, "I have been learning how to listen, all this weekend. To each of you, all of you, to myself. Maybe listening to a sword is another skill." I looked at the bear, feeling myself opening up again. "This is not a quick decision."

"Nor should it be. None of your decisions needs to be quick. The only thing you need to choose now is to acknowledge that you have more choices than you thought you had. One of them is the possibility of joining us, being more formally part of Timewind. We welcome you, always, whether you choose a tribal name or not."

Nodding slowly, I said, "I think I know why you would welcome me into the tribe."

"Oh?"

"Yes." I grinned at him. "You wouldn't be Timewind's oldest member anymore."

* * * * *

After dinner, I washed the pot, dishes, utensils, made sure the rest of the sauce was in the fridge, generally set the place to rights. I chuckled to myself, wondering how long my newly-made good habits would last. Living alone for so long had made me lazy, in so many ways. At Starhold... well, we put away our shopping carts, don't we? The idea made me want to call Lightwing again, but I held off. There's affection, there's romance, and there's clingy, or so it seemed to me. After all, absence makes the heart grow fonder, and there's a cliché for every silver lining.

I laughed out loud, gently giving myself permission to enjoy being silly. I hadn't felt anything even in the same country as "silly" for a very long time, and I realized how much I was liking it.

Moving to the living room, I opened the polished wooden box and took Albion gently from its velvet-lined resting place. I held it properly, resting the business end of the blade on my other arm. I wanted to look at it, not wave it around. I had noted and praised the craftsmanship even before I met the creator-smith. I'm not a connoisseur of any kind of weaponry; with due respect to the famous fictional federal agent's Rule 9, I didn't even carry a pocket knife. Albion was a high-quality piece, even to my inexperienced eye. I had no clear idea of how a blade is forged, short of fantasy films, but it was strangely easy for me to imagine the great bear of Timewind heating the metal, or folding layers, or using some kind of mold, then banging it into its best form, lovingly tending every last centimeter of it. (It occurred to me only then that I hadn't seen any sort of forge on Starhold's grounds. Something more for me to discover, perhaps?)

Could this blade be used for physical defense? If someone were properly trained, yes, although I could also imagine someone being frightened enough simply to impale someone on it. That's the thing about weaponry: With rare exception, someone could use anything to inflict pain and injury on anyone else, possibly with deadly results. History has proven that we sapients can be a bloodthirsty lot. If we weren't, perhaps my "day job" wouldn't be necessary anymore.

"That's not what you were made for," I said to Albion, or to myself, depending on how you look at it. "You could represent 'red in tooth and claw,' but I think you are more like the great symbols of justice. Equality, fairness, taking right action, defending honorably." I sighed quietly into the evening air. "All the ideals that Glover had begun with. He had such high hopes, such noble purpose, but in the end..."

I lay the sword gently in its velvet bed. "No," I whispered. "Let's lay his ghost to rest, peacefully. Let us remember Airdancer. The tiger who dreamed. He didn't really plan to leave the tribe..." I took a breath, gathered myself, remembering Oaknail pledging that we not lose another to the void. Did he mean me? Probably not *just* me, but me as well? He made that statement yesterday morning; this evening, I stood in my home, whispering to a sword, wondering if I really deserved to be the one to keep it. I wasn't entirely sure that I would be part of the tribe, much less...

My chair beckoned me, and I didn't resist. Lightwing's voice piped up in my head, and I smiled to hear it. I gave myself a few breaths to clear my thoughts and realize clearly that it was indeed time to make a phone call. I actually was looking forward to it. I just needed to...

Smiling wider, I answered Lightwing's voice with a very affectionate "Yes, dear." Picking up the candlestick, I pressed star-zero-one and waited for a few moments.

"Hello?"

"Hello, Michael." My voice clearly took my smile with it.

"Dad! Happy Sunday, or at least I hope it is. Howya goin'?"

"Michael, let me ask first: Are you working tonight?"

"I'm at home, actually. Putting my hindpaws up for a change."

Nodding, I continued. "I ask because I have a lot to talk about, if you have the time."

"Of course I do, Dad. Are you okay?"

"It's good news, or at least interesting news. I want to ask your help in organizing the sequence of events into something that makes some sense."

The hesitation was almost comical, but I didn't laugh. I knew very well that I wasn't behaving like "the old me," and the pup wasn't sure how to react. "Sure," he said, after just over one second's pause. "What's happened?"

"You remember the case that I mentioned, last week? It ended up leading me to Timewind."

"*Timewind?*" he exclaimed. I knew that he'd bought some clothing from them, for his RenFaire garb. "How were they involved?"

"The tiger who committed suicide, Glover, was one of the nine founding members of the tribe. He was known as Airdancer."

"How did you make that connection?"

"In his right forepaw, he held a short sword that is called Albion. Oaknail had made it years ago, for Airdancer."

"Okay, hold on." Michael cleared his throat. "I think you lost me at the bakery."

"That's my pup," I chuckled softly. "Now you see why I said that I needed your help in organizing the timeline. I'm not sure exactly where to start. The case is what led me to Timewind, last Friday evening, and I stayed the weekend with them."

"You stayed—" He took a breath, cleared his throat. I could hear the smile in his voice. "You did say that you needed some time to tell this. I think you understated it."

"Let me start at the beginning, and I'll see how quickly I can summarize the background. Make some tea."

"Way ahead of you."

With a chuckle, I launched into the story. An abbreviated summary of the case hit the highlights that got me to Starhold. From there, I slowed down a little, trying to tell what was important without giving him whole new vistas of worry over his sire. For the most part, I emphasized my meeting such good friends, of touring the house and grounds, of learning something of the history of the tribe as well as my exposure to *The Tribal Manifesto*. "Have you read it?" I asked him.

"Actually, no."

"I've read a little, so far, and they were all helping me to learn of its origins and how they use the principles as best they can. Oaknail gave me a copy of the physical book. You know what a Luddite I am." We both chuckled at our long-standing joke. "You can read it on their website as well."

"You've had a helluva weekend," Michael said, a touch of wonder in his voice.

"And I'm going back for more, this upcoming weekend. Lightwing has roped me into helping her, Unicorn, and a few others do some work at the county library in Green Town; Starhold is only about ten klicks from there. If you can get some time off, you could join us. I think you'd like everyone, and they're certainly curious about you, at this point."

"What about you getting time off?"

That was when I told him about Unicorn's and Oaknail's suggestions, and my pup produced a low whistle. "You gonna take them up on it?"

"Some interesting choices." I paused before adding, "I didn't think I had *any* choices, last week. I've got some things to think about now." I stretched in my chair. "Right now, the next thing for me to think about is some sleep. I've pretty well talked myself into a stupor."

We traded a few sire/pup insults over that one before he said, "I'm going to have to visit you soon, with or without a visit to Timewind. For now, sleep."

"I very much want to see you. For now..." I paused before saying, "I love you, Michael."

His voice cracked a little as he said, "I love you too, Dad."

* * * * *

After my call with Michael, I sat in my chair and let myself feel the space around me. How long had it been, since Barb's departure, that I really noticed the house? General maintenance, a sense of keeping things from falling apart or being too much of a mess, but as weird as it sounds, the house wasn't really there. Roof, walls, an enclosure where my stuff was reasonably safe, but not a home. Taking what the tribe had shown me, each in her or his own special way, I tried to look at the house differently, the same way that I tried to look at my life differently. It was going to take some time, I knew that, but the point was summed up in one word: Options. I could sense that I had options now, real choices, that I didn't have be "stuck," which is what it had felt like before. I could breathe, gather myself, notice.

Listening to the quiet, I realized that it really was "quiet," but not like the stillness of Starhold. Between the city (or the 'burbs) and the country, there's always a difference of opinion about what "quiet" actually means. My house had its own creaks and groans, and the street outside my front door had passers-by, some in cars, some having a loud conversation as they padded by or used some sort of off-street wheels. Even the wind, when it made itself known, sounded different here. Was one better than the other?

The smile on my face came from the realization that the sound I missed most was Lightwing's voice. The adolescent pup in me returned, but not for the "naughty bits"; it had the sense of The Crush, that ancient impulse of infatuation, except that this one had more behind it than mere imagination. I still resisted the temptation to call, wondering if I was "playing hard to get" (too late!), or if it was just the sense of quiet calm that told me I'd best get to bed, to sleep, to get ready for going to work with new eyes, wondering just what it was that I would see.

I glanced again at Albion, resting in its box, and I felt over Oaknail's words. Could I be the defender, metaphorically wielding the sword of justice? The idea made me think of an initiation rite I'd read in some book or other, a scene about asking a young male to take the last vows that would bind him to the priesthood, once and for all. The higher-up intoned solemnly, *Father, will you serve?* And the young male, with deep passion, answered, *Yes, my Holy Father, I shall serve.* The scene was carried out with so much reverence and seriousness that the male felt his spirit bound to his God in every way, and I wondered if the character would still be able to see his flock as fallible mortals who need support rather than as God's perfect souls who needed saving from the temptations, corruptions, and horrors of life in this mortal realm.

Of course, I read it during my more impressionable younger days, before I became the police dog who forgot his rabbi's advice to know what to keep and what to let go of. Now, I'm also aware of an idea that one's best self, aided by those he loves and who love him, is the gift that one brings to the world, that your best self is the light that you shine in those otherwise dark places, inside the self or outside, that try to consume us. Maybe that,

I thought, is the pledge to make, the service to provide, in every way that you're able.

"Will you serve?" I whispered to the air. Perhaps. Not a decision to be made tonight. Time for sleep.

Setting the household alarm system raised the metaphorical drawbridge for the night, and I readied the coffee machine to start brewing at the usual time, turned out the lights, all of the routine that I could now see as mere habit. Not good, not bad, just something that I did, not something that I was. That meant I could change it, if I wanted to. I took a moment to thank the tribe for showing that to me, smiling at myself for giving that thanks. That was probably the weirdest thing about this weekend: I wasn't "cured" or "fixed," only more aware of what I was doing. In a way, that was creepy. Maybe just new. I wasn't sure that I could keep it going, but I was going to do my best, and I had a whole group of people who were willing to help, asking nothing more than my own help when they needed it.

I shucked out of my clothes, realizing that they might last another day. I found some hangers for them, thanking Darkstar for his fine laundering. Crawling furclad between the sheets, I turned out the last light and, after settling in, let my eyes rest half-open as I thought sweetly of Lighting. I seemed to remember thinking of my experience with Timewind as something a dog could get used to. *Yes,* I amended the thought, *but never take for granted.*

After a few moments, I had the feeling that something was off. My eyes adapt to darkness fairly quickly, and I was well familiar with the sort of darkness that my house contains — street lights beyond the closed curtains, a few electronics that may have a charging light on them, soft red light from the numbers of an old-fashioned alarm clock on my nightstand, a nightlight from the bathroom down the hall. Nothing I could think of accounted for the muted blue light that seemed to be coming from the living room.

Leaving the bed, I padded slowly toward the source of the light. Perhaps I should have been, but I wasn't surprised by it. It was easier now to remember that same soft glow from the back seat of the car, just before I ran myself off the road to avoid hitting a cow on that rain-soaked Friday evening. Albion lay where I left it, now suffused with a faint aura of blue light that was no sort of reflection, nor was it an illusion. It might have been in my head, yes, but still not an illusion.

Will you serve?

I stood there for a time, with no particular thought or emotion in my head, until finally I turned and padded my way back to bed. Once again under the covers, I lay for a long moment, considering the question as if I had heard it with my ears. As if Oaknail had asked, or Unicorn. As if Timewind itself had asked me. I didn't have an answer yet, or at least not one I could commit to so completely.

Oaknail, I remembered, had told me that the sword might talk to me, if I listened. I wonder if the bear ever *saw* things as well. Something to ask, upon my return to Starhold. My return to the tribe. To Lightwing.

As sleep came over me, my heart felt suffused with warmth. I had never thought of blue as a warm color. I could only imagine that I was still learning.

Epilog: Famous Last Words

That was more than two years ago now. Much has changed since then, and I thought that I should tell you what's happened.

Darkstar informs me that this is called "breaking the fourth wall." That's a construct of narrative, he says. Truthfully, my intent is for this to be more like a letter to you, a postscript to this... well, "novel" is probably the right word, except that it isn't actually fiction. This happened to me, to all of us, as nearly as we can bring the story to you. Darkstar helped me to tell it to him, and the rest of the tribe contributed their words and portions of the stories, and the wonder weaver of words, the lynx himself, put it all together. (I know that he will want to edit that description out; I don't think any of us is going to let him. If you're reading it, you'll know that we won that debate.)

This book came about through a lot of conversation, soul-searching, and general cooperation. My experience of discovering and becoming part of Timewind was unique, in many ways. I am the oldest member of this tribe, and I found them well into my "middle years," proving (if nothing else) that embracing your life is something that can be done at any age. My story became the best way to tell what happened to one of the founding members of the tribe, and how a relative outsider came to be Albion's champion. I discovered what it means to be tribal by learning about it and living it for a few days, then for another weekend, and then for more days, even when I wasn't at Starhold.

As you might have guessed, I read the entirety of *The Tribal Manifesto* shortly after that first weekend, and many more times since then. In its own way, it's a story, too, told through memories and experiences of our many members, from the earliest days to the 25th anniversary. My experience, we all realized, was a true narrative, one that Heartsinger had called my "transformational experience of the tribe." Through me, he said, others can walk in my pawsteps, to see the spirit of the tribe revealed in the same way that I discovered it. This provides a particularly intimate picture of the tribe, and of me. Perhaps you have realized how much I've changed since "Detective Max Luton" was sent to investigate the death of Thomas

Glover. I could not be so open with my emotions back then, even to myself. Choosing to tell this story took some getting used to, and several of my tribe's members (Lightwing in particular) want me to use the word "courageous" in making this choice. I learned, as far back as that first weekend, that one does not challenge that Husky lightly!

On that note, if I may be permitted a brief aside before continuing... I didn't think of this journey as courageous; I stumbled into it, to start with, and I stumbled a lot more when making my choices. By doing all that, however, I finally have come to understand that choosing to love, to be vulnerable, to be open and actively caring, really is an act of courage. It's easy to be fearful, full of fear, to cower down and hide. To quote a song that's even a little older than I am, "Easy to be hard; easy to be cold." Saying "no" to your emotions, your experiences, is easier than embracing them, understanding, opening up. That is another reason why I want to tell this story: I'm my own best example of discovering this, and that's why I want to share it.

With the idea of telling things (mostly) in order, let me start with my return to the precinct on that Monday morning. That was April 8th. Captain Crandall asked if I'd gotten my answers; I told him that I had, and I'd have my final report ready for him by the end of the day. I did, and nothing more was said about the case, my answers, or Albion. For the formalities, it was case-closed, done and dusted. For me, though, it was only the beginning.

My caseload was never "light," but a dog's gotta eat sometime. On Thursday of that week (that's April 11th), I met Chelsea Watson for lunch at the buffet. With Glover's case officially closed, she was able to be far less furtive than the last time that we'd had lunch. I told her about Airdancer, about Timewind, and she seemed both surprised and reassured. She promised to look up the tribal website (not from her office computer, naturally), to get more information, perhaps to read the *Manifesto*. I had two suggestions for her: To read Oaknail's opening comments first (to see the Three Steps to Becoming) and to check the site again in about six weeks. The tribe was planning to post a memorial page for Airdancer, and we wanted to be sure that we had the family's permission to use his given name. Either way, I told her, the remaining eight founders would be offering their fond memories of the tiger, Airdancer, the young idealist that they knew and loved.

The next day, I took a half-day's vacation time (I can tell you how that's possible for a police detective in my city and precinct to do that, but it's boring and unimportant now); I was determined to enjoy my second weekend at Starhold without arriving so late in the day. The weather was sunny and fair, and I got to appreciate the sunset from the roof of the house, along with a full compliment of resident tribal members. Sunrider was back from his Las Vegas retreat, happy to be home and to meet me in the fur. The fennec was in some sort of meeting for his certification credits when I was on that conference call the week before, and it wasn't until that afternoon (our time) that he could retrieve Oaknail's voicemail to call home. I feel that I must include one bit of conversation with him, from that rooftop sunset gathering, that I remember quite vividly. The bright-eyed vulpine put a forepaw to my arm, looking at me with deep sincerity.

"Thank you bringing him home, Max."

"What do you mean?"

"I'm thinking of the stories of a fallen warrior being carried home on his shield. You brought Airdancer's spirit home to rest by bringing Albion here." He squeezed my arm gently, saying, "Thank you for your bravery."

I didn't have the chance to tell him, in that moment, how moved I was. As I've grown with the tribe, I've been able to be more open. I thank him once more, here, for those powerful words.

Summerwind also joined us that evening, returning from her time advising on a project in Houston. She was delighted to be "back in a part of the country that actually has seasons." The lioness had been on that first conference call but had remained quiet, listening. She told me that she had only known the legend of Airdancer, not the tiger himself, and she didn't know what to say. She echoed Sunrider's sentiment and asked about the status of Albion. I told her that no one had asked for it yet, and I'd been keeping a low profile, hoping to be able to return it to the tribe.

"I get the idea," she told me, "that you took a risk, bringing the sword back to Starhold."

"Cops often use loopholes, for better or worse. This one seemed like a good risk." I paused, breathed, took the chance to trust. "You probably know that I was looking for my own answers."

"Yes, but that's not why you brought it back, was it?"

"Let's just say, it wasn't the only reason."

The lioness nodded, smiling at me. "Albion wasn't the only one coming home."

I thank her, too, yet again.

* * * * *

I have Lightwing's permission to phrase this next line in exactly this way: That was the weekend that I discovered what it was like to become her slave. As I'm sure you've guessed, I'm referring to her "whip-cracking" over me, Unicorn, Oaknail, Oray, and Starshine as we were dragged... erm, gently escorted to the county library in Green Town, to help get the annex one step closer to being ready. This MOOR may not have been the one from Venice (I have retained *some* of my education), but she definitely got us motivated. She also pitched in, so don't get the wrong idea. The Husky is driven, in all the best ways, and her enthusiasm is contagious. I also have her permission to tell you that she didn't tire me out too much that day. As for the night... ah, but now I've said enough.

Mention must also be made of the kinkajou head librarian, Mrs. Sudbury, whose threat regarding a trivia contest that day was brought forth with a vengeance. She kindly waited until lunch, so that no one had to think of answers while toting shelving or working on the interior walls of the annex. Overall, however, I was just as glad that no one had bet lunch on the outcome of that contest; cumulatively, we scored a not-terribly-impressive 78%.

The following Tuesday (that would be April 16th, for those of you keeping track), I took my life in my forepaws, along with a copy of a certain volume already known by me, and traveled a way west and slightly south of the city. I found the squatters still there, right where I had left them, and my welcome this time wasn't much more cordial than my first. Truth told, I wished that I'd had Oaknail and Unicorn with me, but I figured that I'd be better off if I didn't appear armed for battle. Pearl, the matronly coyote who seemed in charge of the bunch, kept the big bull in check again, and I told them all that the case regarding Glover's death was closed. I added that none of them was in my final report, beyond my interviewing "the defendants in the last case Glover was assigned to," so their group had no significant presence in the police computers that I was aware of. That helped to mollify them a bit, although they had a new court date looming over them again.

Of course, the *Manifesto* was my real reason for visiting. It included one of Ezequiel's business cards, and I explained the connection between the book and Glover. The pregnant ewe and her mate were the ones who took it from me, she glancing through as the ram examined the card. I knew that there was another county library, further west on the state highway that I'd driven down. They would have internet connections to find the tribal website and get in touch with Timewind or with Ezequiel directly. The bull, Isaac, was suspicious; even Pearl wasn't clear about my motives. I said only that I had met the members of Timewind and that they had asked me to pass along their story of how they had come together to commingle their lives. The attorney had said that he would be glad to answer questions as best he could, but that he was not trying to get fees or solicit new clients. The general consensus by that group was that no lawyer could be trusted, although the ewe looked like she hoped that maybe just one might be trustworthy after all.

I waited until the end of that week before chancing my arm and calling the Glover mansion. Young Allison, the housemaid, answered; with her help, I arranged a visit with her and the cook, Bessie, just to tell them the conclusion of the story as well. We had a nice tea in the breakfast nook in the kitchen (and yes, it made me pine just a bit for Lightwing). The mistress of the house had told them, finally, of her condition. She had also told her kits, when they came home for Glover's funeral. There was still a sense of mourning in the household, yet also a sense of hopefulness. The chemotherapy would begin sometime in October, giving her and her kits a summer to build up their memories and trips together. Both the panther and the white mouse rallied for their mistress, understanding more of what she was going through. As of this writing, two years since, Helena Glover has beaten the odds, medically. She has largely withdrawn from public life, but you will still hear of the tigress helping other cancer survivors rally, as well as getting support not for charity galas but for cancer research. I, and all of us, applaud her efforts.

Dodging back to that May... Ezequiel contacted her about the use of Glover's name on the memorial page of the tribal website. She requested that he not be named, and neither did she have any wish for Albion, once its provenance had been explained to her. However, she did not slam the door in our collective faces; she was very calm toward Unicorn, he told us, and she wished us well. In fact, in the summer after her chemotherapy —summer of last year — she called Ezequiel to ask if she could visit Starhold for an afternoon. The tigress arrived with a driver as well as her kits, who seemed amazed by the shop and the grounds in general. Helena (as she asked us to call her) still tired easily, so a trip up the stairs for the view wasn't in the cards at that time. Tea on the back porch very definitely was, however, and she enjoyed meeting the other founders who live here. It was that day that the tigress gave permission to use Glover's name on the website's memorial to him, making the observation that her mate must have been a very different cat in his youth. We also have her permission also to quote her: "He was better at his job than at his heart."

Helena has grown still stronger over the last year, and we have every expectation of her spending a weekend with us later this summer. Her kits will be joining her; they want to learn how to ride.

* * * * *

For the sake of completeness, the encounter with "William Keaton" was presented accurately, but to protect his anonymity, the name and species was changed for this book. As Unicorn would be the first to remind us, a touch of decorum prevents a metric ton of nuisance suits.

* * * * *

My days as a police detective were numbered as early as that first weekend at Starhold, although I took time to think carefully about it. Unicorn and

I did have our conversation — several, in fact — and plans slowly evolved. The city isn't as large as those that the television cop shows are set in; there are only 33 designated precincts, and as for the small villages and towns edging up next to the city proper, each has its own constabulary force.

I worked out of the 8th Precinct, on the east side of the city. I was one of twelve homicide detectives, with other departmental detectives, patrol units, officers, and the brass making up the rest. All this isn't really relevant, except that it might help to explain why my work load was comparatively light and how, by the time I had formally retired in May of last year — thirteen months after I'd first visited Starhold — there were a few very fine additions to my precinct.

Officer Bernard Shelby Padilla transferred in from the Two-Six when a position opened up for a detective sergeant (which, for our force, meant someone working toward his detective's shield). It was no coincidence; my boss, Capt. Crandall, knew that I was considering retiring even sooner than I knew it myself. It was July 1 of that year that the Shep started to shadow me. He caught on plenty quick, and he's put in time on the job and on the books to make sure all the tests are passed. I usually called him by his last name, although I did call him "B.S." a few times. It was as much "hazing" as I was capable of. I didn't hide my interest in and experience with the tribe; he teased me that I should take a tribal name of "Nosey Parker." That gave him leave to call me "N.P." sometimes. We got along well.

A young Doberman named Nathaniel Lindsay Cole sat for his exams, getting very respectable scores. He became an academy cadet in May of that year, graduating in early September. He had to wait a while for an opening to show up in the force, but his scores from academy, combined with his experience in private security (time spent dealing with the public really does count), put him at the top of the list. I attended his swearing-in on Saturday, November 4th. We stay in touch, and he's doing well as a "beat cop." His "perhaps" turned into "yes."

I should mention that Parsons, the young Labrador I'd met on-scene when all this started, is still on the job. My description of him in this book isn't complimentary; I wasn't sure just how to tell that bit of story, if only because I was so harsh with him. The name is changed here, but even he told me that I didn't lie or exaggerate. He was all too new to the force, at that point. His own story of facing change deserves to be told, and perhaps he will tell it someday. Slowly, "Parsons" found ways to let the job be what it is without actually succumbing to it. He may find something else to do outside of the force but, for now, he's doing all right for himself. He's got more discipline, more "grit" (as they used to call it), than I had given him credit for, and I appreciate his allowing me to tell the story as it happened. He helped me back then, by showing me that I was getting tired of the job. For that, I thank him.

* * * * *

Changes continued through May and June of that year. Perhaps most significantly, Frank had made the commitment to himself to work on his ASE certifications, which would make his knowledge of car repair official. The first test is A1 – Engine Repair, the second is A2 – Automatic Transmission/Transaxle. I joke with him that I have the A0 certification: I can usually figure out how to put a car in gear. For manual transmission, all bets are off.

He began with finding a mentor in a seasoned mechanic in Green Town, and Frank's knowledge and enthusiasm was enough for him to become a sort of journeyman apprentice. Getting that job was made easier because his police record was expunged, just as it should have been a long time ago. With Unicorn's helpful knowledge and persistence, combined with my access to the files, the bureaucratic administration finally gave in to pressure and did the deed. I freely admit that I was within an ace of figuring out some way to hack into the system, but I didn't have the technical skills, and Capt. Crandall balked at the idea of using his own clearance levels to try erasing files. (Neither of us was sure that he could.) In any case, the system finally worked, after enough pressure was applied. From then on, the mountain lion joked, he was only on the tribe's "most wanted" list, because we all wanted him, and rightly so.

Choosing a tribal name was difficult for Frank only in that he — indeed, all of us — wanted to be sure that his name reflected his best self. That sounds corny, but it's true, as I discovered. At first, we teased him about being "Mechanic" or "Wrenchtwister," but that didn't last more than a brief bout of wordplay. He contributed "Torque-inator," to the tribe's delight.

We all began to ask more about what he truly loved in his life, for that would more likely lead to his tribal name. The first, most obvious joke was to choose "Dreamweaver Dreamlover," which the cat came up with himself, and which netted him a fine kiss from his panther lover. No firm decisions were made during that first conversation, naturally enough, but it was during this time that I learned more about Frank. His strong arms and solid upper body, his long-legged running speed, his cross-dominance (right-pawed and left-eyed) had made him a high school hero on the baseball diamond. He got a partial scholarship to college, yet he felt unmoved to continue. He's bright, in so many ways; it was more that he didn't seem to do well with "book-larnin'," as he joked. That wasn't quite true, as he enjoyed reading, and the entertaining lectures from a company called The Great Courses were also sources of his fascination. I suspected that it was classroom learning and testing that gave him issues.

Over the course of several weeks, he talked with us all, singly and in groups. I felt honored when he asked me to take a walk with him on one of the trails through the woods of Starhold, to talk about himself so openly, inviting my help in his search. Ultimately, it was Dreamweaver who helped him find his name. That only made sense, since she knew him more intimately (not just in *that* sense) than the rest of us. What she saw in him was the essence of his best self: His desire, always, to look for new things to learn, to discover interests, to pursue the things that made him better and better with every new day. Thus was born the tribal member known as Seeker.

* * * * *

I spent that summer, fall, and winter considering my future. I wasn't nearly as impulsive as I'd been in my remote-seeming youth, and I got many helpful cautions from my pup, Michael, as well as members of the tribe. Unicorn and I kept up our conversations, and Lightwing and I talked of every aspect of our relationship. I took some vacation leave around

Christmastime that year, to stay at Starhold and meet a great many other members of Timewind who descended on the place for a visit during the hols. I got to meet the other founders in the fur — Stormsinger, Riverrunner, Quicksilver, and perhaps especially Phoenix. I single him out because of the story that I'd heard about him on that first weekend, and because I consider him to be a hugger of Grand Master skill levels (the rest of the tribe agrees). I will admit to joining in with the Christmas Eve furpile in the pit before the fireplace. Three things to mention: Lightwing called dibs on me, so that I wouldn't be smothered by everyone present, at least not all at once; Unicorn was right about Phoenix being a particularly wonderful pillow to cuddle near; and yes, Oaknail does snore like a jet engine. We managed to get some sleep anyway.

New Year's Eve was a Saturday, so I was able to drive up to ring in the year properly. During the drive back, on Sunday evening, I thought about everything once more. Even more than that, I *felt over it,* as Heartsinger quite rightly describes it. I called Lightwing after I got home, for one more brief discussion, and I had a chat with Capt. Crandall on Monday morning, January 2 of last year. The bulldog managed a twisting of his lip that I had grown to recognize as a smile and asked, "What took you so long?"

For reasons of pension (making that 30-year mark), season, and overall preparations, I delayed making the resignation formal until nearer the spring. Conversations with Crandall helped to pave the way for my PI license. There's nothing in the law that says a cop can't also have a PI license, but it's often policy in various law enforcement agencies to prohibit it. The Police Commissioner for my city is a reasonably fair-minded bullmastiff whose all-but-trademarked thick mustache is often given a ribbing, but never seriously (if only because he's not a guy you want to piss off). He and Crandall had a quiet chat about it, and a dispensation was reached. I had given Crandall 60 days notice, to help him and the other precincts provide coverage; the PC said that I could apply for my license when I had 30 days left before my retirement date. That worked out well, since I had racked up a lot of vacation time that I still hadn't consumed by the time I retired; I was officially on the books but out of the office for nearly all of those 30 days. No one had any complaints.

That brings us up to May of last year, when many things happened seemingly at once. My slow transition from city-dweller to Starhold residency included numerous steps that may or may not be relevant to you. I shed some possessions, stored more in a portion of the office next to Unicorn's law office in Green Town and, as you might have guessed, moved some more things into Lightwing's suite in the main house. Just so you know, my pup Michael visited Starhold several times over the year before I made the move. I teased him that it was because he wanted to make sure I wasn't getting involved with "a bad element." He returned the tease by saying that he wanted to make sure Lightwing was good enough for me. That was when he discovered that my sweet Husky can fetch a slap to the arm that's not soon forgotten.

You may have noticed that I mentioned an office next to Unicorn's. Max Luton, Private Investigator, hung out a modest shingle in a small, two-room office that was (like Phoenix) juuuuuust right. I admit that I would love to have had the classic gumshoe office door, a marbled glass pane with my name and title etched in fake gold leaf, but I really didn't need the ambience or the expense. I didn't even keep regular office hours; like the good stallion himself, I set times by appointment, whenever I need to meet a client. Most of my work has been for Ezequiel, as we had discussed. Not as glamorous as Sam Spade, but you should visit the office sometime. Heartsinger made a gift of his rendition of the Maltese Falcon, based on photos of the original, and it looks quite handsome, brooding atop the filing cabinet.

Despite the cliché aspects of the month, it was indeed June of last year that Seeker and Dreamweaver married. Everyone pitched in to get everything ready, including space for the cars that brought tribal members, guests, and relatives from all over. The Saturday was as perfect as could be hoped for, for many reasons. The Artisanry was closed for the day, and a sign at the end of the drive said as much. One couple had driven up and quietly parked in front of the shop, as if not believing that it could possibly be closed. The pumas were found all but peering into the windows and looking quite dejected. Oray had been helping to guide visitors to the parking area nearer the house when he found the couple, asking if they might be related to Frank. He found instead that the couple were on an extended vacation-by-car and passed through to see what the shop was all about. Our firefox made them an offer: If they had time to attend the ceremony itself and perhaps enjoy a bit of the reception, he would come back to open the shop for them to browse. Never let it be said that Timewind are poor hosts.

The ceremony contained both common and uncommon elements. Heartsinger performed the ceremony as an ordained minister, with quotes from poets and philosophers extoling the joys of the union. Expensive and ostentatious garb for the wedding party had been eschewed in favor of the finest clothing and sashes that our tribal weavers and designers ever made. Unicorn had woven a wreath from his flowers, for Dreamweaver to wear atop her head, although we all agreed that she needed no great adornment to compliment her natural beauty. The ceremony was brief and heartfelt, the vows that the two had written were exchanged beautifully, the cheering of their kiss might well have been heard in town, and our visiting puma couple expressed themselves thoroughly charmed. They did indeed stay for a bit of the reception, met as many of us as they could, and we all enjoyed their company as much as they did ours. Oray and Moonsong gave them a guided tour of the Artisanry, along with a few other guests who were pleased by the treat. The afternoon became a jewel in the pumas' travels, and we got postcards from their many stops over the summer.

It was also about this time that I was brought further into the mentoring sessions that our tribe holds from time to time. I had, of course, visited Lightwing on many weekends over the prior year, and that included some Saturdays when the guests were gathered for their banquet. I listened to readings of poetry and stories, to music and songs, watched the occasional dance, and marveled at a few surprising and wonderful celebrity speakers who dropped in for a time. (No name-dropping; all of our visitors are treated with proper discretion. I've been allowed to hint that Rainmist happens to be friends with a former President... well, he portrayed one, at least.)

My original comment here was to say that "I opened my big maw and shoved my hindpaw in it." I was outvoted unanimously for that one. What I did was to comment how much I wished I could feel more part of the proceedings, and I was met with a veritable chorus of, "Great idea!" After my emigration from the Outworld, the discussions began in earnest, and I found myself being poked and prodded... okay, warmly encouraged (and yes, it really was) to join in the planning and participation of a session that took place during the first full week of June last year. I thought that perhaps I would be able to provide a little "riding herd" on our guests, and a certain puma joked, "We don't need a police cordon!" I can confirm that my ability to provide raspberries has improved since I started my happy verbal sparring with Seeker.

What the discussions eventually unearthed was my love of movies, particularly those of the prior century. I'm permitted to jest here that my age is actually a benefit, since I grew up with an entire collection of stars who are (sadly) mostly gone by now; even more, some of their earliest roles were in films with stars who reached back even further. (This includes that un-dropped name a few paragraphs back. Yes, I was quite star-struck that weekend, and he was great about it.) So I arranged a few wholly-optional movie nights during that week, introducing yowens to great films from the past. Not all of our guests were born in this century, but I was certainly the oldest in the bunch and, with Darkstar and Heartsinger's help (film mavens that they are), I got to provide to our guests a glimpse into cinema that they had not considered before. It seemed to go over well.

During that same week, I got into a discussion with a trio of yowens who were lounging on the back porch one afternoon. They got me talking about how I came to be part of Timewind, and when, and what did I do, and was I always a PI, and then it got interesting. All three bristled when they discovered that I used to be a cop. They were polite enough, but they didn't want to stick around. Interestingly, it was Seeker who happened by, to defend me gently, and then to start the conversation: What's wrong with cops?

To the yowens' surprise, I was the first to outline quite a laundry list of problems with the police in general, from militarization of police forces to a lack of accountability. Seeker told his story, and a young weasel guest spoke of getting harassed at his local shopping mall, stereotyping for species and age. For the next half hour, I told about my own experiences, answering questions, giving the three a chance to find out that it wasn't their mistrust that was the problem, that bad apples among "the cops" were fueling a sad but reasonable tendency to make "cops" untrustworthy... but that it wasn't every cop, maybe not even most cops, and that it was they — the "civvies" — who could work to make it better. I hadn't intended to give a lesson in civil disobedience and affecting change in government and authority, but the conversation seemed to go over well.

You can guess, I'm sure. That same week, I had more talks with more of our guests, and I was surprised by the thank-you's and an appreciative bit of applause at that Saturday night gathering. There was never a formal class created over the last year, nor was there a mentoring for yowens wanting to enter the force. The word got around, partly from the tribal blog posts about that weekend, and I made myself available for those discussions with others who came to spend time with us. The Congressional Representative who had visited once before visited again, late last summer, and he joined me with nearly all of our guests to have an amazing discussion. It will take a lot more than mere legislation; however, what surprises me is that there is a slowly-growing number of fursons in public office who are really taking a look at what's needed and doing something about it. Lightwing, in her post as MOOR, has been helping our Representative and some of his fellow legislators look for more and better answers. It comes down to the simple reality that we need to talk, to listen, and for us all to work together. Tribal thought continues to spread, benevolently and (we hope) beneficially.

* * * * *

I could probably go on for another entire book, because I truly love who I am becoming, and I love my tribe of dreamers. I have an enormous quantity of anecdotes and stories already, and it's only been two years; just imagine how many more I'm going to experience. That may become another book someday but, for now, there are only a few things left that you really want to know.

Lightwing and I are considering marriage, as a formal ceremony and a legal bond; our only reason for delaying stems from how we already feel about each other and how we treat each other. We joke and banter, we kiss and cuddle, we talk and support one another, and neither of us has enough property, money, or governmental benefits to make the legal trappings valuable to us. We've joked with our resident minister that we could have the shortest exchange of vows possible.

HEARTSINGER (to Lightwing): You wanna?

LIGHTWING: Yeah!

HEARTSINGER (to me): You wanna?

ME: *Hells* yeah!

HEARTSINGER (clapping his forepaws): Done!

As for the whole celebration, the declaration, the anniversary...

tempting, for both of us. We already have an anniversary: April 6th (as the astute of you might have guessed). We celebrate our love every day, and neither Lightwing nor Moonsong need any excuses to make cakes or other great desserts. To set to rest the minds of any of those who are worried about us "living in sin" (are there any? A show of forepaws...?), we're considering exchanging special words in a formal declaration, and we think that Christmastime would be perfect. Much of the tribe will be here, and the Christmas Eve furpile will be a genuinely beautiful way to deflect any notions of "wedding night happenings." Besides, it will invite a whole bunch of jokes and jests about opening presents, mistletoe, and coming down chimneys. I feel confident that the quick-witted Quicksilver would be making his list of one-liners, checking it twice... yes, the whole metaphor bears consideration. We, as a tribe, will have to let you know what happens. Watch the website.

I, and we, also invite you to the website to read the insights of those who contact us, who talk with us, who learn from us and from whom we learn (thank you, Darkstar, for the proper grammatical structure), and who has joined with us, whether as new members or in gentle spirit. Those include our visiting puma couple (still in touch) and a few members of the city police force. These ideas get around, and we're happy to help it happen.

My general contributions to Starhold have resulted from of a lot of learning. How to wield a pitchfork without destroying my back. When pitching hay from the loft in the barn, how to make sure that Oray and Starshine don't get jabbed inappropriately. (They gave us permission to keep that little jest in here, amid their laughter and blushing.) How to groom non-sapient horses. How to recognize weeds from seedlings and how to pluck them (also without ruining my back). Assisting with the Artisanry, including how to work the Magic Coffee Machine. I am in no way a "kept dog," and my lovely Husky has an arm-slap ready for anyone who makes the accusation.

One last thing that you want to know. It happened about the time of Seeker and Dreamweaver's wedding (I did mention that there was a lot going on that month, didn't I?), and it happened with a lot of conversation, laughter, and love. You're free to guess who offered names like "Gadget" (as in "Inspector"), "Clouseau" (same reason), "Deckard," "Lestrade," "Kemp," "Parker" (including "Nosy Parker")... As with "Torque-inator," it was a source of great fun. Eventually, we all began looking for a genuinely fitting name, and I am proud of and grateful to my tribe for their help.

Becoming is a lifelong endeavor; it never ends. I believe in a spirit, soul, lifeforce, that will keep becoming even after this dog's physical body decides to rest. What this means is that what I am now is made up of all that I have been, and what I will become is shaped from day to day. I was my sire's pup, and I am my pup's sire. I have touched many lives, in many ways; I have made mistakes, and I've done some good, like any and all of us. I was known as Detective Max Luton, and I am known now as Max Luton, Private Investigator. I am proud to be a member of Timewind.

The last defender of Albion led me here, to myself, and now, I am Albion's and the tribe's defender. I found my name through that promise to protect and to uphold what is right. Long years ago, the relatively early days of television had a hero whose theme song called him "a knight without armor in a savage land." My tribal name means "of the palace," and stands for one who defends a cause as a knight defends his liege. It's what I do; it's what I am.

I am called Paladin.

About the Author

Tristan Black Wolf has been a purveyor of anthropomorphic ("furry") fiction since his first National Novel Writing Month (NaNoWriMo) win in 2010. His work has been featured and followed by tens of thousands of fans over the years. His stories have appeared in many anthologies and have won awards through fiction contests (on the SoFurry website) and in publications like *Allasso Vol 2: Saudade* (Editor's Choice for Best Use of Anthropomorphism). His novel *The Laputan Factor,* which includes artwork by Dream and Nightmare, has been featured at dozens of "furry" convention dealer's tables in the US, UK, and Germany. He is also the writer and producer of the SFW webcomic *Natural Habitat* (begun in 2018). If pressed, Tristan Black Wolf will admit that he is the anthropomorphic projection of actor and author Tristan MacAvery, PhD, who may or may not have been found baying at the full moon from time to time.

www.ingramcontent.com/pod-product-compliance
Lightning Source LLC
Chambersburg PA
CBHW030241030726
47493CB00023B/391